THE GATHERING

BLOODMOURE CHRONICLES: BOOK ONE

J.R. SHEPHERD

BLOODMOURE PUBLISHING

CONTENTS

To my son, Ashton

Nosvonia
Asvernia
Temple of Elements
Ruins of Dreaden
meloorne
Trillion
Durvail
Parador
Glendale
Albatra
Ruins of Rocton
Faylorn
Sea of Radon
Satsun
Ruins of Talamar
Azrel
Orc army
Yukomo
Shandar
The Cursed Woods
Kandar mountains
Veridian
Dornel
Tatsuma
Dewbrook
Evermoure
Orc lands
Endendon Forest
Oppack
Idonia
N
W   E
S

PROLOGUE

The Bloodstone

For three hundred years, the monks worshipped the gods under the Kandar Mountains, untouched by the war and strife of the world above. However, few knew that something else lay hidden within the ancient corridors and chambers. The underground complex concealed a hidden secret—a mysterious organization that eluded even the most perceptive monks.

Don listened to the bell of the inner chapel ring for the second time today. Its deep tone resounded through the stone walls of the underground monastery, beckoning the monks of Kalindrea to their mid-morning devotions. He rested on a wooden bench, leaning against the bedrock wall. His long brown hair cloaked his stoic features, partially concealing his youthful green eyes.

Hours earlier, Don had watched the monks walk down an adjacent corridor toward the prayer chambers. Now, as he listened to the call for mid-morning devotions, impatience tightened in his chest at the thought of remaining on the bench for another service, but it was better than the alternative. At ten years of age, Don didn't dare to tell his father about his boredom.

His father, Samuel, sat beside him patiently, his hands folded on his lap. They waited to see the Hands of the Shadow.

Devotionals came and passed, and the monks flowed from the chapel and returned to their chores. Their red robes dragged along the floor, forming the illusion they were floating in the air. Don whispered a silent prayer to any god that might be listening, hoping he wouldn't be present for their evening devotionals.

After the last of the monks disappeared, Don asked his father a question he'd wanted to ask since they had arrived, "Father, why do the monks not speak?"

Samuel leaned closer to his son before answering, "I understand they have part of their tongues removed. Only enough is left for them to chant."

"Why would they do that?" Don asked, his forehead creased.

Samuel shrugged. "I suppose it keeps just anyone from becoming a monk." He straightened and looked into his son's eyes. "I don't feel like asking today, and I wouldn't recommend you inquire either." Samuel winked at Don, something he often did when he felt he'd taught his son something new.

An eerie silence settled over the hall, with the absence of the chanting monks. Several half-melted candelabras lined the hallway, but still provided ample lighting.

Don watched a beetle crawl along the wall opposite him. The act, however mundane, proved to be a valuable distraction.

A door opened at the end of the hallway, breaking the uncomfortable silence, which prompted Don to lean forward. He peeked around his father as a sense of hope flooded over him.

A tall, slender man emerged from the door at the end of the hall and strode toward them. He wore a robe similar to the monks', though his garment was black with dark red embroidery tracing the sleeves and hood, which draped back. His long, thin face narrowed to a pointed chin. Defined cheekbones and a straight nose tightened the lines around his mouth, while his sandy hair fell to his shoulders. His cold, black eyes mirrored the darkness of his attire.

"Who's that?" Don whispered.

"I don't know, but he's no monk," Samuel whispered, "he's a killer; you can see it in his eyes."

"I see it, Father."

"Whatever happens, you stay close to me. Understand?"

"Yes, sir."

The man cupped his hands into the sleeves to conceal them and stopped before Samuel. He bowed reluctantly. "My name is Neacrom. You will accept the Council's apology for the wait. They had...unforeseen business and will see you now. Follow me," he said, devoid of any emotion. Neacrom turned and walked back toward the door.

They followed him down the hall. Don could see the uneasiness in his father's walk, something he had come to understand from years of journeying with him. To his surprise, Don wished he were still sitting on the bench behind him.

Neacrom removed his hands from his sleeves and silently motioned the two through the door as he opened it.

They entered a large, well-lit room. A dozen more candelabras lit the chamber, and a large, ornate ashen wood table sat in the center of the room, making this the brightest and most prominent area Don had seen thus far.

Neacrom closed the door behind them and stood, hands folded in his robe. His face held no expression as he fixed his gaze ahead of Samuel.

Don kept his eyes fixed on Neacrom and stepped beside Samuel. His father stopped him with a subtle touch of the hand. Don nearly stepped into a fresh area of crimson on the floor. A small crescent-moon earring gleamed in a puddle of blood, its shape hinting at the elven family crest, the Shad'arn. He traced the drag marks leading from the gore toward a second door to the left, understanding from his father's experience that they were more than likely dead.

Don turned his focus on a large ashwood table and five individuals in oversized chairs. He'd never seen such a motley crew of individuals sitting together.

Gorgen, an enormous orc, sat in the first chair on the far left. The muscles beneath his green skin rippled with power. His fierce brown eyes held Samuel captive.

Next to him sat Choluk, a dark elf from deep beneath the Kandar mountains. His black skin seemed to absorb the very light in the room, leaving his icy blue eyes to pierce the darkness, cutting through his father like a sharp sword. His long, silky, white hair cascaded over his pointed ears.

In the fourth chair sat Michael, a fair-skinned, middle-aged man. His dark hair and rugged eyes, set above a square jaw, made him the most handsome of the quintet.

Sitting on the far right sat a dwarf, Zander. His almond beard and well-kept hair suggested nobility within the dwarven community. He appeared childlike beside the others, but the wrinkles around his eyes conveyed his actual age.

And finally, another man sat in the center of the group. His finely chiseled features and elegant attire accentuated a regal presence. His name was JoJung, and he oversaw the Hands of the Shadow, presiding over their Council. He hailed from Satsun, a distant and exotic land across the sea of Radon.

Samuel sidestepped the pool of blood and took a step toward the table. He stopped at a respectful distance and bowed before the Council.

JoJung rose from his chair. "Samuel, we had not anticipated your return for some time. Do you have news for us?" he said expectantly.

"Yes, JoJung. Everything has proceeded as we discussed. The information the Council provided has produced rewards for us both."

JoJung raised his eyebrows. "Rewards?"

"May I approach the Council? I have something you may be interested in seeing." Samuel smiled.

"Yes, come forward, Samuel. Your work has been extremely relevant to the Council." JoJung grinned and waved Samuel forward.

Samuel stepped toward them and pulled a tightly wrapped wad of black cloth from his coat pocket. He placed it on the table with a surprisingly loud thump. Samuel pulled the corners of the cloth back to reveal a dark, blood-red diamond roughly the size of a small apple. The gemstone balanced on its tip as if supported by an invisible string.

A gasp broke the silence in the room, followed by whispers.

JoJung's mouth slid open, and he sank back into the oversized chair. His gaze locked on the balancing gem.

Don had never seen the red gemstone his father displayed.

The orc slapped his hands on the table. "Is that?"

"Yes, Gorgen." JoJung lifted his hand to silence the orc. JoJung let his eyes drift from the gem to meet Samuel's gaze. "Where did you find it?"

"The Council's guidance proved to be most helpful. I discovered the gemstone moved between family units, keeping it from being in one location for long," Samuel answered.

JoJung smiled and shook his head. "That's how they've kept it hidden for all these centuries. Tell me, how many of these families have you located?"

"I've located all of them and eliminated all but one family," Samuel responded.

JoJung smiled and slapped his palm on the table. "You've seen to all but one family?" JoJung nudged Michael, the man to his left.

Michael chuckled, and a wicked grin creased his lips. "Today is proving to be a most fruitful day," he said, leaning his head against the chair.

"How did you find all of them?" JoJung asked, resting his arms on the chair.

Samuel leaned away from the table. "The prime male of each family and his eldest son gather after the passing of every other full moon." Samuel shifted. "I discovered the village where they would come together and assemble. We observed the families and tracked them back to their isolated dwellings. Once I found their locations, the rest was simple.

JoJung tilted his head and glanced at Michael while Samuel spoke.

"In total, there were six family units." Samuel continued. "I admit that's more than I expected."

JoJung focused on Samuel. "Tell us more."

"The last male and his oldest have already left to meet with the other families. When none of the others arrive, they'll know something's wrong, return for his family, and try to flee." Samuel tightened his fists. "It will take me the better part of eleven days to deal with their family before they return home. There's no room for error."

Samuel pushed the gem forward, still balancing. "As per our arrangement, the gem is payment for the information you provided."

JoJung moved closer to the table. Balancing on the edge of his chair, he lifted the gemstone from the table and cradled it in his hands, ultimately letting it balance in his palm. A hush fell across the room as he became lost in its brilliance; reluctantly, he returned the red diamond to the table.

Don recognized that the longer he looked at the gem, the more it seemed to change shades and pulsate.

Zander broke the silence. "Now that we…"

JoJung abruptly lifted a hand, silencing the dwarf. He looked at him sternly and spoke. "Have patience, Zander," he said before lowering his hand. JoJung gazed at Samuel. "Before you leave, we'll ensure you have adequate rations for your journey."

Not wanting to spend any more time away from his mission, Samuel responded, "I'm grateful for your offer, JoJung, but that will not be necessary. We have everything we need. We'll take our leave at once." Samuel backed away from the table and returned to Don's side, stepping around the pool of blood.

Don relaxed, thankful to hear his father announce they were leaving.

JoJung stood. "Very well, Samuel, you've accomplished an invaluable service for the realm. Your obligations to the Council are null and void, and we will no longer seek your assistance in the future." He placed his hands together and bowed before returning to his chair.

Samuel nodded and turned toward the door, his hands on Don's shoulders, protectively guiding him. He understood now that the Council had what they wanted. Samuel no longer served a purpose.

Neacrom opened the door and ushered father and son into the hall, shutting it behind them.

JoJung rested his head against the chair as the door clicked shut.

The dark-skinned elf reached for the balancing red gemstone.

JoJung laid his hand on the elf's arm. "We still have much to learn, Choluk." JoJung looked from side to side.

"We must proceed with caution. One slight deviation could bring everything down around us, jeopardizing what the councils before us accomplished."

Choluk pressed his lips together and slid back into his chair.

Still upset from being hushed earlier, Gorgen stood angrily, flinging his chair back, drawing everyone's attention from the gemstone. "You're going to let them leave alive?" he asked, shaking his head. "Call me when we're ready to move forward. I have to clean this mess." The orc stormed off, following the trail of blood through the door, slamming it behind him.

The dwarf spoke first. "That was dramatic."

JoJung regarded Michael and smiled. "There will be no one to stop us when Samuel dispatches the remaining family."

Michael let his eyes drift from the stone. "You presume Samuel will succeed in eliminating the last family."

"You did not believe Samuel would accomplish all he has." JoJung sighed. "People will do just about anything when you convince them they have no choice. Isn't that right?" He placed his hand on Michael's arm. "He will succeed and end them all—finally."

Michael lowered his head. The corners of his mouth curved upward, revealing a pair of sharp fangs. He brought the stone back into view, his gaze filled with desire. "Samuel has brought us the greatest prize of all."

JoJung looked back at the balancing gem. "The Bloodstone."

Chapter One

ALONE

Sixteen years later,

Aticus walked along a narrow dirt path that had been carved out over the years. Gathering water was his favorite daily chore as it gave him a sense of peace and allowed him to escape from the crowded campsite and its people. The sound of water quickened his pace while its calming influence encouraged him. Taking a deep breath, he stepped into a clearing by the creek and wiped the sweat from his forehead, pushing his long black hair away from his face.

As the early morning sun peeked through the trees, it kissed the shimmering surface of the water, forming a whimsical mist. The sweet aroma of flowers drifted in the breeze as nearby birds sang their songs of life, marking the beginning of another day of survival. Aticus knelt beside the water and placed two wooden buckets on the ground before closing his eyes. He leaned forward and pressed his hands to the ground, feeling the gritty dirt between his fingers. Opening his eyes, he gazed at his reflection in the water, his brown eyes reflecting the calmness of his surroundings.

Aticus ran his hands through the water, rinsing away the dirt, and leaned back on his heels, gazing across the creek. He filled the buckets and placed them aside. Suddenly, a distant voice bellowed his name from the serene forest behind him. Aticus sighed, stealing one more glance at the creek before rising to his feet. "I'll be right there," he mumbled to himself.

"Aticus!" The voice was louder and filled with impatience.

"I'm coming, Vandeer!" he shouted back, frightening birds and a nearby squirrel gathering nuts.

He collected the buckets and started up the path.

Vandeer, the leader of the Alarians, called out twice more before Aticus reached the camp. He'd been trying to avoid the man all morning, and now he prepared himself for a verbal lashing.

Vandeer came into view as Aticus stepped into the large clearing and the Alarian's camp. Vandeer stood over six feet tall, towered nearly a foot over Aticus, and was twice as broad in the belly and shoulders. "Boy, where have you been? Terra needs that water to finish the morning meal!" Vandeer shouted, drawing the attention of several Alarians nearby.

"I have the water." Aticus lifted the pails, sloshing some from one of the buckets. "I finished with the horses," he tried to finish as Vandeer interrupted him.

"It worries me you haven't finished what you were supposed to," Vandeer said, as he turned abruptly and stormed off.

Aticus bowed his head and made his way to the large campfire, where Terra prepared the morning meal with the help of her two younger sisters.

"Thank you," Terra said softly without looking at Aticus.

"I'm sorry it took me so long," he responded.

"It's fine," she said. The fresh kindling she placed on the fire ignited with a pop, and the warmth of the flame brought a bronze glow to her skin. "I'm ready for that water now," she said with a smile, holding out her hands.

Aticus couldn't help but admire Terra's delicate features. The sight of her thin face and hazel eyes framed by silky almond hair induced a flutter in his chest. As he found himself lost in thought, the crackling of the fire and the sound of her voice snapped him back to reality.

"The water? You brought me water?" she giggled. She took a pail from him and placed it on the ground. "You know you shouldn't let him get to you," she said.

Aticus handed her the second half-empty bucket of water. "I know, I know, I'm sure he means well, but he's so mean to me," he said, attempting to regain his composure. His face flushed when their hands brushed.

She smiled and turned her attention back to the pot, "Thank you, Aticus. I appreciate you," she added without looking back.

Aticus nodded and regarded her for a few more seconds before returning to his chores.

The Alarians, a band of traveling gypsies, were busy preparing for another long day of travel. The men wore neutral-colored clothing paired with brown leather boots, while the women dressed in vibrant, colorful attire. As the men tended to the livestock and prepared for a day of trading, the women supervised the children and delivered meals. Coordinating the movement of seventy-five people, along with their livestock and wagons, was no small task.

Aticus had finished securing the chicken cages to a wagon when he caught sight of Terra stacking pans to take to the river for cleaning. He realized he'd missed breakfast again; he sighed quietly. His shoulders slumped, and his stomach growled in protest. "Dammit," he muttered to himself.

At the same time, Terra noticed Aticus, grinned, and motioned toward him with a free hand.

He stood taller with renewed hope and made his way toward Terra.

"I knew you'd forget again." She pulled a plate of eggs and potatoes from beneath the lid of the pan beside her. Her smile expanded as she handed him the plate.

"Thank you." Aticus' eyes rounded.

"You're welcome." She gathered the pots and started toward the path leading to the creek.

Aticus shoved his mouth full of potatoes before surveying the remnants of the makeshift village. He knew Vandeer was probably keeping an eye on him after the earlier scolding. He walked over to an oak tree and took a bite. As he was about to take another, he noticed movement in a caged wagon about forty paces away. It was the dwarf settling down in the middle of the cage, crossing his legs. Despite his small stature, the dwarf had a commanding presence that extended beyond the wagon.

The dwarf wore an olive-green, high-collar, long-sleeve shirt tied together in the front with narrow leather strips woven from top to bottom. His pants were made of a fine tan material; in contrast, his boots, nearly worn through on the soles, told a different story. His dark, shoulder-length brown hair, full mustache, and beard were matted from days of neglect. Despite being in an unenviable position, the smile on the dwarf's face reminded Aticus of his adopted father and how he made him feel safe.

Aticus closed his eyes and let out a deep sigh. He was responsible for feeding the dwarf. He tilted his plate of food from side to side and looked at the dwarf, who hadn't eaten anything since the goblins had handed him over the previous day. Aticus walked toward the caged wagon and observed the dwarf as he conversed with the cage ceiling.

The little man looked at Aticus and addressed him cheerfully, "Good morning, young sir."

Aticus nodded as he reluctantly placed the plate of food on the wagon floor and slid it under the bars. "I thought you might be hungry," he said; his stomach growled at the sight of his morning meal sliding away.

The dwarf brought the plate closer, looking at the food, "Thank you! I wasn't worried; dwarves can survive without food for almost forty days."

"Oh, ah, I didn't know that," Aticus said, staring at the food.

The dwarf tilted his head to better view Aticus through the bars. "Now personally, the longest I've been without eating is ten days; the goblins didn't feed me before handing me over to your master," he said as he tasted the eggs and closed his eyes in ecstasy. "Oh my, this is quite delicious!"

Frustrated for letting his meal slip away, Aticus' face flushed. "Wait—master? Who's master?"

The dwarf pointed the fork at the clearing where Aticus had emerged with water. "Your master. The man who yelled at you earlier by the trees," he said, but never looked away from the plate, contemplating what to eat next.

Aticus silently absorbed what the dwarf said.

"Well, at least he acted like your master the way he spoke to you." The dwarf took a bite of the potatoes next.

"He's not my master. He wants us to do our part, that's all," Aticus said.

"You may not realize it, son, but you're more of his prisoner than I am. The only difference is that I'm in here watching while you are out there toiling," he said with a mouthful of potatoes.

Aticus gripped the metal bars, his knuckles turning white. "What makes you think you know so much?"

"I didn't say I know—I said I was watching." The dwarf smiled, potatoes clinging to his teeth. "People can learn a lot from watching."

"Is that so?"

The dwarf moved the food around on the plate.

Aticus inhaled, taking in a calming breath. "What's your name?"

With a mouth full of food, "I'm Bryce; what's your name, son?"

"Aticus."

"Well met." Bryce offered his hand to shake after holding the fork in his mouth. Aticus shook his hand.

"That was the best meal I've had in more months than I can recall," Bryce exclaimed as he looked around thoughtfully. He put the empty plate on the wagon and pushed it beneath the bars. "Your young lady makes a wonderful dish."

"Yes, she does." Aticus smiled.

"Have you told her you like her yet?"

Aticus' eyes widened. "What?"

"The girl," Bryce smiled.

"Terra?" Aticus trembled.

"Yes, if that's her name."

"I don't **like** her like that—I mean." Aticus found himself scanning the camp, but not for Vandeer.

"I can see these things, you know." Bryce smiled and rolled his eyes; crossing his arms, he leaned back against the cage.

"We're friends. She's a friend," Aticus protested unconvincingly, raising his hands defensively.

Bryce chuckled, "You don't have to worry, son. I promise not to divulge our conversation to anyone," he reassured Aticus. "It's not like anyone's rushing over to speak to me. But even if they do, my lips are sealed tighter than the Dwarven stronghold of Kandar." Bryce nodded his head and winked, indicating his trustworthiness.

Aticus noticed Vandeer walking from wagon to wagon, interacting with each family. Vandeer patted the men on the back, usually followed by a hearty laugh. He bowed before the women and then knelt with the children, smiling and rubbing their heads with his big hands. Vandeer repeated this routine with every family. He had proven himself to be a great leader who cared deeply for his people and was willing to do whatever was necessary to ensure their safety.

Aticus saw Vandeer's path would lead him in this direction, so he retrieved the plate. "I need to get back to my chores," he said anxiously.

Bryce studied Aticus. "Why do you stay, son?" he asked calmly.

"This is my home. What do you mean?" Aticus asked.

"It doesn't seem like much of a home," Bryce responded.

Aticus didn't answer Bryce as he turned and walked away.

Aticus moved toward the food wagon and grabbed a sack hanging on the bench. It represented all his earthly belongings. He leaned against the wagon and slid to the ground.

He took out a small knife and held it tightly in his hand. The blade was the only item he had left that belonged to his adopted father, Nicholas.

Nicholas had discovered Aticus sixteen years ago, wandering alone on a path in the forest, wearing simple clothes and a medallion around his neck. He was traumatized and had no memory before that day. The Elders permitted Nicholas to care for the boy while they searched for his family. During this time, Nicholas began calling him Aticus, a name he and his deceased wife had wanted to call their son, whom they never had. After months of searching, Aticus' family was never located, so Nicholas adopted him.

Aticus recalled the beginning of spring three years ago when Nicholas gave him this knife. It was the day he died.

Aticus replaced the blade in the sack and pulled out a small medallion. He rubbed the piece of metal and searched the surface for meaning while he twisted the thin silver chain around his fingers. The disk was inscribed with hieroglyphs around the edges, and the center bore an octagonal inset.

With their teams of horses hitched and the wagons arranged in a single file, the Alarians settled into their traveling formation.

Vandeer walked the line, ensuring everyone was prepared before the long day's journey. They would travel and trade with four nearby villages before venturing back into the forest to find another campsite for the night.

Aticus sat on the wagon bench, keeping the cloth sack hanging nearby. Rictor, an elderly man, sat next to him, holding the reins. Together, they were responsible for caring for the food wagon and its contents.

The wagon in front of them had been Aticus' home up until three years ago. It was the wagon in which his father, Nicholas, died. After his passing, the wagon became the property of a young couple who were wedded soon after. Nonetheless, Aticus was forced to look at the wagon daily, a constant reminder of what he had lost and would never have.

As the caravan advanced, Aticus glanced back at Bryce. The dwarf leaned against the metal bars with a cheerful countenance. Aticus watched Bryce converse with the ceiling of the caged wagon; he suspected something might be wrong with the little man. Maybe he was senile or otherwise mentally challenged. Either way, he recalled their earlier conversation. Even though the exchange was frustrating, Aticus looked forward to speaking with the dwarf again.

Aticus looked up and down the caravan of Alarians. He began a new day with the only people he could remember. Without Nicholas, he felt alone, a shadow amongst the Alarians. These were Nicholas' people, not his.

CHAPTER TWO

GILANTHOS

Gilanthos opened his eyelids as his brown eyes adjusted to the brilliant sunlight shining through the trees. Long sandy hair matted with dried blood clung to his pointed ears. His head throbbed when he sat up and examined his surroundings. A subtle breeze brushed the leaves of the giant oak trees towering above him, and the thick vegetation concealing him rustled against it.

He took a deep breath and looked at this dented helmet lying on the ground at his feet, with a small arrow beside it.

Suddenly, realization slammed into him, like the goblin's arrow beside him. Gilanthos recalled where he was as he tried to get up. Kneeling, he braced himself against the tree, as a wave of nausea came over him. He paused and retrieved his helmet, dropping it to the side, when he noticed his blood on a rock. Grimacing, he touched the source of the pain on his head. His hair was crusted with dried blood from where he'd hit his head when he fell from his horse.

Gilanthos stood, drew his sword, and shouted for his companions. "Eladonia! Aeotus!" he called out. His breaths were shallow and fast. He used the palm of his hand to press his head, hoping to ease the throbbing, and made his way to a small path they had been traveling. "Ela! Aeo!" he yelled again. There was no response except for the sounds of the forest.

That's when he saw a bare foot sticking out of the bushes. He held his breath and cautiously approached, keeping a vigilant eye on his surroundings. Gilanthos paused before using the tip of the sword to peel back the vegetation. It was one of the three elven escorts from Evermoure. Two arrows protruded from their chest and neck, similar to the one near his helmet. He knelt and closed the elf's eyes. His body had been looted of all his possessions. "Damn goblins!" he uttered, and quickly moved on in his search for his friends. "Eladonia! Aeotus!" he yelled, frantic that they had not answered.

He moved around with urgency, pushing the groundcover with his sword and free hand. Again, he called them, but there was no response.

After taking several deep breaths, he began studying the ground, reading it like a book with a story to tell: footprints, the small ones, were goblins. Hoof prints and leather-souled shoes would have been the elves. He followed the tracks down the path that led to two more elven escorts and several goblins. They were all deceased and stripped of their wares.

Goblins had ambushed them, and he wasn't there for his friends. He wasn't there to suffer the same fate, and he loathed himself for failing them. Then he found two more goblins, their charred corpses amidst scorched grass, the result of a magic spell his friend had cast. "Aeotus! You fought back," he said, as he searched for his body, thankfully with no success.

Finally, Gilanthos discovered a second location where another confrontation had occurred. Crushed undergrowth cradled the remains of four more goblins—their bodies dismembered in a macabre expanse of blood. "Eladonia," he whispered.

Hope became his focal point when further investigation revealed no sign of their bodies or effects. Gilanthos scoured the ground cover and path for more clues. It appeared to have been a large party of goblins that ambushed them. He was both embarrassed and angry. His friends had more than likely been taken prisoner.

Sweeping his hair back from his face, he turned and examined the scene behind him. He traced each location where he'd uncovered vestiges of the battle. He had been in the back of the group and was probably down before the battle was fought, lost in the ground cover and forgotten. He would leave the bodies where they lay. Time was of the essence, and they were getting away. He had no idea how long he'd been unconscious, but considering the clotting in his hair, it had been hours. He knew what the elves from Evermoure believed concerning what happened after death. Their souls would be reborn again, and their journey of immortality would continue, but in a new form.

Gilanthos turned south and followed the tracks southward. He would find his friends, free them, and have his revenge.

Chapter Three

MONGOLE

Mongole stood on a small hill, gazing out over the sandy plains of Eldar. The ankle-high rittle weed swayed gently in the evening breeze as the landscape slowly changed from blue to a brilliant shade of magenta, casting long shadows on the horizon. Lightning illuminated the northern sky, suggesting an approaching storm.

Mongole had a broad face and a firm jaw that matched the size of his sturdy frame. His dark eyes, narrowed in thought, were set below bushy brows. His thick, black hair was tied back for comfort, swaying in the evening breeze. His olive-skinned features were chiseled, and he wore a leather tunic, not his preferred armor, but for comfort when off the battlefield. He stood for several more moments, gazing at the southwestern horizon. For now, he was hundreds of miles away with his family and the comforts of home.

Feeling someone approach from behind, he tightened his grip on the hilt of his sword and turned to face a young orc officer.

Chotak stood with his hands at his sides. "Supreme Commander Talmet is summoning you, sir."

Mongole nodded before speaking, "Thank you, Chotak; pass the word that there will be rain tonight. Ensure that the supplies are covered and off the ground this time."

"Yes, Lord Mongole." Chotak turned and disappeared back down the hill.

A gentle breeze from the north flapped Mongole's cape as he turned back towards the darkening horizon. He closed his eyes, and his features softened. The fog of war parted, and visions of his mate and their two children eased his anxieties.

Mongole made his way through the sprawling city of tents. The temporary encampment contained sixty-five thousand orcs, led by Supreme Commander Talmet. At night, the light from the encampment served as a beacon for the orcs on the front lines in the north.

With the goblins help, the orcs, who were determined to conquer the human cities in the north, had pushed the humans back to the grasslands of Panor and their outpost. There, the knights of Meloorne stood as the last obstacle to overcome.

Mongole approached Talmet's Pavilion, which consisted of four large tents that acted as his command center.

Two gnolls positioned at attention on either side of the entrance held halberds against their chests. Their bodies were covered in rusty brown hair, with pale gray skin visible on their hands and faces. They stood tall, their faces resembling those of hyenas. A tiny black nose accentuated their long muzzles, and their razor-sharp teeth gleamed under the light of a nearby torch; yellow eyes peered out from atop their heads, below a pair of pointed ears.

As Mongole approached, the gnolls' ears turned to face him like another set of eyes. Hastily, the guards pulled back the canvas, allowing Mongole to enter unimpeded. Upon entering the tent, he paused, breathed, and focused on two lanterns hanging on wooden stakes in opposite corners. His attention turned to a leather flap leading to Talmet's war ro om.

He walked forward, his footsteps stirring up dirt in the enclosure. Lowering his head, he entered the next chamber, where a large, crude table stood in the center of the room. The table, supported by four barrels, was cluttered with maps and papers.

To Mongole's left sat an unadorned weapons rack holding Talmet's armor and war hammer. Two openings similar to the one Mongole had come through opened to the right and left of the room. One was Talmet's sleeping quarters, and the other was the dining area for the officers.

Talmet leaned over the improvised table, examining an open map. Though slightly smaller than Mongole, his thick head, full of long black hair and large pointed ears, was proportionally set to his robust body. Though Talmet's hazel eyes were a rare color for an orc, an old scar on his neck from a war wolf was the first thing you noticed.

"Mongole, my friend, come in!" Talmet waved his hand as he lifted from the table, letting the map roll in on itself. "There's been a change of plans."

Mongole narrowed his dark eyes, curling his brow as he neared the table. "Change of plans?"

"Yes." Talmet looked through the maps on the table and flattened one so Mongole could see.

Mongole leaned over the table and examined the map for relevance. "This is the southern lands, and the ruined city of Oppack," he said, his jaw clenched. He was staring at Talmet with a look of worry in his eyes.

"Yes, Mongole," Talmet replied, walking around the table to stand beside his general.

Mongole studied Talmet. "This is a region controlled by the necromancer, our ally!"

"The necromancer has something I need," Talmet smirked, puffing out his chest.

Mongole responded, "In a month, we'll be at the tower of Parador. We can defeat the humans there and, within three months, be on the steps of their capital. This Bloodstone you seek—I don't need it to win the war!" He looked into Talmet's eyes for agreement.

Talmet placed a hand on his general's shoulder. "Mongole, if not for your leadership, your guidance," Talmet hesitated, "we would not be this close to victory over the humans. You should have been leading us in my stead. As you may recall, the king appointed you supreme commander, but you declined. You were the one who proposed I lead the armies as supreme commander." Talmet paused again. "You are a warrior, and I am a strategist." He removed his hand from Mongole and looked him in the eyes. His mouth curved into a smile. "From an early age, it's been this way. When we were children, do you remember? I'm asking you to be my warrior again—for your people. The Bloodstone will aid our mages in winning the war with fewer casualties. Saving the lives of our brothers!"

Mongole examined Talmet intently.

Talmet continued, "Your ancestor slew Edendon two hundred years ago. The humans' champion—their god's champion. Your name carries significance among our people, and I need your support now more than ever."

Mongole moaned and looked away. "What do you propose?"

"I sent a small detachment of orcs to Oppack a month ago, and they did not return. I want you to choose your best officer, Chotak, perhaps. He seems to be a promising favorite of yours, if I recall. Send him with a battalion of men to retrieve the stone for me, by force if need be." Talmet tilted his head to the side.

Mongole's eyes widened. "A month ago? And now a battalion of over a thousand men! That group was scheduled to reinforce the front lines! Why do you require so many to retrieve the stone from our supposed ally?"

Talmet turned from Mongole and walked around the table before speaking again. "Two weeks ago, I sent word to Uchak in Azrel. I commanded him to send a few hundred goblins and take the stone by force. To my knowledge, none of the goblins returned. I had the bird master attempt to reach Uchak again, but the messenger pigeons returned from Azrel without being checked. I fear something has happened at the goblin mines. I—we—need someone who will not fail us."

"Uchak, that feeble-minded goblin cleric?" Mongole clenched his teeth. "So you've been trying to retrieve the Bloodstone all this time? With the help of the goblins?" Mongole glared at Talmet, reprimanding him like he would scold his son.

Talmet slammed his hand on the table, shaking maps, ink, and many small items onto the floor. "Mongole, you will make this happen. I command it!" Spittle sprayed from his mouth as he screamed the order. "You will be wise to remember to whom you speak!" Talmet regained his composure and pulled the hem of his shirt down. "Issue the order, Mongole." Talmet looked away and skimmed through his maps.

"Of course, supreme commander," Mongole groaned before exiting the tent. He paused outside for many moments, watching the lightning illuminate the northern sky, trailed by a rumble of thunder.

Chapter Four

THE GOBLIN KING

Aticus took a drink from his waterskin, quenching his thirst from the heat of the day. He sat alone on the food wagon, waiting for Vandeer and a group of Alarians to return from trading at their third and final stop for the day in the village of Diedra on the western side of Shandar. Aticus slid off the bench and approached the prisoner wagon where Bryce sat, legs crossed. "I thought you might be thirsty," Aticus said.

Bryce smiled, resting his elbows on folded knees. He played with a twig, rolling it between his fingers before flipping it. "Yes, thank you!"

Aticus passed the canteen between the metal bars. "We'll be making camp in a few hours. I promise to bring you something to eat." He grinned at the dwarf.

"Thank you, son," Bryce expressed with a warm smile. He looked out over the plains in the direction Vandeer had traveled. "How many villages do you trade with?" He took the waterskin and tipped it up, being mindful not to empty all of its contents before returning it to Aticus.

"We trade with eighteen settlements each month. Of course, there are also the occasional travelers we cross paths with." Aticus shrugged. "Nowadays, we see more goblins than travelers." He reached back for the waterskin and noticed the liquid inside. "You can have the rest." He shook the container to let the dwarf know there was more.

Bryce shook his head. "I'll not finish off your water for the day, son. It was kind of you to offer as it is." He smiled.

Aticus shrugged and acknowledged Bryce. "Okay, but I can always get more from the barrel," he said, pointing to a large container strapped to the food wagon. "How can you be so pleasant?" Aticus asked. "You're in a cage; you don't know when you'll eat again, and you smile at everyone. You know that's not normal?"

"I'm alive," Bryce responded cheerfully, before continuing, "Are you suggesting it's normal to be in a cage?"

"No," he replied, contorting his face. "In a day or so, Vandeer will trade you to the goblins from the north, and they'll probably work you in mines at Azrel," Aticus sputtered. His words did little to break the smile on the dwarf's face.

Bryce leaned forward, rubbed his beard, and searched Aticus' eyes. "Maybe I'm destined to end up there. There's a reason why everything happens to us." Bryce leaned back, a gentle smile spreading across his face as he placed his hands on his lap.

"You're going to slave in the mines, and you could die there!" Aticus was worried about the little man's rationality. He knew he shouldn't be. After all, he was a stranger. Why should he care?

"God will guide and protect me wherever He sends me," Bryce calmly responded, enjoying the conversation.

"What gods do you think will help you?" Aticus asked.

Bryce pressed his eyelids together, his eyebrows curled in on one another. He was confused by what Aticus said. "God, not gods. There is but one God!" He shook his hands in exclamation.

"Well, don't you think you'd have a better chance if you had the help of more than one god?" Aticus smiled, trying to get another reaction.

Bryce scooted back so he could lean against the bars. "I know what you're trying to do." He shook his finger at Aticus. "You're looking for a feather to fluff." Bryce laughed.

Aticus' smile widened, and he held his stomach as he chuckled. It felt strange to him; he hadn't laughed this hard since before Nicholas died. It felt good!

Movement among the Alarians drew their attention. It was Vandeer; he returned with the wagons they'd taken to Diedra. "That didn't take long," Aticus whispered to himself.

After returning, Vandeer asked Rictor to gather the elders and protectors, the ten men tasked with defending the camp. Aticus stood near the food wagon, trying to eavesdrop on their conversation.

"We need to be vigilant," Vandeer said as he addressed the ten protectors. "The goblin presence in and around the forest is growing. I'm not going into many details, but from what we learned in Diedra, it doesn't look good. Prepare everyone to leave as soon as possible."

The protectors dispersed, leaving Vandeer with Rictor and the four elders. The six men moved together and whispered in unison.

Aticus couldn't hear what they spoke about, but it set his mind ablaze with curiosity, so he returned to his chores.

It wasn't long into the afternoon before Vandeer had the caravan moving. Aticus was back on the bench beside Rictor, trying to get information from him about what was happening.

"What has Vandeer so shaken?" Aticus was comfortable asking the elderly man.

"When they got to Diedra, most people had themselves barricaded in their homes. The townspeople said hundreds of goblins passed to the west of the village about ten days ago. These goblins got them scared!" Rictor snapped the reins and looked at Aticus.

"Where do they think the goblins were going?" Aticus asked.

"They were heading south, and they were in a hurry. Something big is going on." He turned his attention to the sprawling caravan ahead of them. "Vandeer got a few men to trade, but most paid no attention. There was even talk about people leaving the village," he said. "The bloody creatures are like rats. It's only a matter of time before the vermin take over the forest. There's nobody to oppose the goblins, so they breed, spreading disease and filth."

"What about the elves or the knights in Meloorne? Aticus asked.

"Those elves are just as bad. They don't care about anybody but themselves! They won't do anything until it's their problem." He slapped the reins. "And the knights are fighting the war against the orcs, trying to save those great cities of theirs." Rictor looked at Aticus. "You've been here, what, fourteen years?"

"Sixteen." Aticus' gaze fixed on the wagon in front of them.

"Well, you've seen how bad it's gotten, even in the last year," Rictor proclaimed.

"I wish we didn't have to keep transporting people for the goblins," Aticus said nervously and peered over at the caged wagon at Bryce for comfort. Bryce laid on his back, legs crossed and hands under his head, humming something that might have been dwarvish.

"Vandeer had no choice. He did what he thought he had to, to keep his people safe." Rictor glanced at Aticus, pulling his gaze from the dwarf. "Vandeer told us all when he decided to work with the goblins. If you give them what they need, then you're valuable."

Aticus interrupted Rictor. "I know, I know. If you have nothing to offer them, then you're expendable."

Rictor nodded. "Exactly." Aticus remained quiet the rest of the afternoon, watching the clouds build in the west.

The Alarians traveled northwest through the forest, following a well-traveled route. The protectors' presence during the day did little to elevate the tension among the people.

Aticus watched as they weaved back and forth between the wagons, paying attention to their surroundings. The dirt path wound through the dense forest, sometimes only wide enough for a single wagon, allowing no warning of an attack. When the path widened, it helped to ease Aticus' anxiety. *The fear of the unknown is far greater than the actual danger itself.* He remembered Nicholas telling him that once when he was young.

Aticus often looked back at the dwarf to reassure himself that he was okay. It was apparent that Bryce was content to remain oblivious to the impending doom most of the Alarians felt.

It was early afternoon when the caravan suddenly stopped on the broadest part of the trail they had traveled all day. Only seven of the twenty-four wagons were visible, with the rest of the caravan out of sight around a bend in the trail. "This isn't good," Rictor said, "not good at all." Aticus looked at Rictor as fear swept across his face, which he had only seen once before on the older man. It was the time when Rictor's brother played a prank, making him believe that the food wagon had caught fire.

Rictor stood from his seat, holding the reins tight. "There's a lot of movement up ahead. I can't see what's stopping us," Rictor said loud enough so one of the protectors riding nearby could hear him. The protector spurred his mount, galloping past them into the caravan and disappearing around a bend in the path.

Aticus glanced over the wagon at Bryce, who was standing, holding the metal bars. A look of concern wrinkled his face as they made eye contact. Aticus was preparing to leave the wagon, but Bryce shook his head and motioned for him to stay put. Even Bryce knew something was wrong.

A few moments later, the protector returned and moved closer to the food wagon, keeping a watchful eye on the forest. "What the hell is happening, Harris?" Rictor asked in a distressed tone.

Harris turned his horse back to keep watch on the path behind the caravan. "Damn goblins." He looked at Rictor and Aticus. "It's Toak himself."

Rictor uttered an old Alarian expletive and stood while trying to view more of the caravan. "I wonder what brings the goblin king out of hiding?" Harris shrugged, turned his horse around, and rode back into the caravan, disappearing out of sight.

Several anxious moments passed before Aticus watched several of the Alarians moving around their wagons. It wasn't long before Vandeer appeared alongside the caravan. He was on foot, and he didn't look happy. Toak followed on his horse behind the leader of the Alarians.

Toak deemed himself a king and carried himself appropriately. He had a small silver helmet that sat high on his head, dinged and tarnished. Over his shoulders hung a dirty black cape, tattered and flapping with each of the horse's steps. *He must be too dumb to know how absurd he looks,* Aticus thought. The year before, after defeating a rival clan of goblins, Toak took the liberty to claim himself "King" of Shandar.

Following behind Toak were two stunning white horses with colorful tassels tied to their manes. Atop the steeds were two individuals tied to their saddles. They were surrounded by eight other goblins.

As they approached the back of the caravan, Vandeer stopped near the food wagon and glared into the forest. He didn't speak as Toak passed, heading for the caged wagon.

As the eight goblins approached with their prisoners on horseback, Aticus made eye contact with the first rider. *They're elves,* he thought, never having seen one in person. Eladonia sat defiantly, her hands bound to the saddle. Her piercing blue eyes cut through Aticus like a sharp dagger, stealing his breath. The late afternoon sun peeked through the forest canopy as she passed the wagon, brightening the long blonde hair cascading over her pointed ears and glistening off a small earring. On the second horse behind Eladonia was her companion, Aeotus. He was slumped over and unconscious. His long brown hair was matted with dried blood.

The goblins led the two elves past Toak to the caged wagon and stopped beside it. "Off the horse, elf," one of the goblins said, shaking his spear at her. Hesitantly, Eladonia dismounted from the horse and glanced back at Aeotus as two other goblins pulled him off his horse. He landed with a hard thud, waking him from his wounded slumber. He groaned and rolled onto his back, revealing a grizzly wound across his face.

"Aeotus! You bastards!" Eladonia shouted at the goblins huddled around her friend. She followed up with more words in an unknown language as she pulled at her bindings. A nearby goblin knocked her to the ground with a well-placed blow from his spear behind her left knee, while another goblin approached Vandeer and retrieved the key to the cage.

"The elf is worth nothing to us dead, Toak!" Vandeer bellowed, looking at the goblin king while handing over the key to the cage.

"You'll take him as he is," Toak barked raspily. "Put them in the cage," Toak ordered his men.

A goblin hobbled to the caged wagon and paused, holding the key tightly. "Back away, dwarf!" the small creature grunted, baring its teeth and sniffing Bryce in disgust. Bryce backed away and let the goblin unlock and open the door. He watched four other goblins dragging Aeotus through the dirt toward the cage. "Eladonia," he moaned.

Eladonia lunged toward Aeotus, but two goblins put their spears in her face. "Get in the cage, or we poke your friend again," one of the goblins said, smiling broadly and shaking his spear at her. She sidestepped to the cage, keeping her sight on Aeotus.

Bryce helped Eladonia into the cage and assisted her in pulling Aeotus beside them. She knelt beside her friend and placed his head on her lap. He moaned again and passed out. Bryce started to untie her hands, but Toak shouted, "The bonds stay on the elves!" Bryce held his hands up and frowned apologetically at Eladonia. She nodded and brushed Aeotus' hair out of his face. The goblin locked the door before returning to Toak's side, presenting him with the key. "For your sake, make sure the prisoners get to where they're going on time," Toak said, throwing the key at Vandeer.

Bryce placed his hand on Eladonia's shoulder, knelt beside the elves, and whispered in her ear.

"We will take food as payment for your safe passage!" Toak shouted at Vandeer and directed his men to the food wagon.

"That was not our agreement," Vandeer responded, watching six goblins rush toward the food wagon.

"Changed my mind. I'll keep the horses, too." Toak paused before leaving. "And mind your tone. I'm king in these woods!" He turned his horse back toward the front of the caravan and trotted off.

Aticus snatched his bag from the bench before meddling hands could reach it. The goblins clumsily pillaged the wagon of any food they could carry, haphazardly hurling items to the ground as they raided.

Vandeer looked disgusted at the caged wagon. He seemed like he might do something brash, and he might have if some of his men had been allowed to return with him. The goblins bared their teeth and growled at Vandeer, running after Toak, each carrying what it could. He looked at Aticus and Rictor, who still held the reins in his hands. "You two clean this mess up so we can get moving," Vandeer said, motioning to the contents of the wagon on the ground.

The thick forest canopy blocked much of the waning sunlight as they resumed their journey, making it seem later than it was. Aticus couldn't take his eyes off the three prisoners in the caged wagon. Aticus was no longer concerned about the narrow paths as the afternoon progressed, but watched Bryce and the elf care for her unconscious companion.

The Alarians arrived at a spacious clearing as darkness covered the land. Over the years, they had cleared many such areas to use as campsites. The wagons were arranged in a large circle to create a secure zone in the center. Smaller fire pits had been dug near each wagon, and a large fire pit in the middle of the camp was where everyone gathered to eat and have fellowship.

Aticus and Rictor quickly unpacked what remained of the food wagon, only to find that the goblins had taken most of the dried meat and bread, leaving only fruits and vegetables behind.

After establishing the camp, the Alarians gathered around the central fire pit. After the goblin king's visit, the mood was solemn, devoid of singing or dancing, and parents kept their children close. As the moonlit night deepened, the light from the campfires cast eerie shadows that danced in the darkness of the forest. Unlike the Alarians, Aticus was not afraid of the night; he was eager. He completed his tasks while keeping a close eye on the three prisoners.

Aticus filled a wooden bowl with water and grabbed a rag. He paused and watched the Alarians sitting around the fire. The full moon cast a grayish, foreboding hue over the people. He turned towards the caged wagon and waited for his eyes to adjust to the darkness before approaching.

The moonlight shimmered through the canopy of leaves, revealing Bryce on his knees beside the elf. He chanted in an unrecognizable language, holding Aeotus' head in his hands. Eladonia knelt beside them, holding her companion's hand.

Aticus lingered near the caged wagon, holding the bowl. Though he couldn't understand the words Bryce spoke, they were beautiful. He admired Eladonia's delicate bone structure and ethereal beauty. When she opened her eyes and looked at Aticus, he diverted his gaze toward Bryce, hoping she hadn't seen him staring.

"Bryce said you would come with food and water," she said softly. "I am Eladonia."

Aticus gazed at her as if seeing her for the first time. Her eyes were a stunning shade of blue, even in the moonlight. "I'm sorry it took so long. I brought you water and a cloth. I'll gather some food for both of you shortly." He approached the cart and placed the bowl and fabric beneath the bars. "I'm sorry about your friend."

She inclined her head to see him better through the bars. "He's strong. He will live," she calmly stated.

"Is there anything I can do?" Aticus considered her shadowed features.

"You can open the door," she said pleadingly, rubbing Aeotus' hand.

Aticus hesitated, "I can't," he struggled to get those two words out.

She dipped the rag into the water and wiped her companion's face, careful not to touch the open wound. "Then there is nothing you can do for us, is there?" she responded harshly.

Aticus didn't know what to say. He idled momentarily and twisted his hands in his shirt as he turned to leave.

"Son," Bryce said, breaking his restlessness. Aticus turned and focused on their dark silhouettes.

Bryce touched Eladonia's shoulder to console her before looking at Aticus. "Thank you for the water and cloth. Bring her food; I'll be fine tonight." Bryce turned his attention back to Aeotus. Closing his eyes, he resumed his chanting. Eladonia continued to clean blood from her companion as the wagon glowed from the light of the moon peaking through the canopy of leaves.

Aticus retreated from the caged wagon to find food. He scoured through what was left from the goblin's raid and found nuts and berries. But tucked beneath a bag of grain, he uncovered dried venison that the goblins had missed. Aticus quickly returned to the caged wagon and, without speaking, pushed the plate of food beneath the bars and backed away into the shadows. He walked over to a small campfire near the food wagon, leaned against the wooden wheel, and thought about the day. *What if I could get the key from Vandeer? Could I help them escape? What would Vandeer do?* Aticus pulled his knees close and rested his elbows on them, holding his head in his hands. The evening progressed as the Alarians retired, and the protectors paced the forest line. Alone, Aticus stared into the darkness. He longed for sleep to take him from this living nightmare until he forgot what was keeping him awake. His eyes closed, and his head sagged one last time.

On the edge of the camp, in the caged wagon, Bryce sat with his legs crossed. He silently observed Aticus struggle to sleep. "I feel for the lad, Lord." Bryce nodded his head in agreement as if listening to someone. "Yes, he has a kind spirit and good heart." He looked at the two elves sleeping beside him, smiled, and answered an unseen voice. "I'm going on a new adventure," he said, looking at Aticus. He placed his hands in his lap and watched Aticus sleep.

Chapter Five

REVENGE

Gilanthos stopped by a stream near the path where he had been tracking the goblins. He tended to his wound before foraging for berries and found a large rock to conceal himself from the trail. It was getting dark, and he understood he wouldn't be much help to his friends in his current condition. He couldn't afford to make any mistakes that might lead him in the wrong direction. Despite feeling anxious, he knew his friends were still alive. With that in mind, he closed his eyes and slipped into a restless slumber.

The sound of a horse's hoof shifting dirt woke Gilanthos. He focused on the morning sunlight filtering through the leaves. "Flack!" He cursed, his body aching. Gripping the hilt of his sword, he moved to his knees, pressing his hand against the rock for support. Gilanthos peered around the stone. Two people had stopped on the path. His world swirled as the pain in his head returned with a vengeance.

One man dismounted. He was a towering monstrosity of a man, nearly seven feet tall. The muscles in his arms and chest stiffened when he landed on the trail. His skin was as dark as the blackest dirt Gilanthos had ever seen. He was Asvernian. He wore tan leather pants, no shirt, and a set of leather bracers inlaid with gold on his wrists. A shadowy leather belt with a large gold buckle helped support a two-handed sword on his hip. The casing, adorned with silver and gold engravings, reflected in the morning light. The absence of hair on the man's head seemed to reflect the sunlight with the same intensity as the inlaid scabbard.

A second light-skinned man sat in his saddle, patting the horse's mane. He was average, perhaps five and a half feet tall, dressed in black from head to toe. He had a sheath strapped to his back, cradling a katana sword, a favored weapon of warriors from the island of Satsun.

The large man removed a waterskin from his saddle and drank what remained.

The man in black retrieved his waterskin and gave it to the giant man. "Would you fill mine as well, Palias?"

Gilanthos looked at the creek; he knew they needed water. That's when he realized there was no vegetation along the stream for refuge. It was barren of bush or tree for at least fifty paces on either side of the stone. He pivoted to listen to their conversation.

"We should be out of the forest tomorrow, Yung Sung," Palias advised, gathering the waterskins.

"Good. I look forward to telling Normain about what we found in Azrel." Yung Sung shifted in his saddle, looking at the towering oak and pine trees.

The large man turned and strolled toward the creek.

Gilanthos adjusted his footing as he pulled his sword from its housing and steadied himself.

The dark-skinned man came into view and knelt by the stream, fifteen paces from Gilanthos. He appeared even more significant than when he stood on the trail.

Palias set the containers at his feet and rinsed his hands.

Gilanthos remained motionless. A bead of sweat trickled down the side of his face.

Palias dipped his hands into the fresh water, wiped his face, and paused before reaching for the waterskins. *He'd seen him!*

Gilanthos lunged forward, pressing the tip of his sword against the Asvernian's chest. "Don't move." He glanced at the trail and checked on Yung Sung. He was on his horse well out of distance to be a threat.

The large man towered over Gilanthos' six-foot frame by nearly a foot. Palias uttered in a deep, resonant tone that vibrated down Gilanthos' sword. "I don't want to hurt you," he said, as he pressed his hands out.

Gilanthos glanced back at the path; his head pounded. The man in black was gone! Both horses sat empty on the trail. Gilanthos looked at the giant in front of him. "Where'd he go?" he asked, as a hand touched his left shoulder and the point of a weapon pressed into his lower back.

"Drop your sword, and no harm will come to you," Yung Sung said, standing behind the elf.

"We won't hurt you; you have my word," reassured the bare-chested Asvernian.

Gilanthos dropped his sword in disgust; it clanged, striking bits of stone in the grass.

"You're safe with us. Do you understand me?" Palias pressed his foot onto Gilanthos' sword, making it difficult for him to retrieve it if he became inclined.

"I understand," Gilanthos responded, his head hung low.

"I'm Palias Bogdani, and this is Yung Sung." He pointed over Gilanthos' shoulder before motioning Yung Sung to come around from behind the elf.

Yung Sung removed his hand and withdrew the weapon from his back. He moved to stand beside Palias, dropping a twig in front of the elf to show what he had used to disarm him. A closer look revealed that Yung Sung was indeed from Satsun.

"I'm sorry. My intentions were not malicious," Gilanthos apologized.

"I know. You could have easily killed me," Palias replied.

Gilanthos nodded and glanced at Yung Sung, "The same could be said for you."

Palias glanced around the forest. "Where is your horse, and why are you hiding behind the rock?"

Gilanthos shifted and recounted what had happened the day before. "My friends and I were attacked by a pack of goblins."

Yung Sung interrupted, "Organized goblins, that's unusual."

Vexed, Gilanthos paused and looked at Yung Sung. "They killed our three escorts, and my friends, Aeotus and Eladonia, are missing," he replied, regarding the two.

Yung Sung closed his eyes and bowed his head. "I am sorry for jumping to conclusions and for your loss." He brought the elf back into view. "I only meant to say it's odd for goblins to be organized about anything, much less a successful attack on five elves," he replied and observed Palias.

Palias nodded. "You can understand our curiosity about your circumstances."

Gilanthos closed his eyes, and his shoulders sank. "I can," he sighed. "You can understand my embarrassment." He touched the side of his head. "I awoke in the brush after the attack with no recollection of what my friends faced."

"So then you don't know it was goblins that attacked you?" Palias inquired.

Gilanthos cut his eyes between the two men. "I know it was goblins. I am a tracker, and I know my friends are alive. They have them and our horses."

Palias retrieved the sword from beneath his foot. "I trust you. You could have killed me when you had the chance." Palias offered the elf his sword back.

Gilanthos looked Palias in the eyes when he took his sword.

"I will help you find your friends," Palias said, outstretching his huge hand and glancing at Yung Sung.

Yung Sung acknowledged Gilanthos, "My name is Yung Sung, and I will also help you."

Gilanthos looked at his sword. He knew he had no choice but to accept the help of two strangers. Aeotus and Eladonia's lives depended on him setting his pride aside. "My name is Gilanthos," he responded, taking Palias' hand. He acknowledged Yung Sung the same. "A stick?" Gilanthos looked down at the twig.

Yung Sung smiled and raised an eyebrow.

"Have you encountered any goblins this morning or last evening?" Gilanthos asked quickly, staying on task.

"No." Palias shook his head. "You're the only one we've seen since we arrived in the forest. Yung Sung and I discussed moments ago how quiet it was."

Yung Sung retrieved the waterskins as the men returned to the path and their horses.

Gilanthos knelt and studied the surroundings, nursing the side of his head. He quickly reacquired the goblins' trail while the two men climbed into their saddles. He thought before asking a question he already knew the answer to. "What direction did you come from, east or west?"

Sung answered and pointed. "We traveled from the west."

"The goblins were moving west. You saw nothing?" Gilanthos asked, rolling his eyes in thought.

"No," Palias replied. "But, there is a crossroads back some ways."

"Perhaps we missed the goblins. They may have taken the other trail," Sung suggested, as if he had solved a great mystery and was proud to do so.

Gilanthos looked at Sung and smiled. "Yes! That has to be it."

Sung held out a hand to help the elf into the saddle. "Let's go. You can ride with me; his horse is full." Sung regarded Palias.

Gilanthos suddenly realized how petite Palias' horse looked with him atop it.

Palias shrugged. "It's the largest one they had."

"You know you're going to kill it, right?" Gilanthos looked into the eyes of the horse.

It was past midday when the trio discovered the creatures. The three men would have passed them had it not been for a screaming goblin barking commands in a small clearing not far off the path.

Gilanthos and Yung Sung crept through the forest to get a better look. They found Toak and thirteen goblins relaxing, but no sign of Eladonia and Aeotus. They did have his and his friends' horses. They quickly decided to return and formulate a plan of attack with Palias.

Yung Sung revealed to Palias, "We counted fourteen goblins. Through conversation, we learned that Toak is their leader, and Gilanthos seems to think several more are missing."

Gilanthos nervously paced back and forth. "Our horses are there, but Aeo and Ela are missing." He locked his jaw and clenched his hands.

"We'll find them," Palias said. "The two of you set up on opposite sides of the clearing. I'll cause a diversion." Palias addressed Sung. "We take Toak captive and question him. What do you think?" Sung nodded. "Let's go find your friends," Palias reassured Gilanthos.

Gilanthos and Yung Sung slipped through the forest, taking their positions, and waited for Palias' entrance. Gilanthos gazed at his bow, which was secured to his horse's saddle. It was a gift from his father when he came of age.

It wasn't long, and Palias spurred his steed down the path. An ominous battle cry ensued!

Toak sat on a fallen log, eating dried meat, when he heard the yell. The goblins in his company soared to their feet, startled by the sound.

Palias came into view from the path. His two-handed sword was held high in his right hand, and a small, round shield was on his left arm, looking out of place in comparison. He spurred the horse into the clearing, leaping into the ground cover and throwing chunks of dirt in the air.

Yung Sung selected his targets. Four goblins stood between Palias and him. The goblins focused on the large man while three reached for their bows. Another looked to Toak for guidance. Sung lunged from the bushes, tossing two shurikens. The metal projectiles zinged past two nearby goblins who clumsily gathered their bows. The stars struck the two farthest goblins in the head and neck, sending them to the ground. Sung unsheathed his katana and charged towards the remaining goblin archers. He swiftly sliced the nearest creature, splattering a fine mist of blood. Then he tumbled to the side and plunged his sword into another creature's chest, finishing his attack.

Gilanthos emerged from the forest on the opposite side of Sung and leaped over a fallen tree. He quickly dispatched two goblins and slashed a third before advancing towards Toak.

Palias made contact using his momentum, striking a goblin in the face with the shield, crushing its skull, and sending its limp body into a tree. Palias sprinted through the undergrowth, kicking stones and brush as he charged at a group of five goblins huddled together for protection. He struck two more goblins on their faces with his shield as he swung it around in a wide arc, going over the heads of the three that evaded. He then spun around and brought his sword down on two additional goblins, causing their tiny bodies to be thrown violently onto the ground. The last goblin tried to run away but was caught by Gilanthos' blade in passing.

Toak was the last goblin standing. He dropped his feeble sword and stumbled backward, tripping over the log he had been sitting on a moment ago. "Please don't hurt me!" he screamed as he retreated against a tree. "Take anything you want, don't hurt me." He held his hands above his head and closed his eyes as Gilanthos approached him. Toak waited for the blow of Gilanthos' blood-stained blade as he wriggled on the ground.

"Where are they?!" Gilanthos yelled, pointing his sword in Toak's face.

The goblin king opened one of his eyes, hoping there might be a chance of survival. "Who?"

"You know who I am talking about! The elves! Where are they?" Gilanthos pressed the tip of the blade into his forehead.

"Oh yes, we gave them to a group of evil gypsies yesterday. Vile creatures!" He closed his eyes tight and cringed.

"Gave?" Gilanthos lowered the tip of the sword near Toak's throat. "What did they want with them, and where are they?"

Yung Sung and Palias approached on either side of Gilanthos. Sung placed his hand on the elf's shoulder to calm him.

When the two men appeared, Toak opened his eyes wide, shuddering and whining. "They went north; they took them north to trade with the goblins from Azrel. That's all I know. Spare me!"

Yung Sung chuckled.

Gilanthos glanced at Sung, irritated as to why the goblin's comment would generate such a response.

Yung Sung addressed Toak, "Azrel, the goblin mines?" Yung Sung smiled, wiping the blood from his sword, as he looked at Palias, Gilanthos, and Toak.

"Yes! That place!" Toak smiled and pointed at Yung Sung.

"No, they won't be meeting anyone from there," Sung declared as he sheathed his sword and grinned.

Palias chuckled, "No, they won't."

Gilanthos turned his attention toward Toak. "I should kill you right here." He tightened his grip on the sword and pressed it against the goblin's throat.

"Please, please, don't," Toak groaned. "Take it all, take my horses!"

"Your horses?" Gilanthos mashed his teeth together.

Yung Sung restrained Gilanthos from killing the goblin king. "There has been enough bloodshed today," he said, glancing at the carnage.

Gilanthos let his gaze drift to the fallen creatures around them. He yielded and lowered his sword. "Fine."

Yung Sung pulled the goblin to the side and grasped a nearby coil of rope. "Consider yourself fortunate." He bound Toak to a tree. "Not a word from you, understand?"

The goblin king nodded vigorously.

Gilanthos reunited with his mount, Capasius, brushing her mane. "It looks like everything's here." He retrieved his bow and draped it over his shoulder before reassuring his companions' mounts. "We'll get Ela and Aeo back; don't worry."

Shortly after, the three men returned to the path and continued east.

Toak watched the trio spur out of sight. The rope held him tight against the tree as the buzzing of flies flittered around the corpses of his men. The goblin king knew the remainder of his troops sent to scout would return soon and free him of his bondages. He would find his attackers and quench his vengeance. Toak considered for a moment; his eyes rolled from side to side. He pondered what his men might do. *Why would they*

set him free? What if they fight among themselves for leadership and kill him? Toak stood, supporting his weight, and began wrestling with the tree and his rope captive.

Chapter Six

FREEDOM

Aticus woke up stiff from falling asleep against the wagon wheel. Dawn brought a sharp chill to the air, signifying the approach of fall. Although temperatures seldom dropped below freezing in the forest and plains, the nights could become chilly. The highest elevations in the mountains had already seen early snowfall.

Aticus stood and rubbed his neck; he could still feel the wheel pressing against him. Terra approached.

"Good morning," she greeted him, a warm smile spread across her delicate face. "You look terrible."

"Morning." He acknowledged her and looked around for Vandeer. The camp was bustling with activity as the Alarians packed their wagons.

"Would you fetch me water?" Terra asked, patting him on the arm. "I'll keep working on meals." She smiled and walked toward the large fire pit near the camp center.

"I'll be right there," he said, running his hands through his hair and rubbing his eyes again. Aticus grabbed the wooden pail from the wagon and filled it from the water barrel. He glanced at the caged wagon. To his surprise, Bryce and the elves were awake and talking. Aeotus, whom he had thought was dead, leaned on the bars with his arm propped on his knee.

Aticus delivered the water to Terra and hurried back to the water barrel. He clutched three cups, topped them with liquid, and filled a small bowl with dried berries. Aticus approached the caged cart with his head hung low. After feeling scorned by Eladonia the night before, he didn't want a repeated altercation with a broader audience.

The three ended their conversation when Aticus arrived at the wagon. He passed the berries beneath the cage.

Bryce nodded and smiled. "Good morning, son!"

Aticus fought the urge to look at the elf he thought was dead. "Morning," he mumbled, forcing a smile for Bryce.

"You met Eladonia last night," Bryce introduced the elf maiden again. "And this is Aeotus." Bryce motioned toward the long-haired elf.

Aticus nodded. He was in awe of Eladonia's beauty by the light of day! She looked rested. Aticus glanced at Aeotus, and the wound on his face was gone!

"What's your problem, boy? What are you staring at?" Aeotus quipped and reared his head.

Bryce placed his hand on Aeotus' shoulder. "He is a friend." Bryce reached for the containers and passed them to the elves.

Aeotus acknowledged Bryce and bowed his head.

Bryce placed the berries between the three of them. "Thank you for the water and food, son."

"You're welcome," Aticus mumbled.

Bryce moved to the cart's edge. "You've been kind." He pressed near the bars and smiled. "Keep your head held high." Bryce nodded and winked.

Aticus turned and shuffled over to help Rictor pack the wagon.

Aeotus leaned near the dwarf. "Why do you care so much about the boy, Bryce?" They watched Aticus work.

"Have you ever believed in someone?" Bryce studied Aeotus. "He's a good person. They're all good people." He motioned toward the Alarians. "They want to survive and live the best they can in a world riddled with violence. You would do the same if you were in their place." Bryce let his eyes drift across the Alarian's camp.

Aeotus scanned the dwarf's features. "You're crazy! You'd live like them if you could. Wouldn't you? You would never catch me alive, merely existing, like these peasants. I'm not passive, and I sure as hell wouldn't let the goblins define me as such."

Bryce shook his head before speaking. "No, you would feel differently if you had a wife and children who could not defend themselves." Bryce looked at Aeotus and considered his words. "Do not judge others based on what you perceive to be a reality you cannot understand."

Aeotus shook his head.

"He's right, Aeo," Eladonia expressed. "Aticus has been kind to Bryce and shows genuine concern. I suspect that the others do not interact because of their shame."

"Eladonia, you are wise." Bryce placed his hand on her elbow and smiled. He studied Aeotus and set his hand on his arm. "We will be fine!"

"Seriously?" Aeotus gazed at Eladonia. "We've known each other since...I don't know, birth!" He pointed at Bryce. "You've known him one night, and you're siding with him?"

Eladonia stared at Aeotus and shrugged.

"That's it?" Aeotus paused and looked into Bryce's eyes. "How can you be sure you can trust him?"

"God tells me." Bryce smiled.

"Oh, God tells you? Well, everything will work out in our favor then, won't it?" Aeotus rolled his eyes and shook his hands.

Aticus sat on the bench beside Rictor as the wagon lurched along the forest path. "What do you think will happen to the three of them?" He glanced back at the caged wagon.

Rictor snapped the reins. "They'll be made to work in the mines for the goblins." Rictor regarded Aticus. "Everything's going to be alright, Aticus. Vandeer spread the word that we wouldn't make any stops today. He wants to set camp early so we can prepare for the goblins."

Aticus studied Rictor but didn't respond. "I'm not worried about the goblins. I'm concerned about what will happen to them after the goblins take them." He stared back at the three in the caged wagon again.

In due course, the caravan reached the northernmost portion of the forest. The path split into two: one led south in Shandar, and the other led north out of the woods. The caravan traveled the northern road. After a short journey, they emerged from the forest into a vast grassy region that stretched for as far as the eye could see. On the horizon, the tips of a small mountain range loomed. Home to the goblins and the mines of Azrel. They established camp within a few hours of dusk. Vandeer visited each family, reassuring them everything would be well. The protectors set up positions around the wagons, keeping their weapons close at hand.

With dusk came a heightened sense of anxiety. Vandeer stood for the longest time and watched the north's grassy pastures for any sign of movement. He would grow tired of waiting and venture into the night, only to return to the circle of wagons.

Aticus sat on the food wagon, watching Vandeer and the three in the cage. More than once, he started to get down from the cart and go to Bryce, but stopped. He couldn't bear to disappoint him. He knew the dwarf would accept the Alarians' transfer to the goblins. The elves would not fare so well with the news they'd be working in the mines, so Aticus chose to stay away.

Darkness fell, and still no goblins. Uncharacteristically, the Alarians spent the evening huddled together in the wagons' center around the fire. Mothers held their children; a man drew in the dirt with a stick, and people trod near the campfires. Terra handed out food and water to ease fears. She stayed busy and kept her mind preoccupied. Rictor sat near the fire and rubbed his hands together. A nervous habit he'd picked up without the reins to otherwise distract him.

"I need to open the cage and set them free," he whispered. *Bryce told me I would do the right thing when the time came.* He reached for his bag. *How am I going to get the key from him?* Aticus looked at his bag. *Maybe I could use my knife to pry the lock.* He opened his pack, reached inside, and felt the knife and medallion as Vandeer disappeared into the darkness of the plains. Aticus knew this was his chance, if ever there was one.

"Hey!" Someone whispered from the far side of the wagon.

It took Aticus by surprise. He pulled his hand from the bag and nearly jumped off the bench.

"Hey, are you going to come with us?" A familiar voice echoed from beside the wagon.

Aticus repositioned to get a better view. "Bryce?" He focused on a small figure in the darkness.

The dwarf stood on the far side of the wagon near the treeline. "Well, are you coming?" Bryce outstretched his hands.

Aticus stood and looked back over the food wagon. The caged wagon was empty, but the door was shut.

"I'm right here!" Bryce whispered louder. Unsure if Aticus saw him, he looked at his hands. "He can see me, right?" he whispered into the night sky.

Aticus sat down and looked wide-eyed at the center of the campsite. *The elves,* he thought to himself, *where could they have gone?*

"Come on, let's go," Aeotus hissed from ten or fifteen paces behind Bryce, near a tree at Eladonia's side.

She waved her hand, inviting Aticus to come.

Aticus moved to the edge and jumped off the bench. "What—but how did you get out?" he asked, realizing how short the dwarf was. The top of his head came to Aticus' chest.

"Quiet now—what do you think? We're escaping." Bryce grabbed Aticus' shirt cuff and pulled him toward the forest line.

Aticus didn't resist and moved into the woods with the trio. His mouth sagged. "How did you get out? I don't understand." He looked back, his steps slow and clumsy. Aticus heard a twig snap beneath his foot and stopped. "Wait."

"What?" Bryce asked; he stared into Aticus' eyes, his hand holding tight to his shirt cuff.

Aeotus placed a finger to his lips. "Would you shut up? I could have done it anytime. I cast a simple spell but had to wait for the right opportunity."

"But, but." Aticus held still. "A spell? I can't go!" He glanced back into the darkness behind them. "I don't know what to do."

"This is his first escape attempt. Give him a break," Eladonia whispered.

"Oh," Aeotus looked at her and rolled his eyes. "Mine too." He shrugged and looked at Bryce before he addressed the dwarf. "And how about you? I suppose this isn't your first?"

Bryce let go of Aticus, shook his head, and counted his fingers.

"Oh, blessed dragon droppings, can we discuss this later? I want to put some distance between them and us," Aeotus hissed, shook his head at the dwarf, and pointed toward the Alarian's camp.

Eladonia chuckled.

Bryce grabbed Aticus and pulled him behind the elves. The deeper they moved into the forest, the darker it became. Soon, Aticus couldn't see but a few feet in front of him. The moon hugged the horizon, hidden by the forest, and wouldn't be high in the sky for days. Several branches slapped Aticus in the face and across his chest.

"Stop," Aticus whispered. "I can't see a thing!"

"Damn, I forgot humans can't see in the dark!" Aeotus whispered.

"We can stop for a few moments," Eladonia added.

"Yes, here, sit. Behind you is a log." Bryce helped Aticus sit down.

"I, I can't go any further. I have to go back!" Aticus exclaimed, studying the darkness behind him.

"No, you don't. Come with us." Bryce shifted closer so Aticus could see his face. "There is nothing there for you. You're free! Free Aticus! Do not fear the unknown." Bryce placed his hands on Aticus' arms to comfort him. "You're not alone anymore."

Aticus struggled to see Bryce, but he recognized the expression on the dwarf's face. "I've never done anything like this," he whispered before glancing back once more into the darkness of the past.

Bryce placed his hands on Aticus' face, turned his head, and looked him in the eyes, "You are not alone."

Aticus opened his eyes wide. "What about Terra and Rictor?"

Bryce smiled. "They will live their lives, and you shall live yours." He patted Aticus' cheeks, aligning their vision again.

Aticus overheard the elves speaking and turned his attention to the voices in the darkness.

"If we keep going in this direction, it should lead us to the southern trail," Eladonia stated.

"Yes, I agree. The more distance between us, the better." Aeotus expressed while he scanned the forest. His features sagged. "Do you think Gil survived? I'm worried about him." He looked into Eladonia's blue eyes and reached for her hand.

"He has to be. I won't let myself." She paused. "I never saw him when the fighting began, which worries me; he would never have let us fight alone." Eladonia closed her eyes. Taking a deep breath, she held Aeotus' hand.

Aticus couldn't see the elves, but he acknowledged the fear in their voices. "I can lead you back where the goblins stopped us yesterday. At dawn, of course, when I can see. If you think it would be close to where your friend could be. I know all the trails of the forest." Aticus addressed the darkness.

"Yes, that would help," Eladonia answered. "We need to get to the trail before daylight."

"I'll guide Aticus through the trees. The two of you lead the way." Bryce placed a hand on Aticus' arm.

"Alright," Aeotus declared. "Let's go."

"Wait," Aticus breathed in deeply and closed his eyes.

"Seriously? Again?" Aeotus questioned as he flung his hands in frustration.

"That is the smell of freedom, son." Bryce smiled and watched the creases in Aticus' face disappear. "This is your new start!"

Aticus opened his eyes and smiled. "I'm ready."

Chapter Seven

DON

Don's wide-brimmed hat was getting battered by frigid rain droplets as the dark, overcast sky gave way. The brim of his hat filled with rainwater, and droplets trickled onto his shoulder, spattering his stern face. The snow was soon to fall, transforming the mountains landscape. Don was cold, but he had something more critical that demanded his attention. He raised the collar of his trench coat to cover his ears.

The cemetery was lined with tombstones and oversized granite statues of all measures and forms. Some resembled angels, while others perhaps favored a deity, paying homage to those who lay below.

He made his way to the front of a large crypt near the center of the cemetery. A rusty iron gate dangled by a single hinge and squeaked under its own weight in the wind. Sedric, a husky man with a thick, dark beard, walked up beside Don; the edges of his beard were covered with a thin layer of ice. The sharp chill in the air made their every breath hang in the air.

Two other men walked near, one beside Don and the other beside the bearded man. Both were dressed alike, each with a hooded cloak pulled over his head. They wore leather armor stiffened by the cold, which creaked with each step they took. Each man carried a hooded lantern that directed the spotlight ahead, causing the rain to shimmer like crystals in the light.

The four cautiously entered, descending a long set of stairs that led to the crypt. They stopped in a small room that preceded the tomb. The lights from the lanterns cast eerie shadows onto the uneven walls, giving them an unnatural appearance.

An ornate archway on the opposite wall led into the vault room. The smell of the wet earth weighed heavily and hung in their throats.

Don examined the room from top to bottom. Careful not to disturb the setting, he knelt and inspected the moist earth, "Lycanthrope."

"Got them a baddy, do they?" Sedric commented, brushing the ice from his beard with his forearm.

"A good-sized one by the looks of it," Don added.

The two men holding the lanterns shifted uncomfortably, grasping their swords firmly. Both remained silent, directing the lamps toward the arched doorway and the stairs behind them.

Don studied the men waving the lanterns. "Calm down and keep your heads."

"I know I'm keepin' mine right where it is," Sedric said with a sarcastic grin. His statement seemed to alienate the two men further.

Don rolled his eyes and shook his head at the comment. "Terrell, you and Frank keep an eye on the stairs. You're both going to be fine."

Frank whispered, lowering his head in Don's direction. "How do you know it's a Lycan?"

Don stood. "I know."

"Could it be in the other room?" Terrell questioned.

"No, it's not in the crypt," Don responded.

"How do you know?" Frank asked.

"If the waving of the lanterns hadn't brought it out to attack, then the pounding of your hearts would have by now."

"They smell too," Sedric whispered, glaring at Don.

"You never said anything about Lycans when you hired us!"

"I said Lycan, as in one."

"But you said it was big," Terrell added, shining the lantern in Don's face.

"Watch the stairs!" Don motioned toward the steps, giving them no more thought, and focused on what he had come to do.

Terrell and Frank glanced at one another. Their expressions sagged as they moved to the bottom of the stairs.

Don reached into his cloth tunic and pulled out a blackened and tarnished silver cross he wore around his neck, letting it dangle on his tunic.

Sedric handed Don a small pack hanging over his shoulder and drew his sword. "You ready, boss?"

Don responded with a crooked smile and nodded at the arched door leading into the tomb. He slung the pack over his shoulder, lifted the lantern from the floor, and advanced through the archway. With his lamp held high, the tomb came into view while the light spread throughout the room. He stopped and studied each shadow.

Sedric raised his lantern to Don's left, dispelling the dancing obscurities.

The crypt measured forty paces deep by twenty paces wide. On the chamber's far side, a small stone pillar supported a metallic urn. Its silver inlay reflected the lantern's light onto the surrounding walls.

Three caskets were angled along either side of the tomb. The head of the coffins angled toward the walls and rested on a richly detailed, intricately chiseled stone pedestal.

Don pointed at the dirt. "Someone's been here, and it hasn't been long."

Sedric studied the earth. "Whoever it was, they were all over the chamber. Where do you want to start?"

Don moved to the first casket on the left. "We'll start here." He placed his lantern beside him and removed his pack. Untying it, he retrieved a wooden stake and a mallet. Don paused and looked at his left hand, scarred by fire as a child.

"Does it hurt?" Sedric asked.

"No. It's one more reminder of why I do what I do."

Sedric moved opposite Don, placing his lantern on the foot of the coffin. "I keep telling you I'm not doing this part anymore. Last time you staked, I got hit." He wrinkled his nose and stared at Don. "Remember?" He opened his mouth, bringing his teeth together, pressing his tongue through a small gap where one of his teeth had once been. "I was struck so hard I swallowed it, so help me, if I get thumped today, I stake from now on."

Don rolled his eyes. "Fine." He positioned himself beside the casket, stake and mallet in hand, prepared to strike.

Sedric reached over the casket and placed his hand on the handle. He lifted the lid, stepping away in one fluid motion. Sedric could tell from Don's expression and relaxed posture that the casket did not contain the prize they sought.

Don quickly moved to the next casket, staying along the left wall. "We need to act quickly, Sedric."

"I'm coming. I'm coming." He placed the lantern atop the casket as he'd done with the last. Again, they repeated the process with the same result. "This never gets old." Sedric smiled, forcing his tongue through the void in his teeth.

The two men moved and repeated their routine on the third and final casket on the left wall. Sedric reached over and lifted the lid.

Don looked puzzled and wiped the sweat from his brow with his arm. "It's empty."

Sedric smiled. "Must belong to the one we got in town last night?"

Don shifted his eyes from side to side. "I would expect that much." He moved to the coffin closest to the urn on the right wall.

Sedric took his place, setting the lantern on the coffin. He reached over the casket to grab the handle when an inhuman howl erupted from the adjoining room. Don and Sedric stopped, and their eyes met.

"Oh, I knew this was going too easy," Sedric remarked.

"We need to finish this. Frank and Terrell don't stand a chance." Together, they moved in perfect unison, as they had done countless times before. Sedric reached for the handle on the head of the coffin. In that instant, the casket's lid flew back into Sedric with such force that it surprised him. He was thrown back off his feet and into the pedestal behind him. The lantern on the coffin smashed onto the ground near Sedric, extinguishing itself on impact.

Two slender hands extended from the casket, the driving force behind the lid. The candles and torches set around the tomb ignited with a brilliant flash. The sudden onset of light that illuminated the tomb left Don unaffected. He stared into the fierce eyes of the vampire while he drove the wooden stake into its heart, followed by a solid blow of the hammer, thrusting the wooden weapon deeper into its chest, ripping flesh and cracking bone. Blood sprayed from the coffin onto the wall, pulling away loose dirt as it crept downward. The creature swung at Don, but he held the stake in place. He beat back the vampire's hand with the mallet, splattering blood throughout the coffin.

Don never looked away from the vampire's eyes, holding his gaze. He didn't know who this person had been or what circumstances had led him to become this beast. He only knew it must die! The work was personal to Don. He felt no remorse for his actions, only a sense of satisfaction.

The creature let out a piercing scream and tried to reach for the wooden stake. The vampire began to turn to dust where the wooden post had entered its body. A tsunami of ash overtook the creature's flesh, spreading until nothing was left to incinerate, leaving behind only clothes.

The lid of the casket above Sedric exploded!

Sedric pressed himself nearer to the pedestal in the hope of concealing himself.

Another vampire arose from the coffin, hurling chunks of the wooden lid into the dirt wall.

Don considered the creature's soulless eyes, unfazed by the vampires' abrupt exit.

The undead knelt in the coffin, raised its arms, and presented its fangs brazenly.

Don held up the stake he used and tossed it over the casket onto the ground beside Sedric as a sign of surrender.

The vampire failed to notice Sedric lying below the casket, pressed against the pedestal.

The Lycan attack echoed from the small room leading to the tomb. Frank and Terrell's lanterns cast desperate shadows through the archway as the two men fought for their lives.

The vampire shifted his eyes and listened to his protector killing in the next room. He smelled the blood pouring from their fleshy vessels as he gazed at Don and licked his pointed teeth.

Sedric gripped the stake tightly, forcing his knuckles to go white. He pressed his tongue into the gap between his teeth. A habit he'd taken up in hopes it might keep his teeth in place or at least out of his throat.

Sedric leaped up, plunging the wooden stake into the creature, using his weight to fall against the vampire into the coffin and over the other side. Sedric fell forward hard, headfirst onto the solid earth; the monster's ash remains did little to soften his impact.

Don moved next to Sedric and helped him to his feet.

The two men stood side by side, focusing on the archway's silent darkness.

Sedric expelled the ash from his mouth and patted it from his clothes while brushing his teeth with his tongue and checking for new gaps. Favoring his right shoulder, he rubbed his elbow and forearm. "I quit! This one's yours."

Don glanced at Sedric, "What?"

"Don't look at me like that. I assumed you were staking. I had to clean your mess." He pointed at Don. "It's your turn!" Sedric replied with a sneer.

"I assumed you'd kill it, not dance with it!" Don quipped.

The werewolf lurched from the darkness with yellow eyes atop a long, hairy snout. It took a deep breath and looked at the open coffins around the chamber. Finally, it laid eyes on the two men, snapping its powerful jaws and revealing large, blood-covered teeth. The stench was overwhelming. The werewolf's muscles tightened, its skin stiffened, and every hair on its body stood on end as it howled, forcing a foul breath into the room. Its hands, covered in blood, flesh, and leather, shook.

Don pulled back his long coat and lifted his leg, drawing a dagger from the inside of his boot. The white ivory handle starkly contrasted with the dullness of the silver blade. He charged around the last unopened casket.

As Don arrived, the werewolf lurched forward into a defensive posture. The monster lashed out with its muscular arms, missing Don's head by inches.

Don thrust the long dagger deep into its chest.

The werewolf winced in pain but brought both arms back and slashed for Don's head again.

Don lowered himself toward the ground, letting his attacker strike the air, missing the crown of his head. Don thrust the dagger in deep, pulling the blade upwards, ripping it from the torso, creating a more massive wound than the first. Hair and blood sprayed onto Don.

Again, the Lycan swung for Don's head. The creature struck his hat this time, knocking it to the ground. The Lycan gasped for air.

Don continued downward on one knee. Lashing out with increased speed, he repeatedly struck the creature's gut while blood poured unobstructedly, sending hair and flesh into the air. He jabbed upward, but the Lycan swung wildly, missing Don.

Suddenly, the creature tried to pull away, moving its hands to block the onslaught. The creature wailed in pain as fingers were severed, trying to stop the thrusts of the dagger. Backed against the wall, it had nowhere to go. With its life force spilling freely, its legs began to buckle.

Don sensed the creature going down, so he stepped back.

Its eyes glazed over. A gurgle replaced the screams as it slid down the dirt wall and came to rest.

Don turned to Sedric, "Check that last casket; it should be a corpse."

Sedric confirmed what Don had asked of him: "It looks like a done deal." He let the casket lid slam shut.

Don stared at Sedric, his brows folded inward. "The empty casket couldn't have belonged to the vampire we killed in town last night. He'd recently turned. We're missing one." Don shifted his eyes from side to side. "Of course. We're missing a female; she's the one who turned all of them." Don pointed to the coffins. "She knew we were coming."

Sedric moved beside Don. "I know who told her about us." He pointed at the werewolf, who had reverted to his human form in death. "Ain't that the mayor of the town? We talked to him yesterday?"

Don glanced down with a huff. "Makes sense. I told him we would finish this today."

"He warned her then. She's gone."

Don looked at Sedric. "We'll find her." He retrieved his hat from the floor, pounding it against his leg.

The two men doused the coffins and bodies with flasks of oil that they pulled from their bags, setting them on fire before leaving the tomb.

Don buttoned his blood-soaked coat. They stood and watched the black smoke billow from the tomb. The smell of burning flesh floated in the wind while large snowflakes danced with the rain.

CHAPTER EIGHT

FOUND

More than once, Aticus stumbled into Aeotus, initiating an awkward interaction between the two men. It usually ended with the elf swearing, which prompted Aticus to look back into the darkness, assuming Bryce would translate.

The dwarf laughed and shook his head. "I'm not repeating what he said, Aticus."

"I can barely see him. I can't help it." Frustrated, he held his hands up and looked for Bryce in the darkness.

Not long after, they reached a main trail and traveled along its edge.

Suddenly, Eladonia took a knee, and Aeotus stopped.

Aticus slammed into the elf again, propelling both men onto the ground.

Bryce covered his mouth to keep from laughing out loud.

Aeotus rolled to his feet, tugged Aticus off the side of the trail, and shook him. "Say nothing and be still, dandelion," he whispered, holding Aticus down.

Bryce kneeled beside Aticus and pressed his finger over Aticus' lips.

Clicking sounds emanated from the dark in the direction Eladonia had been. Aeotus recreated the note and disappeared into the darkness and down the path.

"Remain silent," Bryce whispered, patting Aticus on the arm. "They heard a noise and are looking."

Again, Aticus heard clicks and whistles in the dark.

Aeotus appeared alongside the two men and knelt.

Eladonia's voice, lost in the night, broke the silence. "It's Gilanthos. Come here, Aeotus!"

Once again, Aeotus disappeared down the path into the night.

"Who did they find?" Aticus asked, searching the darkness of the trail.

"They found their dead friend." Bryce helped Aticus to his feet.

"Dead friend? They found his body?"

"No, no, son. They found him alive. Those are the sounds you heard. Gilanthos is their friend they feared dead." Bryce smirked at Aticus. "I see them down the path. They're embracing one another now."

Aticus tried hard to see but couldn't discern anything. "I wish I could see as well as you."

"Yes, well, it only works in complete darkness. Well, a little light, at least. If we had a torch, I would be as blind as you, distance-wise." He patted Aticus on his back. "Here they come now."

Aticus overheard the elves conversing when they approached. "Where have you been?" Aeotus asked Gilanthos.

Gilanthos squeezed Aeotus' shoulder. "Trying to find you and Ela, of course. You'll be happy. I made new friends and a few enemies along the way. We tracked the goblins that captured you and, with a little persuasion, discovered where you were."

Eladonia embraced Gilanthos. "This is Bryce and Aticus." Eladonia considered Aticus during the introduction.

"It's a pleasure to meet you, Gilanthos." Bryce clasped the elf's hand in acknowledgment.

Aticus waved at Gilanthos' shadow.

"You said we?" Aeotus looked at Eladonia before addressing Gilanthos. "When the goblins ambushed us, we saw two Evermoure escorts fall. Did the other survive?"

"No. We lost all of our escorts. Although I did encounter two strangers, they helped me find the goblins. "I'll take you to meet them, they're back where we set camp for the night," he said, pointing behind him. He let out a sigh of relief. "It was difficult to rest, so I came looking, knowing both of you were out there somewhere, alive." Gilanthos placed his hands on Eladonia and Aeotus, his expression relaxed. "We'll sleep well tonight," he addressed everyone in the group. "Come with me."

Gilanthos escorted them down the trail and eventually into the forest, where they saw a campfire in the distance.

"Palias, Yung Sung, I found my friends!" Gilanthos announced proudly.

The two men sitting around the fire stood to greet everyone.

"How did you find them?" Sung asked.

Palias patted Yung Sung on the back and smiled.

Aticus' mouth sagged at the sight of the large Asvernian. His dark, muscular frame towered over him by almost two hands.

Bryce poked Aticus, causing him to bring his jaw back into alignment.

"This is Palias and Yung Sung." Gilanthos acknowledged the Asvernian and the man from Satsun. "These are my companions, Eladonia," he laid his hand on her arm, "and Aeotus."

"I'm glad to see everyone is well," Palias responded.

Sung bowed to the newcomers.

Eladonia proceeded to introduce the dwarf and Aticus. "This is Bryce and Aticus."

Bryce and Aticus shook their hands.

"Bryce saved Aeotus' life. He is a healer." Eladonia grinned at the dwarf.

"He's not a healer. It was magic, and I would have been fine." Aeotus retorted.

"A healer?" Palias asked.

"I am but a humble servant of God and nothing more," Bryce responded.

"You are a rare find if you are a healer, sir dwarf." Sung bowed.

Bryce shook his hands and head.

The elves dismissed themselves and reunited with their mounts, searching through their packs. Gilanthos rubbed his head and had Eladonia and Aeotus look at the wound.

Aticus sat near the fire with Bryce while Yung Sung helped Palias care for the horses. "Bryce, can I ask you a question?" he asked, eyeing everyone else.

"Of course, you can, son. What is it?" Bryce rubbed his hands toward the fire.

"Aeotus, how did he survive? When I saw him yesterday, I thought he was dead." Aticus regarded the elves as he spoke.

"It was not his time to die, I suppose." He shrugged. "I'm sure he has a role to play." Bryce studied Aticus while he crossed his legs.

"What do you mean has a role to play? I don't understand?"

Bryce glanced at the ceiling of leaves. "Perhaps God has a task that only Aeotus can perform, and I was there to help." Bryce pressed his lips together.

"Healed, how could you heal a wound like that? Is it magic?" Aticus pulled his knees against his chest.

"Oh, son. I didn't heal him, and it wasn't magic. God healed him through me. I am but his humble vessel." Bryce's words oozed with pride.

"How did that happen?" Aticus asked.

"Many years ago, God sent an angel to save me. A few days later, He revealed to me in a vision that I would seek the one. My calling is to search for that individual and aid them in any way I can." As Bryce stared into the fire, a calmness smoothed his features. "God speaks, guides, and protects me wherever I go."

"The one? Who is the one?" Aticus inquired.

Bryce looked at Aticus, "I'm not entirely sure. God didn't reveal who or where I would find them. I don't know whether the individual is a man or a woman." Bryce paused momentarily, staring at the fire before continuing, "But I have faith that I'll know when the time comes."

Aticus sat with his mouth ajar. "How long have you been searching?"

Bryce thought momentarily before replying, "Maybe fifty years, give or take a few." He smiled, "It's difficult to recall. It might be, more or less, hard to say." His gaze shifted back to the fire.

Aticus sat for a moment, taking it all in. "Ah, that seems like a long time to look for someone you don't know."

Bryce looked into Aticus' eyes and smiled. "That's where faith comes into play."

Aeotus approached the fire and sat down across from them. He was holding a leather-bound book, inlaid with silver embroidery, that shimmered in the fire's light. An expression of contentment spread across his face as he thumbed through several pages before closing it and holding it tight.

"Is that important?" Aticus found it uncomfortable to be around Aeotus but tried to make conversation.

Aeotus looked up at Aticus. "Yes, this is the one possession that I hold most dear. This book is my Evetrus, or spellbook in your language. It contains every spell I've learned and is a mage's most valuable possession." Aeotus shook the book. "I thought it was lost when the goblins attacked."

"You're a wizard?" Aticus asked.

Aeotus chuckled. "No, I am a mage. Perhaps, one day, a wizard. That will take extensive study and patience." He pondered a moment, considering the fire. "Perhaps I'll have a laboratory of my own one day if I am fortunate." Aeotus nodded his head in quiet confirmation. "Now, that is a mark of a true wizard." A smile creased the corner of his lips.

Aticus moved closer to Bryce and watched the flames dance along the blackened surface of the burning wood for a few moments before whispering, not to attract Aeotus' attention. "If he has magic, why didn't he use magic to escape before tonight?"

Bryce shrugged.

"The mechanism on the door had a lock spell cast upon it," Aeotus responded.

Aticus jerked his head in the elf's direction.

"I can hear more than you think." Aeotus pointed at his ears. "I had to pull a counter-spell from memory before I could spell the lock."

Aticus regarded Bryce. Confusion pulled on his features. "Spell? How can that be? The Alarians have no way to cast spells."

"Perhaps Vandeer had it done without the people's knowledge." Bryce patted Aticus on the knee. "We need to get some sleep. It'll be light soon."

"Agreed, I'll take the first watch," Palias offered in a deep voice, stepping up behind Aticus and the dwarf.

Aeotus looked up from the flames and nodded.

No one offered any opposition to the giant man.

Chapter Nine

THE QUEST

Aticus woke to the sound of boiling water. He sat up and looked around for Vandeer, but instead, he saw Eladonia standing near the tree line, talking to Gilanthos. There was something different about her. Maybe it was the light of day, or perhaps she was just happy. She smiled and laughed whenever Gilanthos spoke. Aticus thought she couldn't be more beautiful, but at that moment, she truly was.

It was strange not to see the Alarians breaking camp. The children weren't running and playing. Terra and her sisters weren't preparing the morning meal.

Palias sat near the fire, drinking from a goblet. His large hands made the cup appear as if it might belong to a child.

Aticus inspected the horses and wondered if he should fetch water from the stream, as it was his job to provide water for the animals.

He found Aeotus nearby, sitting on a rock, flipping through his leather-bound spellbook.

"Would you care for some tea?" Sung asked Aticus and knelt by the fire while he poured a brown liquid into a goblet.

Palias spoke from across the campfire. "It's delicious. I'm unsure what Yung Sung puts in here, but it's good," he said, considering Aticus.

Sung smiled and handed Aticus the goblet. "Let it sit for a moment before you drink it."

The sounds of the forest seemed different today. Aticus couldn't help but smile when he realized Vandeer would not be calling him.

Bryce approached and sat beside Aticus before patting him on the back. "Did you sleep well, son?"

Aticus smiled and nodded while he blew into the top of his cup.

Bryce addressed the large man across from him, drinking tea. "What brought you and Yung Sung through the forest?"

Yung Sung sat down beside Palias and crossed his legs, careful not to spill the cup's contents.

Palias regarded Yung Sung before speaking. "We're on a quest." Palias shifted his massive frame and rested an elbow on his knee, letting his gaze drift toward the dwarf. "We're returning to Veridian to complete our final task."

"And what an adventure it's been," Sung added, smiling at Aticus and the dwarf.

Palias' deep tone attracted everyone's attention. "Yung Sung and I were sent on three separate quests to retrieve parts of a sword." He paused and thought before standing. "Let me show you." Palias set the tea down and walked to his horse. He pulled a tightly wrapped cloth from his saddlebag and returned to the campfire. Sitting down, he crossed his legs and began to untie the bindings.

Gilanthos, Eladonia, and Aeotus approached to stand near the dark-skinned man, eager to see what he had to share.

Palias finished untying the rope and peeled back the cloth, revealing a blade. "This is Seravant, the sword of King Eston."

"What?!" Aeotus spat. "Where did you find that? The sword is legendary; it was lost a hundred or so years ago!" His mouth dropped open.

Palias placed the blade on the ground before him and continued to unwrap the cloth, revealing the grip and crossguard. "This is the hilt of the same sword. These…" he placed the handle on the ground beside the blade and pulled a small pouch from the cloth. "These are the Dwarven gemstones that fit into the hilt." He opened the bag and poured three colored gems into his hand: blue, red, and green. He placed them on the ground beside the sword.

"Impossible! That can't be the Seravant!" Gilanthos added.

"Are you aware of any other magical sword in history that contained that combination of gemstones?" Aeotus responded to his friend.

Bryce was on his knees, looking. "Well, now, let me see, that would be one hundred and forty-eight years, to be exact."

Aticus examined Bryce. "How would you know that?"

"King Eston died a year before I was born. I'm one hundred and forty-seven." A smile spread across the dwarf's lips. "You don't think we're taught world history?" He smirked at Aticus.

Aticus gawked at Bryce in amazement at his age, while the others examined the sword.

Eladonia moved closer, kneeling beside Yung Sung. "We studied King Eston when we were younger, remember?" She gazed at Aeotus. "Do you think this could be his sword?"

Aeotus studied the pieces carefully. "It's possible. I can tell the gems are enchanted. Turn the hilt over." He tapped Palias on the shoulder.

Palias turned the hilt over and laid it down.

"Look at the three divots in the handle. The gems go there." He tilted his head and studied the blade. "*Boren-da-la.*" He spoke the incantation. "The blade is imbued, but not as much as the gems." He tapped Palias again. "May I hold the blade?"

Palias lifted the sword and handed it to the elf. He realized Aticus was still staring at the dwarf in disbelief at his age.

Aeotus shifted the blade from side to side, studying it in earnest. "Yes, this is an elven blade, and it bears the mark of Thereon." He looked at Gilanthos and Eladonia. "The Blademaster, a master forger." He returned the sword to Palias.

"Who is Thereon?" Aticus inquired, returning to the conversation.

"He's the man who forged Seravant," Eladonia answered.

"When did he die?" Aticus asked.

"Oh, he is not dead!" Gilanthos added.

Palias excitedly stared at Gilanthos. "Do you think he can reassemble the sword?"

Aeotus laughed. "No, no, he won't. He's the Blademaster; he forges blades. That's not to say he couldn't complete a sword. This one is special. He wouldn't be able to assemble this particular sword without help. The gnomes are the ones who made this sword exceptional. If I remember correctly, the three gems were offered by the dwarves, the elves donated the blade, and the humans created the pommel, guard, and hilt. The gnomes assembled it, but history does not tell who enchanted the sword or the gems."

"Who took it apart?" Aticus asked.

Aeotus shrugged. "I don't know. It had to be the gnomes before they were slaughtered out of existence."

Palias looked at Aeotus. "Do you think Thereon could tell us who imbued the sword?"

"I doubt he knows. If I had to guess, the blade was forged and taken to another location before completion," Aeotus suggested.

"Maybe Normain can tell us when he examines it?" Yung Sung questioned, tapping Palias on the arm.

"Who is Normain?" Aticus asked.

"He's an elderly man who understands artifacts greatly," Yung Sung responded.

Palias followed up with Yung Sung. "He sends people on quests to gather artifacts. His only condition for the information is that you return to him with the item so that he can examine the artifact." Palias studied the blade before continuing. "Then he lets you take it." He looked at the components spread before him. "A few months back, we came across Normain in a tavern in Veridian. We overheard him making arrangements with others and were intrigued, so we approached to inquire about finding a sword. He shared the sword's history and expressed his eagerness to see it. Normain told us he was an explorer when he was younger. He wants to see as many artifacts and treasures as possible before he dies."

"You've been looking for the sword for some time?" Aticus asked.

Palias nodded. "He sent us out for the hilt first. When we returned with it, he sent us out for the gems. After we returned with those, he gave us an idea of where the blade was. That proved a little more difficult."

"How so?" Bryce inquired.

"We found it in an ancient underground city near the goblin mines you would have been forced to work in," Palias added and smiled.

"The mines of Azrel?" Aticus interrupted.

"Yes, that would be the one," Yung Sung boasted before Palias could.

"Those are the goblins that come and take the prisoners from us."

Bryce placed his hand on Aticus' arm, stopping him. "From the Alarians, son. Not you."

"Well, I'm certain the goblins from Azrel won't be visiting anyone for some time." Sung chuckled before finishing. "Not unless they have another way of making new goblins I don't know about."

Palias chuckled and began wrapping the sword.

Aticus relaxed and glanced at Bryce. A look of peace spread across his face. Thankful the Alarians would not be dealing with the goblins from the north.

"Perhaps the lad and I could accompany you south?" Bryce motioned toward Aticus with his thumb.

Aticus grinned at Palias and Yung Sung.

Palias regarded Sung before he spoke, "It would be a pleasure. You're both more than welcome to come along." Palias looked at the three elves, "The three of you are also welcome to join us."

The three elves looked at one another, each one apprehensive about answering.

Gilanthos scanned Eladonia's face before speaking, "It's up to you. We're due in Evermoure in a couple of weeks. They'll become suspicious when we don't arrive. I'm sure they'll start sending out search parties at that point."

Aeotus looked at Gilanthos sternly. "You understand how she feels. Why force her to go at all?"

Eladonia snapped at Aeotus. "Stop! He knows how I feel! You know that. I have no choice."

Aeotus regarded Gilanthos apologetically, like a scolded child.

"We can travel with them. We're going south anyway, and it'll be on our way." Eladonia considered Aticus while she spoke.

Aticus didn't want to see the elves go; he didn't want to see her go.

Gilanthos favored the side of his head before speaking, "They won't take kindly to us arriving without the escorts! How are we going to explain that?"

"We tell them the truth!" Eladonia glanced at both her companions.

"I don't like it, Ela. Why can't we run?" Aeotus suggested.

Eladonia closed her eyes and shook her head.

Bryce stood, attempting to disarm the situation. "I recommend we be on our way before someone comes looking for us."

"Agreed." Gilanthos nodded and stood. "Bryce and Aticus, you can both take a horse. We have three extras." He regarded Palias before speaking. "You can have the remaining horse if you want it, Palias. She's a little larger than what you have now."

Palias shook his head. "I'm good with what I have."

"If we take the path south from here, we won't run into the Alarians. It will be several days before they pass this way again." Aticus commented.

"I'm more worried about the goblins looking for payback. I don't want a repeat run-in with them." Gilanthos added.

With everyone ready, the seven traveled most of the day on a path that Aticus was familiar with. Later that afternoon, Aticus showed the group a spot to replenish their water and tend to the horses.

Chapter Ten

ALL THE KINGS MEN

In another part of the world.

The waves of the northern sea thrashed upon the rock-laden shore while seagulls flew high over the castle walls, gliding in the brisk morning wind. King Balen Duskwater stood at a window overlooking the city of Meloorne, waiting patiently for his military advisors to arrive. He considered the city and the tens of thousands of men, women, and children he was sworn to protect. His heart was heavy with the news he had received about the orcs earlier in the morning.

Rath Inen, the king's advisor, stood behind King Balen, studying a large map encompassing an entire table. The map depicted the known lands of Idonia, with small flags scattered across the table representing the human and orc armies. Rath moved to stand beside his king. "My lord, how is the Queen? I've not seen her today."

"She's with the children." Balen gazed out the window as he spoke. "It's her birthday today, you know. Thirty-four, and has this notion that she is old." He chuckled and looked at Rath. "She asked me to thank you for the obnoxiously large mirror you gifted her. Rest assured, she will no doubt be critiquing herself more often than not in front of it. Thanks to you, my friend, I will be tasked with reassuring her that she is much more than a reflection."

A rap at the heavy wooden door interrupted their conversation.

"Enter," Balen announced.

Lathal Talos, the general in command of the king's knights, opened the door and bowed as he entered. "My lord, Rath, I have captain Duncan with me."

Following Lathal was Duncan, a young cavalier officer. Duncan's confident, charismatic smile induced a calmness in the room. He wore a light chain mail tunic that covered his lean, muscular frame. "My lord, Rath," Duncan offered a greeting.

"Come in," Balen said, gesturing with his hands. I've called everyone here to discuss our options for preparing for what we all know is an inevitable attack on our cities."

Lathal strolled to the table, placing his hands on the edge of the map. "My liege, I have serious concerns about what's occurring near the forward boundaries. As we briefly discussed this morning, we're running low on food and fresh water provisions. I estimate our troops have twenty-three days before we extinguish the current supplies for our encampment near the front line. We need to increase what's coming from Meloorne. Perhaps declaring an emergency rationing in the cities of both Meloorne and Glendale. As you know, Trillian provides most of the food provisions." Lathal sighed, "I'm not getting what I need from the governors, and I'm afraid we won't unless you're involved.

"I understand, Lathal. We'll make additional plans for supplying the forces on the front line, and these plans will not be open for discussion by the governors. I'll speak to them personally at the Queen's birthday celebration this evening," Balen responded.

"Thank you, my lord." Lathal bowed.

King Balen looked around the room before speaking. "Duncan, this morning, you expressed concerns about new movements by the orcs." The king crossed his arms and rubbed his chin.

"Yes, my lord. Our scouts have reported that the orcs have amassed more troops behind their main lines. It's not a matter of if they advance, but when. I've been to the front line, and you can see the fires of their encampment. I don't understand why they haven't pressed forward yet." Duncan paused to consider his words. "We believe that with their current numbers, when they decide to move against us, they'll easily overcome our forces on the front line. We won't be able to stop them." Duncan narrowed his eyes and scanned the table. He pointed at the small wooden pawn that represented the outpost of Parador. "Parador is our last defense, but it was never designed to defend against a siege." He gritted his teeth and regarded Lathal and King Balen.

"How much time do we have?" Balen asked, studying the expansive map.

"Once they decide to move, we estimate it will be three months before they are here in Meloorne," Lathal said.

"What do our scouts estimate the size of their army to be?" Balen asked Duncan.

"Conservatively, they estimate over one hundred thousand, perhaps more," Duncan added.

Balen closed his eyes, bowed his head, and spoke to anyone who would answer. "How long could the city sustain that kind of attack?"

Rath responded first. "Days."

Duncan leaned over the table before speaking. "My lord, I recommend continued diplomacy with the elves and dwarves. Without their combined assistance," he paused before continuing, "I'm afraid to say that even with their help, there is no viable solution. I don't see an outcome that would be in our favor."

King Balen leaned against the table and sighed. "The elves will not support us. I've offered every conceivable concession, but they still refuse to help. The elves think if they stay out of the war, the orcs will leave them alone. I don't understand how naive the elves could be for a race that has existed long before ours, and the dwarves have offered support in the form of weapons and refuge when the time comes." He turned and walked to the window, peering over the unfortunate inhabitants. "I don't have the answers, gentlemen, and I don't think anyone does."

"My lord, what about the Asvernians? Can they offer any assistance?" Lathal asked.

"King Bogdani reassured me he would supply as many of his ships as required to evacuate the cities. He guaranteed sanctuary for our people if it came to that." King Balen tapped his fingers on the stone slab of the window.

"Damn the elves, the dwarves, and the Asvernians." Lathal cursed. "Don't these fools know that when Meloorne falls, Idonia will fall into chaos?!"

The king returned to the table. "We must be strong for our people. We can not let them feel our helplessness."

"I recommend we draft all men of age for the garrison," Lathal offered.

"Yes, we'll need everyone when the time comes." Balen addressed Rath. "I want you to issue an order by my creed, the drafting of all men fifteen and older to report to the garrison of their city for training." King Balen returned to the table, "I don't know what will happen in the days and weeks ahead, but we must be strong for our people."

Chapter Eleven

BLADECANTOR

Aticus stepped away and gathered berries while the others filled their waterskins from the stream. The sun's warmth radiated through the canopy of leaves and felt good on his skin. He stopped and took in the sunlight, letting it warm his face.

As he stood out of sight from the others, he couldn't help but think about Vandeer and the Alarians. He wondered if Rictor, who was now alone on the wagon, would be okay. He hoped that Terra would find someone to bring her water. Most of all, he wished that Vandeer and the rest of the tribe would find peace.

Aticus heard a rustling in the bushes ahead of him. He looked up, thinking it was Yung Sung looking for herbs. He was wrong! Forty paces away, part of the forest peeled back, and four small creatures emerged. They appeared surprised to see Aticus, but not as surprised as he was to see them. Their pale green skin and petite features allowed them to blend well with the forest. They were goblins, and they kept coming from the brush. Each goblin stopped upon entering the clearing.

Another one stepped out, and another one. There were twelve now, Aticus counted. Still, he didn't move.

One of the goblins shouted something and pointed at Aticus. Another brought his bow up and reached for an arrow from the quiver.

Aticus turned to run but tripped and fell hard. An arrow struck the tree near his face, causing him to shudder. He could hear the goblins heckling as he struggled to gain his footing. Thud! Another bolt struck the ground inches from his hand. Pushing forward, he glanced up and saw Eladonia emerging between two large trees.

She passed him, leaping over a large bush. He hadn't seen her wear a sword before, much less two. They were strapped to her back, supported by a leather harness, tight against her firm torso. The handle of each sword balanced above her shoulders. The steely sound of the blades sang when she pulled them from their casings.

Gilanthos lunged from the forest line and stopped beside Aticus. He knelt and notched an arrow. When he released the string, the bowstring hummed, launching the shaft into the bow-wielding goblin's chest, sending him to the ground.

Aeotus approached Aticus and pushed him to the ground into a sitting position. "She's got this," Aeotus said, kneeling beside Aticus.

Gilanthos lowered his bow with another arrow readied.

"Shouldn't we help her?" Aticus' voice cracked.

The goblins drew their short swords and charged toward her. She caught one across the face with the tip of her sword, sending it sprawling to the ground. Eladonia began to whistle while she twisted her body around, bringing the second sword down on another goblin. The creature slammed into the ground violently.

Aticus heard Eladonia humming, and then she began singing. Her attacks corresponded with the elvish melody she murmured. Each thrust matched a high note in her song. Another goblin fell, but still, they came. She dipped and dodged their attacks, none of which came close. The tempo of her song grew quicker, and so did her actions. She extended her swords outward simultaneously, in different directions, eliminating two more. Her song grew in intensity, and her pace quickened with each kill. She spun around, striking one across the chest, annihilating the goblin.

"Beautiful, isn't she?" Aeotus said and sighed.

Her long blonde hair swirled behind her as she darted up and down. Bright-hued ribbons adorned the hilts of her swords and gracefully traced behind every action of the weapons.

"Yes, she is," Aticus answered, helpless to look away from her. "Shouldn't you help her?" he uttered.

Aeotus' eyes narrowed while he scrutinized Aticus, uncomfortable with his agreement concerning her beauty. "No, we'd be in the way."

For the first time, Eladonia blocked an attack from a goblin. She slid the blade of her sword down the goblin's weapon, removing its hand at the wrist. With her second sword swiping behind her, she lopped off an arm of another; she finished him with the twist of the blade, then spun around. A third creature routed, but she caught him on the neck, ending her melody of death. She stood silent as the goblin slid off the end of her sword. Her elvish theme of cessation continued and was swift for the last two aggressors. The final goblin lost its head between her twin weapons. Her melody finished as swiftly as it had begun, her dance ending in a poetic stance of triumph, swords lowered before her.

Aticus stared at the carnage splattered on the forest floor. There were pieces of goblin and blood everywhere. However, Eladonia had no blood on her except for the crimson dripping from her swords. Her tan leather armor was as clean as when she entered the fray.

Gilanthos shook his head and shifted toward Aeotus. "Were you ever that clean when you used the bladecantor?"

"No, I could never do that. One more reason I failed at it," Aeotus noted. He stood and chuckled. "You okay, Aticus? You look a little pale."

Aticus was nauseous. He attempted to look away from the massacre, but he couldn't. Not while she was standing there. She was beautiful and horrific all at the same time.

Eladonia approached Aticus. "Are you alright?" She placed both swords in her left hand and presented Aticus with her free hand.

Aticus couldn't take his eyes off her. "Yes—thank you." He took her hand in his and pulled himself up.

She nodded and walked back to where she had emerged.

"You can close your mouth, Aticus," Gilanthos said, chuckling.

The three men turned and watched her walk away as she passed Yung Sung, Palias, and Bryce, who had arrived midway through her song.

Yung Sung was the first to break the silence after Eladonia disappeared into the forest. "How can I learn that, and where must I go?"

"You can't unless you have forty years to dedicate to the form as she has. It's the art of the bladecantor, a technique handed down for generations. She will teach it to her sons and daughters, and they will teach it to theirs. Her great-great-grandfather, Armanithia Eveningstar, was the father of the bladecantor. He developed the form and taught it during the Elven Wars." Aeotus answered.

Bryce shuffled past the others to stand near the goblin carnage. He shook his head in disgust. "This is taught to children! The elves teach their children this?!" Bryce took in a deep breath before he looked at Aeotus and Gilanthos. He waited for one of them to answer.

"It's not taught to children and not until the forty-third year. The technique is passed to the next generation within the families, so we will never forget how to defend the elven nation if war comes to us." He looked at Aticus. "The bladecantor is only used when provoked. The boy would have been killed if she had not come to his aid." Aeotus responded to Bryce.

"Both of you know how to kill like this?" Bryce asked Aeotus and Gilanthos.

"No," Gilanthos replied. "I'm Albatra. We don't have access to the bladecantor. Only the Faylorn elves are taught the form. It's exclusive to the bladecantor lineage."

Aeotus declared, "My family has a long line of bladecantors, but I chose not to pursue my apprenticeship. My father disowned me for that choice." He paused to gaze at the destruction around him before turning his attention back to Aticus.

Aticus regarded Aeotus. "My name's Aticus, not boy!" He turned and walked away.

Chapter Twelve

DREAMS

The final raindrops from a receding rainstorm gently fall on the swaying tree leaves as the majestic moon peeks from behind the racing clouds. The moon's radiance casts shifting shadows on the forest floor, creating an unusually eerie atmosphere.

Aticus leaps out of the forest shadows, startling a rabbit drinking from a muddy puddle, causing it to flee into the undergrowth.

The damp ground, softened by a day of rain, sinks beneath his feet as he stumbles into a large tree. He struggles to catch his breath, creating small puffs of mist in the cool air. Suddenly, footsteps and snapping branches behind him propel him forward.

He rushes through the thick foliage. Branches and smaller limbs scrape against him, drawing blood on his face and arms. Something's chasing him, and he can't get free. There's no place to hide. Fear of what's behind him causes him to misjudge, entering an area that abruptly ends near a steep ravine. He glances from side to side before running to his right, searching the ridge for a way down.

Thud! Suddenly, a sharp pain pierces his right leg, sending him to his knees, and his hands sink into the mud. Before he can turn to see where it came from—*thonk*. Another arrow strikes him in the shoulder, shattering bone. The impact twists him around, and he lands face-up, breaking the arrow shaft off in his back. He yells for help, but there's no one to help him. Despair strips his breath away as he tries to get up, but it's too late. His attackers surround him, grunting and snorting. The pain is overwhelming, and he can't catch his breath. Suddenly, someone kicks him in the face, chest, and abdomen. Aticus cries for them to stop.

When the kicking ends, he hears a man's voice. "Stop, get back, you fools!"

Aticus is pushed onto his back and restrained. It hurts everywhere, and his raspy breaths are shallow and challenging. He tries to open his eyes, but all he sees is a blurry shadow—rough shapes of a tall figure standing over him.

The person pulls at his medallion and lets it drop on his chest. The weight of the medallion feels like a rock when it hits him. "This is the one," the shadowed individual replies.

Aticus hears a sword pull free from its casing. He tries to move, but firm hands hold him in place. "Please don't kill me!" he pleads. "Not again, please!" A sharp pain in his chest takes his breath, and everything goes dark.

Aticus trembled, his clothes soaked with sweat. He sat up, resting his arms on his knees, and covered his face. The crackling of the fire comforted him—it was the dream again.

"Are you okay?" Yung Sung asked, leaning against a tree. He had taken the first watch while everyone slept. "It appears you had a bad dream?"

Aticus yanked his hands from his face, unaware that anyone had seen him. "A nightmare is more like it." He settled and wiped the sweat from his face. "You'd think I'd be used to them. It's always the same." He straightened his legs, resting his feet near the fire. He paused for a moment before speaking. "Do you have nightmares, Yung Sung?"

"When I was a child. Although some nightmares don't require sleep." Yung Sung shifted his weight to his other leg. "You say you have the same dreams or nightmares? What happens?"

"I die. It's the same every time." Aticus squeezed his eyes shut and swallowed hard, trying to push the vision out of existence.

"Perhaps the nightmare reflects what you're going through in life." Sung side-stepped a sleeping Palias and moved closer to the fire, sitting across from Aticus. When did the dream start?"

"After my father died three years ago, in the spring." Aticus shrugged and studied the flames. "That was hard to go through alone."

Yung Sung contorted his face. "That could be the catalyst. I recently lost my master, who was like my father." Sung watched the flames lick the wood. "His death is what brought me to this land. For a fresh start, you might say." Yung Sung considered Aticus intently.

"I'm sorry," Aticus responded.

Yung Sung nodded. "When I was struggling with internal conflict, my master would teach me to meditate." Sung settled, crossing his legs. "It would be an honor to share a few relaxation methods. It may help you."

"Thank you. Anything might help at this point." Aticus stared into the fire for several moments before speaking. "I want people to see me for who I am and not pity me." Aticus' eyes glistened when he looked at Yung Sung. "I want to feel like I belong somewhere again."

"I understand." Sung smiled and glanced back at the flames, lost in a memory.

Aticus regarded Sung, wiping his eyes. "How do you understand?"

"Several years ago, I created a rift between my master and me when I associated with an unsavory group of individuals. I am burdened with the fact that my decisions led to the death of Master Tau. I must live with that dishonor," Sung said with a frown and a shrug.

"I'm sorry," Aticus added. "What about your family? Where are they?"

"I am not sure where they are or if they are alive. At five years old, my father took me to Master Tau for training." Yung Sung frowned. "That was twenty years ago."

"Do you remember anything about him? Did you ask your master about your family?" Aticus asked, happy not to be speaking about his dream.

"I remember my father was tall and strong, and I have no memory of my mother. I asked Master Tau many times about them both, but I grew tired of asking the one question he would never answer. I learned to resent Master Tau for that. Again, something I will forever regret." Yung Sung thought a moment. "You have never been taught to use a sword?" he asked, changing the conversation.

"No. I don't suppose that was hard to figure out after what happened yesterday with the goblins?" Aticus regarded Yung Sung.

Sung chuckled, "I would be honored to share a few sword techniques. It may help you feel more confident and ease your anxiety."

"I'd like that." Aticus straightened. "Let me take the next watch. I don't feel like sleeping."

Sung smiled. "Of course."

CHAPTER THIRTEEN

THE JOURNEY

The seven departed from Shandar early in the day, traveling south on a well-worn path. It had taken them the better part of two days to travel through the forest of Shandar, and Aticus was ready to leave it behind. His world opened before him as they exited the forest's shadows and crossed into the southern plains. Aticus stopped his horse and gazed over the land, letting the sun warm his face. He couldn't help but think of all the new and exciting possibilities ahead as he peered over his shoulder at the forest. Bryce passed Aticus and smiled warmly, pulling Aticus' vision away and toward a new life.

After a long day of travel on the dry plains, they stopped for the night. "Tomorrow, we'll arrive in Veridian," Palias shared as he collected twigs and placed them on the ground near Gilanthos.

"I've never been to Veridian," Bryce responded as he watched Gilanthos position the timbers for the campfire.

Yung Sung took Aticus aside and worked on his sword skills. He used two thick branches from a birch tree as practice swords. "Here, hold it tight where the hilt would be. If you hold it too low, you could lose control, and if you hold it too close to the crossguard, it will limit your range of motion."

"Can't we use a real sword to practice with instead?" Aticus held up the remains of the birch tree.

Palias patted his hands together, cleaning off the dirt. "If you keep practicing with Yung Sung, when we get to Veridan, I'll buy you a sword."

Aticus' eyes grew wide. "You'd do that for me?" He asked Palias.

"Of course, if you work hard and do as Yung Sung says." He folded his arms across his chest.

Aticus watched Sung balance the branch on his finger. "How did the two of you meet?"

Sung locked eyes with Aticus. "We met in Dornel three months ago." He glanced over his shoulder at the large man. "Palias saved my life."

Aeotus and Eladonia returned from foraging for food and walked in on the conversation. "Do tell," Aeotus inquired, sitting beside Gilanthos.

"It was late in the evening when I arrived. I was looking for a place to stay when a man ran from an alley and bumped into me. He dropped a knife when we collided and then proceeded to run away. When I examined the weapon, it had blood on it, so I stepped into the alley to see if someone needed help. Unfortunately, the man was dead." He looked back at Palias. "The city guards rounded a corner and found me standing over the body with a bloody knife nearby. They assumed I killed the man and took me into custody."

Gilanthos' expression cringed as he struck the flint and steel together. "I see where this is going."

Sung tilted his head. "By the time they had me in the city prison, I was convicted and sentenced to hang at first light."

Palias interjected. "I had arrived the same night on a different ship when I witnessed Sung and the man bump into each other. The city protectors arrived and dragged him into the street as a mob formed. There was no one to explain what happened, so I spoke with the captain of the night watch and explained to him what I'd seen." Palias shrugged. "There was nothing I could say to change his mind. From the perspective of the captain, he had the killer."

"Turned out the dead man was a well-to-do noble in the city," Yung Sung added.

Bryce crossed his legs and leaned forward. "What did you do?" he asked Palias.

"I went back later when there was one guard and broke Sung out." Palias shrugged.

"So, then you're both fugitives?" Aeotus chuckled and patted his leg.

Gilanthos struck the flint and steel together, shaking his head at Aeotus' response. The spark in the kindling ignited, and he fanned the flame, giving it life. Eladonia sat across from him and handed a few sticks to her friend.

"What brings you to Idonia? Bryce asked Palias.

"I'm on a life quest." Palias approached the campfire.

"What's a life quest?" Eladonia questioned.

"It's custom for a prince of Asvernia to travel the world and gain knowledge before being deemed worthy of the throne. My two elder brothers and I have one year to complete our life quest. Upon returning, our father will decide who will become king." Palias tucked his fingers under his belt. "I hope that by returning with the sword of King Eston and sharing my adventure, he will name me heir to the throne."

"So then we are in the presence of royalty," Aeotus told the group.

"I may be a prince of Asvernia, but I expect no special treatment. I'm a man like you."

"What about you, Yung Sung? Are you royalty as well?" Aeotus inquired.

Sung twirled the stick in his hand and chuckled. "No, I'm doing a bit of soul-searching." He motioned to Aticus to move further away to continue to work on thrusting and parrying with the sticks.

Aeotus looked at Bryce. "I'm curious. What magic did you use to heal me in the cage?"

Bryce puffed his chest and stuck out his chin. "That wasn't magic. It was God's will. I did nothing."

"I find it hard to understand, my friend." Aeotus settled in for a long conversation.

"You find it hard to believe I healed you or that it was God's will?"

"Elves have been around for a long time, and we seem to have done fine without a god." Aeotus glanced at Eladonia and Gilanthos. "We're immortal, we can't get sick, and we're better at everything." Aeotus shrugged, "How do you suppose we have all that without a god?"

Bryce settled back and considered the elf before speaking. "Because you don't believe it doesn't mean there isn't a God."

Aeotus smiled. "Your god healed me, and I don't even believe? Why would he heal me if I don't believe?"

"Perhaps he believes in you?" Bryce smiled.

Gilanthos chuckled.

Aticus and Sung finished sparring and sat down near the fire.

"Can you teach me how to fight like you?" Aticus asked Eladonia.

Aeotus regarded Aticus and leaned back, laughing.

"No—it takes a long time to learn the bladecantor." Eladonia considered Aticus. "The form is passed down within our family and can take a lifetime to master, and even then, you must maintain a strict study regimen."

Aeotus' face became rigid as he glanced past Eladonia. "Something you won't have time for once you wed."

Eladonia glared into the fire.

"Why wouldn't you continue your training?" Palias asked.

"Eladonia and I are Faylorn elves, and we are the only nation of elves with families teaching the skill." Aeotus put his hands together on his lap. "Ela is betrothed to Thrace Silverspell. His family is one of the ruling classes in Evermoure."

"Aeotus, I don't want to talk about it," Eladonia demanded.

"The elves of Evermour prohibit the practice of the bladecantor technique. She won't be allowed to study or teach the skill to her children." Aeotus glared at her.

Gilanthos placed his hand on Aeotus' arm. "She doesn't want to speak about it, Aeo."

"We were being escorted to Evermour when the goblins attacked us." Aeotus nodded at Gilanthos. "We've tried to convince her to run away with us."

"Aeotus! I said I don't want to talk about it anymore."

"Fine!" Frustrated, Aeotus stood up and disappeared into the darkness.

Sensing Eladonia's anxiety, Bryce interjected, changing the topic, knowing the answer to his inquiry. "I have a question. Can you explain to us the earrings that elves wear?"

Gilanthos was happy to steer the conversation towards a new topic and began discussing the family heirloom. "All elves wear the Shad'arn. It's what you might call a family crest." To demonstrate, he pointed at his right ear, which had a bird in flight. "This was my father's family Shad'arn. One day, my mate and children will also have the same Shad'arn. If I have a son, he will wear it in his right ear, and if I have a daughter, she will wear it in her left ear."

He pointed to Eladonia and the crest in her left ear, in the shape of two swords crossed. "Eladonia wears her father's crest on her left ear until she weds." Gilanthos pointed into the darkness behind him. "Aeotus' Shad'arn is a crescent moon."

Gilanthos paused for a second before continuing. "During the wedding ceremony, she will move her Shad'arn to her right ear and wear her husband's crest on her left ear." Gilanthos looked at Aticus and his medallion. "If you see an elf wearing the crest on a necklace, you know they are widowed or a widower. If the woman dies, the man will take his wife's crest to wear around his neck. If the man dies, the woman will leave her crest in her right ear and move her husband's crest to a necklace to show she's a widow."

Aticus widened his eyes and shook his head in confusion.

Bryce laughed at Aticus before looking at Gilanthos. "Thank you. That helps to explain what I've often wondered. In my travels, I've seen elves who wore the Shad'arn on a necklace."

"What if a woman's husband dies and weds a second time?" Aticus observed Eladonia's earring.

"She would continue to wear the crest around her neck until death, and then she would take her new mate's crest and wear it on her ear as before. If her second mate were to die, unlikely that might be, she would wear both crests around her neck." Gilanthos shrugged. "I can only think of a few occasions where that occurred. Elves mate for life, and there have been so few deaths since the end of the Elven Wars."

Eladonia abruptly stood and walked out of the light of the fire and into the woods.

"I didn't mean to offend her," Aticus said after she disappeared.

Gilanthos leaned over the fire closer to everyone and whispered, "You did nothing wrong. She's wrestled with the marriage ever since she found out."

Aticus leaned closer to Gilanthos. "Is she a princess?"

Gilanthos chuckled and shook his head. "No, we do not have royal families like you. A thousand years ago, we were one people living together. Our elders are attempting to reunite the three nations through arranging marriages."

"What are the repercussions if she doesn't go through with the union?" Palias asked.

Gilanthos studied the large man before answering. "The treaty between Evermour and Faylorn could be in jeopardy."

Chapter Fourteen

VERIDIAN

They arrived in Veridian after mid-morning. The air was thick and humid, and a warm wind blew from the west, pulling dark clouds from the horizon. Rain wouldn't be far behind.

Two wagons with men, women, and children passed the seven. Palias turned and addressed everyone. "The local farmers hire townsfolk to work in the fields, sending wagons throughout the day when more help is needed."

Palias and Yung Sung directed the others through the city, passing the residential area to the trade district. The old cobbled paths were busy with people going about their daily routines. Street vendors sold their products, while skilled merchants offered their services. A blacksmith's hammer pounding could be heard above the buzz of people talking.

The crowd in the trade district became so dense that they had to get off their horses and walk them. Aticus was astonished by the number of people gathered here. Although he felt overwhelmed, he pushed on, finding comfort in the fact that none of his companions seemed negatively affected by the masses.

"We're getting rooms at the Skullduggery Inn for the night, and then we'll get something to eat at the Wet Stag," Palias announced to everyone.

Bryce led his horse beside Palias while they talked. "You have been here often?" Bryce questioned, his grip on the reins tightened.

Palias nodded, "Yes, this is where we met Normain." Palias placed a hand on his horse. "Whoa, boy." He kept his mount still while a family passed," carrying their morning bounty from the market. "Collet Duskwater owns the Wet Stag; he declared he won it in a card game from the previous owner. Palias smiled and glanced at Bryce. "He said he won it with a hand of four stags."

"Duskwater, as in Balen Duskwater, the King?" Bryce asked.

"Yes, the king is his brother." Palias nodded, guiding the horse around people.

They passed many stables along the way, but Palias chose to stop at Black Hoof Stables because he and Yung Sung were familiar with their services. Upon arrival, the stable help greeted Palias and Yung Sung by name.

Palias generously tipped the four men and informed them they would need to accommodate seven horses for the night and possibly longer. One of the younger boys rushed to get assistance, knowing that Palias was a wealthy customer who would reward them handsomely. While another boy ran for the nearest farrier, who happened to be his father.

Soon after leaving the stables, Aticus was quickly distracted by new and incredible things. As they walked through a bustling square, he was overwhelmed by the mouth-watering scents of fresh-baked goods and roasting chickens. The vendors were selling an abundance of fruits and vegetables harvested earlier that day. A meat seller was displaying cuts of beef and venison on his cart, loudly announcing the prices for each piece.

Aticus had never seen so many people before. He had only been allowed twice to venture into a village to trade with his father, Nicholas.

As children played in the street, their dogs chased after them. On several corners, bards sang and played their instruments. They offered their services to attend social gatherings for a fee, hoping to share their stories through song and melody.

Eladonia received a job offer from a nearby establishment. The owner assured her she would be a profitable public servant in the area. Aeotus and Gilanthos made playful remarks, promising to remind her of what she could have had if she had accepted the offer. She laughed and promised she'd stab them both in their sleep if they continued.

Bryce prayed for people more than once after witnessing something unsavory.

The seven arrived at the Wet Stag and were welcomed by Collet Duskwater. He quickly cleared the table for Palias and his friends by asking four other patrons to move. The tavern had a warm, inviting atmosphere, with a stone hearth burning on the far wall. Many of the tables were already occupied by other patrons.

Once seated, Collet came to the table and took their drink orders. Palias ordered first. He shifted the sword on the table, still wrapped in cloth. "I'll take an ale and put the rest of the orders on my tab, Collet."

Collet nodded, "Yes, sir, I will. Thank you."

"I will take ale also, please," Sung expressed, raising a finger.

"Water for me," Aticus uttered as he watched Eladonia.

"No, give him ale, and the same for me," Aeotus spat out, patting Aticus on the back with a smile.

Eladonia and Gilanthos both took the same drink. They thanked Collet after they ordered.

"Do you have any Dwarven spirits?" Bryce questioned. "It's been months since I had any good Dwarven spirits and not that watered-down drink, mind you."

"I recently acquired a few bottles and keep them in the cellar for special occasions. Shall I fetch one for you?" Collet asked, glancing at Palias for approval.

Palias nodded, acknowledging that the spirit would cost more than a typical ale.

"Let us pay for our food, Palias," Eladonia insisted.

"Yes, we'll pay for ours," Gilanthos added.

Palias shook his head adamantly. "No, I have this. And the rooms are already taken care of as well."

"You are generous, Palias," Eladonia replied warmly.

Aticus couldn't help but stare at her blue eyes and how they sparkled. The creases that spread around her mouth when she smiled were set perfectly. Aticus had noticed that a single dimple would appear on her left cheek when her smile was genuine.

"I don't usually carry money or food with me," Bryce explained, feeling the need to justify his statement. "It makes me less attractive to thieves and other unsavory characters." He shrugged. "What?" He looked around the table at everyone before turning to Palias. "But thanks for your kindness."

Palias smiled warmly and nodded. "Never feel like you have to defend yourself, my friend. It's an honor to help when I can."

"Is that why you don't carry a weapon? It keeps the riff-raff from killing you and taking your weapon, too?" Aeotus asked the dwarf.

Bryce smiled, welcoming his question. "When you have God with you, you don't require a weapon to defend yourself; He is my shield," Bryce said, sitting a little taller.

Aeotus smiled, preparing to ask more questions, but Eladonia placed a hand on his shoulder to stop him from saying something he might regret.

Kerrn, one of the tavern hosts, took all the food orders and departed the table. Yung Sung pointed across the tavern. "That's Normain."

All attention was drawn to a small table by the bar on the opposite side of the tavern. An elderly man was seated alone at the table, sporting a pair of silver spectacles that had lost their luster. He was bent over the table, engrossed in reading a rather bulky book, carefully flipping through its delicate pages.

"He'll be happy to see the sword." Palias' deep tone drew the attention of a nearby table as he stood up and retrieved the sword from the table. "We'll be back in a few moments. If the food arrives, please don't wait for us." Yung Sung followed Palias' lead.

"Can I come?" Aticus asked.

Palias nodded. "Of course."

Chapter Fifteen

Normain

Palias, Yung Sung, and Aticus approached the table where Normain sat.

Normain looked up and greeted Palias with a smile. "Hello." Normain motioned to the three available chairs around the table, "Please sit."

Palias placed the sword wrapped in cloth on the table. "How have you been, Normain?"

"Fighting a cold, I'm afraid, but I'm making it the best an old man can." Normain straightened himself in his chair. "It's good to see you both again; please sit." Normain insisted, pointing toward the seats again. "And your friend as well. How have you been?"

"We're well, thank you," Palias responded as they sat at the table. "This is Aticus," he introduced his new friend.

Normain greeted Aticus, noticing the medallion hanging around his neck. He studied it until Palias spoke.

"We found the last pieces of Seravant," Palias said, uncovering the sword and being careful not to drop anything.

The old man regarded Palias with renewed excitement and watched with anticipation. "King Eston's sword, let's have a look at it!" Normain looked over at Aticus. "I never believed I would see this one before I died." Normain focused on Aticus' medallion before turning his attention back to the sword.

Palias lifted back the edges of the fabric to reveal a small pouch. He placed it on the table and unfolded the cloth until the sword's hilt appeared.

Normain gasped, then gently patted his hands together. "Oh, yes!"

Finally, Palias peeled back the final layer to reveal the blade. To conclude, he emptied the contents of the small pouch onto the cloth next to the sword. The red, green, and blue gems sparkled in the light of a burning candle on the table.

Normain started to rub his hands together. "Ah, so beautiful; may I touch it?" He looked at Palias through the eyes of a ten-year-old boy.

Palias smiled. "Please, do as you wish."

Normain held the blade of the sword in his hands. He balanced it, feeling the weight of the weapon. "Very light for a blade of this size, I'll say." He turned it from side to side and examined it before returning it to the table. Then he picked up the hilt and studied it in the same way. "Ah, I see this is where those go." He rubbed the indents on the handle with his thumb and picked up the blue gem. He gently placed the blue gem into the top-notch. "Now, I am trying to remember if it is the blue or red one first. You have to give an old man a moment, you know." He contemplated before placing the blue gem down and retrieving the red one, putting it into the top indent. Then he placed the blue rock in the second spot and the green one in the third. "Yes, that's it." He looked at the three men at the table over his spectacles. "I never forget my artifacts. It just takes me a bit longer to remember." His broad smile revealed several missing teeth.

Palias addressed Normain after giving him time to take it all in. "When you first told us about the sword, you said that King Eston had a wizard who advised him. If I remember, you said he disappeared shortly after the king's death. And you suggested he was tasked with disassembling Seravant to keep it hidden?"

"Why, yes, ah, Gildon, ah..." Normain tapped his chin. "Gildon Prather—he was the king's most trusted advisor and friend! If I recall in writings, after the death of King Eston, some believed Gildon took the king's sword for himself and disappeared." Normain pursed his lips together and raised his eyebrows. "But it appears he obeyed Eston's last demand." Normain smiled and looked at the sword with wonderment.

"I'm asking because we found someone's remains where we found the three gems. And we have what seems to be Gildon's belongings," Palias said, grinning at Yung Sung.

Aticus watched as Sung pulled a small black satchel over his shoulder and laid it on the table. He hadn't noticed Sung carrying the bag. Aticus glanced at Normain and realized he was studying his medallion again.

Sung spoke while he opened the bag and pulled out the contents. "We found these items close to the body." Sung pulled out a scroll tied with a green ribbon and an unbroken wax seal bearing the letter E. Then he pulled out a small cloth bag similar to the one the gems were in. Finally, Sung pulled out a thick brown book inlaid with silver and gold.

Aticus recognized the brown book. It was similar to the one that Aeotus had, although considerably more substantial. His eyes grew wide when he saw the tome, recognizing what it was. He looked back at Aeotus, who was drinking and laughing with his friends.

Normain quickly grabbed the unopened scroll. "Oh my, now this is interesting!" He studied it, his eyes wide. "This is a true find, my friends. A document with King Eston's unbroken seal." He sighed and held the scroll in his hands more preciously than he had held the sword. "This is the most fantastic find, I have to say." Normain looked over his spectacles at the three of them.

Aticus leaned near the table. "Why is that scroll so fantastic?"

Normain studied Aticus. "The unknown, of course—we hold something in our hands King Eston wrote. It's never been opened, so it is unknown what he wrote or for whom it was written." He shook the scroll gently.

"Open it," Yung Sung stated.

Normain's eyes grew wide, and he shook his head, gazing at the scroll. "You cannot open it. The value is too great. Revealing what is inside would destroy the unknown." Normain looked at the bag and book as he placed the scroll on the table. He grasped the book and held it against his chest.

Aticus spoke before Normain could. "That's a spellbook!" He looked at the three men with a confident smile.

"Why, yes, it is." Normain considered Aticus and his medallion before he opened the book. The pages were empty; he flipped through the book, letting the paper flick. "This is a Wizard's book and a thick one at that. It must be Gildon's."

"Why are the pages empty?" Aticus was confused.

"Oh, I can assure you they are not empty. Only a magic-user can read the language of magic." Normain smiled at Aticus and tilted his head.

Normain stacked the items together and pushed them toward Yung Sung. "Keep those safe. They are worth far more gold than you or I will see in our lifetime."

Yung Sung smiled at Normain's statement and glanced at Palias. "You told us where we could find the pieces of the sword. If these items were indeed lost, how did you know where we could find them?"

"Excellent question, but I cannot explain in a language you would understand. Let's say I have a method that shall die with me." Normain smiled a crooked, somewhat toothless grin.

"What do you think could have killed Gildon? A powerful wizard would not have been dispatched so easily, wouldn't you say?" Palias asked.

"Curious questions I cannot answer." Normain shook his head and looked at Aticus and his medallion again.

Aticus noticed that Normain's gaze would fall to his medallion whenever he spoke to him; it piqued his curiosity.

Palias wrapped the sword while Yung Sung placed Gildon's belongings in the black sack. "May I ask you one more question? Is there anything special I need to do to reassemble the sword?"

"You need a Gnomish swordsmith that dabbles in the arcane." Normain frowned.

"Why a gnome? I don't understand?"

"The gnomes assembled the sword. Only an expert swordsmith or artificer with the knowledge of magic can make it whole again." Normain scrunched his features together. "Gnomes were the only race with that skill, my friend. And it's unfortunate that..."

"There are no more gnomes alive to do that," Palias finished Normain's sentence. "Alright then, thank you, Normain." Palias shook the old man's small, frail hand.

Yung Sung bowed to Normain.

Aticus shook the elderly man's hand. Normain held Aticus' hand more firmly than expected for a man his age. "That medallion you're wearing. Where did you get it? If you don't mind me asking." His eyes were transfixed upon it.

Aticus looked down at the silver chain and medallion. "It's mine. I've had it for as long as I can remember, but I don't know anything about it. Why?"

"It looks oddly familiar; I can't seem to place it. I'll tell you what: A friend is arriving this evening. He's an expert in such items, and I'm sure he would love to meet you. He may be able to help you understand what the symbols mean. It's not quite my thing." Normain smiled, tilted his head, and studied Aticus intently before he let go of his hand. "I invite you to come to my home tomorrow evening; you can speak with him then."

"I would like that very much." Aticus grinned.

"You can find my shop four streets down on the left, the way the sun sets. There is a sign hanging over the door that says Artifacts."

The three men returned to their table and ate dinner with their companions.

Aticus caught Normain gazing at his medallion more than once in the evening.

Chapter Sixteen

Neacrom

I n another part of the realm.

Neacrom walked down one of the many empty stone corridors in the once-grand palace of Oppack. The shadows cast by the torchlight only served to accentuate his sunken features. His long, silver hair, thick from lack of care, stuck to his face, and he limped with his left leg, causing his movements to be slow and awkward. With each painful step, the blue robe he wore jolted violently around his frail frame. Finally, he entered the spacious central chamber of the palace, which had once been the grand throne room of the now-abandoned, ruined city.

Two marble stairs with embellishments on either side hugged the walls of the circular room. They led to the floors above and spilled into a grand balcony overlooking the throne room below. At the center of the chamber sat a chair, which was not originally part of the palace but was placed there by its current occupant. The throne was made entirely of bones, including skulls, ribs, spines, and other organic material, yet it somehow held together unnaturally.

Neacrom walked out of the corridor and ascended the steps to the raised platform, where he sat on the throne of bones, his breath labored.

Nearly eighty years ago, the water unexpectedly surged from the ground in Oppack, resulting in the vast swamp that now encompassed the entire city. The mysterious flooding forced tens of thousands to flee in a matter of days and probably claimed the lives of many more. The palace, perched on the highest point in the city, was the only structure that remained unscathed by the marshy terrain.

Neacrom sat for several moments before painfully standing and moving to a wall close to the corridor he had exited earlier. He reached above his head, just below a torch, and firmly pressed on an oddly shaped stone. A slow rumble, accompanied by the sound of stone scraping against stone, echoed throughout the chamber as a section of the wall gradually shifted outward, revealing a hidden corridor. He descended a set of stairs hidden behind the secret door, using his hand for support. Slowly, he proceeded down the ten steps before he paused.

He strolled a short distance down a dark, narrow hall. At the end of the corridor, he could see flickering torchlight. Neacrom stepped into a small room carved into the earth.

Standing at the entrance, he clenched his hands and gazed at two men sitting on wooden crates near the wall. Both of them were sharpening their knives and competing over who had killed more people with their weapons. They were assassins who belonged to the Hands of the Shadow. However, they overlooked Neacrom when he entered the room.

Neacrom limped past the assassins and rounded a column to his left. He finally arrived at his underground laboratory, which he had occupied until JoJung and the council decided to use it as a temporary base of operations for their assassins.

The room was quite spacious, with a table placed against each wall. The counters were loaded with vials and jars containing disgusting specimens. Some of the jars had eyes floating in colored liquids, and they seemed to stare at you in an eerie way. Other jars contained body parts of animals, humans, and beasts.

A full-sized mirror leaned against the wall at the room's far end. A heavy wooden chair was placed in front of the mirror, and behind the chair stood a boarded pedestal. On top of the pedestal was a red gemstone that balanced on its tip. The stone reflected the light from the torches, casting a red hue on everything around it. Neacrom gazed at the gemstone and took a deep breath.

A dark-haired man wearing black robes, a mage from the Hands of the Shadow, positioned himself between Neacrom and the red stone. "What brings you here so early in the day, Neacrom?"

Another man to Neacrom's left—an assassin, propped himself up against a table. He adjusted to see Neacrom better as he chewed on a sliver of wood.

Neacrom spotted a mind flayer standing nearby, looming over an unconscious woman on the ground. It emerged from the shadows, its skin a pale cream color with blue-tinted tentacles writhing and twisting where a mouth should be. The creature's large, black eyes made it difficult to determine where it was looking, but Neacrom understood it was gazing at him.

Neacrom looked at the mage. "I require the Bloodstone for a ceremony that must be performed this evening!"

"That sounds dark." He chuckled before answering. "I don't see any trouble with that; she won't be ready again until tomorrow, at the earliest," the mage announced, studying the woman on the ground. She was unconscious, bound by her legs and wrists.

Neacrom moved forward to retrieve the stone from the pedestal.

"Make certain you have it returned by morning. I'd hate to have to inform the council again. JoJung may not be as charitable this time," the mage said, taunting Neacrom.

"Don't test me! You are here entirely because of my generosity!" Neacrom snapped.

The mage chuckled at Neacrom's arrogance. "What exactly are you trying to do?"

"I'm looking for something I lost a long time ago." Neacrom retrieved the stone and limped back the way he had come.

The mage uttered as Neacrom disappeared around the corner, "You know that dark magic is going to kill you, eventually." He chuckled before looking at the mind flayer. "What do I care. Just going to save us the time later." He expressed himself where only they could hear, or so he thought. The assassin laughed and threw the piece of wood he was chewing on the ground.

Neacrom listened to the men laughing in the room behind him, clutching the Bloodstone tightly, he hobbled down the hall toward the steps.

CHAPTER SEVENTEEN

MONGOLE

Mongole's frustration with Talmet was becoming an unnecessary distraction. He watched the pigeon return for the second day with an unchecked message. He mused over his decision to send Chotak and his men to Oppack. He had received word from Chotak seven days ago that they had reached Oppack and were preparing to enter the city to confront Neacrom. Chotak had noted, in his last message, that there was no sign of the orcs or goblins previously sent to similar missions. Mongole understood that Chotak would have sent news by now if he were alive.

His anger with Talmet had been festering over the past few days, and the more he pondered it, the more upset he became. Mongole had been summoned by Talmet earlier in the day, but he considered it wise not to go in his current state. So far, Talmet had sent two separate battalions of orcs and a small army of goblins to Oppack, but they still had nothing to show.

Mongole promised Chotak that they would walk on the ramparts of Meloorne and celebrate the lives of all who died fighting the humans. They would stand in the courtyard and raise their hands in defiance. To think Chotak gave his life for a gemstone that Talmet wanted enraged Mongole.

Mongole's thoughts drifted to his family. He lost himself in the majesty of the Kandar mountains on the horizon. He looked to the southwest and his family for strength: his mate, Chulla, and two children, Leeda and Heden. The latter was named after his great-great-grandfather, the orc who killed Endendon Beramen in the great battle.

Mongole was tired of fighting and wanted the war to end. He was confident that if Talmet focused on the north, they could win the fight against the humans and go home.

Utaka, the bird master, approached Mongole. "Do you wish me to send another pigeon, general?" The bird master was an old hobgoblin, smaller than an orc but more significant than a goblin. His mustard skin was thick with wrinkles and as tough as aged leather; his clothes were dirty and unkempt. He cared more for the birds than for his own well-being, tending to the pigeons and other fowl.

Mongole looked down on the old hobgoblin. "No. If he were alive, he would have responded by now." Mongole waved Utaka away like an insect. "I'm here to fight a war, not look for rocks."

The bird master bowed, holding a pigeon in his hands. "Yes, General."

Mongole gripped the hilt of his sword and twisted around. His anger festered as he focused on the quickest route to Talmet.

When he reached the command tent, he was greeted by Hamael, the goblin servant of Talmet. "Tell Talmet I am here to see him."

Hamael stood waist-high to Mongole. He fidgeted when Mongole spoke to him. "Supreme Commander Talmet has a visitor and has requested that he not be disturbed." Hamael shook as he conversed, avoiding Mongole's glare.

"I don't care; tell him I'm here!" Mongole barked. The two gnolls stationed outside the tent stared at the ground.

"Yes—yes, of course, General." Hamael retreated into the tent.

The gnolls didn't acknowledge the goblin.

Several moments passed before Hamael nervously scampered from the tent. "Supreme Commander Talmet said that he is occupied and will summon you when he is finished, General." Hamael cowered as he completed the sentence. He knew well enough what Mongole's reaction would be.

"Get out of my way!" Mongole pushed the goblin to the ground and approached the tent. The gnolls that flanked the door of Talmet's tent didn't lift the flaps and didn't try to stop him.

Hamael started whimpering incoherently, fearful of what Talmet would do to him. He held his head between his tiny hands.

Mongole burst through the second set of tent flaps and entered the war room. Talmet was standing behind his makeshift table, speaking to a large, muscular orc, as large as or larger than Mongole himself. They looked at Mongole when he entered, distracting them from their conversation.

"Ah, Mongole, there you are," Talmet pronounced in an uncharacteristically calm tone.

It's not what Mongole expected after blatantly defying his summons order for the second time today.

"Mongole, this is Gorgen, an ambassador from the king!" Talmet came around the table to stand next to Gorgen after speaking.

"King Aldamead has sent you to the front lines with orders to advance northward?" Mongole asked Gorgen, his face twisted in disgust.

"No." Gorgen crossed his arms defiantly.

Talmet smiled abnormally as he spoke. "Gorgen has given me orders from the king to retrieve the Bloodstone—myself." There was a morsel of nervousness in Talmet's voice.

"He wants you to retrieve the stone?" Mongole looked at Talmet in dismay.

"Yes, and you are going with him," Gorgen addressed Mongole, his irritation evident.

CHAPTER EIGHTEEN

DEATH'S DOOR

The following day brought clouds and steady rain. Palias had reserved rooms for everyone at the Skullduggery Inn, which happened to be across the street from the Wet Stag.

Aticus felt fortunate to be indoors, rather than sheltering from the rain beneath a tree or a wagon. He could become accustomed to having a roof over his head and a bed to sleep in.

The rooms were modest, with two beds and a wooden table between them. At the end of the beds was a larger table against the wall. On top of the table, set an oil lamp, and on the wall hung a tarnished bronze mirror. Bryce had pulled the sheepskin curtains on the single window in the room back when he woke, revealing a wet, overcast day that allowed enough light to keep him from using the lamp.

Bryce was Aticus' roommate, while Sung and Palias shared the room beside them. Across the hall, Gilanthos and Aeotus shared a room, and at the end of the hall, Eladonia had one to herself.

Aticus was eager to start the day and discover more about his medallion. He chatted with Bryce, who sat in a chair, drinking his tea, "What if Normain's friend can't help me? What if this means nothing?" He sat on the edge of the bed, fiddling with the medallion around his neck.

"Don't you think it's strange that someone recognized your medallion in the first city we come to? I do hope that Normain has your best interest at heart." Bryce tapped his finger on the table before taking a swig of his tea. "Are you sure you don't want me to accompany you?"

"No, it's fine. Yung Sung told me he'd come with me." Aticus nervously swayed from side to side. "Maybe I should go and see if I can find his place. That way, I'll know where I'm going."

Bryce chuckled. "Or—we could go back to the Stag and have a wee bit more of that Dwarven spirit." Bryce smiled. He rolled his eyes and conversed with the voice in his head. "I know," he said, smiling at the ceiling.

Aticus grinned and shook his head at the dwarf. He'd become quite accustomed to Bryce having conversations with himself.

A knock rattled the door to their room. "We're going to explore if anyone wants to come," Gilanthos announced from the other side.

"Yes!" Aticus sprang from the bed and rushed to the door, pulling it open.

Gilanthos, Eladonia, Aeotus, and Yung Sung stood wide-eyed in the hallway. Aticus looked back at Bryce. "Are you coming?"

"No, I'll stay here and appreciate the room and my tea, for a bit longer." Bryce smiled and waved his hand to assure Aticus it was fine to leave him.

Reluctantly, Aticus accepted. He valued Bryce's company and appreciated his benevolence. He held a great sense of well-being with Bryce and respected his opinions.

After midday, they escaped the increasingly heavy rain and found another local tavern. After only one drink, the three elves continued exploring the city, leaving Aticus and Yung Sung alone. Aticus figured the three wanted to be by themselves.

Once the elves left, Aticus glanced at Sung. "Where's Palias? I didn't see him at the inn this morning. I thought he'd come with us?"

"He had business to attend to from a previous visit." The two sat at the bar, sipping a second ale, a drink quickly growing on Aticus.

A man entered the tavern, his hair and coat saturated from the pouring rain. He immediately approached the counter. "Keeper, I'll take mead." He squatted on a stool beside Aticus.

"It's a bad day to be out in this, friend," the barkeeper said as he delivered the man his drink. I appreciate your business, though."

The man took a drink of his mead, then lifted it in salute to the keeper. "Damn good. That hit the spot." He wiped his wet hair back to avoid dripping into his drink. "I'm passing through." He took another sip, swallowing before he continued his conversation with the keeper. "Has there been any word of plague around these parts?"

Aticus and Yung Sung looked at the man when he said plague.

The keeper stopped drying an empty glass. He looked around at his patrons before inquiring, "plague? There's been no word of plague." He leaned in closer before asking a question. He didn't want to scare any of his customers. "Where did you hear there was a plague?" He thought he might be too close and quickly pushed away from the man. Then, he finished drying the glass before placing it on the shelf behind him.

"Something nasty is killing people." The man shifted closer to the bar and whispered to the barkeeper, "Word is—in some of the smaller villages south of here," he pointed with his thumb in a southward direction, "people are dying. They're fine when they go to sleep, but they never wake up." He looked at Aticus and opened his eyes wide for dramatics. "Kills them in their sleep; at least, that's what I heard." He took a big swig of his drink before looking back at the keeper. "I suppose if you're going to go, that's the easy way ou t."

The keeper gulped.

A long moment of silence was broken when the door to the tavern burst open, and a man appeared. "There's a fire! Fire! Up the street! We need buckets!" The man ran to the next establishment, sounding the alarm and repeating his call for help.

The tavern emptied as people ran to help extinguish the fire, including the tavern keeper, who grabbed a wooden bucket painted red. He ran for the door.

Aticus and Yung Sung watched out the window as people piled into the street.

The rain came to an end.

The man who spoke about the plague sat on the stool, drinking his mead and shaking his head. "End times are coming: plagues, fires; what next?" He looked wide-eyed at Aticus and Yung Sung.

Aticus and Yung Sung leaped up and ran out the tavern's door, following the crowd. In the distance, they could see smoke rising. The closer they got to the fire, the more familiar the surroundings became. It was apparent that the flames were close to the Wet Stag and Skullduggery Inn, perhaps a few streets away.

Aticus and Sung mingled with the crowd. They watched the townsfolk using buckets to pass water from a nearby well to the burning building.

"They made a fire line," Sung explained to Aticus, who had never seen such a thing. "Everyone has to work together to extinguish the fire; if not, it could quickly spread to the entire city."

Suddenly, a woman began to scream hysterically. Aticus and Sung couldn't see who was yelling, but they could make out a few words between the wailing. "My baby... my baby—in the burning building!" They tried to make their way toward the screaming, but it was difficult because the crowd had become so dense.

An eerie silence quickly descended over the crowd, and the woman hushed as well. Aticus and Yung Sung pushed through the crowd, stunned by what they saw.

Bryce knelt in the mud of the cobbled street, his clothes covered in soot, holding a small child tightly against his chest.

The child's mother knelt before Bryce. She brushed the baby's black hair with tears in her eyes as she sobbed.

The crowd remained silent, except for the shouting of the fire line. "Bucket, bucket, bucket."

Aticus noticed a rainbow glistening in the clouds on the horizon, over the city's buildings.

Bryce rocked slowly back and forth, his face buried in the child's hair.

Aticus heard Bryce praying while he moved. "Oh, no," Aticus said, looking at Sung.

Unexpectedly, the child began coughing and crying. Bryce stopped moving and held the child out so that her mother could see the baby's soot-covered face.

The woman sobbed as she reached for her child. Regarding Bryce, she held her baby and smiled. Tears gushed down her face as she tenderly touched the dwarf's face. Bryce grinned, nodding in acknowledgment.

The crowd erupted with jubilation as they surged forward and surrounded the dwarf, mother, and child, who disappeared from view.

Aticus smiled, and Yung Sung patted him on the back. "That dwarf has gifts." By the time the two pushed through the crowd, Bryce had disappeared, leaving the mother and child to celebrate with others.

"Where did Bryce go?" Sung asked. The two looked around the crowd for several moments. "I suppose we'll catch up with him later. Hey, it's time for your visit with Normain." Sung smiled at Aticus and patted him on the back again.

Aticus had forgotten in all the excitement. "Let's go find him," Aticus replied, smiling widely before looking around again for his dwarven friend.

Several blocks down the street, past the Skullduggery Inn, they discovered a house with the sign hanging over the door, as Normain had said they would.

Aticus knocked on the door, eager to meet Normain. There was no response. Again, Aticus rapped on the door. He shifted impatiently, watching others walk past. A third time, Aticus beat, still, with no response. "Should we go inside?" Aticus asked.

Yung Sung reached down and turned the knob; the door opened. "Suppose so; it's not locked." Sung smiled.

The two men walked in. "Hello?" Aticus asked; the door closed behind them.

The room, cluttered with tables in every available space, was dark except for a few burning candles. Gadgets and artifacts spilled off the counters and scattered across the floor, making it challenging to walk. Wooden blinds covered the windows, blocking the sunlight. Across the room were two closed doors.

"Hello? Is there anyone here?" Aticus asked, mainly to the closed doors, hoping Normain was in another room and hadn't heard them knock.

Aticus cautiously moved through the room, gazing at the clutter. "Hello?" He stepped around a long table near the center of the room.

The color in Aticus' face drained, and his mouth gaped open. "Oh, no." He swallowed hard.

"Oh no, what?" Sung shuffled around Aticus. "Oh, that's not good." Sung stepped in front of Aticus and cringed his nose; Normain was lying on the floor in a large pool of blood. Flies buzzed around the elderly man's body. Yung Sung walked closer to Normain and leaned over his body to examine him. "He's dead." He looked back at Aticus. "We need to get out of here, now!"

"Maybe he's alive," Aticus suggested as he leaned against a table, trying to keep from gagging.

"No, he's dead." Sung shook his head.

"How can you tell?" Aticus asked.

"Most of his blood is on the outside of his body, he's not breathing, and his eyes—he's dead. We need to get out of here!" Sung pushed Aticus toward the door.

Aticus resisted. "But, but…"

"No, I am telling you from experience, we need to move now." Sung pushed harder on Aticus, guiding him toward the door.

"Fine, I'm going. I can't believe Normain's dead."

The two abandoned the shop, closing the door behind them. "Walk normally," Sung said, touching Aticus' back firmly.

"We need to tell someone!" Aticus stopped and looked at Sung.

"No, we don't. Trust me; it won't end well for us!" Sung started walking.

Aticus followed Yung Sung; his thoughts were about Normain and who killed him.

Chapter Nineteen

DIRECTION

Aticus and Yung Sung roamed the city until darkness set upon them. "I think we need to tell someone about Normain," Aticus suggested again.

"We can't. You don't understand; I've been in a similar situation before. Everyone would suspect we had something to do with Normain's death. Especially if someone saw us coming from his shop." Yung Sung shook his head and turned to look at Aticus. "We can't."

Neither of them spoke while they walked. The rain had stopped long ago, and the sky gave way to a full moon that shone through breaks in the clouds. Lanterns hung on wooden poles, lighting the cobbled street and reflecting in puddles from the rain that had fallen earlier in the day.

They returned to the Wet Stag and stood outside looking through the window at the others sitting at the table. "They're going to ask me questions about what Normain said," Aticus expressed.

Yung Sung avoided answering Aticus as he turned and walked into the tavern. Aticus sighed and followed him through the door.

As they crossed the room, Bryce was the first to acknowledge them. "Aticus, how did your visit with Normain go?" he asked, turning up a goblet of mead. Everyone at the table looked at Aticus.

Aticus and Yung Sung took their seats at the long table. Before Aticus could sit down, he told them. "Normain's dead."

Yung Sung closed his eyes and shook his head as Bryce spat his mead out.

"Dead? What happened?" Palias asked them.

"We found him dead in his shop," Sung said, defeated.

"Where have the two of you been all this time? Did the city guard have any ideas about what happened?" Gilanthos asked.

"No, we found him on the floor, in his blood. We didn't move him and didn't tell anyone." Aticus looked at Yung Sung like a child waiting for a beating.

Yung Sung nodded, reassuring Aticus that what he said was fine.

"You didn't tell the city guard? Why did you not tell the guard?" Eladonia asked.

"It's my fault," Sung added, looking at Palias. "You know what would have happened if we had told the guards. He had a knife in his neck. We would have been the prime suspects. You know I couldn't do that again." Yung Sung glanced around the room.

Palias nodded, understanding that Yung Sung's last discovery of a corpse didn't go well for him.

Aticus glanced at Sung. "I didn't see a knife."

"I saw it. I didn't tell you then because I knew how it would affect you," Sung added.

Bryce stood at the end of the table. "I'm sorry, Aticus," he consoled.

"He's right. There's nothing you could have done for him. They'll find the body, and whoever is responsible will be brought to justice," Aeotus said, taking a drink.

"Sorry, Aticus," Eladonia added.

Palias lifted his cup. "Let us remember him and pray he has found peace." Everyone followed the large man's lead and raised their cups.

After a few more rounds of ale and a well-cooked dinner, Aticus questioned Bryce about his whereabouts for the day, already knowing where he had been. "Bryce, did you get out of the inn today?"

"Well, yes, I did. I managed to go for a walk when I realized none of you were coming back for me." Bryce sipped his mead and let his sight drift to everyone around the table.

"Sung and I saw you earlier this afternoon," Aticus added.

"Did you? Why didn't you say something?" Bryce inquired.

Aticus raised his eyebrows. "We tried, but after you saved that child from the burning building, you disappeared."

"That was you who saved the child?!" Palias blurted out. Everyone at the table gasped and looked at Bryce.

"We heard a house caught fire a few blocks away. Word spread that someone ran into the burning building to save a little girl," Eladonia said proudly.

"It was nothing; anyone would have done it. The Lord had me where he needed me to be." Bryce shrugged and took a drink, attempting to deflect.

"That is very impressive, nonetheless." Palias smiled.

"I heard they put the fire out quickly with little damage to surrounding dwellings. What did everyone else do today?" Bryce redirected the conversation.

"After the three of you left us at the tavern," Yung Sung directed his statement at the three elves, "a most eccentric man came in and spoke of a plague spreading through villages in the south."

"A plague; how exciting," Bryce looked at the ceiling and spoke, but not to those at the table. "You didn't tell me anything about a plague." The dwarf's eyes moved around like he was listening. "Well, what could it be then?" Again, he looked for a response.

"I am telling you, there is something not right about him," Aeotus whispered to Eladonia, tapping his temple with a finger.

Eladonia poked him with her elbow. Everyone tried not to look at Bryce during his episodes, except for Aticus, who found the dwarf most enjoyable to watch.

Bryce nodded and looked at everyone around the table. "I have to go south. I don't think it's a plague that's killing people."

"I'll go with you!" Aticus voiced in support of his short friend. He looked at Eladonia.

"You can count on us for a bit longer," Palias said, patting Sung on the back.

Bryce smiled. "I would be happy to have all of you along." Bryce winked.

The word plague caused uneasiness around the table. "You know that's not something you run toward, right, Bryce?" Aeotus expressed sarcastically.

After an awkward moment, Eladonia spoke. "We will travel south with you for a few more days. My path leads to Evermoure." She looked at her two elven comrades.

A dejected expression grew on Aticus' face that they would be parting ways with the elves soon.

Palias looked down the table at Aticus. "I acquired something for you today." He reached beneath the table and pulled up a sword housed in a black sheath. The blue handle stood in contrast to the black. "This is yours, as I promised." Palias slid the sword down the table in front of Aticus.

Aticus was overjoyed at the sight of the sword on the table. "Thank you, Palias!" A giddy expression stretched across his face. "Thank you!"

Palias smiled. "You're welcome."

Aticus looked at Yung Sung. "Can we practice tonight?"

"I am unsure how the city guard would react to us hacking it up in the streets. We have several more days of the journey ahead of us. Perhaps tomorrow."

Aticus nodded in eager agreement.

Across the room and out of earshot, a man sat alone at a table in the shadows. Don watched the seven dine and talk, keeping his face hidden beneath his wide-brimmed hat.

CHAPTER TWENTY

BAD NEWS

King Balen Duskwater rushed toward the throne room with Lathal close behind him.

"M'lord, what is it?" Lathal questioned, trying to keep up with Balen, "What's going on?"

"I don't know, Lathal. I received word that Rath had important information concerning the Asvernians." Balen looked back at his general. "The Courier said that Rath had just arrived from Trillian with grave news. I told them to have him meet us in the throne room."

"Well, maybe they've decided to help us."

"I very much doubt that." The two men rounded a corner, passing four palace guards. They hurried out of King Balen's way to keep from getting hit. "Where's Duncan?"

"He left yesterday for Parador with the new soldiers," Lathal said, his breath heavy.

King Balen and Lathal entered the throne room briskly. Two men-at-arms saluted their king before moving on either side of the archway from which the two men had entered.

Lathal breathed in deeply, trying to regain his breath. He was nearly twenty years older than Balen, and he felt it.

Balen paced back and forth in front of the throne chairs.

Rath Inen entered through another door on the far end of the room. "M'lord," Rath stopped before King Balen and bowed. "While I was in Trillion, I received troublesome word from Asvernia," Rath paused, ensuring he had King Balen and Lathal's full attention. "King and Queen Bogdani are dead."

"What! How?" King Balen looked at both men. "When?"

"Two days ago, M'lord." Rath considered the two men, his face drained of color.

"Why are we just now hearing about this? And what are you not telling me? How did they die?" King Balen squinted and stared at Rath.

"Assassinated—in their bed chambers," Rath responded.

Balen looked wide-eyed. "Assassinated—who's responsible for this? Do you know yet?"

"You may want to sit down, M'lord," Rath suggested.

King Balen retreated and sat on the throne.

"The Asvernians claim *we* assassinated the King and Queen, M'lord." Rath looked at the stone floor intently.

"What?!" King Balen, threw himself forward out of his chair. "How can they actually suspect we would do that? We've been allies since—before I was born." Balen searched for words. "Have we reached out to his sons yet?"

"They're currently all on life quests, M'lord. They are trying to find them as we speak." Rath cleared his throat. "The oldest daughter, Neierva, has authority of the throne until the sons are located."

"I need to send her a message—reassure her it was not us." King Balen paced. "I need to go there now."

Rath shook his head. "I would advise against it, M'lord. Neierva has already issued a declaration of war in retaliation.

"Send for their ambassadors; perhaps I can talk some sense into them," Balen commanded in desperation.

"Their ambassadors have already left Meloorne. I have no doubt the Asvernians were gone before you were even awake, M'lord," Rath conceded.

"How can this be?" Balen stepped back to the throne and sat down. He rested his elbow on the arm of the chair and held his chin. "I want to know what proof Neierva has. What kind of evidence could there be?"

"That I don't know. I'll continue trying to contact my sources," Rath declared.

Lathal raised his hands, then let them drop to his sides. "What more can we possibly endure? The Asvernians are our best hope of escape if the orcs overwhelm the capital."

King Balen raised his hand to silence Lathal. "We need to worry about one thing at a time." Balen thought before addressing Rath, "Summon the elf and dwarf ambassadors."

CHAPTER TWENTY-ONE

RESPECT

Aticus held his sword tightly with both hands, shifting left and right, looking for an opening to attack.

His adversary moved around Aticus and swung his sword in a broad arch.

Aticus sidestepped and rolled to the side, evading an attack that would have taken his head off. Dirt wafted off him as he stood in the waning sunlight. He lashed out wildly, but his opponent deflected the blows, sending Aticus against a tree. He ducked again, just in time.

His opponent's sword lodged in the tree above his head.

Aticus tumbled forward, approaching the man from behind, ready to strike, but he was too slow. His opponent pulled the sword from the tree and pressed it against his chest.

Yung Sung pursed his lips and squinted his eyes, "Why didn't you strike at me when my sword was stuck in the tree?" Yung Sung questioned, holding the tip of his sword against Aticus.

"I thought I could hit you from behind," Aticus suggested.

"Haha..." Aeotus sat by the fire, laughing. "Sung, I think he likes to roll around on the ground."

Sung let his curved sword drop to his side. "I purposely put my sword in the tree to give you the advantage. If an opportunity ever arises, seize it. Never run away."

"He stays on the ground more since he got the sword," Aeotus bellowed, enjoying the show.

Eladonia poked Aeotus. "Stop it. Leave him alone."

"What, don't you find this amusing?" Aeotus chuckled and rested his hands on his knees. "We never get performances like this back home." He sighed.

Aticus glared at the elf. "I've never seen you use a sword!"

Sung shook his head. "Aticus, ignore him; he's trying to provoke you."

"I'm not sure you could handle this, dandelion," Aeotus patted his chest and looked at Gilanthos. "Watch this," he whispered.

Gilanthos shook his head. "Don't."

"Aeotus, please stop," Eladonia pleaded, seeing the anger festering on Aticus' face.

"Come on, if you think you can teach me something!" Aticus taunted Aeotus.

"Challenge accepted." Aeotus stood, dusting off his pants. Eladonia held on to Aeotus. "I won't hurt him—much." Aeotus retrieved his sword, pulling it from the sheath. "This is a sword," he addressed Yung Sung.

Sung moved to the side. "Aticus. Do what I've shown you. You'll do fine," he said, in a reaffirming tone, and nodded.

Aticus glanced around for Bryce. He'd gone into the tall rittle weed to meditate.

Palias addressed Aeotus, "If you hurt him or use any of that sword singing, you'll be sparring with me next." His tone was quite intimidating.

"Don't worry, big guy; I'll show him a few things." Aeotus held his sword out, placing the point into the dirt and nodding at Aticus.

Aticus held his sword and lunged forward, thrusting it at the elf.

Aeotus shifted his sword upwards, deflecting the attack away from him quickly.

Aticus pulled back and regained his stance.

The elf began moving in a broad arc around Aticus. "Good."

Aticus shadowed Aeotus, keeping himself in front of the elf.

"What are you waiting for?" Aeotus dragged the sword, tapping the blade on the ground.

"He's trying to provoke you. Stay calm," Sung reassured Aticus.

Aeotus sprang forward, then moved back.

Aticus lunged forward, lifting his blade and bringing it down. Aeotus intercepted the sword as before, but Aticus pressed forward. The two men exchanged blows, blocking and thrusting at each other.

Eladonia leaned near Gilanthos. "He's playing with Aticus." She glanced at Gilanthos and realized he was favoring his head. "Are you unwell?"

"I have the head pain again." Gilanthos rubbed his temple.

"Do you think it was from the fall when we were attacked?" Eladonia shuffled near him and placed her hand on his arm.

Gilanthos shook his head. "No, not from the goblins. It'll stop. Always does." He smiled at his friend.

"You're worrying me," she said, studying his expression. "Are these the same headaches you had before we left Faylorne?"

"Yes," Gilanthos answered.

Aeotus saw an opening and pinned Aticus against a tree with his sword. "Yield."

Aticus glanced at Eladonia. She was speaking to Gilanthos. Aticus regarded Aeotus and grinned, confident he could hold his own. "I yield."

"Wise choice." Aeotus let Aticus go and moved back. "Not bad; you did a good job."

"I didn't expect that," Aticus said, surprised that Aeotus praised him. He sheathed his sword.

"Next time, I won't hold back." Aeotus placed his sword in the casing.

"Neither will I," Aticus retorted. "I thought you were going to teach me something?"

"Oh, I did." Aeotus glared at Aticus.

"What?"

"Humility." Aeotus smiled. "And you fight better when you're not rolling in the dirt."

Everyone laughed and gathered around the fire as the sun set on the horizon.

CHAPTER TWENTY-TWO

DEWBROOK

The seven approached Dewbrook, the next village on the road south. Population sixty-five, or it used to be.

As they approached Dewbrook, the flames of a funeral pyre drew Aticus' attention. Nearly a dozen people stood around the fire, paying their respects. "I'm not sure I'd want my body burned after I die," he said, focusing on the flames.

"It's just your body. Not like you need it anymore." Bryce smiled.

Aticus watched the flames reach for the sky. "You'd want your body burned?" Aticus asked Bryce.

"I don't care what happens to my body when I'm gone. My spirit will move on, and I'll be at peace in the afterlife," Bryce expressed, sitting straighter in the saddle.

Aticus shrugged. "Well, I haven't given it much thought."

"If I were you, I would worry more about what comes after death. That's for eternity," Bryce explained.

Eladonia listened to them talk before speaking, "What if there is no afterlife, Bryce? What then?"

Bryce looked into Eladonia's blue eyes. "Is it worth *not* preparing for eternity? Our bodies are temporary vessels for our spirits."

Aeotus couldn't help but offer his wisdom, "There's no afterlife. When it's over, it's over, the end. But we're immortal, so I plan on living forever," Aeotus bragged.

"Well, you are immortal but not invincible. Keep that in mind for future reference," Bryce retorted. "Lord, please forgive them, for they do not know what they say," Bryce declared, glancing into the sky.

Aticus looked to his left; snow-covered mountains lay not far to the east. "Why doesn't it ever snow here? I'd love to see the snow."

Bryce smiled at Aticus. "It doesn't snow down here, only in the higher elevations, like those mountains."

"How far away are they?" Aticus inquired, wonderstruck by the white peaks.

"Oh, I'd say a good two or three days' journey if I had to guess. Why?" Bryce tilted his head in inquiry.

"I'd like to go there." Aticus smiled.

"There may be a few villages we could find refuge from the cold." Bryce smiled. "Maybe we can find you some snow to play in one day."

The people began dispersing from the funeral as the seven entered the village.

Their arrival attracted the attention of the local guard. Before they could get far into town, three men on foot dressed in studded leather armor stopped them. Each man carried a long spear with a short sword fastened to their waist.

One of the men, sporting a full beard and mustache, addressed the group. "What's your business in town?"

Palias responded to the guardsman from the back of his horse. "We're passing through and require an establishment to stay for the night. Perhaps have the horses fed and tended to."

"We don't take too kindly to outsiders." The bearded man looked back over his shoulder for reassurance. "With everything that's happened, we can't be too safe. Especially with people we don't know."

"We'll give you no trouble; you have my word," Palias assured.

One of the other tall, dark-haired, and cleanly shaven guardsmen stepped forward, "We'd prefer if some of you didn't stay." He looked at the elves.

Aeotus was about to contest the statement, but Eladonia knew the short-tempered elf would voice his opposition. She acted quickly and placed a hand on his arm to distract him from what indeed would have been harsh words, understanding that if they had any prospect of spending the night, it would end once he spoke.

Aeotus glanced at Eladonia, her touch calming.

"I can assure you that we have good intentions," Bryce articulated as he positioned his horse beside Palias.

The guardsman mumbled incoherently under his breath.

The bearded guard nodded reluctantly in acknowledgment. "There's an inn at the end of the street on the left, Grogs Inn. There's a stable behind Grogs. They can take care of all your needs. Keep to yourself and be quick at leaving come dawn."

Palias gestured kindly, "Thank you for the directions."

The three guardsmen parted and stared as the seven rode past.

When they arrived at Grogs Inn, Palias, Yung Sung, and Gilanthos took the horses to the stable while everyone else entered the establishment to secure rooms.

The inn was also the local tavern. There were very few chairs and tables, and a small fireplace was near the outside wall.

"Good day, friends. The name's Klan'den; do you need rooms or food?" The innkeeper announced from behind the bar.

Eladonia responded, "We require both."

"Sit anywhere; I'll be right with you!"

"We have three more that will be joining us shortly. We'll be drinking ale, please. And bring bread if you have it!" Bryce exclaimed, waving his hand.

"Yes, sir, I'll have it right out!" The innkeeper disappeared through a door into the kitchen.

A bearded man at the bar watched the four pull tables and chairs together. He lifted his cup, took a drink, and pressed his tongue into a gap between two teeth.

It wasn't long, and Klan'den came through the door with a tray of ale held over his head in one hand and three loaves of bread in the other. "Here we are; I hope it's to your liking. Can I offer you a pheasant or chicken?"

"Chicken, we'll take six birds if that won't put you out," Bryce said.

"Not at all; I appreciate the business. I don't get many customers anymore."

"Where is everyone?" Aticus inquired.

"Well, those that stayed keep to themselves. Most folks are moving east to the bigger cities for safety. With everything that's happened. I swear I'd leave too if I could."

"We were in Veridian and overheard something about a plague or an illness spreading," Bryce said.

"No, not a plague. It's more of a sickness, I suppose. It started some time ago. People went to sleep and never woke." Klan'den let his eyes focus on the table. "The deaths started happening more often."

"We saw the funeral when we came into town," Aticus said.

"Yes, that was a local farmer's daughter, a perfectly healthy little girl." Klan'den shook his head. "We have the worries of war with the orcs. Thank goodness the goblins haven't made it this far south yet. The town's not what it used to be."

"Why haven't you left?" Aticus questioned.

Klan'den gazed around the tavern. "This is all I got. Everything I have is right here. I can't afford to move. You lie in bed at night, scared to sleep, and if you do, pray you wake in the morning. I have to admit that I try not to sleep most nights." He shrugged half-heartedly.

"The city guards welcomed us when we came to town, and they didn't seem happy to see us," Bryce added.

"You met Ular. He lost his brother and father not long ago. Both in a matter of days." Klan'den shook his head in memory. "Good people. Not long after the sickness, well, after, people started to die. Someone began digging the bodies—right out of the graves."

"Grave robbers?" Eladonia asked.

Klan'den clicked his lips and tilted his head. "Well, you see, here's the strange thing. The bodies disappeared, but the personal belongings were left untouched." He shook his head. "I'll get your dinner ready." With that, Klan'den disappeared into the kitchen.

It wasn't long before Palias, Sung, and Gilanthos joined the rest of them in the tavern. Bryce informed them regarding what they'd learned about the cemetery and the deaths. After eating and securing their rooms, they decided to visit the graves on the southern-most edge of the village.

The seven drew strange looks from passing villagers. When they reached the cemetery, they had attracted the attention of the three city guards they had encountered earlier, prompting them to approach.

Gilanthos and Aeotus walked among the tombstones, studying the heaps of dirt littering the ground. Aeotus counted thirty-four disturbed graves. Everyone else stayed outside of a rod-iron fence surrounding the cemetery.

"What brings you to the graveyard, strangers?" the bearded city guard asked. They were understandably aggravated to see outsiders walking into the cemetery.

"You need to get out of there now!" the cleanly-shaven city guard barked at Aeotus and Gilanthos. "Get out of there!" He pointed with his finger.

Palias stepped forward to calm the three guards. But his size only seemed to unnerve them more. "We're trying to understand what happened here," Palias added.

Eladonia stopped beside Palias. "We want to help find who desecrated your burial site."

"How do we know you didn't dig up the bodies, and now you're back for something else?" The third, and until now silent, guard asked.

"The bodies were not dug up," Gilanthos said.

"What, what did you say?" the first guard barked.

"The graves were not dug up. That's what I'm trying to say," Gilanthos pronounced suspiciously. He knelt and studied the ground. Then, he followed the tracks out of the iron fence. He stopped and looked at the southern horizon.

Aeotus watched his friend, cautious not to interrupt him until he was outside the fence. "What, what is it, Gil?"

Eladonia pivoted toward Gilanthos waiting for his response.

"The dirt was not dug out of the ground," Gilanthos responded, returning to the cemetery, he stood over a grave.

Everyone gathered against the iron fence, waiting for him to complete his investigation.

"The dirt was pushed up. The bodies in the ground dug themselves out," Gilanthos said, almost in disbelief. He pointed at the dirt piled around the top of the grave. "Look here. See the dirt pushed back and away?" Gilanthos followed tracks out of the cemetery. "These depressions leading from the graves—they all go south." He pointed at the southern horizon and looked at everyone. "These are footprints of the dead."

"How can you tell? Everyone in the city has been in there," the clean-faced guard said, irritated. "You're making this up."

Gilanthos responded as he scanned the ground, "Every one of these graves has footprints leading out the gate and moving south." He pointed at the ground adamantly.

The guard with the full beard responded, "That's absurd to say they would dig themselves up and walk away."

Eladonia responded, "If he says they dug themselves up and walked away, that's what happened."

The three city guards moved off to the side and spoke quietly.

"What does he mean, dug themselves up and walked away?" Aticus asked Bryce.

Bryce looked at the displaced dirt in the cemetery. "Something or someone raised the dead."

"A wizard?" Aticus questioned so everyone could hear.

"No, not a wizard but a necromancer; this is dark magic. It's the kind of magic that sucks the life out of you and destroys everything it touches. No, this is the opposite of magic," Aeotus asserted, shaking his head. He looked southward.

Gilanthos looked at Aeotus. "No. You don't think that's possible, do you? A necromancer?"

"I can find no other explanation," Aeotus responded.

"What are we doing about it?" Aticus asked.

Aeotus glared at Aticus. "Nothing; this doesn't involve us. We stay as far away as we can." He looked at Gilanthos. "Far away, like the opposite direction."

Gilanthos nodded. "Agreed."

"What do you think, Bryce?" Aticus asked.

"Aeotus and Gilanthos are right. We can't help the dead now." He looked at the guardsmen. "Is that why you're performing cremations?"

The bearded guardsman nodded. "We thought there might be grave robbers." He looked at the other two guards before continuing. "We know of two other nearby towns with the same situation."

"If I were you, I'd find somewhere else to live," Aeotus added.

"Everyone who can leave is gone. The rest of us have nowhere to go," the cleanly-shaven guard said. "What do we do?"

"I would continue burning the dead and hope that you never have to deal with this again," Palias suggested.

Yung Sung stopped next to the Asvernian. "What is killing the people in their sleep?"

Palias looked down at Sung. "Good question."

The guardsmen turned and walked away in dismay.

Bryce looked at the sky and shook his head in confirmation. "I feel like I need to stay for a few days," Bryce said, looking at Aticus.

Aticus nodded. "Then, maybe we can check out the mountains and that snow?"

"We need to leave for Evermoure in the morning." Eladonia glanced at Aeotus and Gilanthos. Doubt etched into her features.

Aticus looked at Eladonia. "You could go with us to the mountains. Have you ever seen snow?" He wasn't asking as much as pleading. He looked into her blue eyes. "Please?"

"We can't, I can't." Eladonia looked at her two elven friends. "Neither of you needs to go with me. My obligation should not define your paths." She smiled at Aeotus and Gilanthos.

"I go where you go," Aeotus added, his voice cracked uncharacteristically.

"What kind of friend would I be if I didn't follow you both?" Gilanthos smiled.

Palias separated himself from the group and moved to look out at the southern plains and the tracks the dead left behind.

Yung Sung moved to stand beside him while everyone spoke. "You're worried about these people, aren't you?"

Palias looked down at Sung. "I am."

Sung shook his head and gazed at the horizon.

Chapter Twenty-Three

The Visit

Neacrom sat upon his throne of bones, his breathing labored. He had rested from a long night of work in his laboratory when, suddenly, the stone slab of the secret door began to open. He opened his eyes, shifted in his chair uncomfortably, and straightened himself the best he could so that his condition would not be noticeable. He was surprised to see who emerged.

A tall man dressed in a long, green cloak stepped into view. He pulled the hood of his cloak back to reveal shoulder-length, black hair. His dark eyebrows and long eyelashes only seemed to accentuate the clarity of his blue eyes. His confident smile infuriated Neacrom. "It's been some time, hasn't it, Neacrom?" Michael stopped and let his eyes drift across the massive chamber. "You like isolation, don't you?"

Neacrom stood from his throne. "What brings you here, Michael?" Neacrom inhaled and took two steps forward.

Michael tilted his head while he looked around the room; his smile faded. He blinked slowly and looked at Neacrom. "I have a favor to ask of you."

"So, JoJung sent you?" Neacrom took another painful step forward. "He can't have it back; I'm not finished with the Bloodstone yet."

Michael straightened his head and waved his hand dismissively, "No, JoJung didn't send me, and no, I'm not here for the Bloodstone." Michael smiled. "JoJung doesn't know I'm here." He took several steps toward Neacrom and pointed his finger. "I'm here for the favor you owe me." He paused and studied Neacrom's feeble frame. "I have no doubt you remember what I am speaking of."

"That was a long time ago..." Neacrom raised his voice angrily.

Michael held his hand up to stop Neacrom before he continued. "Did I, or did I not get you and the woman out of the Hand?" Michael grinned and looked at the stone floor. He waited for Neacrom to speak.

"You did, but JoJung found me twelve years later. He killed my family!" Neacrom squeezed his hands tightly. "I'm confident you helped him find me!" Angrily, Neacrom took a painful step forward. He nearly went down but regained his balance.

"I can assure you, Morgan, I didn't have anything to do with their deaths." Michael gazed into Neacrom's eyes with certainty.

Neacrom was shocked; he hadn't heard his name spoken in years. He was at a loss for words, "I...I..."

"I know it must have been difficult. I did care; you must know that. I felt great remorse for your loss; she was a good woman." Michael looked up. "What was her name? I can't seem to remember." Michael knew her name. He wanted to hear Neacrom say it.

Neacrom let his gaze drift from Michael as he focused on the past, "Claire, her name was Claire."

"Claire, yes, I remember now." Michael smiled. "Now for that favor."

Neacrom looked into Michael's eyes fiercely. "They're dead; I owe you nothing." He turned and walked back to his chair.

Michael knew what Neacrom was doing in Oppack: using the Bloodstone to raise his family from the dead. He took two steps closer before speaking sympathetically, "Neacrom, what are you actually doing?"

Neacrom sat in his chair, looking down at Michael. "I know you have an ulterior motive for being here. What is it, Michael? You never do anything without it benefiting you."

Michael advanced, ignoring the question; he stopped at the first step. "You're attempting to use the Bloodstone to bring them back? Claire and the children?" Michael tilted his head to the side. "You can't find the right combination of incantations, can you?"

Neacrom didn't respond; he stared at Michael, resolute.

"I have something that may be able to aid you, but I require something from you." Michael slid his hand beneath his cloak and retrieved an object.

Neacrom watched his hand disappear cautiously.

Michael pulled out a small, black leather book inlaid with purple embroidery.

Neacrom's eyes widened when he saw his spellbook. JoJung took it from him many years ago as leverage.

"You remember this?" Michael let his lips crease on one side.

"What do you want?" Neacrom didn't take his eyes off the book.

Michael bent over and placed the book on the top step of the raised platform where Neacrom's chair sat. "I give you the book in good faith—but I will require something from you."

Neacrom looked at Michael. He waited silently. He knew the price would be steep, but he understood the book would contain what he needed to bring his family back from the dead.

Michael moved up the three steps onto the platform where Neacrom sat. "In seven days, Talmet and his general will arrive and try to take the Bloodstone from you. I want you to kill them, all of them. I don't want one survivor; do you understand?"

Neacrom laughed at Michael's demand. "You expect me to kill the orcs?" He laughed again before speaking, "I've killed every army that orc has sent. One more will make no difference." He looked at his book, lying on the marble platform behind Michael. "Consider it done."

"That's one part of the favor." Michael smiled. "After adding the orcs to your undead army, I want you to send them into Evermour. Attack the elves. Do what damage you can." Michael shrugged. "That's all I require."

Neacrom studied the floor.

"Do we have an accord?" Michael tilted his head.

"I need the Bloodstone every night. Tell your henchmen in the other room not to trouble me." Neacrom felt he was in control now, and his demeanor changed.

Michael nodded in agreement, "We'll see what can be arranged."

CHAPTER TWENTY-FOUR

DUNCAN'S STAND

It was late afternoon, and the sky was clear, except for a few high clouds. Duncan and his men were en route to Parador and would reach the fortress midday tomorrow. Splotchy patches of rittle reed drifted with a light northwesterly breeze, relieving the day's heat.

Edden, Duncan's first officer, traveled on his horse beside him. "One hundred and fifty men." Edden glanced at the newly conscripted soldiers walking behind them. "Do you think any of them, or us for that matter, are going to make a difference?" he challenged Duncan, his shoulder-length black hair fluttering in the wind.

Duncan regarded Edden for a moment before speaking. "I believe every individual can make a difference," he said before looking at the eastern horizon and finishing his thought. "Hope is all we have, my friend. Perhaps one of these men will tip the balance in our favor." Duncan grinned. "It was done before, but in the enemy's favor."

"I suppose. I wish I had your optimistic viewpoint of people," Edden commented sarcastically.

Duncan smiled. "We'll set camp over that rise," he signaled ahead of them.

Edden smiled, "Good. I'm getting hungry," he commented.

Duncan let his vision drift south before stopping his horse and raising his hand into a fist, halting the caravan of men behind them.

Edden stopped beside him. "What is it?"

"Someone is riding towards us. I think it's one of our scouts," Duncan said to himself.

"I don't see anything," Edden expressed, jutting his head forward. "Oh, wait, I see now."

The rider approached as quickly as he had appeared. It was, indeed, Thain, one of the two scouts assigned to Duncan for his trip to Parador. "It's orcs!" Thain yelled before calming his horse beside the two men: "It's a raiding party of orcs! Somehow, they've snuck behind the lines!" He was spilling out words faster than he could breathe.

"Slow down," Duncan said, trying to calm Thain.

"They killed Ri'Jel! Shot him in the back! They almost hit me!" He looked at Duncan. "They came out of nowhere."

"Take a breath. How many?" Duncan asked.

"Fifteen, maybe twenty."

Duncan glanced at Edden. "We need to take care of this." He looked out over the conscripts. "I know these men have never seen combat, but you know as well as I do that a small raiding party of orcs can cause a lot of problems if left unchecked."

"What are you thinking?" Edden asked. "You're thinking about doing something we shouldn't. They're not ready." Edden glanced at the men.

"There aren't that many orcs," Duncan commented before addressing his scout. "Thain, I want you to ride to Meloorne. Tell Lothal he needs to double the patrols. Let him know a raiding party got through, and we'll handle the situation before continuing to Parador." Duncan waited for Thain to ride off, but the man sat on his horse thinking. "Go!" Duncan motioned toward the west and Meloorne.

Thain nodded and spurred his horse, kicking up a cloud of dirt as he rode away.

Sarack, Duncan's second officer, made his way to the front of the caravan by horse, stopping beside Duncan and Edden. He'd seen combat with them several times.

"Sarack, I want you to take the wagons and half the men over that ridge; set camp there. The rest of us are going orc hunting," Duncan declared.

Sarack nodded and turned toward the caravan to gather the men and wagons. He shouted for the rank of men on the right to follow him with the wagons. Although the conscripts had never seen combat, they understood the importance of following orders. "The rest of you are going with captain Duncan. Let's move." Sarack lifted his hand in the air, moving it in a circular motion.

"Are you sure this is a good idea?" Edden questioned as he adjusted in his saddle. "They're not ready."

"Were any of us ever ready?" Duncan asked Edden with raised brows.

The sun had dipped below the horizon, casting long shadows over the land. Duncan and Edden had taken seventy-five conscripts, clad in chainmail and armed with swords and shields. Duncan had hoped they would have come across the orc camp by now. He certainly didn't expect the orcs to find them first.

A single arrow struck the earth not far from Edden. Then, another hit the ground behind Duncan. They were taken by surprise when the first volley fell. A barrage of arrows rained down, striking all around them. Two conscripts nearby were hit in the head and neck, toppling to the ground. "Everyone, spread out! Prepare for battle!" Duncan yelled as the sounds of swords pulled from their sheaths echoed in the night.

The next salvo of arrows came, striking Edden's horse multiple times, throwing it to the ground, and trapping the knight's leg beneath his mount. Somehow, the barrage missed Duncan's horse, Stoubil, as more of his men fell around him. "That's more than fifteen or twenty orcs!" Duncan yelled and dismounted. He pulled his shield from the saddle. "Go, boy." He slapped his horse on the rump, sending him back into the darkness and out of range of the attack.

The orcs' battle cry came from all around them. Duncan rushed toward Edden and dug at the soft dirt around his leg, freeing Edden from beneath his horse and helping him to his feet. Orcs and humans clashed around them as the sound of steel on steel echoed in the evening air.

Duncan watched an orc approaching from the high weeds, not far from where he stood. He dodged the creature's attack, brought his shield up under its chin, and knocked it backward. With a forward thrust of his sword, he impaled the orc and used his foot to push it off his weapon. "This is no scouting party! It's a large detachment of orcs!"

Edden confronted an orc emerging from the shadows. "There's too many!" he yelled, sidestepping to prevent his head from being displaced. Before the fourth volley of arrows struck, Duncan rushed to his friend's side, pushing the orc to the ground. He held his shield high, covering himself and Edden—the torrent of missiles killed more orcs than conscripts, including the one at their feet.

"I need to get to those archers, or they're going to kill us all!" Duncan shouted before issuing his command. "Edden, I need you to get to the rest of our unit!"

Edden sliced an approaching orc across the chest, sending a crimson mist into the air and across Duncan's face. "I'm not leaving you here with the men to die!"

"You have to warn them!" He whistled loudly and parried a strike from an approaching orc before bringing his weapon around and dispatching the creature. The smell of blood and sweat permeated the air.

Stoubil appeared out of the darkness, side-swiping an orc, sending it sprawling. "Go! Someone has to warn them if we fail!" Edden nodded reluctantly before climbing onto the back of Stoubil. "I'll be back with help!" Duncan pressed against an approaching orc to keep it off of Edden. He stepped on the orc's foot and pushed him back onto the ground, piercing his chest.

Edden spurred Stoubil, glancing back again before disappearing into the darkness. Duncan watched Edden ride away. "Good luck," he whispered before turning to find the archers. Duncan ran into the darkness, leaping over the bodies of the fallen and around skirmishing soldiers; the heavy plate armor he wore did little to slow him down. He tasted the blood of his enemy; it was sweet yet metallic.

Duncan found ten orc archers standing ready with their bows pointed at the sky. He caught them off guard, striking down two before they could lose their arrows. The remaining eight bowmen released the strings on their bows, launching the arrows into the night sky. Duncan quickly dispatched six more archers before the remaining orcs routed.

Three larger, heavily clad orcs suddenly appeared out of the darkness, pausing when they saw the cavalier. These orc soldiers were Loden, an elite unit trained to withstand pain and fatigue through herbal concoctions created by shamans. Consuming the tonic rendered them resistant to pain with the added benefit of enhanced strength and agility. The Loden were trained to make the potion themselves from herbs found in the wilderness.

Behind the three Loden and atop their horses sat four orc officers, the architects of the raids.

Duncan swallowed and paused, taking a deep breath. He grinned as a set of fangs slid from the corners of his mouth, and he licked his lips. Duncan tasted the blood of man and beast as he tightened his grip on his shield and sword. He sprinted toward the Loden, his weapon ready.

CHAPTER TWENTY-FIVE

SHADOWS

> *"As children, we're fearful of the dark. But as we grow older, we realize it's not the dark we should fear, but what lurks in the shadows."*
> -Bryce

Aticus sat up, covered with sweat. *It was the nightmare again.* He let his legs hang off the bed and focused on the dark surroundings. He could hear Bryce snoring from across the room. He sighed, knowing it would be difficult to sleep again after the dream. As his sight adjusted to the lack of light, Aticus saw an odd glow around Bryce. "That's new," he whispered.

He placed his bare feet on the wooden planks of the second-floor room. Trying not to wake Bryce, he walked across the room toward the slumbering dwarf, curious about the blue aura. The floor was cold to the touch and creaked with each step. He hovered over the dwarf, studying his features, illuminated by the glow. That's when he heard the scream from outside.

Bryce opened his eyes and was startled at seeing someone standing over him in the dark. Defensively, he swung his hand, slapping Aticus across the face, sending him back onto the floor. "I'm sorry, son!" Bryce apologized and sat on the edge of the bed.

Aticus rubbed his jaw, astonished at how hard Bryce had hit him. "That hurt."

"What was that? I'm sorry I hit you. Where did that scream come from?" Bryce pushed off the bed, landing with a thud. He offered no further condolences as he shuffled to the window. "Did you hear that scream?"

"Yeah, I heard it." Aticus stood, moving his jaw from side to side. "Why did you hit me?"

"Why were you watching me sleep?" Bryce looked at Aticus. "Was I snoring?" His eyes widened.

"Yes, but there was this…" Aticus was interrupted by another scream from the other side of the closed window.

Bryce drew back the curtains and opened the shutters. "It's coming from the house on the other side of the street."

The door to their room swung open. Startled, Aticus flinched as if he'd been hit again. It was Yung Sung. "Did you hear the screams?"

"Yes. Something's happening across the street." Bryce pointed out the window.

Gilanthos appeared behind Sung. The scream came again, more prolonged and filled with pain.

"I need to get over there!" Bryce said, running across the room, leaving his boots behind. Gilanthos and Yung Sung moved aside to let the dwarf pass.

Palias and Aeotus emerged from another room at the end of the hall. "What's happening?" Palias asked.

Bryce moved as quickly as his small legs would carry him down the stairs and out the tavern door. Palias and Aeotus trailed behind the dwarf, trying not to trip over him.

Gilanthos quickly caught them in the street as Sung and Aticus stopped outside the door to the inn. The townspeople slowly began to file into the street, never moving far from the front door of their homes.

Klan'den, the tavern owner, strode through the door onto the front porch with Aticus and Sung. "Bloody hell. It's happened again."

Aticus studied Klan'den. "What?"

"Someone died; that's what happened." Klan'den looked at Aticus. "Welcome to hell."

Sung and Aticus glanced at one another before moving to the edge of the street.

Bryce crossed the street and entered the home, followed by Palias and Aeotus.

The woman was still screaming and lamenting. Aticus found it painful to listen to her wails.

An older man stepped from the open door of the house. Gilanthos backed away, giving him room to move. "I saw something!" the man said, confused. "I saw it over my little girl. There was a shadow. It was there, and—then it was gone. She's dead. My baby's dead!" He fell to his knees and began to sob.

Gilanthos stared at Sung and Aticus from across the street, an unfamiliar vulnerability etched into his features. He could make life-and-death decisions in seconds and fight goblins without hesitation, but he stood before this sobbing man, at a loss for what to do.

Palias stepped from the doorway of the home. He made eye contact with Aticus and Sung and shook his head, his expression dismal. Then he placed his large hands on the sobbing man, uttering compassionate words; his deep tone resonated so even Aticus could hear him from across the street.

The screams from inside the house stopped; no doubt, Bryce was with her now.

Aticus waited for Bryce to walk out the door with the child in his arms. But it didn't happen—not this time.

Aeotus emerged from the house and approached the crying man. He knelt, looked into the grieving man's face, and shook him.

"There he is," Aticus commented, shaking his head. "Aeotus has no shame."

"You saw what? What did you see? You need to tell me exactly what you saw!" Aeotus shouted. Palias placed his hand on the elf's shoulder, but Aeotus shrugged it off. He continued interrogating the man more intensely. Once he felt he had all the necessary information, he stood and began to walk in circles, contemplating what had happened. Meanwhile, Bryce emerged from the house and sat by the door, not making eye contact with anyone.

Suddenly, Aeotus paused. He glanced around at everyone. "Where's Eladonia?" Everyone looked around. "Where is Eladonia?" His voice cracked. "She'd be here with the rest of us."

Aticus and Sung glanced around, understanding she wasn't there. They were the first up the stairs. Aeotus was behind them when they reached the door to her room. Aticus pushed open the door and saw the shadow. It hovered over Eladonia, holding her face in its dark hands or what looked like hands. The spectral shadow had no face. It was dark and opaque but humanoid in shape. "Eladonia!" Aticus shrieked.

Sung looked around for something he could use as a weapon.

Aeotus burst through the door, pushing the two men out of his way. "Ela!" He quickly brought a spell to mind and spoke, *"Tera'lack,"* and six small spheres of light sprang from his hands. They passed through the shadow and impacted the wall behind it, sending splinters flying and wisps of smoke from the burnt wood.

The shadow moved away from Eladonia and hovered near the bed, facing the three men. It extended its spectral arms toward the trio.

Aeotus raised his hands again. He uttered the word of another spell, *"Dothrok."* A burst of wind erupted from his hands, blowing anything loose around the room. It didn't seem to affect the spectral form.

Suddenly, Bryce shoved his way through the door beside Aeotus and held out his hands. *"Gabil!"* he said as a bright light illuminated the room, emanating from every fiber of the chamber. The glare was so great that Aticus covered his eyes.

Bryce paused, but the light continued to pulsate. The spectral form was nowhere to be seen. "Nothing will bother us here now," Bryce stated. He hobbled to the side of the bed and took Eladonia's hand in his. "My dear, Ela." He rubbed her hand in his.

Aeotus made his way to the other side, grasping her other hand. "Ela!"

Aticus and Sung leaned over the foot of the bed. Palias and Gilanthos entered the room to stand beside the bed as well. "Is she..." Sung started.

Aticus' heart skipped, and a knot formed in his throat. It was hard to breathe.

Aeotus felt for a pulse. "I don't feel anything. She can't be." He frantically searched for her breath, listening to her chest for a heartbeat.

"I do not sense her spirit." Bryce stared at her. "Without a soul, your body cannot survive." He looked up and began to chant, placing his hands on her head and chest.

Aeotus looked up at Bryce. "She's not dead; I hear her heart. Barely, but I hear it." Aeotus uttered, his head pressed against her chest.

Aticus caught his breath when he heard Aeotus speak the words. "How did you know something was wrong?"

Aeotus straightened. "What the man said reminded me of my studies. I didn't put it together at first, but—this is all tied to the necromancer." Aeotus caressed her hand and arm. "That was a soul reaver."

"What is a soul reaver?" Palias inquired.

"They're the result of a powerful necromantic spell. A side effect of failed attempts at completing a spell." He thought for a moment. "There's a price to pay when using the dark arts. Reavers are souls pulled from hell when the spell fails. When they're pulled back onto our plane, the souls lack individuality. They're only seeking to escape by feeding off the living spirit…" Aeotus' shoulder sank when he realized how helpless he was. "When touched, it removes your soul, binding the spirit to the soul reaver."

"Is it dead?" Aticus asked.

"No." Aeotus studied the chanting dwarf. "He merely pushed it outside of the light."

"Then it's still out there," Yung Sung inquired as his vision drifted to the walls.

"Yes," Aeotus responded.

"Then how do we kill it?" Aticus asked.

Bryce continued his soft chanting.

Aeotus looked at Aticus. "We can't kill it. Nothing on the mortal plane can touch the soul reaver."

"There has to be some way?" Gilanthos asked, his features sagging as he placed his hand on her leg.

"The child across the street, no doubt, was touched. All of these deaths…" Aeotus hesitated. "The people that died…" Aeotus looked around at everyone before continuing. "The people who died were probably not dead at all. They were likely alive when they were buried or burned." Aeotus swallowed hard when he said it out loud.

Everyone remained silent.

"We have to help her. There must be something we can do, right?" Aticus requested. "There has to be."

"The only way to banish a soul reaver is to destroy the necromancer. Theoretically, the souls would be released from bondage and returned to the body upon death. If the body survives."

"Then, there's a chance?" Yung Sung interjected.

"We don't know where the necromancer is or how long it would take us to find this person. The body can only go so many days without nutrition before…" Aeotus paused.

Bryce stopped chanting. "You can find this—necromancer, and you can save her." Bryce looked at everyone. "I'll stay here. But you have to go now."

Hope spread across Aeotus' face. "We can, and we will."

"Let's go," Aticus blurted out.

"No, you need to stay here. We can't risk your safety," Aeotus stated, seeking agreement from the rest of the group.

Palias agreed, "You're needed here to help Bryce."

Bryce acknowledged Palias, "Yes, I'll need help spreading the word to everyone. I'll speak to the family across the street and let them know there's hope for their child."

Palias and Yung Sung departed for the horses while Aeotus and Gilanthos gathered their belongings.

Bryce left the room to comfort the grieving parents. "Stay here with her, Aticus. Nothing will harm you in the light," Bryce reassured him.

Aticus sat on the bed beside Eladonia and tenderly grasped her hand. "Don't worry, Ela. You're going to be alright. I promise."

Chapter Twenty-Six

THE PIECES MOVE

Rath Inen woke to someone banging on his bedroom door. He sat in his bed and placed his feet on the wooden floor. "Cursed damnations." He could see the flickering light from a torch glowing from beneath the door. His eyes adjusted to the darkness, hoping they might go away. They knocked on the door again and called his name. "This had better be good," he grumbled as he stood and pulled his robe off a nearby chair. "I'm coming!"

He reached the door, turned the handle, and pulled the door back, fully prepared to immerse someone with colorful metaphors. Instead, he paused when he found General Lathal Talos holding a torch in the hall. His complexion was devoid of color.

"King Balen and the queen are dead," Lathal whispered the words, fearful that if said louder, it might be true.

Rath stood in the doorway, unable to speak. The crackling of the torch filled the silence for what seemed like an eternity.

"Rath, did you hear me?" Lathal asked, clearing his throat.

"How?" Rath asked.

"They were killed in their sleep. We have no suspects, and there's no evidence implicating anyone," Lathal revealed.

"Do you think the Asvernians could have done this?" Rath was grasping for answers. "The children?" His voice cracked.

"They're fine. But the youngest, Celest, found them," Lathal uttered.

"By the gods. She must be so scared." Rath placed his hand on his abdomen.

"Timan and Loren are both with the priests," Lathal said.

Rath considered Lathal. "It could be someone who sympathizes with the Asvernians. It had to be someone close to the king." He stepped into the hall. "There's no way anyone outside could have entered the palace at this time of night." Rath ran through scenarios before looking at Lathal. "How many people know?"

"The royal coroner, two priests, three of the king's guards, myself, and you. As well as the children," Lathal declared. "Why?"

"Too many people know already. I need to see the chamber; perhaps we can find more information before the area's cleaned and any evidence wiped away." Rath started to close the door and go with Lathal, but stopped. "I need to change. I'll meet you in the royal chambers."

Lathal nodded and left.

Rath returned to his bedchamber and shut the door behind him, lighting a candle on a nearby table. He quickly changed into his everyday garments before pausing at his writing desk. He retrieved a golden clasp from the drawer and placed it in his pocket.

Rath arrived outside the royal chamber, pausing. He braced himself for what awaited him on the other side. Upon entering, he found that the coroner had already removed the king and queen, leaving behind a gruesome scene.

The first thing Rath focused on was the queen's mirror, which he had gifted her for her birthday.

Lathal waited at the end of the bed, staring at the bloody carnage. "I can't believe this is real."

Rath examined the chamber. "The furniture is not out of place, there's no sign of a struggle." He studied the blood-covered bed before walking to the window and looking out. "There's no way anyone could have climbed the tower wall."

"No." Lathal shook his head. "I looked as well," Lathal said, scanning the room for something he might have missed.

Rath wandered around the royal chamber, examining everything. He looked under chairs and behind tables.

"I've looked everywhere, Rath. I don't understand." Lathal paced back and forth. "The children are too young to rule. Timan's the oldest—he's only nine." He stopped and watched Rath. "The only other family Balen has is an estranged brother in Veridian."

Rath listened but didn't answer.

"Rath, you are the commander of the kingdom's defenses. We are at war with the orcs and now quite possibly the Asvernians." Lathal paused. "You have to supervise the kingdom's administration and oversee Timan until he comes of age in a few years."

Rath shook his head. "No!" He considered Lathal. "That is not an option."

Lathal proceeded to stand beside Rath. "It's our only option—the kingdom's only choice."

Rath stopped searching the room and slumped into the nearest chair. His expression sagged, and he paused before speaking. "For the kingdom." Rath stared at Lathal.

"Yes, for the kingdom," Lathal whispered reassuringly.

Rath's vision drifted toward the blood-stained bed where his king and queen died. He focused on the stone floor beneath the bed. Rath stood, placing his hand in his shirt pocket, and approached the bed.

"What—what do you see?" Lathal asked.

Rath knelt beside the bed. He withdrew his hand from his pocket and reached under the bed. He pulled his hand back and revealed what he held. "I think we have our proof!"

"I searched under the bed; how did I miss that?" Lathal's face contorted.

"It's fine, my friend. It's been a difficult night for us all." In Rath's hand lay a clasp for a cloak. The gold element shone in the torchlight. The clasp consisted of a pair of roses intertwined. "It's the Asvernian crest."

"Then it was the Asvernians," Lathal stated. "They did this out of revenge!"

Rath held the clasp in his hand and gripped it tightly. "We need to prepare for a possible attack from the Asvernians."

"We can't fight a war on two fronts, much less one. I leave tomorrow for Parador with reinforcements from Trillian." Lathal shook his head. "I'm at a loss for what to do."

"We must lay the king and queen to rest; you cannot leave until then," Rath replied.

"Agreed." Lathal nodded. "You must address the people at first light."

Rath walked to the window and stared over the city of Meloorne, shrouded in darkness.

"I have preparations to make if I stay a few more days. You should try to get some sleep. It's going to be a long day," Lathal reassured Rath.

"I don't think I can sleep," Rath replied. "Go do what you need; I'll meet you later."

Lathal left the chamber, leaving Rath standing at the window.

Rath shifted and examined the blood-stained bed before walking to the large mirror. He gazed into it, but not at his reflection. A smile spread across his face as he inspected the tiny golden clasp in his hand.

CHAPTER TWENTY-SEVEN

LIFE OR DEATH

Neacrom entered a makeshift laboratory on the second floor of the south tower. He'd been forced to use this area since the Hands of the Shadow had confiscated his primary laboratory. He paused inside the room and glanced at the three tables in the center. Each one was covered with old, tattered material. Lightning flashed through a boarded window on the far end of the room.

He proceeded to a table against the wall and placed a black leather book on the wooden surface, then pulled the Bloodstone from his pocket. He marveled at the mist swirling within its crystal confines.

"Tonight, my love, we will finally be reunited," Neacrom said, taking a deep, painful breath. He placed the Bloodstone on the table and reached for his book. "I have everything I need to make our family whole again, Claire," he added, opening the book and scanning several pages.

His lips curved into a smile as he spoke. "Our family can live without fear. We will return home, and everything will be as it was before JoJung found us." His smile vanished, and his face slumped. "JoJung will pay for what he did, my darling. They will all suffer for their murderous actions."

Neacrom retrieved the Bloodstone and flipped through the book as he lurched toward the table at the center of the room, flanked by two others. His lips curved up as he remembered a time when he was in love. "The autumn flowers will soon be in bloom. It was your favorite season."

The sudden crack of thunder brought him back to the present. He resumed flipping through the book's pages until he discovered the missing piece. "This is it. The missing incantation," he said to himself, tightening his grip on the Bloodstone. Approaching the central table, he pulled back the cloth, revealing the mummified remains of his beloved, Claire. Despite her ghastly appearance, he tenderly stroked her coarsely matted hair.

Neacrom studied her features before addressing her, "Michael suspects that I intend to direct the undead into Evermour as a means of attacking the elves." He stroked her hair once more. "All this while, they believe I am acting as their pawn. I did create an army of the dead, but not for their selfish motives."

Neacrom examined the Bloodstone he held tightly in his hand. "They betrayed us, and now they want me to create an army of the undead for them. I will give them what they want, but they will regret it. I will destroy the Hands of the Shadow entirely. JoJung and Michael will pay with their lives first," he spoke resolutely, and tightened his grip on the red gem. "I won't let them use the Bloodstone to achieve their objective, whatever that is.

Neacrom gazed at the two covered tables on each side. "I promise, Claire, I will protect you and the children."

Neacrom pulled the book closer and began reciting the words written on the page aloud. He held out his hand, the Bloodstone balanced in his palm as he started to chant. The stone began to glow brightly, and the mist inside swirled violently. After reading one page, he turned to the next and continued speaking in a language only he could understand. Once he finished the second page, he placed the book on the table beside Claire and began reciting other unholy necromantic incantations.

He repeated the words over and over, and the stone glowed brighter, casting a red hue through the room. The tip of the vibrating Bloodstone pricked his palm, drawing blood.

His eyes drifted over her corpse as the skin on Claire's face stretched and softened, returning to its youthful plump appearance. Her hair regained its almond hue and grew as delicate as silk. The cloth covering her body swelled as her figure returned to its earthly form. The blood defied gravity as it seeped from the wound in his hand and streamed up the edges of the Bloodstone. He would give every drop if it brought her back.

Claire's body trembled as she opened her eyes wide and gasped for a breath that she could not catch.

"Claire," Neacrom whispered as tears ran down his face. He had done it; she'd returned to him.

Clair struggled to pull air to fill her lungs, her brows furrowed, and her body convulsed on the table as she tried to scream, but no sound came out. She thrashed, knocking Neacrom's spellbook to the floor.

He reached for her as he held the Bloodstone out and spoke the incantation repeatedly. Her skin dried and collapsed over the bones. Her eyes, devoid of life, sank into her skull.

Neacrom cried out in despair, "NO! NO!" He dropped the Bloodstone on the floor and reached for her with both hands. Her body decomposed, crumbling to dust before his eyes. "No-no-no! Please don't leave me, Claire, come back! Come back!" He raised his hands and watched as her remains crumbled through his fingers.

Neacrom's legs buckled beneath him as he tumbled to the floor, his hands grasping hold of her ashen remains. He lay defeated, sobbing uncontrollably. "What have I done, Claire?" His anguish reverberated through the tower halls as thunder shook the walls violently.

Meanwhile, the Bloodstone balanced on the cold floor of the tower, absorbing the necomancer's blood into its hard surface, feeding the mist within.

CHAPTER TWENTY-EIGHT

HOPELESS - DAY THREE

It had been three days since Palias, Yung Sung, Gilanthos, and Aeotus departed in the middle of the night. They were following the trail of the deceased, hoping it would take them to their necromantic creator. It was a race against time, as they needed to locate the necromancer before Eladonia's body failed her. Aticus couldn't shake his thoughts of Eladonia's body fighting to stay alive, her soul ripped away and trapped by the soul reaver.

So much had happened in such a short time. The idea of being with the Alarians and watching Nicholas' wagon lurch ahead of him while sitting beside Rictor seemed insignificant now.

Bryce and Aticus had devised a plan to protect the townspeople. They gathered everyone in the tavern before dusk. Before, two soul reavers, driven by their insatiable thirst for the souls of the living, would materialize with the shadows of darkness. Bryce stayed up all night. His prayers illuminated the tavern, creating a divine barrier between the people and the supernatural creatures. As dawn approached and the darkness receded, the soul reavers vanished, and life in the town returned to a peculiar form of normalcy.

Aticus opened the door to Eladonia's room. Bryce was asleep, slumped over in a chair beside Eladonia's bed with his head resting in his hand.

Aticus slowly shut the door and listened to Bryce breathing. The late morning sunlight filtered through the window as he studied Eladonia's features. At first glance, it appeared she might be in a deep, peaceful sleep. If only that were true. Her complexion had softened significantly over the last few days, and her lips had taken on a blue hue. He crept into the room and sat in a second chair beside the bed opposite Bryce.

Bryce woke as his arm buckled and his head jolted from the lack of support. "Aticus, I didn't hear you come in."

"I just stepped in." Aticus considered Eladonia before continuing, "When will they find the necromancer? When are they going to kill him?"

"I don't know, son," Bryce said, shifting in his chair.

"It's so hard waiting. I wish I'd gone with Palias; at least I'd feel like I'm doing something."

"You are; you're helping the people of Dewbrook," Bryce reassured him.

"I don't see how. All I do is sit." Aticus took Eladonia's hand in his; it was cold.

"That's not true. You've been here for the people. Helped organize everyone at night, ensuring we're all safe in the tavern." Bryce smiled.

"You make sure we're safe. I gather everyone downstairs before it gets dark. You're the one who sits awake all night, keeping those things away from us." Aticus swallowed hard.

Bryce moved to the edge of his chair, nursing his aching muscles. "Look at me, son." Aticus looked at him with tears in his eyes.

"You are much stronger than you think. When the soul reavers come back at dusk, you're the one who helps give these people hope. You play with the children, distracting them from what's in the dark. You sit with her all day while I sleep. She knows you're here, and she can hear you." Bryce brushed Eladonia's hair over her pointed ear. "She's not alone. Not as long as we're here."

"You think she can hear us?" Aticus wiped his eyes dry.

"I know she can." Bryce nodded his head with confidence.

After a brief silence, Aticus looked at Bryce. "What if they don't find this person in time? What if something happens to them?" he asked.

"Life is full of uncertainties, most of which are out of your control. Regardless, what truly defines you is how you react to and learn from those moments. We must have faith that they will succeed."

Aticus smiled weakly.

"Go downstairs and get something to eat. I'll try to sleep a little more. You know when to wake me."

Aticus stood and placed Eladonia's hand on the bed. "Do you want anything?"

"I can manage without," he said, winking.

Aticus proceeded downstairs to the tavern. He found Klan'den behind the counter, serving a man something to drink.

"Aticus, are you ready for something to eat?" Klan'den asked.

"How about some eggs?" Aticus sat down at the counter beside the stranger.

"I'll be back." Klan'den tossed the towel in his hand on the counter and disappeared into the kitchen.

The stranger at the counter took a drink of his mead. "Having a bad day?"

Aticus looked at the bearded man. "You could say that."

"The name is Sedric," the bearded man said, presenting his hand to Aticus.

"Aticus, pleased to meet you." Aticus shook Sedric's hand. "You were here when we arrived a few days ago. I haven't seen you around since then. Are you passing through?"

"Aye, I am. Thought I'd take a break before heading out to hunt." Sedric took a drink.

"Well, you might want to rethink staying here," Aticus said, contorting his face.

"Klan'den was speaking to that." Sedric smiled and pressed his tongue into a space between his teeth. "He said something about shadows that come out at night; how everyone in town comes here for safety." Sedric scrunched his mouth together and raised his brows. "Sounds scary."

"The soul reavers are scary," Aticus confirmed.

"I was talking about everyone in town fitting in this room; that's scary," Sedric smiled. "I can imagine the smell."

Aticus chuckled. "It gets a little crowded."

"Klan'den told me that these soul reavers hurt one of your friends and a little girl?"

Aticus nodded. "My friends are trying to find the necromancer who summoned the shadows. They have to kill this person to save them."

"Helping these good folk out is noble of you all. I reckon I could stick around and see how the story turns out." Sedric finished his mead and placed the goblet on the counter.

Klan'den stepped out of the kitchen door and handed Aticus his eggs. "You're going back up, I suppose?"

Aticus nodded. "Yes, so Bryce can rest. Nice to meet you, Sedric." He stood and walked toward the stairs.

"Likewise, hero," Sedric replied.

Chapter Twenty-Nine

THE LIGHT - NIGHT THREE

Aticus watched Eladonia, willing her to wake. He rubbed his fingers over the wooden arm of the chair. "How long will it take them to find where they are going?"

Bryce looked up from his chair. "Gilanthos said it could take them days to find the necromancer. We must be patient and have faith." Bryce studied the waning light coming through the window. "Why don't you begin gathering the townsfolk downstairs?"

Aticus glanced at the window. "I'm sure they understand what to do by now."

Bryce stood and stretched at the edge of his chair. "Come on, I'll help you gather everyone."

"I can do it; you get something to eat before you do your thing." Aticus pushed away from his seat and glanced at Eladonia. He took a deep breath before turning and going downstairs.

Klan'den leaned over the counter and acknowledged Aticus. "I think a couple of nights of this, and everyone's figured out where to go."

Aticus glanced around the establishment. The tavern was full of townspeople quietly sitting at tables. "Is everyone here?" he asked Klan'den.

"We're still waiting for Jasmine and her family." Klan'den stepped around the counter and addressed everyone. "If I could have a few volunteers to help with the food, we can get everyone fed before dark."

Several people stepped forward as Aticus approached Sedric, sitting at the bar. "I see you decided to stick around."

Sedric nodded, "Why not? It looks like we might get some rain tonight. I'd sooner be inside where it's dry."

Aticus smirked. "Fair enough, but to be honest I'd rather sleep in the rain far from here."

Sedric grinned. "Is there anything I can do to help?" he asked before taking a drink.

"After we eat, we'll move the tables and chairs out toward the walls and make pallets for everyone to sleep on in the center of the room." Aticus articulated with his hands. "If they can sleep."

"Putting everyone in the same room? Isn't that going to make it easy for these soul things to find us?" Sedric scrunched his brows together.

"No, we need to be near Bryce for him to protect us," Aticus acknowledged one of the townspeople as they passed by.

"Your dwarf friend cast a spell or something?"

"Something like that. I can't explain what Bryce does," Aticus answered.

The door to the tavern opened, and Jasmine's father entered, carrying her lifeless body. She suffered the same fate as Eladonia.

"I need to help," Aticus pardoned himself.

Sedric settled back on his stool and drank his ale as he watched Aticus interacting with the townspeople.

Aticus dashed over and assisted Jasmine's mother in moving a table so they could place a blanket on the floor for her daughter. "Thank you, Aticus, for your help. Where's Bryce?" Jasmine's mother inquired, laying her hand on his shoulder.

"He's upstairs."

"What can I do to help?" Jasmine's father questioned as he tucked the linens around his daughter.

"Nothing until after we eat. Klan'den is preparing the food now. After everyone's taken care of, we'll do like last night and put the furniture against the walls."

"We'll help in the kitchen," Jasmine's mother said as she pulled her husband away toward the bar, glancing one last time at her daughter.

Aticus nodded and turned to go and get Eladonia.

Before Bryce could take the last step into the tavern, three children ran over and threw their arms around him. He smiled and patted the kids on the head. "It's good to see you, boys and girls."

Aticus stepped into Eladonia's room and stood over her bed for several moments, considering her features. "It's time to go downstairs." He knelt over, wrapping her in the bedding before lifting her into his arms and cradling her against his chest. He glanced out the window at the developing hues of the horizon. "I'm glad you're not awake to see what happens at night; it's horrible." He rested his chin on her forehead before going downstairs into the tavern.

Bryce cleared an area beside Jasmine for Aticus. "Place her here."

Aticus knelt beside the little girl, tucking Eladonia next to her as Klan'den and those who helped in the kitchen distributed stew and bread to everyone.

With darkness came an uneasiness in the tavern as everyone huddled close together and prepared for the storm. Bryce wobbled into the center of the crowd and sat down, crossing his legs. "Everyone needs to try to get some rest if you can. It will be a long night, but do not fear; you are not alone."

Aticus smiled at Bryce as he tossed a ball with a group of nearby children, hoping to keep them occupied.

Bryce winked at Aticus before closing his eyes to meditate and prepare himself for a night of prayer.

Sedric examined the candles and lanterns on tables and chairs around the room. "Is that enough light to keep the soul reavers away?" Sedric questioned Aticus.

"The candles and lanterns are mainly for the children. Bryce summons the light that keeps the creatures away," Aticus responded.

Sedric pursed his lips together and pressed his tongue between the gap in his teeth. "I see," he nodded and sat down near a couple. "Don't worry, I've seen a thing or two. I won't let anything hurt you," he clicked his lips together and winked.

Aticus stood and stretched. "It's time to get comfortable," he suggested to the five children, shifting his eyes toward their parents.

As the wind grew more robust and the distant thunder rumbled, rain began to pound against the tavern's front windows. A strong gust shook the shutters, extinguishing two candles on a table by the windows. The approaching storm increased anxiety in the room, but Aticus tried to reassure everyone, "It's just the wind; everything will be fine."

Bryce's chanting became rhythmic as an azure light spread throughout the tavern. A flash of lightning illuminated the window, and thunder followed, vibrating the building. Everyone huddled together, hoping they were close enough to Bryce.

Aticus knelt next to a little boy and brushed his hair. "It's going to be alright, Blake," he said. At that moment, he was reminded of how Vandeer would comfort the Alarian children during storms. Aticus retrieved a ball from the floor and gave it to the child.

Two more candles extinguished, darkening an area of the tavern nearest the front door. Exultations resounded through the room as everyone tightened toward Bryce and the two bodies that rested near the dwarf.

Sedric gripped the hilt of his sword tightly, prepared to pull it free from the confines of the casing.

"The sword won't help you, mister." A young boy sitting on his father's lap commented calmly, observing Sedric.

"Is that so?" Sedric responded, releasing his grip and crossing his arms. "Thank you for your confidence," he replied, pushing his tongue between his teeth.

A burst of wind rocked the front of the tavern as lightning spread its luminous fingers through the cracks of the shutters, a precursor to the dissonant clash of thunder.

Blake let go of the ball he was holding and instead clung to his mother and father. The round toy rolled past Sedric and continued outside of the mystical boundary toward the tables and chairs lined against the nearby wall. Sedric quickly jumped after the ball, stopping it before it went under the furniture. Suddenly, he felt the air around him vibrate, making the hairs on his arms stand on end. A blast of cold air crept up his body and brushed his face.

"Sedric!" Aticus screamed.

Sedric looked at the table before him and noticed a dark, shadowy figure that appeared out of nowhere, passing through the wall. Its ghostly appendages reached out toward him as if trying to take something from him. Hastily, Sedric pushed back, landing on his backside. A soul reaver had pierced through the wooden wall of the tavern and reached out to him. The sound it made was like a dying animal intertwined with the wailing of a baby.

Sedric backed away from the ghostly creature and returned to the safety of Bryce's protective shell of light. The soul reaver followed Sedric but stopped short of crossing the holy boundary. The high-pitched screeches cut through the night, prompting the young townspeople to cover their ears and close their eyes. Sedric stood defiant inside the divine bubble, examining the barrier and the shadowy creature howling just out of reach. "Well, isn't that interesting?" He turned and tossed the child his ball. "Don't drop it, cause I won't get it again." He glanced at Bryce and scrutinized the dwarf chanting his otherworldly words of protection.

A second soul reaver appeared on the opposite side of the room, adding its tormented shrieks. It approached with outstretched, shadowy arms, a mist of darkness drawn to the living, desiring a soul to cling to. The soul reaver hovered near the barrier, yearning to escape the nightmarish realm between life and death.

As everyone squeezed closer together, Sedric asked, "How long will this go on?"

"All night," Aticus added.

CHAPTER THIRTY

SOUTHWARD BOUND - DAY FOUR

It was mid-afternoon when the four men stopped on their journey south.

Gilanthos knelt, studying the soil. "More footprints are converging here from the east. Klan'den said there were more villages with burial sites disturbed." He pointed at the tracks. "They meet here and continue south with the ones from Dewbrook." He stood and looked at the horizon. "There's nothing else south of here besides Oppack." Gilanthos glanced at Aeotus.

"I can't think of anywhere else I'd go if I were a necromancer than a ruined city, mostly submerged in swamp water," Aeotus responded.

"How far is it from here?" Palias asked.

"Maybe a day and a half," Gilanthos answered.

"That will put us at almost six days. How much time does Eladonia have?" Yung Sung asked Aeotus.

"Seven days, maybe," Aeotus answered, his features sagging as he stared at the southern horizon.

Gilanthos returned to Capasius, leaping into the saddle. He patted her neck as he studied his friend's features. "Aeotus, she'll be fine."

Aeotus didn't answer as he spurred Konnos into a gallop. The three quickly filed in behind the elf.

It was nearing dusk when the four encountered a small caravan of traders traveling from the west. Three covered wagons, each hitched to a single horse, approached. Two men were visible per wagon.

Palias, followed by the others, approached the first group cautiously. "Greetings. Where do your travels take you?" Palias asked.

The man in the lead wagon pulled on the reins reluctantly, stopping. A second man on the wagon pulled a crossbow from behind him, resting it on his lap. "We're traveling toward Rivereach. We ain't got anything of value." He brushed his dark beard, cautiously examining the four men.

Palias held up his hands. "We're looking for information."

"What is it you need to know?" the man with the beard asked.

"We're tracking some suspicious characters. Have you seen anything questionable?" Palias looked back at his friends, unsure of what word to use to describe the dead.

The bearded man looked over at his companion, holding the crossbow in his lap. "Yeah, we did see something. A day back, we saw a couple of thousand orcs traveling south. We barely made it into a patch of woods before they passed. Thought it strange how they were so close to elf territory." The man paused. "Other than that, we ain't seen anything else."

"Orcs?" He looked back at Gilanthos. "That's not what we're looking for, but thank you for the information." Palias nodded and moved his horse to the side. "We won't keep you any longer. Safe travels."

The men on the wagons remained vigilant as they passed.

"Orcs; that's kind of far east for them. That puts them this side of Evermour," Gilanthos stated.

"I don't like the added threat of orcs," Aeotus added.

"What are we going to do about the orcs?" Yung Sung asked.

Aeotus glanced at Sung. "We can't worry about them right now," he said, spurring his mount southward.

Yung Sung glanced at Palias as they filed in behind Aeotus and Gilanthos. "Suspicious characters?"

Palias chuckled and shrugged as he focused on the Endendon bow draped over Gilanthos' back. "When did you acquire your bow?" Palias asked as he pulled his mount beside Gilanthos. "I admired the elven craftsmanship of the Endendon bow and have only ever seen a few, but yours is extraordinary."

Gilanthos smiled. "Thank you. My mother gifted it to me in my seventieth year." He motioned with his eyes at the bow. "It was my grandfather's bow. He died when the minotaurs attacked our homeland."

Palias nodded. "That was nearly eighty years ago. I remember studying the unprovoked attack on your people and the forest of Albatra. It was after the cataclysm that destroyed their island. It drove them to the mainland and your forest."

Gilanthos looked at Palias. "Invasion and now occupation. A few years after the invasion, my father sent my mother and me to live in Faylorn." He nodded toward Aeotus. "That's where I became friends with Ela and Aeo. They've been like siblings to me since being displaced. My mother is still in Faylorn, teaching ancient elven text to newblings." He glanced at Palias and Sung. "That's what we call our elven children." He smiled. "My father is still fighting in Albatra with the elven resistance."

"Seventy years," Sung interjected. "How long has it been since you've seen your father?"

Gilanthos looked at Sung. "It has been seventy years since I've seen my father. We would occasionally receive messages hinting that progress was being made. But it's been years since we heard from him. I had hoped to have returned by now and found my father. I wish to help fight against the minotaurs and liberate our homeland." He smiled and looked at his friend, who was riding ahead of him. "Aeotus plans on joining me after we take Eladonia to Evermour."

"I'm sorry, Gilanthos," Yung Sung commented.

"There is no need for you to be apologetic. I will see my father again." Gilanthos smiled.

"It's difficult for me to comprehend ten years, much less seventy. It seems like such a long time." Palias added, staring at the waning sun as it faded on the horizon.

"It would be for you, but when you think about it from my perspective, seventy years is a short time." Gilanthos watched Aeotus pull away from them. "We'd better pick up the pace. We've got a long way to go."

The three men prodded their mounts to catch Aeotus.

CHAPTER THIRTY-ONE

THE STORY - DAY FIVE

The sunlight filtered through the window over Eladonia's bed, casting warmth throughout the room.

Aticus paced at the end of her bed, rubbing his hands together. He paused and considered her ghostly complexion. "I feel so lost." Aticus leaned on the wooden support of the bed. "I want to help you, but I don't know what to do." He ran his hands through his hair and sighed before collecting another blanket. Adding it to the two quilts already covering her form, he sat on the edge of the bed and smoothed the hair over her pointed ear.

"I've sat here for days and told you about my life." He gazed out the window at the clear blue sky. "If it hadn't been for Bryce and you, I'd still be with the Alarians." Aticus admired her features. "I could have died, but you saved me from the goblins." He stared at the ceiling. "I remember the day Nicholas found me in the forest and how safe I felt afterward. I remember when he died and how my life changed. Everything good was stripped away, and I became an outsider." He shrugged. "I know I was never one of them, but when I was with Nicholas, it didn't matter. I belonged."

Aticus pulled the blanket to cover her neck, tucking it behind her shoulders. "I feel safe with you and Bryce—like I belong again." He put his hands on his lap. "I don't want you to die, Eladonia." He took a deep breath. "I haven't known you long, but that's how I feel." Aticus touched her arm beneath the blanket.

He focused on one of the chairs beside her bed and studied the four marks carved into the arm. Aticus stood, reached into his pants pocket, and pulled out his knife before walking over and collapsing into the seat. He sat for a long moment before rubbing the markings with his finger and glanced at Eladonia. "Day five, and I'm not going anywhere, I promise."

He carved a fifth line in the wooden arm. "I don't want you to go to Evermoure when you wake. You should listen to Aeotus." He stopped carving and looked at her. "I don't like Aeotus; he reminds me of Vandeer. But I agree that you should run away from whatever is in Evermoure." He started etching again.

The door opened, and Bryce walked in. "Good afternoon, son."

"You didn't sleep long," Aticus smirked. "You should be proud of me; I didn't wake you today."

Bryce chuckled. "It doesn't bother me." He sat in the chair beside the bed and laid his hand on Eladonia's.

"I have a horrible feeling, Bryce."

"About?" The dwarf sat back in the chair, settling in.

"I don't think…" Aticus paused. "I tell her she's going to be alright, but I don't believe it," he whispered, looking at Bryce.

"Do I look worried?" Bryce added, his confident demeanor unchanged.

Aticus shrugged. "No. I've never seen you worried about anything."

"That's not true; I choose not to show it." Bryce placed his elbows on the arms of the chair, putting his hands together. "I have faith."

"Where do you think they'll take her… if—well, you know." Aticus scrunched his brows together.

Bryce pressed his lips together. "I imagine they'd take her back to her family in the forest of Faylorn."

Aticus thought silently before speaking, "I'd like to rest with Nicholas. The Alarians have a place in Shandar."

Bryce smiled and let his hands rest on the chair. "That sounds nice, Aticus."

"What about you, Bryce? Where would you like to go?"

Bryce pondered for a few seconds before speaking. "There is a lake near the northern hills of Kandar. When the sun sets behind the mountains, it's beautiful—the sky changes to the most brilliant shades of rose and lavender. That is the most alluring landscape I have ever seen in all the land. It beckons to you and is very charming. I would love to share it with you one day." Bryce smiled.

"Did you grow up there?"

"I did, yes. I almost died there as well." Bryce took in a deep breath and let his face relax.

"Almost died? What happened?" Aticus moved to the edge of his chair.

"It was a warm summer day." He looked at Aticus. "Very hot. I was…" Bryce looked up and rubbed his chin, contemplating. "Forty-four or thereabout. Several of my friends and I were swimming in the lake I mentioned. I suppose I got out a little too far. I was never a strong swimmer; I'm still not today, but that's neither here nor there. My mates headed to shore, but I presumed I would try to impress a certain young lady." Bryce wiggled his eyebrows and smiled. "Needless to say, it didn't have quite the results I had envisioned. I made it halfway across the lake when my body decided it had had enough. I panicked and began taking on water. Eventually, I lost consciousness. My friends later told me a man came out of nowhere and saved me."

Bryce paused for a moment for dramatics. "Not any man, but a human. Now, you need to understand that no humans lived in the area, nor did they travel to that side of Kandar. He swam into the murky lake water, dove into the darkness, and found me. He pulled me to shore and revived me. They said I spit out half the lake." Bryce squinted his eyes and smirked. "I know that part's not true."

A curious look spread across his face. "I'll never forget his appearance, not until the day I die. He stood there over me, the sun at his back. At first, I thought he had wings, but it was his shadowy silhouette blotting out the sunlight. He knelt over me, patted my chest, and told me I'd be fine. I had never seen things as clearly as I did that day." Bryce glanced upwards as he recalled. "I could see every stubble on his chin and the blue of his eyes—like the sky on a crisp fall day. The hair on his head was as brown as dirt."

Bryce blinked his eyes. "He stood, gathered his pack, and disappeared around the lake. I never saw him again. A few days later, I heard His voice in my head. It was God who saved me." Bryce smiled proudly.

"Do you hear the man's voice or God's?" Aticus asked.

"The man was God, so, yes, He speaks to me all the time," he said with a smile, glancing to the ceiling.

The hair on Aticus' neck stood on end. "That's an incredible story."

CHAPTER THIRTY-TWO

THE ARRIVAL - DAY SIX

Talmet sat on his horse on a hill outside Oppack overlooking the partially submerged city. "So, this is the ruined city of Oppack, waste-deep in muck? I find it hard to believe this was touted as one of humanity's greatest accomplishments." Talmet adjusted in the saddle. "The port city of Oppack and its marble streets." He glanced at Mongole and chuckled.

"Yes," Mongole said, looking out over the ruins. Neacrom will no doubt be in the palace," he said, pointing to the tallest structure standing in the distance.

"Of course he will," Talmet said, examining the palace. "It's the only land high enough not to have succumbed to the rising waters."

Talmet looked at the army behind him, straightening in the saddle. "I will take half the troops with me, and you will stay here with the remaining battalion." Talmet pulled at his chain armor, adjusting its position on his torso. "Once I reach the palace, you will reinforce us, do you understand?" Talmet nodded at Mongole, expressing his expectations.

"Of course," Mongole retorted.

Talmet issued the order to move forward. He regarded Mongole one last time. "When we've finished with Neacrom, we will double our efforts to take Meloorne. You will see, my friend. All of this will be worth it." With that, he turned toward Oppack and the Bloodstone.

Mongole nodded. He had become resentful of the supreme commander and was suspicious of what Talmet would do with the Bloodstone once he had it in his possession. Regardless, Mongole was satisfied that this would soon be over.

Talmet was little more than a speck in the distance when he and his battalion came under attack by an onslaught of undead that clawed from the swamp water. Arms of the dead reached out and grasped hold of the orcs, pulling many beneath the muck, but Talmet and his men fought fiercely. The assault was coming from all sides.

Mongole and his men watched the ghastliness. "Is this how Choluck and his men met their fate?" he whispered.

One of Mongole's officers, Hunthar, guided his horse near Mongole. "Did you say something general?"

"Ironic, is it not?" Mongole mumbled, watching the battle.

"What is?" Hunthar inquired.

"How many of those rising from the swamp were our brothers sent here to die by Talmet?" Mongole glanced at Hunthar.

Unsure whether to respond to the comment, Hunthar remained silent and watched the troops react nervously to the disturbing scene unfolding before them.

Mongole's four remaining captains moved closer, waiting for the order to join the fray.

"Should we help Talmet? What are we waiting for?" Another of Mongole's officers, Dothroal, questioned.

Mongole glanced at Dothroal. "You will hold here until I give the command."

"They need our help—Talmet ordered it," Dothroal retorted as he looked around for support.

"Shut your mouth, or you will go and help Talmet by yourself; do I make myself clear?"

Dothroal lowered his head in submission before the general.

They watched as more undead pulled themselves free from the swamp, sweeping across the living army of orcs.

Talmet and a small group of his men broke away and advanced toward the palace.

Dothroal found the courage to speak. "Let me take my army; we can help with their flank, there." He pointed out where he thought he could help.

Mongole took a deep breath and placed his hand on his sword. "Question me again, and you will find it hard to help anyone." Mongole watched Talmet make his way to the palace, cutting through the undead with his warhammer.

Dothroal swallowed, looking around for support from the other officers.

Talmet and his band of orcs made their way to the palace. As they approached the main entrance, they began ascending the stairs. The rest of his troops remained engaged, protecting the supreme commander. Despite their valiant efforts, it seemed that two more undead clawed free of the swamp for each one defeated.

Frustrated at watching orcs fall to the undead, Dothroal turned his back on Mongole, hoping to inspire others to follow him. "Larn, bring your men with me, for today we will be remembered for defeating the powerful necromancer of Oppack."

Mongole never looked at Dothroal. He pulled his sword free and swung it to the side at his officer. The orc's head tipped to the left and slid off his shoulders, striking the ground with a thud. Mongole dangled his bloody sword to the side and watched Talmet enter the palace. Dothroal's body toppled off the horse, his mount shuffling to the side.

"Or today you will be remembered as those who joined the ranks of the undead," Mongole exclaimed, listening to the silence of his officers and soldiers who witnessed Dothroal's decapitation.

"We do not move until the undead stop. Then, and only then, will Neacrom be dead; do I make myself clear?"

"Yes, commander," resounded a unified affirmation from his four remaining officers.

Chapter Thirty-Three

Oppack - Day Six

I t was late afternoon when the four men moved cautiously through the swamp, weapons in hand. The dense, humid air helped to feed the sweat running down their faces. Small insects buzzed around, and buzzards patrolled the sky, lingering for the next meal. They had decided to leave the horses behind on drier land to keep them out of harm's way.

In the distance, they could see an orc army assembling on a hill overlooking Oppack. "That has to be several thousand orcs," Palias commented.

"Or more," Gilanthos added.

They tried to remain hidden by scurrying across the roofs or the rotted remains of taller homes that protruded from the quagmire. The smell from the marsh was pungent, causing Yung Sung to gag and nearly lose the contents of his stomach, but he mustered the fortitude to continue.

Gilanthos pointed at the orcs. "Look, on the hill." A large number of orcs began moving into the swamp toward the palace.

"Do you think they saw us?" Yung Sung asked.

"No. However important I feel I am, I don't think the orcs would send an army that size if they saw us trudging through the swamp," Aeotus commented. "This is about something else for them entirely."

The four were almost to the palace when the orcs were attacked by the undead clawing free from the marshland. The orcs were overwhelmed. Palias, Yung Sung, Gilanthos, and Aeotus took cover, climbing onto the roof of a half-submerged house, watching the battle unfold.

Yung Sung looked around at the muck. "Is there more undead in there?" Nobody answered. They watched the horror for several moments.

"This could be a good distraction to get us inside." Gilanthos looked for a clear path to the palace. "It would be wise if we moved now."

"We know where all the bodies from the graveyard disappeared to," Palias said.

"It would appear so," Gilanthos answered. He scanned the soggy ground beneath his feet, uncertain what might lie below. "It's hard to believe this was once the greatest port city in the realm."

They hastened their advance and ascended a set of marble stairs. At the top were two archways, each of which cradled a set of rusty iron doors that led into the palace. They chose a set of doors out of the line of sight for the orcs. The sound of battle on the opposite side of the palace seemed to grow nearer. "I think the orcs may have the same idea as we do. They appear to be fighting toward the palace," Palias stated.

"I never thought we'd be using orcs as a diversion, but I'll take all the help we can get right now." Aeotus pushed on the iron door. The door creaked as it opened, revealing its decrepit state.

They entered a large chamber. Several ornately broken windows allowed the swamp's stench to linger. The ceiling height extended to over thirty feet. The room wrapped around the front of the palace to another set of doors. "That will be the door the orcs are fighting to reach," Sung said. He rushed across the room and pressed his ear against the iron door. "Maybe we'll get lucky, and they'll kill each other." Sung shrugged.

"We could only be so lucky. You think we could get the orcs to kill the necromancer, too?" Aeotus said as he swung his sword from side to side. He looked for an exit from the room.

"You're welcome to step outside and ask if you'd like, but I don't think they're faring well." Sung presented the closed doors to the elf.

"We got this," Aeotus retorted. There were two corridors, one to the left and one to the right. They were smaller, measuring eight feet wide and ten feet high.

Palias moved down the corridor to the left. "I found a door."

Gilanthos notched an arrow and moved to stand beside the door. "Let's move; we're running out of time."

Palias advanced on the wooden door and opened it.

Gilanthos pushed into the room, ready to defend himself. "It's clear," Gilanthos confirmed. "Dead end." A broken table and chair littered the center of the room. Shattered remains of a cabinet leaned against a wall in the corner. The putrid smell continued to haunt the abandoned palace.

Palias moved down the second corridor and approached another wooden door.

Gilanthos readied his arrow and stood prepared.

Palias turned the handle and pushed the door. It creaked open. "Empty."

Gilanthos slid in and surveyed the room, arrow drawn. This area was more significant than the previous and contained only an old, tattered rug. "I have two doors."

The four filtered into the room. Sung remained near the open door so he could keep watch. He held his curved katana tightly while he stood guard.

"Which door?" Gilanthos asked Palias.

Palias looked at Aeotus.

"Don't look at me; I forgot my map," Aeotus retorted.

Palias shook his head. "That way." He pointed at the left door.

Gilanthos stood at the ready.

Palias turned the handle. This entry was locked. "Should I break it down?" Palias asked Gilanthos.

"No, move to the other door," Aeotus answered before Gilanthos could. "Let's break all the doors down; let them know we're here." Aeotus shook his head in frustration.

Palias made his way to the second door and opened it.

Gilanthos rushed in; his bowstring pulled tautly. "Clear." This circular chamber was massive. Palias and Aeotus followed Gilanthos. Yung Sung remained in the room to monitor the hallway. "I think we're close." Gilanthos pointed to the center of the room, where a grotesque throne of bones sat upon a raised platform.

Palias moved cautiously, his sword lifted. Two sets of stairs ascended on opposite sides of the room, following its curvature, spilling onto the second-floor balcony.

There were three more entrances to the chamber. Another door, identical to the one they came through, and two more passages led off to the south. Suddenly, the sound of stone scraping stone resonated through the room. It was a secret door opening between the passages leading south.

The three looked around for somewhere to go. "Up—go up," Palias declared, pointing at the stairs as he ran to the door to get Sung. "Sung, come quickly," he whispered.

Aeotus and Gilanthos sprinted up the steps. Palias waited for Sung to enter the room before following the elves. Sung stopped at the bottom of the steps; he realized he'd forgotten to close the door.

"Forget it," Palias said.

The sound of scraping stones stopped.

Gilanthos and Aeotus had made it to the second floor, huddled behind the waist-high marble wall. Palias and Sung made it part of the way but were forced to drop on the steps. They hid behind the marble wall that traced the outside of the stairs.

Gilanthos peeked over the wall while Aeotus motioned Palias and Sung to stay down.

The elves watched a man emerge from the secret door. His long silver hair hung over his face in disarray. His violet robe was tattered and burned on the edges around his feet. He limped in pain as he dragged his left leg. In his blood-stained hand, he carried something the size of a large melon. It was a head.

Gilanthos nudged Aeotus with his elbow, holding his bow and arrow tightly. He nodded, confirming he had a shot.

Aeotus places his hand on Gilanthos' arm, stopping him.

The necromancer who emerged from the secret door was not alone. Six badly decomposed undead corpses followed the man. One had an arm missing, and another had only half a head. The creatures made no noise except for the scuffling of their feet across the dusty marble floor. When the last walking corpse stepped from the hidden room, the man in the robe reached above his head and pressed a stone that closed the stone door.

As the door closed, the necromancer turned his attention toward the throne of bones and began painfully moving toward it.

Gilanthos clenched his teeth.

Aeotus shook his head in defiance. "Not yet," he mouthed.

The six undead positioned themselves around the necromancer before dropping lifelessly to the floor.

The limping man approached the steps leading to the raised platform where his chair was situated. He climbed the steps in pain and reached the chair. He dropped the object in his hand on the floor. It was the head of a dark-haired man. He sat down on the bone chair.

Yung Sung and Palias stayed motionless, watching the elves for instructions.

The man in the chair started to speak to the head lying on the floor, eyes open, even in death. "JoJung has no control over me, and neither do his pets." The necromancer spat at the head and chuckled. Neacrom realized a door to the room was open. He wrinkled his brow.

Aeotus prepared to signal his friend to fire when the door opposite the one they had come from flung open, slamming against the wall.

The elves dipped below the wall.

CHAPTER THIRTY-FOUR

DEJAVU - DAY SIX

With the arrival of daylight, the soul reavers disappeared, and the townsfolk returned to their homes, leaving the tavern hauntingly silent. Everyone understood that the reavers would return when the dark fingers of night grasped hold of the world and plunged it back into darkness.

Aticus carried Eladonia to the room and placed her into bed, covering her with blankets. Her face was devoid of color, and her body had become rigid. Aticus no longer left her side, even when Bryce came to sit. He'd lost his urge to eat and was irritable when anyone spoke to him.

A steady rain beat upon the window over Eladonia's bed as Aticus lit a candle on a nearby table.

He returned to her bedside, brushed Eladonia's hair, and touched her cheeks. "I'm here, Ela. You're going to be fine. They're going to save you; I know they will."

Aticus sat down in the chair beside the bed and watched her. He tried to calm himself by listening to the rhythmic pitter-patter of the rain striking the roof. Its calming sounds lulled him into a restless sleep.

Aticus woke several hours later when a distant clap of thunder shook the walls. He pulled himself to the edge of the chair and stretched. "I'm here, Ela," he whispered. He rubbed her arm and felt her face. He knew she'd be cold, but did it out of habit. Day six, and Aticus was close to losing hope, but he wouldn't speak it into existence.

The door opened, and Bryce ambled in.

"Couldn't sleep any longer?" Aticus asked.

"Yes, and no. I thought you might want something to eat before gathering everyone."

"I don't need a break. "It can't be that late already." He glanced out the window.

"Yes, you do. I'll let you know if there are any changes. Now go," Bryce pleaded.

Aticus agreed reluctantly and proceeded downstairs to the tavern. He paused at the bottom step and acknowledged that this was the longest he'd been in one place since leaving the Alarians. It was beginning to feel like home.

"Afternoon, Aticus," Klan'den greeted him.

"Klan'den." Aticus acknowledged the barkeeper. He noticed Sedric sitting at the bar, drinking. "Sedric."

"Aticus," Sedric nodded as he lifted his glass of mead.

"I've not seen you around. I thought you might have moved on after that first night." Aticus sat beside the man.

"I've been out hunting."

"Have any luck?" Aticus questioned.

"I always find what I'm looking for, so yes." Sedric took another drink.

"Do you want anything, Aticus?" Klan'den asked.

"No, not hungry."

"Let me know when you want to eat." Klan'den stepped into the kitchen, carrying Sedric's empty plate and utensils.

"I found something in the woods near here that might interest you." Sedric rubbed his beard.

"What's that?" Aticus inquired.

Sedric finished off his mead before finishing. "There are these stones with symbols etched in them. Never seen anything quite like it, and I've seen a lot." He pushed his empty glass forward onto the bar. "I could show them to you. It might have something to do with these soul reavers. You know, it might not be a necromancer. It could be something you could take care of right here."

Aticus thought for a moment. *Wouldn't it be wonderful if it were that simple? If he could help Eladonia, and it wasn't a necromancer. What if Aeotus was wrong?* "That sounds interesting, but Bryce needs me."

"I'll help you figure this out. Besides, we'll be back long before it gets dark. I can help you gather everyone when we return." Sedric patted Aticus on the back. He bobbed his head toward the door.

"I don't know."

"Come on. You're the only person I know here. I'm dying to show someone."

"Alright, but we need to hurry," Aticus said.

"I'm your man." Sedric patted Aticus again and smiled as he reached for a bow and quiver of arrows from a nearby table.

Klan'den stepped from the kitchen. "Heading out for a while?"

"Sedric wants to show me something in the woods. If you see Bryce, tell him we're going to the forest."

"Sure, I'll let him know." Klan'den nodded.

The rain had ended, leaving behind an overcast sky. The two men engaged in small talk as they walked west into the forest.

Aticus grew impatient. "How much farther? We've been out here for too long."

"Not far," Sedric said without turning around.

Another half-hour passed, and Aticus was ready to return to the inn. "Sedric, we need to go." Aticus stopped and started to turn around.

"Wait, we're almost there." Sedric looked around.

"You've been telling me that all afternoon." Aticus pointed at the sky. "If we don't quit now, it'll be dark before we get back."

"It's right here." Sedric pressed his tongue between the gap in his teeth.

"You said the stones are here, but I don't see anything. I don't think you know where it is, do you?"

Sedric took a deep breath and let it out. "I'm going to tell you the truth." Sedric walked beside Aticus and drew his sword. "I'm sorry, boy; I like you."

Aticus reached for his sword. He'd forgotten to get it before leaving the inn.

"We're going to walk a little longer," Sedric said with a tilt of his head.

"Don't do this, Sedric. I don't know what you want, but they need me," Aticus pleaded as Sedric reached for his arm. He pulled away and ran.

Sedric caught hold of Aticus and threw him against a tree. As the two men struggled, Sedric was careful not to use his sword to hurt Aticus. Aticus tripped over an exposed root in the tussle, his hand landing on a fallen branch the size of his arm. In a desperate move to escape, he seized the branch and swung it at the bearded man, striking Sedric in the head and sending him to the ground. Sedric clutched his face and grimaced in pain.

Aticus reacted and ran toward the city.

The overcast sky made it seem later than it was. Aticus leaped over a fallen tree, scaring a rabbit that drank from a mud-filled puddle, causing it to scurry into the undergrowth. He nearly tripped as the ground, saturated from a day of rain, gave way under his feet. He paused to take a quick breath as water droplets struck him in the face. 'This is so familiar.' His warm breath met the rain-cooled air, forming small puffs of mist with each exhale. He steadied his breathing and listened for Sedric's footsteps. Suddenly, he heard branches snap and leaves rustle.

He ran through thick foliage, branches, and smaller limbs, scratching his face. *Why was this so familiar? He was trying to get away. He needed to hide. Watch out for the ravine,* he thought.

Aticus entered a clearing that ended abruptly near a steep ravine. He had seen this before. Aticus looked from side to side before running. He kept glancing over his shoulder. *The nightmare, this was the nightmare that had haunted him for so long.* He tore through the brush, frantically gasping for air. Fear gripped its cold hands around his heart and squeezed. He panicked! He knew what happened next, and there was no stopping it.

Thud! Suddenly, a sharp pain pierced his right leg, sending him to his knees. *No, this isn't happening!* "Eladonia!" he shouted. "Bryce!"

He stood, pain shooting up his leg. Thonk! A second arrow struck him in the shoulder from behind, shattering bone. The impact twisted him around, landing on the wet ground; the shaft of the arrow broke off in his back. The pain was intense as he rolled on his side and looked at the treeline, willing Eladonia to save him again.

"Help!" he yelled, the pain seizing his breath. He tried to stand, but the last thing he saw was a boot.

Chapter Thirty-Five

BLOOD AND STONE - DAY SIX

The door on the wall behind Neacrom's chair slammed open, and Talmet bolted into the room. "Neacrom! How dare you attack me!" Talmet's rage echoed throughout the throne room. "We were allies."

The necromancer stood, keeping the throne of bones between him and the orcs. "It was you who drew first blood, Talmet!" Neacrom spat at the orc. "You finally mustered the courage to meet face to face."

Aeotus and Gilanthos peeked over the wall. They witnessed an orc in heavy chainmail. The remains of undead rot dripped from his armor and weapon. He clenched his warhammer tightly by his side. Two orcs clad in chain armor emerged from the door behind Talmet.

"Where is Bloodstone?" Talmet took a step forward. The orcs behind Talmet moved outward on either side of their leader to surround Neacrom.

"I will kill you, Talmet, and your little army," Neacrom regarded the advancing orcs.

Aeotus watched as the necromancer placed his hands behind his back, magically tracing the air with his fingers. Aeotus knew he was preparing a spell, so he put his hand on Gilanthos' arm to prepare him for his shot.

"I will kill you—and tear this place apart to find the Bloodstone." Talmet signaled his men to advance. The cries of his orc comrades fighting outside echoed through the door behind him.

Neacrom threw his hands up and spoke, *"G'lorn-duthra-veldar."* The green light from his hands reflected off the marble walls where the dust was disturbed. The six corpses on the floor leaped upright and lunged at the three orcs.

Talmet quickly advanced toward the raised platform, taking two steps with each stride.

Neacrom moved back from the orcs, letting the dead pass; he moved back to the platform's edge, keeping the chair between him and his attackers. Waving his hands, he spoke another incantation, *"Val-tare-oom."* Neacrom pressed his hands out at the chair as a burst of wind, accompanied by a flash of magenta, blew from his palms. The force struck the skeletal chair, tearing it to pieces. The fragments of bones became deadly projectiles, striking the three orcs. Upon impact, they were tossed against the wall like dolls. Sharp bone fragments blanketed the marble wall, shattering the larger pieces.

Talmet's soldiers were killed by the impact of the bones and slamming into the wall. Five of Neacrom's undead were torn apart and scattered in the wind.

Talmet was able to prepare himself by covering his face and sidestepping before being slammed against the wall, sustaining severe wounds.

Aeotus and Gilanthos watched from the second floor. Palias and Yung Sung positioned themselves to peer over the stone wall of the stairwell.

Talmet lowered his arms from his face. Fragments of bone protruded from his cheek, forehead, and arms. The force was so great that shards of the dead had even pierced his chain armor. Talmet winced as the blood ran from his wounds. "Arrr!" he screamed and ran toward his nemesis.

The last of Neacrom's undead threw its body in front of Talmet, but did little to slow his advance. Its arid body disintegrated when it met his warhammer.

Neacrom braced himself for Talmet's attack.

The orc brought his hammer down on the frail man, but Neacrom grasped Talmet by his wrists, holding his arms steady. Locked in a stalemate, the two grimaced at one another, inches apart.

Talmet winced, surprised Neacrom could hold him, as he pushed to bring his weapon down.

Neacrom taunted Talmet, his expression sublime.

"I'll kill you," Talmet whispered, spittle spraying from his mouth.

"Not today, coward," Neacrom began to chant. *"Talor-oon..."*

Talmet brought his knee into Neacrom's chest, taking the wind from him and his words.

Neacrom was forced back down the steps, losing his balance. He fell to the ground, and the impact pushed the air from his lungs.

Talmet started down the steps as he pulled another fragment of bone from his face and tossed it aside.

Neacrom rolled on the floor. "*Lortal-Toe-mor*," he frantically hissed, trying to stand.

Talmet lunged at Neacrom with his hammer, striking the necromancer in the arm, but not before Neacrom could issue his spell.

"Now?" Gilanthos whispered to Aeotus.

Aeotus looked defiantly into Gilanthos' eyes. "No," he whispered.

The dark-haired head on the raised platform behind Talmet became a projectile and slammed into the orc. The impact sent Talmet to the floor, his hammer forced from his hands. The head locked its mouth onto Talmet's neck and bit fiercely, severing the jugular vein. Talmet grabbed at the head, but the more he pulled, the more damage it did.

Neacrom got to his feet and stood over Talmet. He held his broken arm and watched as the orc's life ran from his body like sand from a broken hourglass.

Talmet's strength waned; he let his hands drop beside him. He regretted coming to Oppack for the Bloodstone. He questioned why Mongole had not come to help. He wanted to see the human cities fall. He listened to his men dying outside and knew he'd failed. He desperately wanted to wrap his hands around Neacrom's neck, but that was the closest he would get. His eyes shifted to the side as they relaxed, and he took his final breath. His eyes locked over Neacrom's shoulder. The last thing he saw caused him to smile as he toppled to the side.

Neacrom grinned at his victory. The orc's line of sight caused Neacrom to pause, curious why Talmet smiled. He turned and looked at the open door behind him. The door hadn't been opened in years. Movement on the second-floor balcony drew his attention one last time.

An elf stood tall behind the marble wall. Bow in hand and arrow notched.

Neacrom's stomach twitched, followed by a violent jolt to the head—and darkness.

The necromancer's body dropped to the ground, resting beside Talmet. One man had a smile on his face; the other did not.

CHAPTER THIRTY-SIX

AWAKENING

It was late afternoon when Klan'den knocked on Eladonia's door, waking Bryce.

Bryce wrenched from the chair. He looked around the room at Eladonia and the window. It was getting dark.

A rap at the door sounded again. Bryce realized it was the knock that woke him. He knew it wasn't Aticus; he would have come in. "Who is it?"

Klan'den pushed the door open. "Ah, most everyone's downstairs already." Worry sank into the innkeeper's features. "Aticus has been gone for a long time. He said he'd be back before dark, but—it's getting dark."

"Where did he go?"

"He went with Sedric into the woods to look at something. He said it might help your friend." He pointed at Eladonia.

"Who's Sedric?"

Klan'den shrugged. "He's the hunter that's been hanging out downstairs off and on for a couple of days."

"Oh, God." Bryce stood, shuffled out the door, and rushed down the stairs.

Klan'den followed behind him.

Suddenly, Eladonia sat up, infusing her lungs with air. She gasped, and tears filled her eyes. "Aticus," she whimpered. Eladonia threw back the covers and put her feet on the floor. She searched the darkened room for her belongings on the floor in the corner, including her swords. She stood, but her legs couldn't support her weight. Eladonia fell to the floor with a loud thud. "Bryce!" she screamed, her voice husky.

Bryce heard her scream and stopped, nearly tripping Klan'den. Bryce turned and ran back up the stairs and into the room with Klan'den behind him. "Ela, thank God you're awake!"

Eladonia floundered across the room and retrieved one of her swords from the sheath.

"What are you doing?" Bryce knelt, steadying her.

"Aticus, he's in danger! I need to help him!" She trembled, short of breath.

"Danger?" Bryce held her arm. "What are you talking about? You're in no condition."

"They're trying to kill him!" She pulled away from Bryce and staggered toward the door and down the stairs. She wore only her trousers and a woolen shirt.

"You're too weak, Ela. Let us look for him!" Bryce yelled.

"I know where he is!" Her voice was dry and scratchy. She staggered out the door of the tavern, dragging her feet.

Bryce ran upstairs and retrieved his boots. She was nearly out of town when he made it outside. She stumbled forward, driven by an invisible force, even in her weakened state, giving her the strength she needed to get to Aticus. Bryce ran as fast as he could, trying to keep her in sight.

Eladonia pushed through the exhaustion, teetered through the brush, and hobbled around trees. She saw movement in the distance. Two men stood over someone. Eladonia knew it was Aticus on the ground. Her insides wrenched with renewed anxious anticipation; she pressed into a clearing near a steep ravine. "Stop!" she yelled hoarsely, falling to one knee twenty paces away from Sedric and Don. She fought back nausea and nearly passed out.

The two men stopped and looked at her. Sedric held his sword out with one hand and rubbed his bloodstained face with the other. "Stop right there, girl. We have no quarrel with you," Sedric said.

She presented her sword in a warning and wobbled, nearly going to the ground again. Eladonia looked at Aticus. He wasn't moving. "If you have a problem with him, you can take it up with me." She took another uneasy step forward.

Sedric took a step toward her. "I'll not tell you again."

Eladonia watched as a second man, wearing a wide-brimmed hat and a long coat, stood over Aticus. He held his sword to the side, knelt over Aticus, and lifted his medallion. After studying it, he let it drop to his chest. "I remember you," he said, rising to his feet.

Eladonia's heart raced. Her legs buckled, but she steadied herself against a tree. "Leave him alone, please. Sedric, help Aticus. You know him," she said, pleading with Sedric as if she knew him.

Sedric paused, confused by her words.

"Where were you, Sedric?" Don asked as he regarded Aticus lying on the ground.

Sedric jerked his head toward Don. "Where was I?" Sedric pointed the tip of his sword at Eladonia, letting her know he was still aware of her. "Where was I? Where were you, Don?" His eyes widened at Don's question. "I took Aticus where you told me to, but you weren't there. I led him around the woods for over an hour, looking for you."

Don ignored Sedric's response and studied Aticus, then abruptly slapped him.

Aticus jolted awake, wrenching in pain as he fought to catch his breath.

"Aticus!" Eladonia shouted.

Aticus looked for Eladonia's voice; fear pulled his eyes wide. "Ela." He sobbed.

Don poked Aticus in the chest with the hilt of his sword. "You don't remember me, do you, boy?"

"Don't touch him!" Eladonia took two steps forward and knelt down again.

Sedric moved between Don and Eladonia. "You best stop where you are if you know what's good for you."

Aticus looked at Don; his body convulsed. "No." He coughed painfully.

Don frowned. "That's a pity. It'd mean so much more if you did." Don knelt beside Aticus and pressed the tip of his sword into the ground, using it as support. "You remember when your family died?" Don wrinkled his brows together and looked at his scarred hand from burns he had sustained when he was ten. "I remember when mine did."

Aticus shook his head, his eyes glazed, chest pounding. "I don't know what you're talking about; I don't know. Please." He reached out.

Don stood and kicked Aticus' arm away. He tilted his head to the side and moved the tip of his sword over Aticus' chest.

"Don't," Ela cried. "Please, don't." She tried to stand, but her body had nothing left to give; she threw her sword to the side. "Please."

Aticus looked at Eladonia. Tears streamed down the side of his face.

The sound of leaves and twigs snapping attracted everyone's attention. It was Bryce. He stepped from the brush beside Eladonia. "Stop; leave him alone. We can give you whatever you want." He held out his hands pleadingly.

Sedric pointed his sword at the dwarf.

Don looked at Aticus as he addressed the dwarf. "You have nothing to give me that I cannot take." He pressed his sword downward into Aticus' chest. Bones cracked as the sharp, cold steel pierced Aticus' chest.

Aticus heaved and gagged. He lifted his hands pleadingly toward Don.

Don slapped Aticus' hands away and stared into his eyes. A look of profound satisfaction crept across his face as he knelt beside him.

"No!" Eladonia stumbled forward, tumbling to the ground, her sight never leaving Aticus'.

"No!" Bryce shouted and selflessly rushed toward Sedric.

Don twisted the sword, pushing it forward and backward, widening the wound.

Aticus gagged on his blood, and his body shuddered from the pain. He tried to scream, but no sound escaped his lips. Aticus looked at Eladonia as his body trembled and tears gushed down his face. He stretched his hand out in painful desperation for Eladonia and Bryce. Aticus' eyes glazed over as the last breath left his lungs. His hands dropped into the grass and relaxed as his eyes lost focus. Don raised his sword over Aticus' head and prepared to strike again.

Bryce screamed, "God, no!" He knelt on one knee and slapped his hands together. A deafening clap of thunder sounded, and an invisible force knocked Sedric and Don away and down the ravine, disappearing into the trees below.

CHAPTER THIRTY-SEVEN

AFTERMATH

Gilanthos' arrow found its mark. The necromancer dropped to the steps beside the orc.

Aeotus, overjoyed, struck Gilanthos on the back. "Nice shot!"

Yung Sung leaped up and ran towards Gilanthos to congratulate him. Suddenly, Sung's mood changed. "Eladonia! Do you think you killed him in time?"

Palias stood and looked over the marble wall of the stairwell.

Gilanthos lowered his bow and looked at Aeotus' pocket.

Aeotus reached into his pocket and pulled out a small green emerald the size of a walnut. It glowed softly. "Yes, she's alive." Aeotus smiled; his expression softened.

Palias approached from the stairwell onto the balcony beside the others. "What's that?"

"A life stone," Aeotus responded.

"Life stone?" Sung inquired.

Gilanthos placed the bow over his head, letting it hang on his shoulder.

"I cast the spell before we left. As long as it glows, I know Ela is alive," Aeotus said, holding the emerald out in his hand so everyone could see.

"You could have told us you had a way of knowing she was okay. It would have eased our tensions," Sung added.

Palias looked at the emerald in the elf's hand. "That would have been nice to know," Palias declared condescendingly.

"He knew." Aeotus pointed at Gilanthos.

Gilanthos rolled his eyes.

"Besides, if I'd told you, then all I would have heard would have been, Is she alive? Is she okay? Can I see it?" Aeotus shook his head. "I didn't see the value in adding more stress to my life."

"Is she awake?" Gilanthos asked.

Aeotus rolled his eyes to the side and looked at Palias and Sung. "See, that's what I'm talking about. I don't know; this is a life spell. I would assume she'll wake with the necromancer's death and the soul reavers hold on our existence broken."

"We need to get out of here before more orcs come," Palias interjected.

Aeotus looked at the secret door the necromancer had exited. "I want to know what's in there." He pointed.

Gilanthos looked over at his friend. "Do you think that's wise?"

"When have you ever known me not to be wise?" Aeotus asked, walking around his friend. Gilanthos tilted his head and raised his eyebrows.

Palias placed his large hand on Aeotus' shoulder. "We should go."

Gilanthos lifted his hand to silence the men as his eyes darted to the open door through which Talmet had entered. They watched from the balcony as the sounds of armor clanging and deep, muffled voices grew louder. "Orcs!"

They knelt behind the marble wall. Gilanthos pulled his bow free and notched an arrow.

The throne room echoed with the sounds of orcs entering through the door, drawing Palias' attention over the marble wall.

Aeotus stopped Palias. Then, silently, he drew an imaginary line around his head in a broad arc in the hope he could convey his message that Palias' head was too large and shiny to look over the wall.

Palias let his body sink back to the floor. He nodded.

They heard more orcs pour into the chamber.

Aeotus softly patted Gilanthos on the chest, letting him know he could look over the wall.

Gilanthos looked at Palias with a blank stare.

Sung put his fingers to his eyes and pointed down the rounded stairwell below them. He pulled four shurikens from his shirt and maneuvered to get a better view of the stairs. Then he held a thumb to let them know he would watch the stairs.

Gilanthos took a breath and glanced over the wall. He had seen over twenty orcs so far, not counting the ones that had made it below the balcony where he couldn't see.

The orcs were clad in chain armor. All of them carried a long sword; some held shields. None of them had bows. That, at least, would play in Gilanthos' favor. Their olive skin and armor were dark from the ebony remains of the undead.

Gilanthos watched more creatures enter the palace chamber. They congregated around their fallen leader, their expressions filled with horror and their sighs filled with dismay. The flood of orcs entering the room continued.

The orcs' shock of seeing Talmet lying on the steps next to Neacrom kept them preoccupied and prevented them from going upstairs.

Several moments passed, and silence spread across the room as the orcs began clearing a path for someone. Gilanthos watched as another, more massive orc strolled through the door. The others in the room stepped away, giving him a wide berth toward the fallen orc.

One of the orc soldiers spoke, "Lord Mongole, General Talmet is dead." He pointed to where their leader lay.

Mongole approached the steps and examined Talmet. He shook his head. "I told you this Bloodstone would be the death of you." Mongole studied Talmet's face; his blank stare and smile puzzled him. After he closed Talmet's eyes, he examined Neacrom's body.

"This isn't one of our arrows," Mongole stated. He took a knee and ran his finger over the feather on the shaft.

Calmly, he looked around the throne room, taking note of every entrance. "This is an elven arrow." Mongole glanced at the stairs leading to the second floor.

Gilanthos ducked when he saw the orc looking in his direction. He pressed his teeth together and scrunched his nose while shaking his head at Aeotus. "He saw me," he mouthed.

Mongole scanned the area above them. "Is there someone else here with us?"

The orc soldiers glanced at one another, wondering who Mongole was talking to.

"Did anyone check upstairs?" Mongole asked, looking at the second-floor balcony. "If there is someone here, I suggest you show yourself."

"There are too many," Gilanthos whispered. The four looked at one another, unsure of what to do next.

"Look upstairs," Mongole commanded his men, and pointed to the set of stairs rounding the outside wall.

Three orcs standing near the stairwell began ascending the steps hastily.

Gilanthos stood and drew his arrow, aiming at Mongole.

Everyone followed his lead and stood up beside the elf.

Mongole's men stopped a few steps up. They watched Mongole for further orders.

Yung Sung walked to the top of the steps and looked down at the orcs. "Wise choice."

Mongole held his hands out. "I am confident that will be the last arrow you ever fire."

"No, I'm somewhat guaranteed I'd empty my quiver before it's over," Gilanthos added confidently.

"It doesn't matter. You may kill me, but I can assure you that none of you will make it out alive," Mongole retorted.

"I'm sure it won't matter to you if it comes to that point then," Aeotus added sarcastically.

Palias stepped away from Gilanthos and lifted his hands. "I think we can come to some arrangement." He tried to diffuse the situation, which wouldn't end well for either side.

Mongole examined the large man. "How do you recommend we proceed, Asvernian?"

"You obviously came to kill the necromancer, as we did." Palias pointed at Gilanthos. "He finished what your general could not."

Mongole glanced at Talmet and Neacrom, then lowered his hands.

"Kill the elves," expressed an orc, and then another, as unrest began to take root in the chamber.

"Silence!" Mongole commanded.

Palias examined the room nervously. "Mongole. That's your name?"

Mongole looked at Palias, disdain chiseled across his face.

"I overheard one of your men say your name when you entered," Palias added. "My name is Palias." He lowered his hands to his sides.

Mongole considered the circumstances before replying. "We are at an impasse. Perhaps it would benefit both groups if we were to go our ways amicably."

Palias smiled and nodded. "I agree."

Mongole examined Talmet one last time before addressing the room. "We leave Oppack. No one is to harm the necromancer killers." His face relaxed. "Take Talmet's body." He commanded four orcs near the body.

Gilanthos lowered his bow as the orcs began to retreat from the throne room. Aeotus was about to say something when Gilanthos kicked him.

Mongole turned and left the throne room as the orcs carried Talmet behind him.

CHAPTER THIRTY-EIGHT

DISCOVERY

"We could have beaten them," Aeotus said as he leaned against the marble wall of the balcony, studying the secret door.

"I'm glad you waited until they left before saying that aloud," Palias replied.

"Trust me: he would have if I hadn't stopped him," Gilanthos exclaimed.

Aeotus shook his head. "One day, Gilanthos, you won't be there to stop me."

"Sounds like they're gone," Sung said, dashing down the stairs to check the exit. He cautiously poked his head out, then disappeared through the door.

Everyone else made their way down the stairs. Palias stood over the necromancer; the dead man's eyes frozen in time. "I wonder who he was?" The question fell on deaf ears.

Gilanthos stood anxiously beside Palias and watched for Sung to return, bow in hand.

Aeotus wasted no time moving to the secret door. He pushed the stone Neacrom had pressed near the torch sconce. The sound of the hidden door shifting vibrated the floor.

Sung returned through the door. "Mongole kept his word. They're moving back toward the hill, and there's no sign of the undead."

"Good," Palias declared.

The secret door came to rest, revealing a set of stairs descending into an underground chamber. Aeotus turned to the others. "Are we ready?" He drew his sword and smiled as he started down.

Gilanthos walked close behind, followed by Sung and Palias. The four navigated down a narrow hall and entered a small room. They witnessed the body of a man clothed in black, lying in a broad expanse of blood, his arms pulled unnaturally behind him, and his head contorted.

They entered another, more significant room on the left. It appeared to be a laboratory.

"Whoa." Sung stood with his mouth gaping open in horror.

Palias surveyed the room, taking in the carnage that littered the floor, walls, tables, and ceiling. "They put up a fight," Palias added.

Gilanthos covered his nose and looked at the dead sprawled before them. Parts of undead creatures covered the dirt floor of the room.

Aeotus put his sword away. "There's nothing left to fight here."

Palias pointed to two more men, "They are dressed like the man in the hall."

"This one's a mage," Aeotus said as he pointed at a man in a black robe, his head missing. He knelt over and searched his robes.

"What are you doing?" Sung asked, repulsed by Aeotus' actions.

"Looking for his spellbook, of course," Aeotus answered Sung like he should have known.

Against the wall, wedged between two tables, was a mind flayer. Its soulless black eyes reflected their movements like looking into a wet mirror.

Yung Sung, fascinated, moved closer to investigate the creature. He nudged its leg with his foot, if only to reassure himself that it was, in fact, dead. "I've never seen anything like this. What is it?" Sung knelt and gazed into its eyes.

"It's a mind flayer, and they're rare," Aeotus said. "Usually, they don't associate with other races." He glanced at the others, dressed in black, and stood, placing the dead man's spellbook in his pocket.

"I feel like he's watching me." Sung moved closer to the flayer.

"I wouldn't get any closer if I were you!" Aeotus interjected.

Yung Sung jumped away. "Why?"

Aeotus laughed.

Gilanthos shook his head. "He's playing with you, Sung. It's dead; it can't hurt you."

Yung Sung straightened. "I know."

Aeotus pointed at the far end of the room. "What's this?" he said, intrigued.

Ahead of them was a large, intricately designed, full-length mirror propped against the wall. Two torches hung on either side, illuminating the corner of the laboratory. Lying in front of the mirror was an overturned wooden chair. Behind that was a stone pedestal. Broken vials and other items were pushed from the tables during the conflict.

Aeotus' gaze fixed on the object set upon the pedestal: a large red diamond balanced on its tip, reflecting the light of the torches. He pushed across the room. "Now, this—is interesting."

Gilanthos moved beside his friend. "It's stunning."

"It's powerful," Aeotus exclaimed as he examined it from every angle. Cautiously, he reached for it.

"What are you doing?" Gilanthos asked his friend.

Aeotus stopped and looked at Gilanthos. "I'm taking it, of course." He picked up the red stone. "It's heavier than I thought."

"It's not yours," Gilanthos expressed, understanding it didn't make a difference.

Aeotus shifted his eyes and smirked at his friend. "It's not theirs anymore." He pursed his lips together.

"I swear, you should have been a thief," Gilanthos declared.

Palias knelt and picked something up, drawing Gilanthos and Aeotus' attention away from the stone. "That's odd." He lifted a small buckle and examined it. "This is a Meloorne buckle to a sword belt." He sifted through debris on the floor, revealing more trinkets. "These are dwarven coins and an elven dagger."

Gilanthos moved beside the large man. "Let me see that dagger."

Palias handed the elf the dagger and continued scrounging around on the table.

Gilanthos examined the dagger. "This is from Evermoure." He looked at Aeotus, puzzled.

Palias picked up a small black book. He opened it and skimmed through it. "It looks like a journal of some kind." He turned a few pages. "Someone references opening portals to Meloorne, Kandar, and..." Palias scrunched his eyes together. "Asvernia."

"Your homeland," Gilanthos stated.

"Yes," Palias glanced at the elf, curiosity painted across his face.

Aeotus distracted the two when something caught his attention on the table beside him. "Oh, I've wanted one of these for a long time," he said as he retrieved a black book.

"Is that a spellbook?" Palias asked.

Aeotus nodded. "No, this is an arcane ledger." He smiled and placed it in his pack. His expression froze, and he raised his hand to stop Palias from asking about the ledger, then looked at Gilanthos. "Did you hear that?" He placed the red diamond in his pocket.

Gilanthos nodded. "Just now." He turned and looked at a closed door behind Yung Sung, hidden in the darkness.

"What?" Palias inquired as he closed the journal and put it in the pocket of his trousers.

Aeotus focused on the door. "Something's moving behind that door," he whispered.

Palias and Sung glanced at one another as the elves moved cautiously past them and toward the door, drawing their swords.

Aeotus tightly gripped the hilt of his weapon as he reached for the doorknob.

Gilanthos took his place beside his friend and nodded.

Sung readied two shurikens.

Aeotus turned the doorknob until he heard it click. He slowly pressed the door with his foot, spreading light into the dark room, revealing a woman lying on the dirt floor, bound at her legs and hands. She was unconscious.

Aeotus rushed into the small room. It was large enough for her and a medium-sized cage against the wall. He reached down and checked her neck for a pulse. "She's alive," he addressed Gilanthos.

Gilanthos entered the room and knelt beside them. He began to untie her legs.

Palias and Sung moved into the doorway, casting long shadows across her body.

Aeotus brushed her black hair from her face. The smell that wafted across his nose told him she hadn't bathed in a long time. Her face was attractive despite being heavily soiled. He could see movement through her eyelids. Her small nose and full lips were placed perfectly above her pointed chin. Her overall physique reminded him of an elf, but her ears spoke to her human heritage.

A small, child-like voice surprised everyone from a dark corner. "Master. Master?"

Aeotus sidestepped Gilanthos, moving toward the little voice.

"Master! Is it you, master?" Two tiny eyes reflected in what little light made it into the room.

A partially covered cage was set against the wall, not far from the woman. Little slate-colored hands grasped the iron bars.

Aeotus knelt beside the cage. "What have we here?"

"Master, master, you come!" The tiny creature, no more than two hands tall, jumped up and down in the cage excitedly. "Master!"

"What is it?" Yung Sung asked. He moved into the room and approached the cage.

Palias aided Gilanthos by scooping the young woman up in his arms. "I'll carry her."

Gilanthos was content to let the giant man do the heavy lifting, mainly because of how she smelled. He knew Palias could carry her around all day. In her current state of malnutrition, she might have weighed ninety pounds.

"Master?" The creature uttered. It looked at both Sung and Aeotus.

"Does he think we are his master?" Sung suggested.

Aeotus pursed his lips and thought for a moment. "This is a familiar."

"A what?"

"A wizard's familiar." Aeotus looked at Yung Sung. "When a wizard casts potent spells, there is a rare probability that a familiar could be conjured. It's loyal to the magic-user." Aeotus focused on the wall, thinking.

Sung raised his eyes. "That is interesting. You think it was the necromancer's?"

"No, necromancers don't have familiars. The power they draw from is destructive, not creative like a magic-user's." Aeotus opened the cage. "There you go, little one," Aeotus said.

The tiny creature crept to the edge of the door and stepped out of the shadow. Its skin was greyish blue, with large green eyes that seemed unnaturally large for its small head, no larger than a man's fist. Its small neck was the size of a quill pen, ending on tiny square shoulders. The creature's rib bones protruded, pushing against its leathery skin.

Sung watched its chest thump with every beat of its heart. The tiny hands had three fingers and what appeared to be a thumb. It wore no clothes and had no hair on its body. The thin, frail legs ended on two feet with three toes.

"Is it a boy or a girl?" Sung asked Aeotus.

"It's neither; it's magical." Aeotus looked at Sung, watching the wonder in his eyes.

"Master, you come, master, you come." The tiny creature wrapped itself around Aeotus' leg.

"He likes you."

"What's your name, little one?" Aeotus asked the familiar.

The creature backed away and tilted its head, "Portel, Master! Portel." He took his bony finger and pressed it into his leathery skin.

"Portel," Aeotus nodded and smiled. "It's quite funny."

Gilanthos stood beside Palias. "What's so funny?" Gilanthos asked.

"It was a familiar, similar to this one, that piqued my interest in magic when I was young. I found it near the end of its life, not far from my home. It died in my arms." Aeotus smiled and rubbed the creature's bald head.

The creature cooed and spoke in a self-soothing tone, "Master."

"Then it was a creature of this race that you found?" asked Palias.

Aeotus looked at the giant man. "No, you don't understand; this is not a race of creatures. It's one of a kind. No familiar is the same; each is an individual, created by the magic-user."

"Then why does this one look like the one you found when you were young?" Sung asked.

Aeotus shrugged. "Don't know." He pulled the cooing creature off his leg. "You're free—go, go on." Aeotus pushed the creature away.

"Yes, free master, free master!" It looked at the four with its large green eyes.

The woman began to stir in Palias' arms. "We need to get her out of here."

Gilanthos put his hand on Palias' arm. He could feel the muscles rippling beneath his dark skin. "Let's go."

"Portel, stay. This home." The tiny creature cowered toward the cage.

"No, you're free, Portel." Aeotus knelt. "Free to go anywhere you want."

Portel's eyes opened wide with excitement at the thought. Then he looked at the cage and the room. "No, Portel, stay here." He spoke adamantly.

"Very well," Aeotus stood and smiled at the familiar. "You are free to make your own choices."

They left the palace and began their trek out of the swamp.

CHAPTER THIRTY-NINE

DECISIONS

Eladonia woke and glanced at the empty chair beside the bed. The freshly chiseled wood reminded her of Aticus. She could feel him sitting in the chair and hear the dagger digging into the wood as it left its mark. A tear ran from her eye.

Her emotions were raw, and the memories from the last six days haunted her, like an open wound she thought may never heal.

Bryce stepped through the open door of the room. "I'm sorry, I couldn't save him." His face was uncharacteristically fatigued.

Eladonia looked at the dwarf, and tears filled her eyes. She didn't understand why Aticus' death upset her; it wasn't like she'd known him that long.

The last seven days felt like years to her, and he had been there with her throughout the whole nightmare. The voice she heard and the face she saw were his. He held her hand, caressed her face, and brushed her hair. Aticus shared his life. His pain.

"I don't remember much after you clapped your hands together," she shared with Bryce.

"You passed out," Bryce replied as he walked across the room and stood beside the empty chair. "Klan'den came with Ular; we were able to get the two of you back."

Eladonia let her gaze stray back to the chair where Aticus spent his days. "What about the two men..." She paused, not wanting to finish the sentence.

"We couldn't find them."

There was a long, uncomfortable moment of silence before he spoke. "Do you remember anything?" Bryce asked.

Eladonia explored Bryce's eyes before she answered. "I remember everything during the day." She looked at the chair. "I could see and hear you both." Eladonia let her eyes drift over the bed. "I was floating above my body—looking down in the room."

Bryce looked intrigued. "Fascinating. Only during the day?"

Eladonia's eyes lost focus as she remembered. "At night, everything was dark. There were flashes of memories that were not mine. Pain, and there was an urge to kill. I couldn't make out faces or voices. Everything was a dark shadow." Eladonia looked at Bryce. "You were my light—and Aticus. When the daylight came, you were both here. I clung to that light for hope when everything went dark."

Bryce rested his hand on Eladonia's arm. "You're safe now. It can't hurt you anymore."

She closed her eyes, and tears flowed freely down her cheeks.

After another long silence, Bryce explained his plans to Eladonia. "Tomorrow, I'm going to take Aticus back to Shandar. He told me how Nicholas was buried there..."

"I know. I heard Aticus tell you where he wanted to be put to rest." Eladonia wiped her eyes and looked at the dwarf. "I'm going with you."

"No. It would be best to stay here and rest until the others return." Bryce patted her arm.

Eladonia sat up. "I've rested enough. You can't take this from me, Bryce. Please don't."

Bryce shifted his head and studied her features. "It will take me four days to reach the forest, and then I must find where Nicholas is buried." He could see the pain in her eyes. "Alright then, we'll leave at first light."

The following day, Bryce didn't bother to look in on Eladonia. With the help of Klan'den and Ular, he prepared the horses for their journey.

A nearby farmer lent a small cart to transport Aticus, who was covered in textiles to shield him from the weather.

Bryce stood at the counter, talking with Klan'den, waiting for Eladonia to come downstairs. "When our friends return, if you don't mind, fill them in on where we've gone and what happened."

"I will, and I'm sorry about Aticus; he was a good kid." Klan'den clicked his lips.

"I'm sure Palias will make us even for the rooms," Bryce added.

"You've given us our city back. That's payment enough for me." Klan'den shrugged. "Maybe at least when word spreads, people will come back." Klan'den fidgeted his hands nervously on the counter. "It's going to be quiet without you here. You'll always have a place in Dewbrook, Bryce. That goes for all of you."

The sound of footsteps caught both men's attention, and they looked towards the stairwell.

Eladonia stepped into the tavern. Her tan leather armor fitted loosely on her. She wore her double short swords strapped to her back; the colorful ribbons wrapped around the handles. Eladonia's face showed no emotion.

"Are we ready?" she addressed her dwarven friend.

"Aye, we're ready," Bryce responded.

Chapter Forty

DUNCAN

Duncan stood on the ramparts of Parador, gazing at the morning sun as it rose in the east, peeking from behind drifting clouds.

He arrived last night from Meloorne after attending the funerals of King Balen and the queen.

Duncan had a difficult time believing that someone could have scaled the tower's wall, gained access to the king's chamber, and murdered him without detection. However, such thoughts were inconsequential with war looming on the horizon.

Rath Inen was declared the temporary guardian of the realm until Timan, King Balen's eldest son, reached adulthood. Rath's duty was to mentor and educate Timan for the next three years.

Duncan believed in Rath's leadership skills, but knew it might not make any difference. It seemed probable that Meloorne and the sister cities would be conquered before Timan's next birthday. He closed his eyes and basked in the warmth of the sun.

Edden, Duncan's first officer, stepped beside him. "What are you thinking? Got any brilliant thoughts?"

"I was hoping you could contribute for once," Duncan replied.

"Alright. I was thinking about our choices," Edden said as he leaned his elbows on the rampart wall.

"Oh, you have options? I'm intrigued." Duncan turned and faced his captain.

"Well, there's only one I'm leaning toward right now," Edden smirked. "We abandon our post and head east to live out the rest of our lives. Find some honest women, have kids, and die old, looking at the sunrise."

Duncan nodded his head. "You understand that's treason, and I should report you to your superior." Duncan looked back at the passing clouds.

Edden sighed, "Yeah, suppose you'll have to put me in shackles somewhere safe." The two men chuckled.

Their attention was drawn to the southern skyline as an advancing drake appeared. Its smooth black scales reflected the sunlight.

"I see the morning report from the front lines is right on time," Edden uttered as he leaned against the wall, admiring the sizeable winged beast and its rider. "Before I met you, I wanted to be a Kabatra." He nodded his head at the approaching drake in the distance.

The Kabatra were trained to ride the drakes, a lesser cousin of the rarely seen dragon. They were trained by the elves of Evermour hundreds of years ago. At one time, the skies were filled with hundreds of winged creatures, but now their numbers had substantially dwindled from years of war, leaving only eight drakes in the service of Parador.

Duncan turned and watched the beast approaching. "I can't see you on the back of a drake."

The creature soared above the fortress, which was shaped like a triangle. The rider guiding the drake tugged on the reins, causing the beast to veer to the left as it circled the three towers and the linked walls. The beast spread its wings broadly and hovered over the northern tower. It lowered its sturdy legs, tucked against its body, and landed delicately on a raised platform in the tower's center.

Edden clicked his lips and shook his head. "Suppose we'll never know." He quickly changed the subject and tapped Duncan on the shoulder. "I am sorry about Balen. I know you were close to the king and his family."

Duncan turned around and faced the eastern sky. "I still can't figure it out. If the Asvernians had killed them, why would an assassin be careless and leave a gold buckle behind? It doesn't add up."

Edden shrugged. "You think Rath will do right by the king?" he turned and looked at the swaying rittle weed in the fields below them.

"I do. Rath has been King Balen's advisor for a long time, and he knows what to do." Duncan looked south and took a deep breath. "We need to stop the orcs here."

"You didn't tell me what happened when you sent me running the other night. How'd you escape the battle without a scratch but lost nearly half the men?" Edden inquired.

"Luck, I assume." Duncan elbowed this captain. "Let's get some food. We have a long day ahead of us."

The two men walked along the ramparts, admiring the drake.

As the rider descended the stairs to submit his report in the command tower, the creature lifted its head, bared its teeth, and let out a piercing screech. The roar echoed through the walls of Parador.

CHAPTER FORTY-ONE

DON

Don sat beside the campfire, watching the dancing flames starve as they fought for air, reaching toward the heavens.

Sedric paced back and forth on the other side of the fire. "Why can't you let this go?"

Don pushed his hat back on his head to see Sedric from under the wide brim. The glow of the flames cast eerie shadows across his face. "You know damn well why I can't stop." He rubbed his hands together near the fire. "I suggest we wait until their friends return and follow them. Surely, they'll lead us to the boy and the dwarf. Then I can finish what we started."

"It's a fool's errand, man." Sedric stopped pacing and looked at Don. "You are not your father. You never will be."

Don glared at Sedric and abruptly stood. "Sedric!" he spat, clenching his fist.

"What! What are you going to do?" Sedric relaxed his stance and presented himself as less of a threat. "Look, I've known you for a long time. We've been through some sticky situations and always come out the other side." Sedric shook his head. "But this is something else, and you know it." He pressed his tongue between his teeth.

Don relaxed and tossed his hat on the ground where he had been sitting. "Dammit, Sedric, I know, I know." He sat down beside the fire and retrieved his hat. He looked at the tarnished silver cross that hung around his neck. It was Samuel's, his father's cross. Don folded his legs and let his hat hang on his knee.

"That cross won't help where you're going, Don," Sedric commented as he knelt by the fire. He found a stick lying on the ground beside him and picked it up.

"We've fought for so long to make a difference, Sedric." Don twirled the cross between his fingers.

"Yeah, we have, but maybe it's time to stop, "Sedric said, looking into Don's eyes.

"I have to finish what my father and I started. I owe it to him, and Mother." Don studied the dancing flames and let the cross lie against his chest.

"I didn't know Samuel, but I know you. Hell, I'm your only friend." Sedric paused. "I don't want to see you wind up like your father." He raised his hands in front of him and let them drop. "But, Don, you'll do what you want." He held the stick out and showed it to Don. "People only bend so far..." Sedric bent the stick until it cracked, "...before they snap." He threw the broken pieces into the fire and stood. "One day, Don, you're gonna go too far."

"I won't let that happen, Sedric." He looked at his friend.

"I know because I'm not sure how much longer I'll bend for you." Sedric shrugged. "They're good folk. I watched Aticus and Bryce protect those people. The dwarf is some kind of healer or holy man. But you didn't see that. I was the one who was there, not you, but then that's how it always is."

"I know what Aticus is." Don studied Sedric. "I think they killed Normain! I watched them come from his shop." Don waited for a response.

Sedric shrugged and turned away. "I can't see Aticus killing that old man." He lifted his hands. "I'm not sure I can help you if you continue." Sedric looked back at Don.

Don let his head sink, and he closed his eyes. "My father told me that when we killed the last Bloodmoure, it would kill everyone infected by the vampirism disease." Don looked at the stars spread across the night sky. "He's the last one. I kill him, and the vampires will be gone forever."

"That one. That one is going to kill you, Don." Sedric looked back into the darkness.

Chapter Forty-Two

HANDS OF THE SHADOW

A bright light illuminated Neacrom's laboratory as the rats scurried from the scattered bodies. A dazzling sphere of azure began to form and expanded, creating a magical door that opened in the center of the room, cutting through any object within its radius.

A shadow began to form in the center of the light, and a foot appeared, then a leg, and the body of someone shrouded in black carrying a lantern. He was an assassin from the Hands of the Shadow. Behind him came another, his dagger drawn, lantern held out. They stepped away from the portal, securing the room from any threats that might still be lingering in the darkness.

Another individual stepped through. The dark grey, studded armor came into focus, as did the black of his skin and white shoulder-length hair draped over pointed ears. Choluk surveyed the area around the portal. His icy blue eyes cut through the darkness as he looked into the shadows, where the lanterns could not reach. "Go look for Neacrom, kill him if you find him," the night elf commanded the two assassins.

Three more assassins emerged from the portal and hurried upstairs to help search.

Choluk looked at the pedestal for the Bloodstone. It was gone!

Another set of boots emerged from the portal. Choluk knew who stepped through the doorway behind him. "Everyone is dead." He did not turn around to acknowledge JoJung.

JoJung looked around the room, using the light from the portal to find what he had come for. "Find the Bloodstone?"

"It is not here." Choluk surveyed the bodies that littered the room. "There is only death." He concentrated on the surroundings, shifting his eyes to the side before speaking. "We are the only ones here."

"The Bloodstone, where is it?"

Choluk squinted, "I've already told you. It is not here! It is not on the pedestal where it should be, and I do not sense its power."

An assassin returned from upstairs. "Neacrom is dead in the throne room. An arrow to the head." The lantern he carried wobbled back and forth, casting shadows across the laboratory walls.

"Talmet succeeded at something," JoJung declared. "The Bloodstone? Does he have it?"

"No, we didn't find it on him."

Choluk shook his head. "I said it wasn't here," he whispered.

Michael emerged from the portal and examined the chamber. The doorway closed behind him.

"Light some torches!" JoJung commanded the assassin, holding the only light source in the room.

Choluk moved to the dead mind flayer resting between two tables. He knelt and gazed into the creature's vast, wet, black eyes. "I may be able to witness what transpired here." Choluk looked back at JoJung.

"Do it then. You need to find the Bloodstone," JoJung bellowed.

Choluk stood and faced JoJung. "Remember, it was you who gave the Bloodstone to Morgan. We unanimously voted against it, but you did it anyway, so do not lay the sole responsibility of finding the Bloodstone on me," Choluk said firmly.

"Yes, JoJung, you overruled the council concerning the Bloodstone," Michael said, tilting his head as he watched the assassin ignite torches around the room, shedding light on the gore.

JoJung softened his tone. "I know what I did. Just tell me where it is. Can you do that?"

Choluk crossed his legs and sat down in front of the mind flayer, putting his back toward the creature. He closed his eyes and adjusted his breathing, preparing himself for the psionic link. "I may be able to see what the flayer saw in the last few moments of its life, and after."

Michael walked around the lab, examining the empty pedestal, the overturned chair, and the large mirror against the wall. He paused and glanced at a table, searching for something else. "They have the arcane ledger as well," he whispered.

JoJung remained silent as he watched the night elf concentrate.

"The mind flayer is a powerful psychic creature, capable of capturing images even after death. With no eyelids, they are capable of sight, even after death, for a short period of time." Choluk conveyed without opening his eyes.

Michael strolled over and stood beside JoJung. He leaned his head and looked where the Ancient woman should have been through the open door.

Choluk's body jolted, and his head thrust back. He opened his eyes. His icy blue pupils were now black, like those of the mind flayer. "I see undead. Neacrom sent the undead in first to fight the Hand." Choluk moved his head from side to side. "Neacrom is here—fighting with his undead monstrosities."

"The Bloodstone, what about it?" JoJung interjected.

Choluk ignored JoJung's question as he continued to describe the vision. "Neacrom defeated the Hand and returned upstairs." Choluk lowered his head and looked around the room, his eyes still glazed black. "The Bloodstone is still sitting on the pedestal." Choluk pointed to the empty pedestal. "Neacrom left it there and returned to the throne room." Choluk paused, looking around the room.

JoJung paced back and forth impatiently.

"Where is the Ancient One?" Michael asked calmly.

"I don't know. Obviously, she's not here," JoJung said sarcastically.

"Someone else came downstairs," Choluk said, pausing and jerking his head to the side. "It's becoming difficult to see now that the mind flayer is dead," he added, moving his head forward, trying to pierce through the darkening memory. Choluk paused and stared silently for several moments.

"What is it?" JoJung stopped his pacing and approached the night elf.

"He is here," Choluk said softly, tilting his head.

"Who is here?" JoJung inquired.

"Your son. He is here with an Asvernian and..." Choluk creased his mouth in disgust, "two elves."

JoJung knelt in front of the Choluk. "Yung Sung was here?" His voice was thick with anticipation. "We've found him?"

"Yes."

JoJung stood and stepped away. He rubbed his chin and looked at Michael. "Yung Sung was here." JoJung spun around to look at Choluk. "Does he have the Bloodstone?"

Michael clenched his teeth and tried not to say anything.

Choluk looked back at the empty pedestal. "It is becoming difficult to see faces. No. One of the elves placed the Bloodstone in his pocket."

JoJung glanced at the empty pedestal on the far end of the room, near the mirror. "Yung Sung is with them, and they have the stone." He paced, clearly disturbed.

Choluk looked at the open door that led to a small room. "They took the Ancient One as well."

JoJung's face went pale, and he knelt when he heard what the night elf said. "They have the Bloodstone and the Ancient?"

"I told you something like this would happen, JoJung," Michael scolded, stepping toward him. "Neither should have ever left our protection."

Choluk looked in the direction from which he heard JoJung speak. He couldn't see him while he was linked to the mind flayer. "Yes, they have them both, and they left last night."

"We need to bring more of the Hand through to go after them. They couldn't have gone far." JoJung stood, turning in circles. "We need to find my son and the Bloodstone before it's too late."

Michael walked in front of JoJung. "This is your fault, JoJung. You know what could happen if they..." Michael's face reddened as he continued to speak, "If they find out what she is and what they have." He tightened his hands into fists, which did not go unnoticed by JoJung.

"I know, Michael! I'll get them both back, along with Yung Sung." JoJung tried not to make eye contact.

Michael moved to the side near a table. He struck it with his closed fist, collapsing the wooden furniture into rubble. Dust and splinters flew around him. Michael looked at JoJung, his mouth open, fangs showing in the torchlight. "You will make this right."

Fear etched itself into JoJung's features.

Choluk closed his eyes and released himself from his psionic hold on the mind flayer. "I will signal for a portal," he said, glancing at Michael.

Michael closed his eyes, took a breath, and straightened his robe. "Thank you, Choluk." His tone was considerably calmer, and he approached the small room where the woman had been held. "They will be running north. We need to dispatch units to Veridian and Dornel." He stood in the doorway. "The Ancient must die, as I said before."

"We need her!" Choluk said.

"She has served her purpose in pitting allies against one another." Michael put his hands behind his back, grasping them tightly. He continued to gaze at the cage in the small room, where the empty shackles lay on the floor.

"But what about the elven and dwarven kings? We still have more of them to eliminate," Choluk added.

JoJung remained silent, letting them talk.

"We have caused a sufficient imbalance in the realm to give us time," Michael boasted.

"But without her, we will not be able to open the final door," Choluk stated.

"She is the key to only one door—and some doors should never be opened," Michael replied as he turned and looked at JoJung.

CHAPTER FORTY-THREE

LORNA

The dawn brought with it a chill to the air, as the rittle weeds of the plains bowed under the weight of the morning dew.

Yung Sung huddled near the fire, wrapped in his blanket. He watched the woman they had rescued the day before rest peacefully, covered in extra blankets to keep warm and dry. "Why is she still sleeping?" Sung asked Aeotus.

"I assume the flayer caused significant damage to her mind," Aeotus suggested. He sat down beside Sung and watched the woman breathe. Her soiled face grimaced, and her eyes raced behind her eyelids.

Palias walked beside Yung Sung and Aeotus, pulling a blanket around his chest. "She may never wake then?" Palias asked as he sat down near the warmth of the fire.

"It's possible. I've never known anyone who encountered a mind flayer," Aeotus added, tilting his head and studying her features further.

Gilanthos appeared from the waist-high rittle weed. "I found the berries you needed, Sung."

Sung removed his cloak and folded it beside him before he retrieved the berries from Gilanthos. "It will take a few moments to make; sit by the fire." Sung placed his hand on Gilanthos' shoulder.

"You have the headache again?" Aeotus asked. He started to stand but stopped when Gilanthos began to speak.

"Yes, it's not that bad; I just need to catch it before it gets worse," Gilanthos acknowledged with a wave. "Sung's mixture seems to help."

"Why didn't you tell me? I would have searched for the ingredients," Aeotus urged.

Gilanthos looked at his elven friend, then at Palias, before speaking. "I'm fine."

"Yung Sung, where did you learn to make that concoction?" Aeotus asked.

"Master Tau taught me how to make several herbal remedies." Sung crumbled dried herbs from his pouch and smashed the berries before placing them in the pot of hot water.

"Did Master Tau teach you how to fight?" Aeotus inquired.

"He did, and much more." Sung knelt by the fire regarding the pot. "I regret that I did not appreciate what he had to tell me before he was gone." He considered Palias, with whom he had already shared much of his story over the past several months.

"Regret? Why would you regret it? He sounded like an excellent teacher." Aeotus inquired.

"I regret not understanding the last lesson, Master Tau was trying to teach me." Sung poured herbal tea into a cup and handed it to Gilanthos. "Perhaps if I had listened to him, he might still be alive today."

Gilanthos acknowledged Yung Sung when he took the cup. "Thank you. What happened to Master Tau?" Gilanthos asked as he sipped the tea.

Sung nodded and sat down before speaking. "Barbarians destroyed our village and killed everyone, including Master Tau."

"I take it you were not with Master Tau when the attack happened?" Aeotus asked.

Sung regarded Aeotus and shook his head. "No, I was not there."

"You believe you could have made a difference if you had been there?" Aeotus questioned, raising his eyebrows.

"Not at all. I would have at least died with honor," Sung replied, his expression sagging.

"Why weren't you with your Master?" Gilanthos asked before he took a sip of his tea.

Sung was silent for a moment, reluctant to answer. "I was robbing the home of a nobleman with a group of people I thought were friends." Sung lowered his head. "Master Tau told me they were using me for my skills." Sung let his eyes drift to the woman they rescued. "I desperately wanted to belong to something other than my training. It wasn't until he was gone that I realized what I needed had been there all along." Sung took a deep breath. "Master Tau was protective, moving me from village to village, hiding me from a father I did not know."

"Why would he hide you from your father?" Gilanthos asked.

"Master Tau said my father would return for me when my training was complete." Sung lifted an eyebrow, watching the woman sleep. "When I got older, Master Tau expressed his desire to protect me from my father and keep me hidden. He said he was an evil man who had corrupted everything he had ever touched. As time passed, I resented Master Tau for hiding me." Sung looked at Aeotus. "I had dishonored my Master by not heeding his warnings concerning the individuals I associated with. What if he was right about my father, too? After Master Tau died, I ran away as far as I could and came here to Idonia."

Palias scanned the flames licking the air.

Gilanthos remained silent as he sipped the tea and gazed out at the morning sky.

Aeotus, however, was not as discreet. "Stealing from an aristocrat, that's not how I saw that going."

Gilanthos looked at Aeotus; his shoulders sagged.

Aeotus recognized Gilanthos' disappointment. "It's not what I would have thought. I never suspected you of being a thief. I thought it might have been a girl or something like that." He was trying to be friendly for what it was worth.

"Aeo, please," Gilanthos pleaded.

"What?" he mouthed, looking at his elven friend.

Trying to change the subject, Palias pulled out the black journal he found in Neacrom's lab the night before. "I skimmed through the book last night and found some interesting references about world leaders." He glanced around at everyone before continuing. "Whoever scribed the book named all the realm's rulers, including my father."

"Why are their names mentioned?" Sung inquired.

"They are all referred to as targets." Palias' face sagged; concern for his father became the anchor.

After several long moments of awkward silence, the woman lying beneath the blankets began to stir. She opened her eyes and glanced at each man without moving. "Who are you?" she asked, her voice husky and dry.

"We're here to help you," Palias expressed; his deep voice drew her attention. "I am Palias." The large man placed a hand on his chest. "You are free from those who were hurting you." He gestured to the others. "These are my friends, Aeotus, Gilanthos, and Sung."

Yung Sung slowly stood.

The woman's eyes focused on him, watching his every movement.

Sung pointed at the waterskin lying on the ground. "Are you thirsty?

She looked at the water container beside Sung and swallowed hard, then nodded.

Sung knelt and retrieved the water. "I will pour you a cup." Sung offered.

She continued watching the men cautiously.

Palias was about to stand to help when Aeotus grabbed his arm. "Let me; you're a little intimidating." The elf scrunched his nose repeatedly.

Palias sighed and glanced at Gilanthos.

Gilanthos shook his head, rolled his eyes, and sipped tea.

Palias sat down, opting not to hit Aeotus. He understood that first impressions were lasting impressions, and if he'd struck Aeotus like he wanted, she might never trust them.

Aeotus moved around the fire and approached her, "Let me help you." With Aeotus' support, she sat up and watched the refreshing water pour from the container into a clay cup.

The blanket fell off her head, revealing sullied, long black hair twisted in knots. Aeotus held his breath while he steadied her, the odor overwhelming. Their gaze met; Aeotus noticed her eyes for the first time. They were a brilliant shade of amber, almost gold.

She looked into his eyes, her brows folded in on one another. "Don't leave," she said, her voice cracked.

"I have you. I'm not going anywhere." Aeotus felt a cold chill creep up his neck, and the hair on his arms stood upright. Uneasily, he looked out over the reflecting sunlight that sparkled on the damp rittle weed.

Yung Sung knelt and gave the woman the cup of water. "Here, you must be thirsty."

She took the cup with both hands and turned it up, emptying its contents. The woman swallowed hard and returned the cup to Sung. "More," she whispered.

She studied Aeotus while Sung refilled the cup. Aeotus avoided her gaze.

Sung gave the woman the water. "Do you have a name?"

She held the cup to her mouth, "Lorna," she said before drinking the water, watching Sung the whole time. She returned the empty container to Sung. "My name is Lorna."

Sung nodded. "Good. Lorna, would you like more water?"

Lorna nodded; her hair fell across her face.

"You may want to take it easy with the water," Aeotus suggested.

Lorna gazed into Aeotus' eyes. She started to say something, but couldn't remember what. She examined the crescent moon Shad'arn in his ear. "You are elf," she mumbled.

"She knows her name and that you are an elf. That's a good start, I guess," Sung stated.

Lorna looked at Sung like she couldn't understand him. Her eyes narrowed; she glanced back at Aeotus; tears filled her eyes. "Menilith," she whispered over and over as she looked into the sky.

"Why does she keep saying that?" Gilanthos asked, still holding his tea by the fire.

Aeotus shook his head. "I don't know." Aeotus wiped the tears from her cheek.

"Something has her troubled. What is she saying?" Palias asked.

Gilanthos looked at Palias. "That is the elven word for remember."

"The mind flayer messed her up badly," Aeotus said as he helped Lorna lie back down.

She watched the four men quietly as they saddled the horses and prepared to break camp, her gaze fixed on Aeotus.

CHAPTER FORTY-FOUR

NORTHWARD

The afternoon sun warmed Bryce's face as he chatted with Eladonia.

She tried to acknowledge him, nodding when she thought it required a response; it was challenging to focus on anything Bryce said during their journey north. Her thoughts remained confined to the memories of the last eight days.

Her memory of Aticus was a stark comparison to the despair of being trapped by the soul reaver, but it was enough to keep her distracted.

"We'll be in Veridian tomorrow, although it would shave a day off our journey if we pass the city altogether; what do you think?" Bryce stated.

Eladonia didn't answer.

Bryce studied Eladonia's features before answering his own question. "That's true. If we stop, everyone will have time to catch up. They would want to be there when we lay Aticus to rest." Bryce considered Eladonia as he pulled the reins, stopping his horse.

It was the sound of the cartwheels stopping that made Eladonia pause. She pulled on Kora's reins, settling her. "What's wrong?" Eladonia asked as she glanced back at Bryce. She couldn't help but look at the cart hitched to the dwarfs horse.

"It's acceptable to talk about him, Eladonia." Bryce studied her intently, then shrugged and looked at the sky. "God knows I don't know what you're going through, but I want to help you." He let his shoulders sag. "If you'll let me."

She paused and studied the tarp covering Aticus before speaking. "I followed Aticus out into the woods with that man. I knew he was going to do something to him. I could feel it." Eladonia turned Kora so she could see Bryce better. "I couldn't tell him—couldn't get him to hear me. I screamed not to go, tried to pull him back." Eladonia looked at her palms. "No matter how many times or how hard I tried. My hands passed through him."

"You said you suspended over your body, but you could also roam willingly?" Bryce asked, shifting in the saddle.

Eladonia nodded. "The first day, I hovered over my body. Watching myself lie there helplessly was confusing and difficult. It wasn't until the second day that I watched you sleep in the chair beside me. There was a glimmer around you that pulled me toward you. Before I knew it, I was standing beside you in the warmth of that light." She sighed. "The first few days, I tried to get you both to notice me, but nothing worked." Eladonia glanced at the rittle weed dancing in the breeze. "You both stayed with me, talked to me. I'd stand beside you in the light while you slept and listened to Aticus tell his stories and share his pain. I watched him etch in the arm of that chair with each day that passed. I saw the despair on his face for me." She looked Bryce in the eyes. "Those conversations helped me hold on and not give up. You both helped to calm my fears of being alone, all the time knowing what came with nightfall."

"I am sorry, Eladonia," Bryce sympathized.

A tear found its way from the corner of her eye. "When darkness came, I was so cold and alone. I couldn't control myself, trapped in the shadow as it lusted after your souls, as it had mine. I couldn't help but feel that if I—we could touch the living, we might be free." Eladonia swallowed hard. "My fear was if we were to have taken another soul, then where would mine have gone?" She looked at Bryce before whispering, "Somewhere much darker, I fear. It was your light that saved my soul."

"My dear, it wasn't I who saved you. It was God," Bryce articulated with a smile.

"Your God didn't save him," she said coldly.

Bryce's smile faded, and he remained silent.

Eladonia guided Kora beside Bryce. She studied the cart and the burlap that covered Aticus' body. "I heard you both speak of a little girl who suffered the same fate that I had." Eladonia looked at Bryce. "Did she make it?"

Bryce nodded. "She did." Bryce let his head lean to the side while he studied her. "I didn't know you knew about her, or I would have told you. You did not see her in your corporeal form?"

She shook her head. "No." Eladonia forced a smile. "I'm glad she lived. I hope she has help dealing with what I know she's going through."

"She will. Her parents seemed attentive to her needs." Bryce studied the swords on Eladonia's back and observed the ribbons around the hilts move with the wind before he spoke to the sky, "I know she will. It will change her." He glanced back at Eladonia and smiled.

"It will change her? Are you talking about the little girl or me?" Eladonia questioned Bryce.

"I'm sorry, dear. Sometimes, it isn't easy to carry on two conversations at the same time." Bryce smiled warmly and spurred his horse forward.

The sound of the wagon wheels drew Eladonia's gaze. She glimpsed something out of the corner of her eye suspended over Bryce, but it seemed to disappear when she turned in his direction. It reminded her of the days she stood in the light. She looked up and watched a lone vulture circle.

Chapter Forty-Five

LORNA

As the day progressed, the sky had become overcast, and a gentle breeze blew from the southwest. Gilanthos decided to lead them on a more direct route toward Dewbrook, hoping to shorten their trip by half a day.

Aeotus caught Lorna watching him countless times while seated behind Yung Sung on his horse. Whenever Aeotus looked their way, Lorna would redirect her gaze to the horizon or turn around to face the opposite direction. Sung had eagerly offered to share his horse with Lorna after she bathed and before anyone else had the chance.

Palias rode up beside Aeotus and handed him a brown book inlaid with silver and gold.

"Where did you get that?" Aeotus' eyes widened.

"We think it was Gildon Prather's spellbook."

"The wizard, Gildon Prather? King Eston's advisor? The one that went missing over seventy years ago?" Aeotus straightened in his saddle and eagerly opened the book.

Palias nodded, "Normain seemed confident that the book belonged to Gildon, especially after discovering other items alongside it. That's where we stumbled upon the gems for the sword near his remains. Sung and I want you to have the book, as it has no value to either of us."

Aeotus was stunned as he flipped through the book. "These are potent spells," he said, pausing to look at Palias. "Thank you."

Palias nodded, "You're welcome." He glanced over at Lorna before addressing Aeotus again. "Do you have any idea why she keeps watching you?"

"You've noticed that as well?" Aeotus glanced around the big man, closing the spell book. Lorna rested her head on Yung Sung's back, looking in the opposite direction. "It could be that I remind her of someone." Aeotus relaxed his voice to a whisper and drifted nearer. "I believe she is a Lamarian, or an Ancient One." Aeotus tilted back in his saddle and placed the book in his saddlebag.

Palias glanced at Lorna. She was still looking in the other direction. "Ancient," Palias uttered. "Weren't they a myth. A child's tale?" Palias scrunched his brows together, looking at the elf.

"They were real and existed long before us," Aeotus replied.

"How can you be sure?" Palias asked.

"Her eyes; only one kind of people were said to have a golden hue to their eyes that she does." He gestured toward her with his finger.

Palias narrowed his eyes. "I'll admit, she's unique. However, I find it unlikely that we've discovered a Lamarian." Palias expressed.

Aeotus stared at the large man. "It's improbable that I'm mistaken," he said sarcastically.

Palias looked down on Aeotus, "I didn't say you were wrong. I feel like you're looking for something that's not there."

"You're an oaf!" Aeotus said.

Palias shook his head and spurred his horse forward beside Gilanthos to keep from striking the elf from his horse.

"You want your book back?" Aeotus reached into his bag and lifted the spellbook over his head.

"Don't let him irritate you, Palias," Gilanthos said, glancing at the large man with a smile.

"Has he always been like this?" Palias asked.

"No. Aeotus changed after his father disowned him for turning from the bladecantor to the arcane," Gilanthos explained. "He puts up a wall to protect himself from the people he cares about."

Aeotus muttered under his breath so that only Gilanthos could hear him. "I don't care for that big oaf."

"You know you do," Gilanthos smirked, responding to Aeotus' comment.

Palias looked over at Gilanthos. "Do what?" he asked.

"What will you do with the sword now that you've collected all the parts?" Gilanthos asked.

"I had hoped to retrieve the sword and bring it home. My father would be delighted to hear about the challenges I faced in gathering the pieces. Unfortunately, it appears I won't be able to assemble the sword without the help of the gnomes," explained Palias.

"So what is the purpose of the life quest you and your siblings were sent on?" Gilanthos asked.

"It's a tradition that our ancestors have held for generations as a rite of passage," Palias explained, looking at Gilanthos. "The experiences we have in life are what shape our character. Without them, we can only rely on what we have learned from books or stories. Life quests are designed to provide experiences one would not encounter within the walls of our city. How can you effectively lead if you do not understand other cultures?"

Gilanthos nodded. "That's admirable. Do you think the sword will help sway your father?" Gilanthos asked.

"Perhaps. I have under a year remaining on my quest." Palias paused before changing the topic. "I've never given it much thought until now, but perhaps you could clarify something for me?"

"Of course," Gilanthos smiled.

Palias asked, "Why does the entire realm follow the elven eighteen-month cycle for a year?"

Gilanthos heard Aeotus chuckle, and it brought a smile to his face. "When I was young, I asked the same question, and the explanation was quite simple." He looked at Palias with a broad grin spreading across his face and continued, "The gestation period for an elven pregnancy is roughly eighteen months. Our ancestors created the calendar, and everyone else blindly observed it."

"You mean, thousands of years ago, an elven woman created the calendar, based on the length of her pregnancy?" Palias looked out over the landscape, letting the simplicity of his statement sink in.

"I assure you I wouldn't lie about the calendar year." Gilanthos chuckled. "I couldn't make that up myself."

Palias curled his lips in disbelief. "Fascinating." He looked back at the elf. "Even the orcs, goblins, and beasts of Idonia follow that same calendar?"

"Yes. Amusing, isn't it?" Gilanthos added.

While everyone laughed, Aeotus glanced over at Sung and Lorna. She smiled at him while they laughed. Aeotus smiled back.

CHAPTER FORTY-SIX

VERIDIAN

Bryce and Eladonia arrived in Veridian before the rain. They dropped the horses off at the stable and, with Eladonia's help, bribed the boys into holding Aticus' body and cart in one of the empty stalls for the night.

The boys expressed their concern to Bryce that if the stable master found a body in one of the stalls, it wouldn't be good for them or the dwarf. Bryce reassured them that they would be back for Aticus and their horses before dawn.

The two sloshed through the wet streets and entered the Wet Stag. When they walked in, the near-capacity tavern offered only a few tables. The heavy rain had encouraged weary travelers inside, seeking shelter.

Collet Duskwater recognized Bryce and Eladonia when they entered. "Bryce," he bellowed from across the noisy room, waving his hands to get their attention.

Bryce and Eladonia approached Collet as he was about to evict six patrons from the table he had, for some reason, thought needed to be reserved for them.

"No, no, that's not necessary, Collet; there's only the two of us today," Bryce announced to the barkeeper.

"Never mind, you can stay there—put everything down." Collet scolded the people into sitting back down. "Sorry about that, folks."

Collet turned to his two new customers. "Here, I have a table over by the hearth." He put his hand on the dwarf's shoulder and led them to the nearby warmth of the fire. "Where's everyone else? Will they be joining you?"

"It may be a few days before they arrive," Bryce answered. "We've got some bad news, Collet." Bryce glanced at Eladonia before continuing. "We have Aticus with us, but he's passed on—we're taking him home for burial."

Collet knelt beside the table; sadness spread across his face like a shadow. "Oh no. Aticus was a nice kid." Collet clicked his lips and rocked his head from side to side. "Sorry about that." He grimaced and flashed a sad smile between the two. "Drinks are on the house tonight, to celebrate his life." He patted the table.

Bryce placed his hand on Collet's arm. "That won't be necessary; I don't think either of us feels like drinking."

Eladonia swiftly reversed Bryce's comment. "I do; bring me a bottle of ale," she said, staring at Collet.

"Of course, I'll have it right out." Collet stood and shifted, snapping his fingers until one of the servants noticed him. "One bottle of ale." He pointed at the table and knelt beside it. "I suppose you've both heard the news?" He eyed each of them, waiting for a response.

Bryce and Eladonia silently regarded one another. Bryce shook his head. "I'm sorry, Collet, we're not sure what you mean. We just arrived in town."

"I apologize. I assumed you've probably been away from civilization. They found my brother, Balen, and the queen assassinated while they slept."

Bryce's features sank. "I regret hearing that, Collet. I'm sorry for your loss."

Collet nodded. "It is what it is. I haven't seen him in years, and we were never close."

"Nevertheless, he was your brother," Bryce added.

Eladonia watched Collet speak, her demeanor stoic.

The table maid arrived with a bottle of ale and two glasses.

Eladonia immediately took the ale, poured a drink, and then emptied it. She was tired of death.

Collet regarded Bryce sympathetically. "There's more, I'm afraid. This information strikes closer to your company." He gazed at Eladonia. She drank and studied the fire, trying not to listen. He paused a moment before finishing. "Palias' father and mother met a fate similar to my brother's. It happened over a week ago. Assassinated in their sleep as well."

Bryce leaned back in his chair. "Oh my. I'm sure Palias hasn't heard yet. We left Duskwater yesterday, and there had been no news of the deaths." Bryce examined Eladonia as she stared into the fire. He heard Collet speaking, but wasn't listening; his attention was on her. Until Collet mentioned something about a war between the Asvernians and Meloorne. "What? War?"

"Yes, the Asvernians say that we killed their king, and we are saying they killed our king in retaliation." Collet shook his head.

"Thank you, Collet. I appreciate you catching us up on everything, but we need some time to process this information." Bryce straightened and adjusted his shirt.

"Hen or ham?" Collet asked.

"Eladonia, what would you prefer?" Bryce asked, waiting for her to answer.

She stared into the fire and held her glass near her mouth, lost in thought.

Bryce gazed back at the innkeeper, "Hen and the fixings, please." Bryce answered Collet.

Collet nodded as he arose and returned to the kitchen with the order for the cook.

"I do not plan on going to Evermoure when we are finished laying Aticus to rest in Shandar." Eladonia gazed at the fire, which warmly lit the corner where they sat.

"Will you return home to Faylorn?" Bryce inquired.

"No. I do not want to squander my life wed to someone I do not know." Eladonia regarded Bryce.

"I understand. It would be best to find what you are meant to do and embrace it. Life remains short even if you think you are immortal. Nothing lasts forever except death." Wrinkles creased the sides of Bryce's eyes as he forced a smile.

"Near-death experiences tend to change us, don't they?" Eladonia questioned.

Bryce furrowed his brows and tilted his head. "I don't think it changes us. I believe our existence can be somewhat simplified; we find direction in the clarity of that experience." Bryce filled his cup with ale and sat back in the chair.

Eladonia became lost in thought as she focused on the crackling of the fire, blocking out the sounds of the tavern.

Bryce studied Eladonia during dinner; he didn't try to initiate any further conversation, nor did she.

CHAPTER FORTY-SEVEN

DEWBROOK

It had taken Palias and the others only four days to reach Dewbrook, arriving mid-morning.

Aeotus was the first to enter Grog's Inn. Vaulting from his horse, he ran through the doors of the establishment. "Ela!" He scanned the room for his friend. There was no one here. The tables and chairs of the tavern were neatly pushed together. "Ela," Aeotus uttered as he ran toward the stairwell.

Hurriedly, he made his way up the steps and approached the room at the end of the hall, where he had last seen Eladonia's unconscious body.

Aeotus shoved the door open, "Ela?" Instead, he found a man sitting in a chair reading a book. "Who are you?" Aeotus demanded harshly.

The man shut the book and considered the elf before speaking. "Don, can I help you?"

"Where is Eladonia?"

"I'm sorry, I don't know who Eladonia is." Don placed the book in his lap.

Aeotus bounded back through the door and descended the stairs into the tavern.

At that instant, Gilanthos came through the door of the inn, followed by Sung, Palias, and Lorna.

Klan'den walked from the kitchen, holding a towel. "You're back already?"

Aeotus approached the bar and slapped his hands on the counter." Where's Eladonia?"

Klan'den frowned at Aeotus, "You all may want to sit down."

Instinctively, Aeotus reached into his trousers and pulled the life stone free. He looked at the glowing rock, satisfaction spreading across his face as his brows folded inward. "Why do you want us to sit?"

Gilanthos sidestepped Aeotus to get a better view of Klan'den. "What happened?" He glanced at the stone in his friend's hand. "Where are Ela and the others?"

Palias and Sung approached. Lorna was the only one to take the innkeeper's suggestion and sit at a table.

"Eladonia's fine; don't be concerned." Klan'den placed the towel on the counter and folded the corners.

Aeotus sighed, and his features relaxed. "I don't understand."

Don walked down the stairs and stood on the last step. He folded his arms and listened.

"Aticus is dead." Klan'den's gaze drifted to the dark oak countertop.

Gilanthos turned and faced the wall. "We left him here to protect him." He kicked a nearby chair.

Aeotus looked at Gilanthos. "Dead." He shook his head as he replaced the stone in his pocket. He squinted his eyes together as he processed what Klan'den said.

"What? How?" Sung asked as he sat in a nearby chair, his voice cracking.

Palias sat near Lorna; his face sagged at the news as he shook his head in disbelief. "Bryce is okay?"

"Yes, Bryce is fine," Klan'den responded.

"How did...how?" Yung Sung tried to ask, but he found it difficult to articulate his words.

"A man arrived in town a couple of days after you left." Klan'den shifted while he recalled. "Sedric said he was a fur trader and was passing through the village. He was only here a few days, off and on." Klan'den swallowed hard, "Seemed like a nice man." He paused. "The afternoon before Eladonia woke, he convinced Aticus to look at something in the woods; told him it might help your friend." Klan'den paused as he leaned on the counter.

"Aticus said he would be back before dark. When he didn't return, I told Bryce; that's when Eladonia awakened and ran out the door, yelling that Aticus was in danger."

"That must be when we killed the necromancer," Gilanthos suggested as he sat in a chair and placed his head in his hands.

"Bryce chased after her. By the time we found them, it was over. Eladonia was unconscious, and Bryce was praying over Aticus, but he was already dead." Klan'den shrugged.

"This man you spoke of, Sedric, killed Aticus?" Palias inquired, his booming voice resonating as he clenched his hands into fists.

"No. Bryce said another man killed Aticus. Sedric kept them out of reach."

Aeotus turned and glanced at Don standing on the stairs before he walked over and sat beside Palias, placing his hand on the large man's shoulder to console him.

"Bryce wanted me to tell you that they were traveling north to Shandar, where they would lay him to rest. He mentioned they might stop in Veridian before continuing. Their time will be limited before nature takes its course, and Aticus—well, you know."

Klan'den attracted Don's attention when he spoke of where Bryce and Eladonia were going.

"We should leave right away," Sung announced as he stood, the chair scraping the wood floor.

"We need to tend to the horses and gather supplies before leaving. It would be good to have a meal before going; then, we could continue without pause," Palias suggested.

"I've got a stew I can start if you're interested," Klan'den stated.

"Who is Aticus?" Lorna asked Palias.

"A friend," he responded, resting his hands on the table.

Sung glanced at Klan'den and nodded in agreement; he noticed the man on the stairs watching him. "Who are you?" Sung asked.

"My name's Don."

Everyone in the tavern analyzed the man on the stairs.

"I apologize. I couldn't help but overhear about your friend." Don let his arms hang at his sides. "I'm traveling north today for Shandar. If you'd let me ride along, I'd be happy to purchase any necessary provisions. There's safety when traveling in numbers." Don raised his brows and glanced at everyone for approval.

"There's no need to buy our supplies. However, you are welcome to accompany us to Shandar or wherever your travels lead you." Palias considered his friends for approval.

Everyone shrugged or nodded in agreement.

"Thank you." Don nodded and clasped his hands. "I'll prepare my things so I don't slow you down when you're ready to leave." Don turned and walked back to his room, smiling.

Aeotus sat at a table in the tavern of Grog's Inn. He held the red diamond, observing the mist swirling inside. He explored its surface for something that could help him learn what it was.

Lorna sat at the table across from him, her feet in the chair, knees pulled to her chest. She silently watched the elf fidget with the red stone.

Aeotus presented the stone before Lorna, "Do you know what this is?"

Lorna regarded the mist-filled gemstone with her golden eyes and shook her head. "No, but it does look familiar. Beyond that, I am not sure."

"It should look familiar. We found it where we found you." Aeotus pursed his lips together and studied her eyes. "Whatever this is, it possesses a great deal of magic." He shifted his jaw from side to side. "Do you remember what you were doing there? In that room?"

"That's where they kept me when they weren't using me."

"Using you. What do you mean, using you?" Aeotus questioned.

"They woke me long enough to open a door using the mirror." She uttered.

Aeotus rolled the stone around. "A door to where?"

Lorna shrugged, "I don't know." Her golden eyes reflected the sunlight that spread into the tavern through the open windows. Her delicate features accentuated an air of innocence.

"Like I told Palias and Sung, they would pull me out and sit me in the chair. The mind flayer would dig into my consciousness and make me open a door through the mirror. Men would go through and come back. After they finished, they would take me back and shackle me."

"A magical door? How can you open a portal?" Aeotus questioned as he looked around the empty tavern.

"It's my gift, or curse." She paused, looking him in the eyes. "You know who I am; I heard you tell Palias."

"I was under the impression that all the Ancients perished eons ago during the end times," Aeotus asserted.

"If it truly were the end times, you wouldn't be sitting here," Lorna declared.

"Most ordinary people believe the Lamarians never existed and were stories created by bards or old elven elders to inspire those who cared to listen," Aeotus stated. "Where've you been all these years? Are you a descendant of the ancients?"

"Honestly, I don't know. I'm surprised I remember my name." She rolled her head from side to side. "I have moments of clarity, and then things become cloudy."

"Are there more of you?" Aeotus couldn't help but ask.

Lorna tapped her temple, "I told you. I don't know."

Aeotus glanced at the table and nodded. "Fair enough. Why do you consider your gift a curse?"

"It's obvious they used me against my will. In that regard, I would consider it a curse." She sniffed and sat back, placing her feet on the ground. "What's your curse?" She asked.

Aeotus raised his brows and turned the red jewel in his hands. "Right now, it's sitting here with you." He looked at Lorna with a confident smile.

She looked deep into his eyes and smiled.

The sound of footsteps descending the stairs drew their attention. Don appeared and stepped into the tavern.

Aeotus quickly moved his hands below the table to conceal the red jewel.

"What sort of work do you do, Don?" Aeotus asked.

"I'm a hunter of sorts." Don placed his saddlebag and pack on a table before sitting beside Lorna.

Lorna tilted her head and watched the two men speak.

"Small game or big game?" Aeotus questioned.

Don leaned on the table, admiring Lorna's eyes and delicate features before responding. "Big game, of course." He looked at Aeotus. "I track and kill vampires."

"Vampires." Aeotus chuckled and widened his eyes. "I wasn't aware we had a vampire problem." He sank back into the chair.

"You're welcome." Don crossed his arms and leaned on the table.

The door to the tavern opened as Gilanthos and Sung walked in.

"Palias said we're ready. He's collecting the horses now," Gilanthos announced.

Aeotus stood and nodded. "Well, let's not keep him waiting."

Don rose from his chair and retrieved his bags. "I'll meet you at the stables."

Chapter Forty-Eight

LIFE

The morning sunlight poured in through the open windows and door, filling the room with radiance. The stillness of the morning made it seem all the more brilliant, or it was something else entirely. The dust particles floated gracefully, sparkling like silver pieces in the house's entryway.

The little boy looked through the knothole in the wall. It was the same hole he used to cheat while playing hide and seek with his siblings.

But not today, today, the six-year-old hid between the walls of his home to block out the screams of his family and servants.

Time seemed to move so slowly to him as he watched his baby sister, red-faced and crying, cradled in his mother's arms.

He watched his mother's lips move, but there was no sound. She pleaded for their lives, her hand outstretched, begging for mercy. Her face contorted in agony as tears ran down her cheeks.

The man standing before her held his sword by his side. The wide-brimmed hat on his head cast shadows across his stubbled, stern face. There was no sound as his lips moved, but the saliva spattered from his mouth glistened in the sunlight. He shook his finger at the woman.

She knelt before him, placing the baby on the floor beside her. She pleaded again—but now with both hands outstretched.

Suddenly, and without warning, the man with the wide-brimmed hat swung his sword, removing her head.

The boy watched as her head drifted like a feather to the floor. He looked away from the hole and screamed, yet there was no sound. The horror of what he had seen caused him to retch uncontrollably.

The little boy knew they heard him, even though there was no audible sound to his screams. Out of fear, he forced himself to look back through the hole. He avoided looking at his mother, but instead looked for his sister.

The man with the sword knelt and grasped the infant, lifting her. A silver cross slipped from under his tunic, reflecting the morning light.

The man handed his baby sister to a second person who appeared from an adjacent room and quickly disappeared out the front door.

The boy in the wall watched someone else enter the house behind the man with the sword. He was an older boy who looked him in the eye. He pointed at the hole in the wall and yelled something to the man with the sword.

The boy in the wall had been seen. Quickly, he moved back and replaced the knot in the wall. He screamed, holding his head in his hands, but there was no sound.

Aticus sat up, gasping for air. Painfully, he forced air into his lungs, fighting to live. He frantically kicked at the tarp draped over his body, or was it the shadowy figure of a man? Aticus reached for his chest, where he'd been stabbed, as the tears streamed down his face. The cart he sat on wobbled back and forth as he exerted himself and struggled to breathe. His vision was blurred, a kaleidoscope of vivid colors and glare. Aticus tried to scream, but all he could muster was a whine.

"Aticus!" He heard someone shout. It felt like his name, but it wasn't his name. That name drifted into obscurity as he heard someone shout again. "Aticus!"

He calmed himself and searched for the indistinct voice, his hands pressed against his chest. "Mother?" Aticus coughed and looked at the shifting form beside him, and then she touched him. "Mother?" he said again, envisioning her brown eyes forever burned into his memory.

Aticus shuddered as a cold, prickling sensation returned to his hands and feet. The vision played over and over of the sword glistening in the sunlight, striking his mother.

Or was it the sword he remembered impaled in his chest, and the man with a wide-brimmed hat standing over him?

His head pressed against someone; the sound of their heartbeat was soothing, and the warmth began spreading around his midsection. He felt a squeeze against his chest. Someone rubbed his leg. He saw blurs of color, but nothing made sense to him. The warmth felt right, and it became easier to breathe; the pain eased.

"Aticus, you're alive! Eladonia repeated, holding him close. "How is this possible, Bryce? How?" She stared at the dwarf, held Aticus near, and brushed his hair.

"I have no idea," Bryce commented, looking at the sky. "Thank you, God, thank you."

"He's cold," she said as she pulled the cloth tarp around him, holding him close. "How is this possible?" she uttered, staring around the dwarf.

"It's God's grace, my dear. A miracle." Bryce smiled as he rubbed Aticus' legs.

Veridian

Palias, Yung Sung, Lorna, Gilanthos, Aeotus, and Don arrived in Veridian early in the evening, before sunset.

Don excused himself to tend to a few essential matters that couldn't wait. He told them he might see them at the tavern later.

After dropping the horses off at the local stable, they went to the Skullduggery Inn to procure several rooms for the night.

Palias and Sung would share a room, as would Gilanthos and Aeotus.

Against Aeotus' judgment, Palias made it clear Lorna would have her own room for privacy. "I'm not sure that's a good idea, Palias. Someone needs to keep an eye on her."

"She'll be fine," Palias peered down at Aeotus. "Besides, will you share a room with a lady?" He pushed three gold coins across the counter as payment for the rooms and looked back at the innkeeper.

Aeotus narrowed his eyes, preparing to verbally assault the Asvernian when the innkeeper beat him to it.

"The cost of the rooms is three gold coins per room." He regarded Palias sternly.

Palias lifted his hand to stop Aeotus from talking and addressed the innkeeper, "What are you talking about? The rooms have always been one gold; the person you helped in front of us paid a single gold for their room."

"For you, it's three gold each; you're lucky I'm even letting you stay." The keeper stated callously.

"Palias leaned over the counter, "I'm lucky? What do you mean, I'm lucky?" His voice was low yet stern.

"You're Asvernian. That's what I mean." The keeper placed a hand beneath the wooden counter, reaching for a weapon.

Everyone in the lounge area of the inn watched Palias with disdain.

Aeotus touched Palias' muscular arm before speaking to the keeper. "Let me pay for the rooms, one gold each."

The keeper regarded Aeotus with similar disrespect. "If you're with him, then it's three gold." He tilted his head and cleared his throat, his hand still beneath the counter.

Aeotus' eyes widened, and his face flushed.

Gilanthos and Sung eyed one another, curious about the sudden disrespect of such a wealthy patron.

Palias reached into his pocket and pulled out six more gold coins. "It's fine, take them. We don't need any trouble."

"Trouble! He's an ass, Palias!" Aeotus looked at the large man with disbelief.

Palias glanced down at Aeotus while taking the room keys from the keeper. "He's not worth the trouble." He turned and walked away from the counter.

Aeotus lingered, leaning over the counter. "You want to wager I can take your arm off before you pull out whatever you're holding under the counter?" Aeotus ground his teeth together.

"We're out of hand towels and anything else you need, so don't come asking."

Gilanthos grabbed the back of Aeotus' tunic before he lunged over the counter.

"Da-ranato!" Aeotus swore at the keeper while his friend pulled him back.

"Aeo, stop! What do you think you're doing?" Gilanthos demanded, clenching his jaw, "Take a breath and calm down." He looked around the room at all the unwanted attention.

Aeotus moved to the side with Gilanthos and took a deep breath. "Sorry." He noticed Palias and Sung were already ascending the stairs to the rooms. Lorna stood near the steps, watching Aeotus.

Gilanthos tapped his friend on the chest. "Look, Palias put it behind him already. Let's put our gear away and get some food. Yes?" He looked into Aeotus' eyes for confirmation.

Aeotus nodded and frowned before letting his gaze drift back to Lorna. Her confused expression shifted to one of compassion. A nearby candle on the wall sconce illuminated Lorna's face, highlighting her golden eyes, which shimmered like a multifaceted emerald.

Aeotus felt a calmness settle over him as he looked at his friend. "Let's stow the bags and get to the Wet Stag. The night can't get any worse."

After dropping their belongings in their rooms, the five walked across the street to the Wet Stag. Palias and the others witnessed several disgruntled expressions from people passing by.

Yung Sung was the first to acknowledge his discomfort with the unwarranted attention. "I feel like I've done something wrong. Is anyone else getting the same impression?"

"Yes, I feel the people's distress," Gilanthos added.

"Everyone seems to be looking at you mostly, Palias." Lorna put her thoughts into speech.

When they entered the Wet Stag, an uneasiness settled in the room; they found a table in the center, close to where Normain had once sat.

Lorna gazed into a mirror on the nearby wall. Her face went pale, and her expression trembled.

Sung leaned closer to Lorna while the others chatted around the table. "Are you okay? You look sickly."

Lorna swallowed hard and glanced at Sung. Her eyes twitched, and a bead of sweat ran down her cheek.

Sung glanced in the mirror and back at her. "What is it?"

"I'm good. I don't like mirrors." Lorna wiped her face and looked around the tavern uncomfortably.

Sung got up and removed the mirror from the wall, placing it on the floor against the wall.

Lorna's posture relaxed, and she nodded at Sung in appreciation.

Uneasily, Palias glanced around for Collet. The patrons at nearby tables whispered in hushed tones and gasped when their eyes met the large man's.

"I feel like I need to walk out and come back in by myself," Aeotus stated, trying to break the uneasy atmosphere around the table. Suddenly, he scrunched his brows together as confusion formed on his face. His keen, elven ears picked up on a conversation nearby.

Gilanthos stared at Aeotus, "I heard them too, Aeo, let it be."

Aeotus glanced at Gilanthos before directing his attention toward a couple, two tables away. "This man is no murderer! Do not speak as if you know him because you do not!"

The man and woman promptly left the tavern, leaving payment on the table.

Palias watched Aeotus, surprised the elf would come to his defense for a second time tonight.

Gilanthos held his head in his hands, studying the table's wood grain.

"Does your head hurt again?" Sung asked.

"No," Gilanthos whispered.

Aeotus took in a deep breath and looked at Gilanthos. "No, his head doesn't hurt. I embarrass him."

Palias continued to analyze Aeotus. "What did they say?"

"It's not what they said. It's what everyone is saying." Aeotus looked at Palias. "I've heard more than one person accuse you of killing the king."

"What?" Palias met the gaze of several patrons before inquiring, "King?"

Gilanthos answered before Aeotus could, his head still in his hands. "King Balen Duskwater, lord of the seven cities and protector of the realm, guardian of the gateway into Idonia, and father of the future king Tamen." Gilanthos laid his hands on the table, looking into Palias' dark eyes. "They say the Asvernians killed their king."

Uncomfortably, Lorna let her gaze drift around the room. The atmosphere was palpable with contempt. A part of her felt thankful she was not the center of attention.

Aeotus nodded and sat back in his chair, content with what Gilanthos shared.

Sung looked around the tavern. "I wonder if that's why we haven't seen Collet." He looked at Palias. Their eyes met. "He and the king are brothers."

"You mean were, that's what you meant," Aeotus interjected.

They sat at the table for nearly half an hour, and no one came to see if they needed anything. Palias was about to suggest they go when Collet bolted through the kitchen door. He searched the room and found them. Collet hurried over, nearly knocking someone out of their chair.

"My friends, how are you doing?" Collet raised his hands out wide. "When did you get in? I came as quick as I could when I heard you were all here."

Palias remained silent.

Sung was quick to answer. "We haven't been here long."

"Good, good." He patted Sung on the back. "Anyone got your drink orders yet?"

"No, not yet," Gilanthos stated, his eyes darting between Collet and Palias, neither of whom had acknowledged the other.

"Have you seen Eladonia and the others come through in the last few days?" Aeotus couldn't refrain from asking any longer.

Collet's composure changed. "They did two days ago. Bryce said you'd be along." He put his hands on Sung and Palias' shoulders. "I'm sorry about Aticus." He shook his head and glanced at the table, hesitant about what to say next.

"It was quite a shock to us all, but thank you, Collet, for your kindness and generosity," Sung commented.

Collet addressed the group, avoiding eye contact with Palias. "How are the rest of you doing?" He let his gaze rest on the large man when he finished his question.

Palias let his eyes drift to the side and over to Collet. He wasn't sure how to apologize for the death of Collet's brother, the king, without sounding like it was his fault.

"Palias, could I speak with you in private?" Collet asked.

"Of course," Palias responded, his eyes narrowed.

"You can help me get the ale; I've got a special bottle of gnomish mead you might enjoy." Collet and Palias walked together toward the kitchen.

"He's quite cheerful for someone who's lost his brother," Aeotus vocalized after Collet was out of earshot; he sneered at a patron sitting at a nearby table.

"We all deal with loss in different ways," Lorna added.

"Now, you're going to speak?" Aeotus criticized her.

"Aeotus, why do you have to be so blunt?" Sung challenged, leaning on the table.

"I am not blunt; I simply say what I mean." Aeotus inclined on the table, mimicking Sung.

Gilanthos put his head back in his hands, resting his elbows on the table. "My head hurts."

Collet and Palias walked through the kitchen door and downstairs into the cellar. Collet started the conversation as they stepped into the cellar. "I wanted to speak with you alone, Palias." He turned to face the large man towering over him by nearly two hands." I needed you to know that I hold no ill will toward you or your people."

A look of confusion washed over Palias' face. "I've never gotten the impression from you, Collet, and I'm sorry for the loss of your brother, King Balen."

Collet nodded, "And I'm sorry for your loss."

Palias' forehead creased.

Collet rubbed his chin and squinted his eyes. "You haven't heard yet," he uttered to himself.

Palias' eyes narrowed. "I don't understand."

Collet shifted where he stood before he placed his hand on Palias' arm, "Your mother and father were killed. I was afraid you didn't know yet. I'm sorry, Palias."

The large man's face contorted, "How?"

"Murdered in their sleep." He moved back to give Palias space. "I'm sorry."

Palias ran his hands across his bare head and looked around the room. His breathing became rapid and profound. "Who? Who did it? I have to return home—find my brothers." He mumbled to himself, thinking aloud.

"There is more." Collet took a step back.

Palias let his hands drop as he focused his attention on the innkeeper. "What?"

"After your parents died, Balen was accused of ordering their assassination. Not long after, my brother and the queen were found assassinated. From what I understand, they obtained incriminating evidence indicating it was, in fact, your people who killed Balen."

Palias turned in place. "I don't understand; our people have always had peace." The large man looked around the room, thinking. "Father always communicated openly with King Balen and even offered our ships if war came to Meloorne and the other cities." Palias sat on a crate; it creaked under the strain of his weight. "I don't know what to do. I'm sorry about your brother, Collet, but we did not do this. You have to believe me." He placed his hand in his trouser pocket and felt the outline of the book he found in Oppack.

"I do, my friend, I do." Collet patted Palias on the arm.

"I need to return home; I have no idea if my brothers know." Palias looked at Collet. "Do you have a way of contacting Meloorne? I may have proof that someone is assassinating the authorities of the realm."

Collet looked around the room. "I may know someone who can help us."

Chapter Fifty

VERIDIAN

Aeotus abruptly stood from his chair, causing Lorna to flinch. "I can't take the waiting, and the incessant mumbling is more than I care to deal with." He looked around the tavern. "We won't get food or drink tonight, so I am retiring." He glanced at Gilanthos and moved from his chair.

"Agreed. I have some rations in the room, we can eat." Gilanthos stood from the table, his chair scraping along the floor.

Sung studied the elves and Lorna, "I'll wait here for Palias."

Lorna looked at Sung. "I think I'll stay as well—for the food."

"Fine by me, suit yourself." Aeotus turned toward the door. "She has a room of her own." He commented, walking away.

Gilanthos shrugged and followed his friend.

Sung sighed and glanced at Lorna, his forehead creased, "What?" He noticed Lorna watching the elves as they left the tavern.

"There's something about him that's so familiar."

"Aeotus?" Sung asked.

"Yes."

"It must be difficult not remembering," he added.

"I see reflections of faces and locations, but not much makes sense. Occasionally, I have clarity of thought, but it escapes me as quickly as it comes." Lorna glanced up. "Here comes Palias."

Sung turned to see his friend shuffling across the room. His shoulders drooped low, eyes glossed over. He looked like a broken man. Concerned, Sung arose from his chair to meet Palias as he approached the table. "What's wrong? Is everything alright?"

Palias sat down and rested his arms on the table. "Collet informed me that my parents are dead." He took a deep breath.

Aeotus and Gilanthos crossed the street and entered the inn. The innkeeper was draped over the counter, smirking. Aeotus scowled at him and proceeded toward the stairs.

Four men sat around a table in the lobby, drinking and playing cards, none of whom acknowledged them.

The two ascended the stairs and approached their room. "I hate human cities," Aeotus uttered so only Gilanthos could hear.

Aeotus opened the door to their room and observed a man in brown pants and a green shirt digging through his pack bag. "What are you…" Aeotus didn't see what struck him in the face. The impact thrust him into the door, hurling it open and knocking him onto the floor.

Before Gilanthos could react, someone pushed him from behind. Even with his keen elven hearing, he hadn't heard anyone ascend the stairs, and he knew none of the other doors in the hall had opened. The elf slammed into the door facing and turned to meet his assailant. There were two men behind him; both were playing cards downstairs a moment ago. One man sported a trimmed beard; the second was bald.

Inside the room, Aeotus struggled to stand. His jaw throbbed from the contact with an unseen assailant's hand.

A man with a large scar above his left eye emptied the contents of Aeotus' bag onto the bed—he was looking for something.

Aeotus rolled to the side and stood in time to fend off an attack from the man who slammed him into the door. He had a similar build to the one rifling through his belongings, but he was from Satsun, the same island as Yung Sung. Aeotus blocked a left-handed attack but was not so lucky when his ribs took a direct hit from the man's right foot. The impact lifted Aeotus into the air and back into the door again.

Gilanthos rushed the bearded man in the hall. He swung his fist, but the individual easily dodged to the right, letting the force of Gilanthos' momentum throw him off balance. The bearded man landed a barrage of fist strikes on the elf's side and back, taking the breath from him. Gilanthos attempted to bring his elbow down, but the man sidestepped. Now, Gilanthos had an attacker behind him and in front of him.

Aeotus bounced back and stooped, avoiding another left hook. He brought his fist around and contacted the assailant, pressing him back long enough to glimpse the man rifling through his belongings. He held the red gemstone in his hand.

Aeotus reacted swiftly, searching for something to use as a weapon. He grabbed an oil lamp resting on a nearby table and hurled it at the man holding the red diamond. The glass container struck him in the face, shattering on impact, blinding him. He dropped the gemstone onto the bed, backing away, grasping his face.

Aeotus lunged forward, pushing the man through the second-story window, smashing the shutters as he fell to the street below. The last thing Aeotus saw was the red gemstone balancing on the bed when a well-placed foot to the head robbed him of consciousness.

Gilanthos landed a punch on the bald man's face, but his attack was short-lived as the bearded man quickly grabbed him from behind, trapping him in a headlock. Gilanthos struggled to break free while he kicked at the bald man to keep him at bay.

Sung heard screams from outside and ran to the window.

"What is it?" Palias inquired.

Sung pushed around a patron sitting near the window for a better look. "Something's happening across the street at the inn. A man's lying in the street, and it appears someone has fallen out of a window." Sung turned to face the two; his eyes widened in surprise. "It's Gilanthos and Aeotus' room." Before he could finish his words, he bolted for the door.

Palias stood and glanced through the window. From his vantage, he could see little.

Lorna watched Sung run for the door.

Sung had to squeeze sideways as he ran through the door to avoid knocking over two men entering the Wet Stag. The two men were dressed in black, one in a robe and the second in black leather armor with two long daggers fastened to a belt at his side.

Lorna's eyes widened when she saw the two men Sung slipped by, and they recognized her.

Gilanthos took copious punches to the abdomen. Pain shot through his midsection, stealing his breath as he deflected several strikes with his knees, but the bearded man held him fast from behind. His assailant pulled Gilanthos down the hall and away from the steps. He kicked, using the man who held him as leverage, but the fatigue set in. It was only a matter of time before Gilanthos would lose consciousness, and he knew it. Continuing to be pulled down the hall and past their room, he noticed Aeotus sprawled on the floor, face down. Another man stood over his friend's body. He held the red stone in his hand with a look of satisfaction etched on his face.

Lorna leaped from her chair, her mouth twisted. "Palias!" She pointed at the two men who stopped inside the door. "They're here for me!"

Palias looked at the two men before peering out the window. He knew Sung would need his help.

The man in robes settled into a defensive stance and started chanting, shifting his hands exaggeratedly as if he were tracing an invisible line that only he could see.

Palias knew he was preparing a spell and acted. He lunged forward as people scattered to far corners of the tavern, overturning tables and chairs and spreading food across the floor.

In black leather armor, the second man sidestepped around the mage and placed himself between Palias and the spellcaster. He removed two long daggers from his belt and planted his feet. A green hue emanated from behind him.

Sung entered the inn. The keeper stood behind the counter, a look of fear carved deep across his face. Sung could hear a struggle coming from upstairs. Two men sat at tables in the lobby. Sung knew from their expressions that they had no connection with what was happening.

He sprinted for the stairs, taking two steps at a time. When he reached the second floor, he observed a bald man striking Gilanthos. A second bearded man had the elf in a headlock, pulling him down the hall. That man saw Sung, but Sung was on them before he could warn his comrade.

Palias rushed the man, brandishing the daggers. He preferred to have had a weapon on him, but used what he could and grabbed a chair to bring to the fight. He pulled the chair back, prepared to hurl it, but before he could, a burst of jade light spread over Palias; instantly, he lost consciousness. The giant man crashed onto the floor with such force that it knocked objects off the wall. He came to rest at the feet of the duel-wielding adversary. The chair he dropped slid into a nearby table.

Lorna started to back away as the two men advanced on her.

Sung struck the bald man below his ear, stopping the blood flow and dropping him to the ground.

The bearded man threw Gilanthos aside and pulled out a small knife, then threw it at Yung Sung.

Sung sidestepped left, letting the knife pass him. The blade slammed into the ceiling of the stairwell as it clattered down the steps behind him. He advanced, removing a small metal star from his shirt, and hurled it at the bearded man.

The bearded man lifted his hand, deflecting the shuriken with two fingers and thrusting it into the wall near Gilanthos' head.

Sung closed in on the man. The two exchanged punches, but neither seemed to have an advantage.

Gilanthos held his neck, gasping for air. He noticed another man stepping into the hall behind Sung, and he had the gemstone. Gilanthos realized Sung wouldn't know about the incoming threat. Pressed against the wall to keep from getting struck by the two men fighting, he grabbed the shuriken embedded in the wall and thrust it into the bearded man's leg.

Sung took advantage and struck the man with an open palm, breaking his nose.

Gilanthos grabbed the man's legs, tripping him. "Sung, behind you!"

That was enough time for Sung to dodge to the side and bring his foot up, striking the assailant, causing him to drop the gemstone behind him. Sung turned to face his new attacker.

Gilanthos climbed on the collapsed man, ready to strike. His glazed expression revealed he was no longer a threat.

Sung and the man in black exchanged punches.

Gilanthos turned to see the bald man wake, then retrieved the gemstone that had been balancing beside him on the floor. He had it and was down the stairs before Gilanthos could stand. "Sung, he's getting away with the gem! I can't get to him!"

Sung found himself evenly matched against the new opponent, who used the same technique that Master Tau had taught him.

Lorna struggled to pull away from the leather-clad man. He had her by the hair, yanking her toward the tavern door. She screamed for help, but no one came to her defense. She reached for Palias as they dragged her past.

Collet burst from the kitchen, small sword in hand. "Let her go!"

The man in leather threw one of his daggers across the room, striking Collet in the shoulder and knocking him down behind the bar.

"Stop! Let me go!" Lorna fought to pull away. "Help me!" she yelled at a man cowering behind a chair.

"You've got unfinished work," the mage remarked as the assassin dragged her toward the door.

"Palias!" she yelled, hoping her cries would wake the slumbering giant.

"He won't be helping you," her assaulter commented as they passed through the door and into the street.

"Sung, I need to get past!" Gilanthos struggled to find a way around the onslaught of feet and hands, but couldn't.

Sung slammed into the wall, trying to avoid getting punched. He crouched, avoiding his opponent's right foot.

The man in black flicked his hand, and a small knife emerged from beneath his sleeve. The two continued to exchange blows, slamming into walls.

The confident smile of Sung's attacker troubled Gilanthos. Sung wasn't smiling; it was all he could do to avoid being struck.

Sung moved his head to the left. His assailant's knife embedded itself into the wall beside Sung's face. He took advantage of the mistake and struck his arm, dislodging the knife mechanism from his wrist and leaving the weapon stuck in the wall.

Although the action helped disarm his opponent, it left his right side vulnerable to attack. Sung took a blow to the ribs, cracking more than one. Cheated of his breath, Sung fought the pain and exchanged another volley of palms.

Don stood in the street as the assassin dragged Lorna out of the tavern. "I suggest you release her," he said defiantly.

The assassin inspected Don and threw Lorna to the ground. He lifted his dagger, challenging her new champion.

The man in the black robe appeared behind the assassin and chanted in a rhythmic tone.

Lorna scrambled away, backing into a vendor cart in the street.

"Don't go far; this won't take long," the leather-clad assassin addressed her.

The people in the street retreated out of harm's way but remained spectators.

The assassin lunged at Don, leading with his dagger.

Don leaped to the side, hoisting his sword to deflect the deadly assault. He glimpsed the mage, casting his spell from the open door of the tavern, and acted. Don pulled a silver dagger from his boot and threw it at the robed figure, striking him in the chest. The impact pushed him back into the building and out of view.

The assassin lunged with his dagger, but Don blocked the attack and sidestepped left. Regardless, the man landed a solid kick on Don, pushing him further into the street. Don regained his footing, only to see a bald man emerging from the inn across the street, similarly to his current adversary. He drew a dagger, ready to join the fight and help his comrade.

Sung grabbed the man's arm and used his knee to parry a kick. The assassin had an open hand and began striking Sung in the torso. More ribs cracked, and Sung buckled to one knee.

Gilanthos rushed to help, but before he could get to the man, the tip of a sword emerged from the assassin's chest.

The assailant coughed blood and gasped at Sung. His body went limp, revealing Aeotus standing behind the assassin, holding his sword.

Sung slumped to the side as the man fell forward, crumpling against the wall.

Gilanthos glanced at Aeotus and pointed at the stairs, "They have the stone."

Aeotus glanced back at the steps as he rushed back into the room toward the window, sword in hand. Don was in the street, fighting with another assassin. Aeotus climbed out the window on the roof and jumped onto the street, landing near the bald man, holding the gemstone. The assassin, taken by surprise, paused at the sudden appearance of the elf.

Don used the distraction to roll to the side of his opponent, stabbing the assassin in the side and ending the fight.

Aeotus sprang at the bald man, swinging his sword. The two parried one another before Gilanthos emerged from the inn, tackling the assassin to the ground, knocking the gemstone from his hand, and onto the street.

From a crouched position, Don watched the red diamond land near him, balancing on its tip. His brows folded as he recalled the last time he saw the Bloodstone. He was ten, and his father passed it to the Hands of the Shadow.

Gilanthos and the bald man rolled in the dirt until it ended with the assassin straddling him, his knife poised to strike.

Aeotus swung his sword across the assassin's back, cutting deep and allowing Gilanthos to overpower the wounded man, pushing him to the side. The assassin stumbled away and retreated down the street and between two buildings.

"Thanks," Gilanthos said, dusting himself off.

"He was going to kill us for that." Aeotus pointed at the gemstone balancing on the dirt street. That's when he realized Don's gaze was fixed on the gem. Kicking dirt, Aeotus rushed and retrieved the artifact, placing it in his pocket.

The two men stared at one another awkwardly. "What's that?" Don asked.

"Nothing. A family heirloom," Aeotus responded.

Gilanthos glanced up at the window and saw Yung Sung holding his side in pain.

Don stood, patting the dirt from his pants and placing his sword back into its casing. He recognized something on the assassin's neck. He knelt over and pulled his hair to the side, revealing a tattoo of a black hand. "You've pissed the wrong people off, friend."

"What is it?" Aeotus approached, favoring his jaw and temple. "What is that on his neck?"

"You don't want to know." Don looked at the elf, resting his gaze on his pocket containing the Bloodstone.

Chapter Fifty-One

SHANDAR

Aticus knelt over the campfire, warming his hands. The morning brought a familiar, calming coolness he didn't anticipate. The forest of Shandar was the last place he wanted to be, but he was okay with that today. He was pleased to be anywhere after waking from the dead.

Aticus watched Eladonia sleep, paying attention to her gentle breathing. His mind wandered back to the days in Dewbrook, when he anxiously waited for any sign of life from her. He sat down, took a deep breath, and placed his hand on his chest. He felt the thumping of his heart as memories flooded his mind of the last moments he recalled before everything went dark.

"Why didn't you wake me for my watch?" Eladonia asked. She sat up, pulled her legs close, and rested her arms on her knees.

Startled, Aticus looked at Eladonia. "I didn't know you were awake."

"You seemed distracted." She looked at Bryce, who was still snoring. The hairs in his beard and mustache shifted with each breath.

Aticus crossed his legs. "I didn't feel like sleeping."

Eladonia tilted her head and regarded Aticus. "I know what you mean. What did it feel like for you?"

He shook his head and stared into her azure eyes. "I forgot how blue your eyes were," he said, trying to avoid the question.

Uncomfortable, Eladonia avoided his gaze and watched Bryce. "What was it like?"

"Nothing," Aticus said, with a huff. "It was like there was nothing." He swallowed hard before speaking. "Everything went dark, and then I woke. What was it like for you?"

"I remember everything." She regarded Aticus through squinted eyes. "I remember everything you said. You talked about memories of when the Alarians found you and how Nicholas took you in."

Aticus' face flushed while he watched the flickering flames dance.

"I remember the pain you spoke of when he died and the helplessness you endured." Eladonia tilted her head, trying to see into his eyes. "You shared with me how alone you were. Aticus, know that you are not alone."

He looked at her with glazed eyes, his mouth contorted to the side. "I didn't know you could hear all that."

"I'm sorry, Aticus. I'm sorry I couldn't help you like you helped me." Eladonia's shoulders sank.

Aticus straightened himself and wiped his eyes. "You were there for me; you were the last person I saw."

A sniffle from across the campfire distracted Aticus and Eladonia. Bryce sat with his legs crossed. "That was beautiful," Bryce commented, wiping his eyes and looking into the trees above.

Aticus glanced at the dwarf and chuckled.

"Good morning, Bryce," Eladonia added.

"Is anyone else hungry?" Bryce asked. "I have some dried meat and fruit in my pack." Bryce stood up awkwardly and shuffled to his bag near a tree.

"Your bag!" Eladonia exclaimed, looking at Aticus. She hurried to her saddlebag, draped over a fallen log, and pulled out Aticus' brown sack. It held all of his belongings.

A wave of relief washed over him when he noticed the pouch.

Eladonia handed it to him. "This is everything."

Aticus opened the bag and rummaged around inside. He removed his knife and admired it. Next, he pulled his medallion out and placed the silver necklace around his neck. "Thank you," he said with a smile.

Bryce returned with dried beef wrapped in cloth and a container of dried fruit. "Let's have some breakfast before deciding where we're going."

"Where are we going?" Aticus inquired.

"I said after we eat," Bryce declared with a warm smile.

Aticus ignored him. "When are you going to Evermoure?" he asked Eladonia, fearful of her answer.

She looked at Aticus, and a smile spread across her lips. "I'm not going."

Aticus' eyes widened. "What? Why not? I mean, good—I..."

Eladonia's smile broadened at his response. "I thought I might see what Aeo and Gil wanted to do."

Aticus' chest felt like it had dropped into his stomach. "Oh. Aeotus and Gilanthos?" he asked, realizing she didn't expect to stay with him and Bryce.

Bryce, oblivious to the conversation, handed out meat and fruit. Aticus heard the dwarf speak, but didn't listen to what he said.

Aticus' brows folded in, and he sniffed. He tilted his head around, trying to capture the aroma. "Can you smell that?"

Bryce looked at the dried meat. "I smell the beef."

"No, it's something else. Burnt wood?" Aticus questioned. A breeze carried the scent.

"I smell it," Eladonia added.

Bryce was about to speak, but Aticus held up his hand. "Do you hear that?"

Eladonia and Bryce looked at one another.

"I don't hear anything," Eladonia said.

Bryce shook his head, "Me either."

"There it is again." Aticus turned from side to side as he stood. "I hear someone screaming!"

CHAPTER FIFTY-TWO

HANDS OF THE SHADOW

S omewhere in the world,

Deep beneath the mountains of Kandar, hidden among the tunnels of the Kalindrea monastery, the Hands of the Shadow remain hidden from the world.

JoJung sat in his chair behind an ornate desk. He gazed at the fire that burned in the stone hearth.

His room was filled with exquisite furniture from across Idonia. The desk from the halls of Rocton was once used by King Eston. His chairs and bed, made by a gnomish woodworker, were gathered from the ruins of Talamar. Other items included a table given as a gift by the orc king, Aldamead, with paintings from Dreandan and artifacts collected from the undead city of Satsun.

JoJung contemplated his next move when a knock at the door distracted him.

"Enter," JoJung said.

Zander stepped inside and closed the door behind him. The dwarf wore a brown tunic and leather pants. His expression was void of emotion. "They found them," he said.

JoJung stood, supporting himself with his hands on the desk. "Where? Did they recover the Bloodstone?" He clenched his teeth. "Is my son with them?"

Zander brushed his almond beard with his hand. "Our scouts found them in Veridian. We had the Bloodstone, but lost it."

"Lost it; how?" JoJung raised his voice.

"Now, now," Zander pleaded and held up his hands. "We had a second group of scouts that engaged them this morning outside Veridian, though they also failed to retrieve the Bloodstone; we severely injured several of them."

"A second group failed to seize the Bloodstone as well?" JoJung asked.

"We have them on the run. The group had no sleep and left Veridian before dawn. There were two elves, an Asvernian, the Ancient woman, and Yung Sung." The dwarf walked over to the desk. "There's another individual who unexpectedly helped them as well."

"Another? Who?" JoJung asked.

"The vampire hunter's son, Don." Zander took in a breath.

"Samuel's son?" JoJung questioned and sat down.

"Yes."

JoJung waved his hand, dismissing Zander's concern about Don. "Yung Sung is with them?" JoJung asked more to himself than Zander.

"We've dispatched another Hand to Veridian should they return." Zander tilted his head to the side to get a better view of JoJung. "Did you hear me?"

"Yes, I heard. You've sent a Hand," JoJung repeated back.

"We have a contact in Veridian who suggested they're traveling north toward Shandar. Several villages surround the forest, so I dispatched additional Hands if they stop."

JoJung shook his head. "What's Michael doing?"

"He's feeding again. The same thing he always does when he gets upset with you." Zander strode in front of the hearth and watched the crackling flames.

"I've told him to be careful about gorging here," JoJung voiced angrily.

"Since when has Michael listened to any of us?" Zander shifted. "You know you were wrong. Letting Neacrom use the Bloodstone was reckless." The dwarf looked into JoJung's eyes while he spoke.

"I know. I hoped Neacrom would've given us the army of undead we needed." JoJung slumped back in his chair.

"You burned that connection when you killed his family," Zander added.

JoJung took in a deep breath. "I understand that, but he was never supposed to discover it was us. We still have no idea where the leak came from."

"You, not the council." Zander corrected JoJung. "It was your pride that put us in the situation we're in now."

JoJung closed his eyes and raised his chin, letting his head roll back into the chair. "Everything I've—we've done has been undermined somehow." He opened his eyes and looked at Zander. "I assume it's Michael working against us for his own agenda."

Zander ignored JoJung's statement by deflecting the conversation. "I was going to wait until our meeting to update everyone on Meloorne, but I can tell you now. Rath contacted me to let us know everything is going according to plan. He has the ear of Prince Timan and control of the northern kingdom." Zander smiled. "At least one thing is working according to plan."

"And the Asvernians?" JoJung asked.

"Reports from Asvernia indicate their kingdom is still reeling from the deaths of their king and queen. However, our spies report that one of the royal sons has returned and taken guardianship of the throne." Zander tapped his finger on the desk. "It's imperative that we retrieve the Bloodstone and the Ancient. We have the dwarven king to deal with in Kandar." Zander held his fingers still. "What are we going to do about Michael?"

You let me worry about Michael. You find the Bloodstone."

Zander nodded, "That's what concerns me."

Chapter Fifty-Three

DEATH IN SHANDAR

Aticus looked from side to side, searching for the screams. "The cries are coming from that way," he said, pointing toward the northern trail.

"I hear the sounds, but it's drifting with the wind." Eladonia glanced at Bryce.

"I hear it, too," Bryce added, nodding.

"How did Aticus hear that before me?" Eladonia questioned Bryce.

Bryce shrugged, looking out the corner of his eye.

"It sounds like a woman." Aticus moved around, hoping to understand better where the scream was coming from. He stared at Bryce and Eladonia. "The screaming—it stopped."

Eladonia shifted her eyes, trying to reacquire the sound. "I can't hear anything now."

"The two of you go, I'll break camp and catch up," Bryce said, gathering items and throwing them in his pack. "What are you waiting for?" Bryce questioned.

Aticus stared at Bryce. "Do you smell something burning?"

"No." Bryce straightened. "Go now; someone may need help."

Aticus nodded and considered Eladonia.

"I don't smell anything burning." Eladonia studied Aticus, a look of concern etched on her face.

Aticus retrieved his sword, strapping it around his waist. "You'll be okay, Bryce?"

"Yes, I've been by myself for far longer than you've been alive; now go." He waved the two away with both hands and thought about what he said.

Eladonia fastened her swords to her back and leaped onto Kora. She rubbed the horse's neck and spurred her forward.

Aticus climbed in the saddle and urged his mount to follow Kora and Eladonia.

Bryce shook his head. "God be with them."

Aticus and Eladonia galloped down the trail for some time before a trace scent of smoke turned them down a westward path.

It wasn't long after that when they entered a clearing in the forest used by the Alarians. The sight of smoldering wagons confirmed Aticus's worst fear.

Eladonia stilled Kora. "I'm sorry, Aticus."

Aticus held the horse's reins tight as he navigated into the ruined campsite and counted all the wagons. His chest pounded. "They're all dead," he said, leaning against the neck of his horse as he fought to breathe.

The surroundings were eerily silent as Aticus scanned the bodies, tears streaming down his cheeks. The Alarians were all dead, felled by an arrow or struck down by the sword.

He recognized everyone: men, women, and children. Terra's two sisters rested in their mother's arms, and their father lay nearby.

Aticus examined the carnage. "They fought back," he said, looking at goblin bodies near some of the protector's corpses.

"Aticus," Eladonia said, trying to get his attention.

He slid out of the saddle and stood beside his horse. Aticus swallowed hard, took a deep breath, and began sobbing.

"Aticus," Eladonia pleaded, her heart ached for him.

He walked into the center of the wagons and examined each gruesome scene. Aticus played out what happened as he said their names. He knelt to regain his composure, or at best, to recover his breath.

Among the dead were Cantor and Sophia, his back opened and face down in her lap. The tip of an arrow had extinguished her spark. His father's wagon, or what remained of the newlywed couple's belongings, was smoking behind them.

Aticus noticed Talon, a middle-aged protector. He was near his oldest son; no doubt they had gathered together for reassurance when the end came.

Eladonia stayed on Kora's back and watched Aticus pass from corpse to corpse, wagon by wagon, as he knelt and sobbed. Her eyes glossed over as she watched him.

Aticus found the food wagon where he had sat all those years with Rictor. That's when he heard movement on the other side. He drew his sword and cautiously moved around to investigate.

Eladonia reacted and dismounted, pulling the twin swords from their sheaths as she moved in his direction.

Aticus stepped around the wagon and found Rictor slumped against the wagon wheel. Rictor coughed. He ran to the old man and dropped his sword. "Rictor!" Aticus tenderly cradled the man's face in his hands. "Rictor, it's me."

Rictor moaned and tried to open his eyes. His breaths were shallow, and fresh blood trickled from the corner of his mouth.

"What happened?" Aticus asked Rictor, realizing the wound he had sustained was to his gut. Rictor rested his hands on his abdomen, wincing with each painful breath. Eladonia walked around the end of the wagon as he examined the wound.

"Goblins..." A painful cough prompted Rictor to contort in pain, and fresh blood poured from his mouth. "They took...Vandeer...Terra." He swallowed the blood in his mouth to speak. "Everyone dead?" he asked, closing his eyes.

Aticus nodded before speaking. "Vandeer and Terra were alive?" Aticus questioned, touching Rictor on the arm to keep him alert.

Rictor slowly nodded, his eyes shut as he spoke. "They were...when the goblins took them," he whispered. His head slumped to the side as his last breath escaped.

"Rictor! Rictor!" Aticus cradled Rictor's head, willing him to open his eyes. "Rictor."

"He's gone. I'm sorry." Eladonia tried to console Aticus. "What can I do?"

Aticus slumped back onto his backside and crossed his legs. He rocked back and forth as he sobbed into his hands.

Eladonia stepped near him; she wanted to hold him. "What can I do?"

Aticus stopped rocking and looked at her through tear-filled eyes. "Help me kill them. Kill them all."

Aticus, Eladonia, and Bryce gathered the Alarians and placed them in their wagons, with each family together, and then began filling the wagons with dried brush and wood.

Aticus threw a handful of twigs into the back of a wagon. "When the goblins see the fires and return, we'll be waiting." Aticus studied his friends. "I need to find Terra and Vandeer. They have to be alive."

Bryce took a deep breath while he gathered sticks. "Revenge should not be an option," Bryce said.

"It's the only option, Bryce." He regarded the Alarian wagons around them. "They can't avenge themselves, so I'll do it for them."

"Eladonia, you must talk sense into Aticus. Help him understand this is wrong," Bryce pleaded with her. "We have no idea how many goblins there are."

Eladonia watched Aticus collect more vegetation. "I'm going to help him, no matter how many there are." She glanced at Bryce. "We need to stop the goblins, or they will continue killing innocent people who come into the forest."

"Killing never resolved anything," Bryce added. "Killing leads to more killing."

"They're vermin," Eladonia whispered as Aticus approached with a handful of branches and tossed them in a nearby wagon, pausing after he finished.

"They are living creatures." Bryce waited for Aticus to walk away before he continued. "I care about what happened to these people. They should not have died, but I cannot in good conscience encourage further bloodshed in the name of vengeance." Bryce shook his head. "Not every goblin is bad."

"I've never met a good one," Eladonia added.

Eladonia and Bryce continued looking for dried wood.

"Bryce, I respect what you advocate and do not hold you in contempt for your beliefs." Eladonia knelt alongside the dwarf. "It makes you who you are, and I would never expect you to change." She squeezed his arm gently.

Bryce looked into Eladonia's eyes and straightened. "Good, because I won't change."

"I think you should return to the path near the forest's edge and wait for the others," Eladonia said.

Bryce let his brows crease inward, "I can't leave the two of you alone again."

"I assure you, I won't let anything happen to him." Eladonia let her eyes drift to Aticus. "Not again."

As midmorning approached, the three finished preparing the bodies, and Aticus set the wagons on fire. He stopped at each wagon one by one in remembrance of each family.

As the wagons burned, the three stood silently, paying their respects to the fallen Alarians. Aticus had no tears left, only resolution.

Bryce said his goodbyes before retreating the way they had come, back to the forest's edge. "Both of you, be careful," Bryce exclaimed, adjusting in the saddle.

"We will," Eladonia responded reassuringly.

"Remember, our choices define us," Bryce told Aticus.

Aticus nodded. "I've made my choice, and I'm fine with that."

Bryce pulled on the reins and spurred his horse down the path.

Aticus glanced at Eladonia. He watched her golden hair fluttering in the breeze. "Are you ready?"

Eladonia nodded and placed her hands on her hips. "I'm ready."

Aticus knelt and watched as the flames engulfed the wagons. "My memories of these people, my people, have brought me pain. I was never really accepted by them, but they tolerated me. Is it wrong that I feel so much anguish for their loss yet feel free?"

Eladonia did not answer. She knew there was nothing she could say that would make a difference.

"What if we're too late to save Terra and Vandeer?" Aticus asked, standing up and looking at her.

"If they were going to kill them, we would have found them here." Eladonia placed her hand on Aticus' back. "Come, we'll hide on the other side of the clearing over there." She pointed toward the eastern trail.

Aticus and Eladonia tied their horses in the forest north of the clearing and took a watchful position near the path. The whining and popping of the wagons burning was the only sound in the forest clearing.

Aticus and Eladonia sat behind two towering oak trees, using them as camouflage. Half an hour had passed, and still, there was no sign of the goblins. The flames from several wagons had collapsed, creating multiple pyres, and dense smoke billowed above the forest.

Aticus sat with his legs crossed, elbows on knees, supporting his head. "I don't understand why we haven't seen anyone. The fires should have worked," he said without looking at Eladonia.

"It was a good plan, Aticus, and it may still work. We need to give it more time." Eladonia considered her swords lying on the ground by her side.

"Maybe we should go look for Terra and Vandeer." Aticus nervously stood and used his sword to strike a bush near his feet. "It shouldn't be hard to track their trail."

"Give it more time." Eladonia tried to calm Aticus. "If we don't hear anything soon, we can go looking."

Aticus ran his hand through his hair. "Fine." He sagged against the tree and peeked around a bush. "What am I doing?" He let his head lean against the tree and watched ants crawl among the wooded ridges in the bark. "Why did they have to die?" He glanced back at the flames in the clearing and followed the smoke drifting into the sky. "Why does it hurt so bad?"

"They were the nearest thing you had to a family. It is natural for you to feel this way." Eladonia moved beside Aticus.

Their eyes met. "Is it normal for a family to treat each other like they treated me?" Aticus asked.

"For some families, yes."

The footsteps and high-pitched chattering drew their attention back to the path. "It worked," Aticus whispered, gripping his sword.

Eladonia retrieved her swords. "Get down," she whispered.

The two watched as a group of eight goblins entered the clearing.

"See, I say I see a fire," the tallest goblin confirmed.

"Who makes these fires?" another asked.

The eight goblins stayed close as they proceeded into the clearing, scanning the area for movement.

"Where are the bodies of the humans?" spoke a third, much smaller goblin. The question had the creatures looking around the area.

The goblins split up and watched the wagons engulfed in flames. "I not see them."

Another goblin knelt beside the smoldering pyre. "The gypsies are here, in the fire. I smell them." He inhaled and used his tongue to taste the air.

"Who burned them?" asked one of the creatures.

"Some of them lived!" One goblin hissed as they drew their swords and snorted at one another.

"We tell Toak; he needs to know someone lives," one goblin with a limp said, cautiously moving onto the path.

Aticus was about to rush the goblins when Eladonia stopped him.

"If we follow, they might lead us back to the others and your friends."

Aticus grimaced and glanced back and forth between her and the goblins. "Fine." He locked his jaw so he wouldn't say anything.

The two watched as the other creatures stepped in behind the lead goblin and ambled back down the trail.

Aticus and Eladonia followed through the forest, keeping off the path and out of earshot.

The constant rambling between three goblins helped to cover any sounds they might have heard from their shadows in the forest.

CHAPTER FIFTY-FOUR

DON

Don stood in the tall grass near the remains of an old fountain. Large portions of the two stone lions, no longer spewing spring water, had broken and fallen to the side. He removed his wide-brimmed hat and placed it on the granite ledge, then sat down. "It's been a long time, Father." He reached for a fragment of stone that lay on the ground, rolled the particle between his fingers, and threw it at the ruins of a house consumed by fire sixteen years ago. Grass, trees, and other vegetation had overgrown the area, making i t difficult to see what lay beneath or who.

After several moments, he stood and approached the collapsed house, where he knew the door would have been. "I swear, Father, I won't stop until I finish what you started." Footsteps behind him pulled him back to the present.

"Reinforcements should be here anytime," Sedric announced as he rubbed his beard. "We probably need to get back to the main path where they can find us." He paused before continuing." I can't talk you out of this, can I?"

Don fixed his gaze on Sedric. "He's the last Bloodmoure. No matter how innocent he may appear, he has to die." Don glanced back at the remains of the house. "I thought we killed them all that day, but he must have escaped the fire." Don looked at his scarred hand.

"You're talking about Aticus?" Sedric questioned.

"Yes. When I looked him in the eyes, I knew he was the Bloodmoure, and he had the medallion they all carried." Don told Sedric.

"I could have asked where he found the bloody necklace before you killed him?"

"No, I knew when I saw him in the tavern. The day Normain died."

Sedric tilted his head. "You were a kid the last time you saw him."

Don stared at Sedric intensely, "For years, I knew one of them had to have lived. That was the only explanation as to why there were still vampires. I thought my father died for nothing." Don glanced over the ruins and clenched his jaw. "I wrestled with that for a long time until I saw Aticus in Veridian," Don said, meeting Sedric's gaze. "I have renewed hope that I finally have a chance to avenge my family and eliminate vampirism forever."

Sedric let his gaze drift to his feet. "I hope you're right. I pray you didn't kill an innocent boy."

"He's not dead, Sedric. When we find him alive, that will be all the proof you need to know that he's Bloodmoure." Don looked over the rubble remains of the home. "Father gave his life here to avenge my mother.

Sedric shifted his weight onto one leg and pressed his tongue between his teeth. "Look, I've told you before, I'll hunt vampires all day long, but killing the kid for the possibility that he may create more of the undead bloodsuckers someday."

Don gazed at the vegetation-covered rubble, ignoring what Sedric said; he focused on the past. "After my mother died, my father went before the Hands of the Shadow. He learned that the Bloodmoure created the vampires; with that information, his quest to kill them began. In return for the council's help, he had to find the Bloodstone for them."

Sedric studied Don. "The Bloodstone, that's the red gem you told me about before. You've already told me this."

Don glanced at Sedric. "I saw it again yesterday in Veridian. They had it."

Sedric let his brows sink inward. "Who had it?"

"Aticus' friends. The elf, Aeotus, retrieved it from an assassin." Don turned and studied the fountain's remains. "The Hand was in Veridian, fighting them for the Bloodstone."

"How did they get the Bloodstone?"

"I don't know. There's something else. I never told you about the blood." Don touched the granite statue. "There has to be a connection," Don spoke to himself in remembrance.

"A connection? You're not making any sense."

Don glanced at Sedric, "When I was six, we went before the council. There was blood on the floor, and a Shad'arn lying in the blood." Don shook a finger at his ear.

"I know what a Shad'arn is," Sedric responded sarcastically.

"The Shad'arn was the shape of a crescent moon, the same as Aeotus'. Whoever the council killed that day had to be a family member of Aeotus."

Sedric cocked his head to the side, "What does that have to do with anything?"

"The elf has the Bloodstone now. Why him?"

Sedric shrugged.

Don rubbed his chin, "I made a mistake killing the assassins; it was the wrong thing to do."

"Why did you help?" Sedric asked, crossing his arms across his chest.

Don walked over to the fountain. "They were after Lorna, and I stopped them from leaving with her." Don looked back at Sedric. "You don't want to cross the Hands of the Shadow. They don't tend to forget and never stop once you're marked. The Hand is the only thing my father truly feared."

"You saved the woman? What's wrong with that?"

"She's not just a woman. She's an Ancient. I didn't know the Bloodstone or the Hand was in play when I helped."

Sedric let his hands drop to his side. "One more reason not to get involved in whatever's happening."

A look of clarity etched itself across Don's face. "Aticus should be awake now; we need to find him before his friends show up." Don looked skyward.

Sedric sat down on the edge of the stone fountain. "This is a lot to take in, boss."

Smoke rising in the distance caught Don's attention. He smiled. "Where there's smoke, there's fire."

Chapter Fifty-Five

THE WOUNDED

B ryce couldn't stop worrying about Aticus and Eladonia. He fidgeted with the reins, undecided about leaving his friends, as he hoped to find Palias and the others. "I shouldn't have left them; they need me." Bryce tugged the reins of his horse and stopped. He peered toward the warmth of the afternoon sky. "Why shouldn't I go back?" Bryce scrunched his eyes together and tilted his head. The forest was silent except for the wind brushing against the leaves. "I don't understand?" He let his head droop in frustration. "I know I shouldn't question." Bryce tapped the stirrups, spurring his mount forward.

Bryce glanced skyward again. "I do trust You. With all of my being, I trust You." Bryce concentrated on the trail ahead and urged the mount onward. "You're right; Aticus and Eladonia will be fine."

Not long after, Bryce reached the campsite they had abandoned, only to find Palias and the others nursing their wounds.

Gilanthos was surveying the area for signs of who might have camped there, while Lorna tended to the wounds and broken bones the best she could. She didn't understand how to treat injuries, but offered a comforting word to her protectors.

"Palias!" Bryce shouted, galloping near his friends. "What happened to everyone?"

"Bryce!" Palias limped toward the dwarf, his left arm in a sling. He grabbed the horse's bridle so Bryce could climb out of the saddle. "We seemed to have attracted unwanted attention. It's a long story; we can discuss the situation later."

Gilanthos hobbled over and placed a hand on the dwarf's shoulder. "It's so good to see you, Bryce," he said, his mouth twisting. "We're sorry about Aticus." Gilanthos glanced around at everyone. "We were shocked to hear what happened."

"Oh!" Bryce smiled and grasped Palias and Gilanthos, pulling them down to his level. "Aticus—he woke! Last evening!"

The two men regarded one another, puzzled by the turn of events. Palias turned and announced the good news to everyone, "Aticus, he's alive!"

Gilanthos tilted his head. "Back from the dead? How?" He asked Bryce and looked back at Aeotus.

Palias searched the dwarf's face for an explanation.

"It was a miracle." Bryce gloated.

Yung Sung glanced up, his face bruised and battered. "Good," he noted in a husky tone and a smile.

"Maybe he wasn't dead to begin with," Aeotus retorted.

"They would know if he was alive or not," Lorna whispered.

Irritated, Aeotus stopped Lorna from blotting dried blood from his forehead with a wave. "Eladonia, is she okay?"

Bryce nodded and grinned. "She woke, I presume, after you found the necromancer." He glanced around at everyone.

Aeotus coughed painfully, holding his chest. "Where are they?"

"Let me help," Bryce announced as he walked beside Yung Sung. He examined the wounds and knelt on one knee. "Son, you've taken a beating."

"We were ambushed twice last night in Veridian. Both times, they tried to take Lorna and the red gemstone that Aeotus has." Sung groaned and looked at the elf.

Bryce regarded the newest member of the group. "You must be, Lorna?"

She flashed a smile and nodded.

"Where's Eladonia?" Aeotus asked, with a quiet intensity, making eye contact with Bryce.

Bryce held up his finger, stopped Aeotus from saying anything further, and closed his eyes. He placed his hands on Sung and began to chant. A soft azure light ebbed from his fingertips, slowly enveloping his hands and spreading across Sung's bruised and swollen face.

Sung regarded Bryce while he prayed, "It feels warm," Sung stated, and looked at Palias, knowing the large man understood what Bryce's healing words could do.

Aeotus curiously studied the dwarf, attempting to ascertain what form of magic he used. Lorna remained behind Aeotus and witnessed Bryce's healing power. Gilanthos and Palias watched with fascination.

Free from pain, Sung began to take deeper breaths as the broken ribs healed, and an expression of wonder replaced the contusions across his face.

Bryce concluded his chanting; he opened his eyes and patted Sung on the arm. "Better, son?"

Sung placed his hand on the dwarf's arm. "Thank you, Bryce."

"Where's Eladonia?" Aeotus asked impatiently.

Bryce scooted beside Aeotus and looked him in the eyes; his expression swelled with compassion. "She'll be fine; she and Aticus are together. Let me take care of you, and I'll answer all your questions."

Lorna moved alongside Aeotus and knelt before Bryce. "You are a healer!" She yielded, placing her head on the ground before him.

"No, no, child," Bryce exclaimed, patting her head. "Please, don't kneel before me."

Lorna nodded but remained on her knees and watched with wonder in her eyes.

Bryce focused his attention on Aeotus.

Aeotus nodded his head at Lorna's reaction concerning Bryce's power. "What magic do you use to heal? It's not arcane."

"My words are spiritual." Bryce considered the elf. "You are skeptical of the divine, and that's fine." Bryce smiled. "We are all nonbelievers in the beginning."

Aeotus' eyes narrowed. "For me to believe that a god grants you these healing powers contradicts everything I know to be true. I am Faylorn; we do not believe in gods."

Gilanthos knelt behind Bryce. "Aeo, does it matter if what Bryce does is magic or divine? He's trying to help." He cocked his head to the side, "He healed you once before."

Aeotus looked at his friend. "I wasn't awake to remember the event."

Gilanthos chuckled, "Kobold, baby."

Aeotus stared into the dwarf's eyes for several seconds before nodding. "I'm not a Kobold baby."

Bryce laid his hands on the elf and started chanting; the azure spread from his hands onto Aeotus' chest. There was a soft humming sound to the light, almost hidden by the toned chanting.

Aeotus gazed at Gilanthos, and a look of uncertainty spread across the recesses of his face.

Bryce finished mending Aeotus and patted him on the chest. He winked his eye and turned to look at Palias and Gilanthos. "Who's next?"

The two pointed at one another.

Palias urged Gilanthos toward Bryce with his large hands. "He goes next," Palias commanded.

Gilanthos moved alongside the dwarf. "Thank you, Bryce," he articulated with a hoarse whisper.

"Where were you struck?"

"The left side, it hurts here." Gilanthos guided Bryce's hand to his side.

Bryce closed his eyes and repeated the chant. Again, the soft radiance illuminated his hand, enveloping the elf's torso. Gilanthos focused on Aeotus.

Aeotus regarded his friend with a blank look.

"Better?" Bryce inquired with a smile as the light receded into his hands.

Gilanthos nodded. "A little bit."

"Your head still hurts?" Concern creased Bryce's forehead.

Gilanthos stood, "It's okay. Nothing I don't live with every day."

"You should have no pain," Bryce announced.

Gilanthos said nothing and turned to check on Yung Sung.

Bryce motioned to Palias, "Your turn, my friend."

The large man knelt on one knee so Bryce could reach his arm.

Bryce observed Palias; he recognized another pain in the large man's eyes. "I am sorry to hear about your mother and father."

Palias lowered his head. "How did you find out?" His eyes glistened in the sunlight.

Compassion washed over Bryce's features. He placed his hands on the large man's arm. "Collet informed Eladonia and me when we passed through Veridian with Aticus." He nodded, closed his eyes, and began to chant, and the warm glow enveloped Palias' arm, shimmering in his eyes.

When Bryce completed his chorus, he stood, "You need to return home?" he asked while he straightened his shirt.

Palias extended his arm, stretching. "Collet has a contact who heard one of my brothers was found and is returning home. Unfortunately, with high tensions, all water routes from Idonia will be blocked from landing in my homeland of Nosvonia." He glanced around at everyone, letting his gaze stop on Yung Sung. "When we're done, I'm returning to Veridian, and with Collet's help, I'll contact my brother. Perhaps then, I can procure a clandestine ship home."

Sung nodded, disappointed his friend would soon be departing.

After several silent breaths, Bryce glanced at everyone. "We need to help Aticus and Eladonia."

"Help how?" Gilanthos asked.

"We found Aticus' people, the Alarians, murdered: men, women, and children. It was goblins," Bryce revealed.

Aeotus stood. "What are we waiting for?"

CHAPTER FIFTY-SIX

SHANDAR

Don examined one of the smoldering pyres. "Looks like a mass cremation." He looked at the remains of the burnt wagons around the campsite. "Sedric, on the ground near you. Is that an arrow?" Don brushed his hands off on his coat. "I see three sets of fresh tracks around the fire, two adults and a smaller one, a dwarf presumably. That's three of them upright and moving."

Sedric paused and looked at Don. "So he's alive then." He reached for the wooden shaft on the ground. "It's an arrow." He pressed his tongue through the gap in his teeth as he flipped the arrow from side to side. "It's poorly made, so I'd say goblin."

"These people must not have put up a fight. I don't see any goblin remains," Don said as he approached Sedric.

"Maybe they torched the goblins, too." Sedric knelt over and examined a set of footprints. "These tracks are fresh and lead down the trail in that direction." He glanced at Don. "They're small. I'd say goblin."

Three men approached on horseback.

"Reinforcements are here. I'll see if I can find anything else." Sedric backed away and began surveying the area again.

Don walked toward the path as the men approached. "Cade, Galder, Dorian, thanks for coming on such short notice."

Cade, the man nearest to Don, spoke first. "When Don calls for help, we know the job will pay well." He spread his hands up before him matter-of-factly. His broad face and stubbled, square jaw helped frame a crooked nose and brown eyes. His long, almond hair partially covered a scar across his forehead that only deepened when he scrunched his brows together. He wore a leather tunic and brown pants with two short swords fastened to either side of his waist. "Sedric!" He shouted in greeting.

Sedric raised his hand in response but continued searching for more clues.

Galder, to Cade's right, nodded at Don in greeting. His small, dark eyes were set back in his skull, giving him a sickly appearance, and his crooked smile exposed his lack of teeth. His freshly shaved head and face revealed numerous old scars. He wore a leather tunic and leggings. He had a short sword strapped to his belt and a wooden crossbow draped across his back.

Don smiled at Galder before speaking, "What happened to all your hair?"

"Lice, he had lice," Dorian pronounced from the opposite side of Cade."

Galder stood in the stirrups and barked at Dorian. "Shut up, halfbreed!"

Dorian smiled and leaned his head to the side. His long sandy hair flowed over his pointed ears, tied against the back of his head. Dorian's thin face and chiseled bone structure exposed his partial elven heritage. His dark eyebrows and thin nose set above a sharp jaw made him the most charismatic. The smile he presented offered a small glimpse of his confident persona. He wore only a green shirt and brown leather pants. A small sheath on his belt held a knife, and a simple wooden bow hung across his back. A quiver of arrows hung on the side of his saddle.

Cade chuckled. "What are we here for, werebear or another vampire?"

"I'm after a man about my height and black hair, and he'll have a gray medallion around his neck. His name is Aticus, and he'll likely be with an elven woman and a dwarf. I need the three of you for backup."

"You need help with fighting off a dwarf and a woman?" Galder added, rubbing his bare head and smiling.

Don gazed at Galder, "They have companions that may be here later in the day. I may need help with them."

"Don, I found something!" Sedric exclaimed as he emerged from the edge of the forest. He led two horses from the trees into the clearing.

"Where are the riders?" Don asked. He glanced at the tree line. "Keep looking for signs. They may have moved through the forest," he told Sedric.

Don peered at Cade. "This appears to be an attack by a group of goblins, and the freshest tracks I've found are leading down the path ahead." Don pointed. "The three of you follow the trail and see what you can find."

Cade readjusted himself in the saddle. "What do you want us to do with the goblins?"

"Kill goblins, but don't engage Aticus and the others before us." Don adjusted his wide-brimmed hat.

Sedric shouted. "I found tracks. They camped out here briefly before moving parallel with the trail."

Don nodded and addressed the three on horseback. "Sedric and I will follow the trail in the forest and meet up with you."

Cade nodded, and the three spurred their horses, disappearing around a corner in the path.

Sedric tied the horses to a nearby tree by the path.

"Are these their horses?" Don asked.

Sedric grimaced. "Not sure, boss. If they had horses, they were stabled, so I never saw them. We could be wasting our time; this may not even be Aticus." Sedric offered. "Besides, there should be three of them. Bryce, Aticus, and the elf. If that's the case, then where is the third horse?

"I know; you may be right, Sedric." Don shook his head. "It feels right to me, though."

The two heard more horses approaching from the opposite direction, which Cade and the others had gone.

Don moved so he could see who was approaching from around a bend. "Sounds like several horses."

Sedric advanced to the path beside Don. "Goblins?" Sedric reached for his sword and pulled.

Don caught Sedric's arm, preventing him from drawing his weapon. "No, not goblins." Don recognized who it was as they came into view. It was Palias and his group; Bryce was behind the large man. "It's them; they shouldn't be here until later."

"Crap." Sedric let his sword slide back into the casing. "There's Bryce, but no Aticus or elf."

"This may work in our favor then," Don commented.

Sedric gave Don a sideways glance. "How?"

Palias, followed by Bryce, Yung Sung, Lorna, Aeotus, and Gilanthos, slowed and approached the two men.

"That's them, the ones that killed Aticus!" Bryce exclaimed.

Palias slid off his horse and held his hand up to calm Bryce. "Don, what's the meaning of this?" He glanced around at the destruction and smoldering pyres.

Sung joined Palias and stood in front of Sedric.

"Palias, what are you doing? They killed Aticus!" Bryce became aggravated.

"I've never seen you so angry, Bryce; it's amusing, to say the least." Aeotus chuckled. "Besides, I thought you said Aticus is alive?"

Bryce shot the elf an angry glance.

Gilanthos punched his friend and shook his head.

"I can explain everything; let's keep calm." Don looked back down the trail, hoping to see Cade, Galder, and Dorian return. Don raised his hands.

Sedric followed suit.

Bryce pointed at the two horses tied to the tree. "Aticus and Eladonia's horses. What have you done with them?" Bryce's expression became rigid, and his face flushed.

"Where are they, Don?" Palias asked and took an intimidating step forward.

Gilanthos slid off Capasius and helped Yung Sung disarm the two men.

"They weren't here when we arrived," Don answered.

"Where are they?" Bryce demanded again.

Don ignored the dwarf's question and redirected. "None of you understand what you're dealing with." Don looked at Aeotus. "The people after you want the Bloodstone, and they won't stop until you're all dead."

"Bloodstone? Is that what it's called? "Why would you care what happens to us?" Aeotus asked and wobbled his head. "And how do you know so much about the Bloodstone?"

"You're good people, and I don't want to quarrel with you." Don regarded Palias. "I've gotten to know you and even helped her." Don eyed Lorna. "That has to mean something."

Palias ignored Don and looked down on him. "Did you try to kill Aticus?"

Don didn't answer.

Aeotus regarded Don smugly. "My friend asked you a question. Did you try to kill Aticus?"

"I was there when he stabbed Aticus. I saw the pleasure it brought him," Bryce commented. "He's evil."

Again, Don ignored Bryce and studied Palias. "You had another run-in with the Hands of the Shadow last night, right? After I left, did they find you again? You fled town in the middle of the night, and that's why you're here so soon." Don asked Palias. The companions looked at one another.

Don studied everyone before speaking, his gaze on Lorna. "You're special, Lorna? Why are they after you?"

Yung Sung pivoted and kicked Don in the chest, knocking him to the ground and dislodging his wide-brimmed hat. "Stop playing us for fools. Palias asked you a question. Answer him!"

Don gazed at Sedric and remained silent.

Aeotus slid out of his saddle, kicking dirt when his feet hit the ground. "Where is Eladonia? I won't be as nice as Sung." He clicked his fingers and summoned a sphere of energy in the palm of his hand, forming an arcane dagger.

Palias placed his large hand on Aeotus' chest, stopping him from advancing further.

Don focused on the trees behind the elf and said nothing.

Gilanthos finished inspecting the pyres and ground of the campsite. "It looks like Ela and Aticus went through the forest here." He pointed.

"What are we going to do with them?" Lorna questioned from the back of her horse.

"They'll come with us," Palias responded. "We'll tie them to their horses, and I'll take them back to Veridian and turn them over to the authorities for attempted murder."

Sedric glanced at Don. *It could work to their advantage,* he remembered him saying. Sedric let his face scrunch together.

Gilanthos established that Eladonia and Aticus traveled through the forest, probably following a group of goblins walking along the path.

Palias decided they would travel the path while Gilanthos followed Aticus and Ela's path through the forest.

Palias and Bryce started down the path, followed by Don and Sedric, bound to their horses. Yung Sung followed closely behind, followed by Aeotus and Lorna in the rear.

"What do you think Don meant about the Bloodstone and me?" Lorna whispered to Aeotus.

The elf shrugged. "I think Don likes to hear his voice."

"There has to be something to what he's saying. Those men had the Bloodstone and used me to open doorways. For what purpose, I don't know or even remember why." Lorna focused on the dirt pathway, trying to remember what the Hand did to her.

"I won't let anything happen to you, I promise." Aeotus glanced at Lorna. The anxiety weighing heavily on her features. "You can't remember anything else besides the mirror and portals?"

"I know my name; I don't like the cold. I love when the sun warms me during the day and hate the darkness that follows." She glanced at Aeotus. "I prefer speaking to you because I feel like you understand me. Like I know you.

Aeotus scrunched his face. "Me? You prefer speaking to me?" He chuckled. "I've never had anyone tell me that."

"When I look at you, I feel like I belong," Lorna expressed. "Do you know more about me than you're not sharing?"

Aeotus pursed his lips together. "I know you're Lamarian, an Ancient."

Lorna cocked her head back. "That makes me feel old."

He smiled. "No, you don't look old." Aeotus thought about what to say for once. "Your people were called Lamarians."

Lorna looked at the elf; her face wrinkled in disbelief. "How would you know this?"

"I read and studied ancient history when I was younger. I tend to remember everything I see."

"I don't understand what you're saying. Why would you say I am who you say I am?" Lorna questioned.

"Ancients, or Lamarians, were said to have a gold tint to their eyes. You exhibit that trait. Also, I see a magic aura around you at times. Again, this lends credence that you are unique." He thought for a moment. "The Lamarians were said to be the oldest known beings and the first immortals. Elves were nothing more than simple creatures with a short lifespan." Aeotus raised a hand. "We have since evolved." He smiled shrewdly.

Lorna listened to what Aeotus said intently. "None of what you're saying sounds familiar to me."

"Likely a result of what the mind flayer did to you, if I had to guess. I hope that with time, your memories will return."

"What else can you tell me?" Lorna's eyes widened.

Aeotus smiled; the weight of secrecy lifted from him as he spoke. "Every Lamarian was born with a gift or an ability, each different and unique." Aeotus' voice swelled with excitement as he shared his knowledge with her. "It is possible that the Hands of the Shadow used you to their advantage. It appears you can open portals through reflective materials. Your other memories, pushed back into the recesses of your mind by the flayer's psionic assaults." He held up a hand. "That's all I can deduce."

Lorna smiled. "Thank you."

"For what?" Aeotus asked.

"Talking to me."

"Certainly, I enjoy speaking with you." Aeotus relaxed and smiled.

"I have to pee!" Sedric said, breaking the conversation.

"Hold it," Aeotus barked.

"I can't. I need to stop." Sedric glanced over his shoulder at Aeotus and Lorna.

"We're not stopping, so you can go anytime."

"I'm not pissing myself," Sedric said.

The argument ended when the sounds of fighting rang out in the distance from further down the trail.

Palias glanced at Bryce. "Aticus and Eladonia?"

Bryce looked into the forest at Gilanthos to get his perspective.

"I hear the fighting," Gilanthos responded.

"What are we waiting for?" Sung asked.

Don and Sedric looked at each other when they realized it was probably their hired help doing the fighting.

CHAPTER FIFTY-SEVEN

THE CAPTURED

Zander stepped from the magical portal into the lush landscape of Shandar. The undergrowth snapped beneath his feet as he studied the scouts standing ready. They had arrived before Zander to clear the area of any potential threats. The dwarf stared skyward, examining the leaves swaying in the breeze. He took a long, deep breath.

The mage standing next to Zander bowed his head.

"Did you find the goblins?" Zander asked while he straightened his dark robe from the static, arcane energy from the portal.

The shadow mage closed his hand around the portal stone, sealing the magical door behind Zander. "We did."

"Good, well done." Zander glanced at the two assassins standing behind the mage and raised his bushy almond brows. "Lead the way."

Aticus and Eladonia crept through the forest, shadowing the goblins who walked the trail. Aticus stepped on a fallen branch more than once, producing a sound he thought would have given the two away. Each time, Eladonia would grasp hold of Aticus' arm and squeeze.

Fortunately for Aticus, one of the shorter goblins chatted the entire time.

"Methinks Toak is greedy," the short goblin said.

Another goblin shook his head adamantly. "No, no, he's keeping what he deserves. Toak is our king."

Aticus watched as the lead goblin stopped and turned to face the others. "He's not king. Our king lives under the mountain in Azrel."

"Your king is not feeding us! Toak is feeding us!" The short goblin threw his hands upward. "So, I call Toak king!" He looked around for support from the other goblins.

Another creature near him silently nodded its head in agreement.

Aticus watched as the lead goblin huffed and turned to face the shorter creature. "You stupid!"

"No, you stupid!" said the tiny, green being.

The lead goblin punched the smaller, mouthy creature, casting him to the ground. The other goblins nearby began striking and pushing one another.

Aticus covered his face and shook his head. "What is happening?" he whispered.

"They're simple creatures," she mumbled.

Aticus' eyes opened wide, and he shook his head. "A bird is a simple creature." He pointed at the goblins. "They're stupid."

Eladonia smiled and rolled her eyes.

A paler goblin walking near the rear of the formation approached and induced a calming demeanor. "Stop arguing and get to camp. All of you know Toak will be angry if we fight." He walked by and took the lead on the path without another word.

The goblins reluctantly gathered their belongings, which they had lost during the struggle, and trailed behind, cursing under their breath.

Aticus and Eladonia continued to follow, cautious not to alert the creatures to their presence. After what seemed like a half-hour, a makeshift camp came into view. The goblins had established an encampment that spilled over into the trail. Several bonfires burned in the large clearing. Aticus and Eladonia knelt behind a fallen tree and watched the creatures assimilate themselves into the camp. "How have they not burned the forest down yet?" Aticus questioned.

Eladonia shook her head and shrugged. "Are you alright?" she whispered, concerned for his well-being.

Aticus glanced at Eladonia, "I feel fine. Why do you ask?"

Eladonia leaned her head to the side. "I watched you die. Then you wake up days later. You've lost everyone you ever knew. I'm worried about you." She shook her head and watched Aticus' features tighten. "When I woke, it took me several days before I felt better. I still don't feel the same as I did."

Aticus focused on the ground. "I feel fine, I do," he replied with a nod, his expression betrayed his words.

Eladonia forced a smile. "Alright, let's see what we're facing."

The two peeked over the log, considering the campsite.

Aticus discovered the caged cart on the far side of the camp on the dirt path. "There I see, Terra and Vandeer. They're lying in the cage." His voice was almost raised above a whisper.

"I see them too." Eladonia placed a hand on his arm to calm him. "We can make our way around when it gets darker. There are too many goblins right now to do anything."

"I count thirty-five, but they keep coming and going," Aticus commented, scanning the forest.

"We need to move back; it's too dangerous," Eladonia asserted.

"I don't see Toak," Aticus said to himself, ignoring what she suggested.

"We can't engage them by ourselves." Eladonia's voice reflected her doubt as she nudged his arm.

"What do you mean? I've seen you fight. We can do it," Aticus pleaded, searching her eyes for the confident warrior he'd seen the last time she killed goblins.

"I can't fight and worry about keeping you safe."

"I can handle myself; Sung showed me how to fight." Aticus clenched his jaw.

"Not enough. You're not ready." She shook her head, peeking over the log.

He exhaled sharply and contorted his mouth, absorbing her comment.

"Aticus, I can't lose you again." Her features sagged as she met his gaze. "Not again."

Aticus swallowed hard. "You'll lose me when you leave for Evermoure."

Eladonia looked away uncomfortably, searching for Toak again. "That's different."

"How is that different if we don't see each other again?" he questioned, admiring her eyes as she scanned the campsite.

She looked at Aticus, but didn't make eye contact. "We bonded during a difficult time, and I am thankful for that. I care about you the same as I would any friend. But when this is over, we will all go our separate ways. Though our paths may cross again someday." She looked at a pair of goblins arguing over something. "That's all I'm saying."

Aticus peered over the log at the goblins. "Either way, it's the same to me."

Eladonia gazed at him, her frustration apparent. "Aticus, we hardly know each other. You're fascinated with the idea of being near me. That's all this is."

"I can't help the way I feel." Aticus fixed his eyes on the fallen tree they hid behind. "I couldn't do anything to help you." He gazed into her blue eyes. "I've felt helpless my whole life, and I'm tired. Like now, I can't do anything to help them." He jutted his chin toward Terra and Vandeer.

"Aticus, you were there for me the whole time. You did more than you'll ever know." She desperately looked for something to focus on in the encampment. "We can still help them; we need to be smart." Eladonia almost touched Aticus' arm, but stopped. "We should move back, go out wide, and come around the other side." She started to move back and stopped.

Aticus held a blank look as if he didn't understand her. He concentrated on something else.

"Aticus, did you hear me?" she whispered.

He looked her in the eyes. "Do you hear him?"

She scrunched her brows together and listened before shaking her head. "I hear the goblins."

Aticus peeked over the fallen tree and scanned the area. "I hear, Toak."

Eladonia examined Aticus. He seemed different. More confident and aware. "Wait, I can hear a shrill voice now."

"There." Aticus pointed and narrowed his eyes.

Toak appeared between two large trees and walked into view, followed by three men dressed in black. One in robes and two in black shirts and pants, a sword draped over their shoulders.

Behind the three men in black was a dwarf; his almond hair was well-kept and braided. His brown tunic, leather pants, and black robe partially covered the leather armor while the hood hugged his shoulders. He rubbed his beard and shuffled behind the three.

The four approached what appeared to be the center of the camp. Toak sat down on a log. "You want me to help you, Zander?" Toak studied the ground and glanced at the dwarf, who stopped before him. The three men moved protectively behind the dwarf.

Eladonia slid adjacent to Aticus. "You can understand what they're saying?"

Aticus nodded, "Yes, can't you?" He squinted his eyes and concentrated on the discussion. "The dwarf's name is Zander."

Eladonia turned her head, expecting to hear better. "How can you understand them from this distance? I hear mumbles, not words," she whispered, studying Aticus' expression.

Toak pushed out his chest proudly, "You need me?"

Zander huffed. "We need more eyes watching for a group of individuals traveling through the forest within the next few days." He used his hands for added dramatics as he spoke, folding them together when he paused. "You will be compensated for your time, of course."

"Of course, but what's stopping me from killing you and taking the payment now?" Toak leaned forward and smirked.

Zander glanced at the three men behind him and rolled his eyes. "I can assure you, we have nothing of value on us." He lifted his hands, tilting his head. He pulled open the robe he wore. "Does it look like we're carrying a large sum of gold?" He added in a condescending tone.

Toak relaxed his posture. "Well, I suppose you're right. When would I be paid?"

"Once we capture or kill these criminals, you will be paid whether you play a role in catching them or not. All I'm asking is for you to be my eyes in Shandar. You will tell my men if you see something, and they will engage the enemy."

"Your men are staying here? With me?" Toak motioned his hand toward the three men behind the dwarf.

"Yes," Zander responded.

"I will help you." Toak nodded his head, confirming his decision.

Eladonia leaned closer to Aticus. "We need to get around the other side and stay clear of whatever fight is coming."

Aticus nodded, and the two stepped away from the fallen tree and traveled in the opposite direction. Once out of sight, they crossed the trail and worked closer to the caged wagon around the camp.

"We have a couple of hours until dark, and neither has moved." Aticus studied the cage. "What if they're dead?"

"Aticus, we can't move until it's dark."

Aticus huffed. Something caught his attention on the other side of the camp, where they had been earlier. Several goblins emerged from the trail, waving their hands and screaming. "We under attack!" One creature sprawled into the dirt when an arrow pierced its back.

Three men on horseback appeared around a bend in the trail, chasing the goblins. They stopped when they realized they had stumbled into an encampment, drawing the attention of the goblins, Toak, and his visitors.

Four goblins near the caged wagon ran toward the new threat, leaving the cart unguarded.

"We have the distraction we needed," Aticus exclaimed and blindly ran toward the wagon.

"No," Eladonia whispered and chased after Aticus.

Chapter Fifty-Eight

THE FALLEN

Toak stood when he heard the screams. "What is the meaning of this?" Toak pointed with a stubby finger.

Several goblins moved to intercept the three men on the trail.

Zander stepped around a tree and examined the intruders. "They're not the people we're looking for." He regarded Toak, "They're not my concern."

"What do you mean—not your concern; we are being attacked!" Toak spat at the dwarf.

One of the assassins stepped around Zander, prepared to pull his sword.

Toak flinched and stepped back, "Ahh!"

Zander placed a hand on the assassin's leg, "Leave it be."

Toak swallowed stiffly.

Zander wiped the spit from his face and considered Toak. "They're not who we're after, either." He pointed behind the goblin king at the caged wagon fifty yards away.

Toak turned and screamed when he saw Aticus and Eladonia nearing the cage. "Ahhh! Stop them!" He grabbed two nearby goblins and pushed them in their direction, "Stop them all!" Toak spread his arms out before him.

Zander relaxed and cupped his hands behind his back.

More goblins appeared from the forest. Toak commanded five of them to reinforce the wagon, three toward the already crowded pathway, and the three men on horseback.

Aticus reached the wagon and rattled the door. "Terra!"

"They know we're here. Get the door open. I'll buy you some time." Eladonia freed her swords. The colored ribbon flowed behind the hilts as she twisted them free and advanced on the first two creatures, leaping over a collapsed tree. Her deadly melody started.

"Terra!" Aticus frantically pulled on the door. She didn't respond, but Vandeer lifted his head. "Vandeer!"

Cade shouted, pulling his short swords free, "What's Don got us into?" He kicked his mount's sides and thrust his horse toward the oncoming goblins.

Galder laughed, rubbing his bald head, "Let's kill some goblins, boys." He pulled the crossbow from his back and yanked back the lever, readying the weapon. Pulling the trigger, he launched a wooden bolt into the nearest goblin, advancing on Cade, sending the creature sprawling. "That's how you kill a goblin!"

Dorian pulled the bowstring taut, prepared to let loose a second arrow before Galder could get off another shot. "The goblins remind you of something, Galder?" His arrow struck its mark.

"What?" Galder chuckled while adjusting his mount's position for a better shot.

"Lice!" Dorian laughed as he found another target.

"Screw you, half-breed pixie lover!" Dorian missed his mark as the horse pulled to the side.

Cade intercepted two goblins, knocking one to the side with his horse and striking the other in the shoulder with his sword. An arrow zipped past his face. "Archers! Get the archers, Dorian!"

"I'm on it!" Dorian sighted six goblin archers taking a position not far from the tree line. He leaped from his horse, wrapping the quiver onto his back. "Galder, you have me? I'm on the archers!"

"Yeah, half-breed, I got you covered."

Aticus beat on the lock with the hilt of the sword. "Vandeer, can you hear me?"

Vandeer glanced at the wooden door. "Aticus?" He wondered whether his eyes were deceiving him. "Is it you?"

Aticus reached for Terra and shook her. She didn't respond.

"Terra's gone, Aticus." Vandeer struggled to lift his head. The white of his eyes starkly contrasted with the dried crimson covering his features.

Aticus paused and considered her body, "Terra," he mumbled, his face contorted.

"She died this morning. Leave me, Aticus. Get as far away from here as you can." Vandeer tried to focus on Toak, who squealed instructions to a steady inrush of goblins emerging from the forest.

"No, she can't be gone." Aticus tightened his jaw and fought back the impulse to cry.

"I'm sorry, Aticus—for everything." Vandeer coughed up bloody phlegm, spattering the floor of the wagon. "It's too late for me, but not for you. Run, Aticus, leave me." Vandeer lowered his head to the wagon's floor and whispered, "I'm sorry, Aticus."

Aticus regarded Vandeer, and he saw a broken man. "I'm getting you out of here."

Eladonia drifted to the left and whistled to the right. She struck oncoming goblins, removing limbs and spattering the dark bloodstain on the green foliage. She hummed her song but kept a close eye on Aticus when she twisted, never straying far from him. Goblins poured from the forest; her only hope was that they wouldn't be archers.

Toak pleaded, "If you don't help me, how will I help you if they kill all my men?"

Zander creased his brows and huffed. "Very well." Zander lifted his hand and waved one assassin toward the three men, and the other assassin and mage toward Eladonia and Aticus.

Both assassins freed their swords and advanced on their new targets as they leaped over brush and cartons of supplies.

Zander contorted his hands and fingers in a swirling motion as he spoke unrecognizable words. An emerald cast illuminated his hands and quickly dispersed onto the advancing assassins, hastening their movement.

Toak stood with his mouth agape at the dwarf's display of magic. "You're a user?"

Zander did not respond to the goblin's words.

Aticus slammed the hilt of his sword into the lock. "I can save you."

"You can't break it. It's magically locked. You need the key." Vandeer coughed up more blood. "Leave me, Aticus. Save yourself, please." He winced in pain as he pulled his hand away from his chest. The bright crimson coloring covered his large hand. "Aticus." Vandeer beckoned Aticus to look at his palm.

Aticus glanced at Vandeer's chest and his blood-soaked shirt. The coughing exacerbated the bleeding. He looked at Terra's body. "I can save you." His face sagged as he battled internally with the choice he had to make.

"Aticus! You need to get the door opened now!" Eladonia dodged to the left; her song ended as she removed the goblin's sword from his grasp, displacing the small blade with his hand in the bright-colored grass.

Aticus caught sight of a man dressed in black advancing on Eladonia at a stunning pace. "Eladonia!" He gripped his sword tightly and sprinted toward Eladonia and a group of goblins outside the reach of her sword.

She spun around and lurched forward, intercepting two of the five goblins nearby.

Galder aimed at a creature advancing on Cade and pulled the trigger on his crossbow—it jammed. "Flack!" He swore.

Dorian dispatched four of the five archers before one could connect with Cade's left arm. His next arrow struck the lucky goblin in the chest. "Cade!"

Cade spun around, using the force of the impact to propel his sword down on a goblin coming from his right. "I'm okay. Incoming in black!" He kicked another and deflected a goblin's swing.

Galder spurred his mount beside Cade and struck a goblin with his jammed crossbow. "The damn peddler said the crossbow was new!" He slid from the saddle and blocked a sword strike on Cade's left. "New my ass!" He threw the wooden scrap at another goblin.

Dorian noticed a man in black dashing toward Cade and Galder. He reached and pulled an arrow from the quiver, notching it in his bow. He held his breath and released the shaft. The arrow narrowly missed the assassin, passing behind him.

Eladonia advanced on the next creature as it swung its sword, running the goblin through. Three more approached from her left.

Aticus locked his eyes on the advancing assassin and charged past Eladonia.

"Aticus, no!" She yelled as she bent, taking the legs off of another goblin. "Don't!" Two more goblins engaged Eladonia as she tried to pursue Aticus.

Aticus ground his teeth together, "I have him." Rage surged inside him, knowing he failed to save the last of the Alarians.

Cade stumbled to the side and planted his feet, preparing for the assassin's attack. "Galder, get behind me and cover my back."

Galder did as he said and dispatched an incoming goblin.

Dorian reached for another arrow, considering that the assassin was magically hasted, he needed to aim ahead of his quarry. One chance was all he had before the man reached Cade.

Dorian's hand grabbed at the air—his quiver was empty. "Flack," He whispered and launched to his feet.

The assassin reached Cade.

Cade's stroke missed the assassin when he folded back, allowing the sword to pass over him, avoiding his nose by inches.

The assassin slid past the mercenary. The curved blade opened Cade's leather tunic and sliced deep into his rib cage, exiting below his shoulder blade.

Cade dropped his sword, losing control of his limb.

The assassin turned and pushed the sword into Cade's back and out through his chest.

Cade toppled forward into the ground cover, as the assassin faced Galder and presented the crimson-stained sword.

Galder glanced at his comrade after dispatching a rogue goblin. "Cade!"

Several other goblins saw what the man in black did as they retreated out of Galder's reach and studied the assassin eagerly.

Galder's hands shook as he presented his sword and swung it wildly at the assassin, glancing over his shoulder as the goblins taunted him.

The assassin lurched forward and sank back, antagonizing Galder.

"You flacker, stay back!" Galder surveyed Cade's body behind the man in black. "I'm gonna kill you!" he yelled.

Two goblins ran up to Cade and began joyfully poking his corpse with their swords.

Dorian dropped his bow and drew his knife as he ran toward the assassin. He knew Galder was outmatched.

Galder lunged at the man in black; his sword raised above his head one last time. His final act would be a futile attempt to avenge his friend.

The assassin rolled to his left, allowing Galder's forward momentum to propel him past. The assassin turned and slid his sword through the mercenary's back and into his heart.

The neighing of horses on the path attracted the assassin's attention. Pivoting, he observed a tall, dark-skinned man on horseback appear on the trail. He furrowed his brow and turned toward Dorian, the greater threat.

Aticus pressed as hard as he could to intercept the assassin. He raised his sword and parried an assault.

"Aticus!" Eladonia yelled. Anxiously, she struck down the last goblin near her and ran after him.

CHAPTER FIFTY-NINE

THE MONSTER

Dorian advanced toward the assassin, glancing at Cade and Galder's bodies. He gripped his dagger with a firm hand and swallowed stiffly. Dorian understood his weapon would do little against the katana of the trained killer; these were his last breaths, and he knew it.

The assassin planted his feet and prepared to strike.

Dorian knew he had one chance and threw the blade to distract the killer momentarily.

The assassin sliced at the dagger, deflecting the projectile into a nearby tree.

Dorian landed a punch, but a sharp sting from the katana pierced his side; he coughed up blood. His right arm went numb and flopped as he stumbled forward. His feet gave way as he tumbled into the groundcover. Dorian tasted blood in his mouth as he rolled over and looked into the assassin's eyes one last time.

Dorian's killer smirked as he glanced at the trail and the new arrivals on horseback.

Dorian's breath became labored as he looked at his companions' bodies. He watched the goblins approach; they laughed and taunted him. Dorian coughed up more blood as he focused on the path. The last thing he saw was Don and Samuel tied to their horses.

Zander approached the assassin, "We finish this now. I will support you."

The assassin nodded and turned his focus on the new threat.

The assassin swiftly thwarted Aticus' attack; his forward momentum carried him past the man in black.

Aticus pivoted swiftly and caught a glimpse of the assassin's curved blade. He raised his sword, deflecting the blade. But, Aticus didn't see the assassin's foot, striking him in the abdomen. The blow was so forceful that it left him gasping for breath, stumbling backward, and bewildered. He dropped his sword and fell against a tree.

"Aticus!" Eladonia screamed as she approached her new target. She wouldn't lose him again, not today.

Her call enticed the assassin's attention from Aticus.

The killer moved swiftly, kicking Aticus' sword out of reach and into the thick brush.

Eladonia engaged the man and swung her left sword, hoping to create an opening for her second weapon.

The assassin's form was precise, deflecting each attack Eladonia launched. "Pretty swords, elf," he taunted. "You're a bladecantor?"

Eladonia ignored the assassin.

Aticus frantically scurried through the thick foliage, searching for his sword. "I'm coming! I'm coming!"

Eladonia parried the onslaught as she backed away, pulling the killer toward her and away from Aticus. "No! Stay there!" she shouted.

The assassin flashed a smug smile as he drove his sword into the dirt and began slapping her wrists. His hands became his weapon as he guided her attacks to the left and right.

Aticus watched the katana teetering behind the killer.

Eladonia retreated, pulling the assassin toward her and separating the killer from his weapon and Aticus.

Aticus thought he heard his name called in the distance over his shoulder, but fought the urge to look. He knew this was his only chance. He lunged for the katana, hoping to use it to help her.

"Aticus!"

He heard his name again and refused to look. He had to help her. Aticus wrapped his fingers around the katana's hilt and pulled it from the dirt. His head pounded with every heartbeat as he felt the blood rush through his body.

"Aticus!"

Again, he heard his name, but focused on what he was about to do. He raised the blade and prepared to strike the killer from behind. His heart pounded like never before. He'd never taken a life, but he would do it for her. One more step, he'd do it for her.

"Aticus! Watch out!"

"Bryce?" Aticus whispered as the sword came down on the assassin's head, but came short, stopped by an invisible force inches away.

Unaware, the killer continued to pull away from Aticus and toward Eladonia as she retreated.

"No! No!" Aticus screamed. He tried to press the blade forward and move his feet to follow, but he couldn't move.

"Aticus! Behind you!"

It was Bryce. Aticus knew Bryce was calling him in the distance, but he couldn't turn to look either. He was held in check by an unseen force.

The assassin landed a solid strike on Eladonia's left wrist, dislodging the sword from her hand.

Aticus could hear twigs cracking and brush moving behind him. Someone drew closer. He could smell them; there was more than one. His heart palpitated as he watched the assassin push Eladonia further away from him.

"Kill them. What are you waiting for?" Kill them!"

Time seemed to slow as Aticus recognized a shrill voice. It was Toak, yelling in the distance, intermingled with the sounds of steel and chanting. He heard Bryce yell his name again and smelled more goblins approaching from behind. He could feel the blood pumping through their veins and listened to their breath. There was another, a larger and stronger heartbeat coming.

Eladonia stumbled over a tree root and lost her balance. She didn't go down, but it was enough for the assassin to take advantage.

The killer struck her with an open palm to the chest, forcing the breath from her lungs and sending her into an oak tree, easily dislodging her second sword with his other hand.

"No!" Aticus screamed. He feared for Eladonia's life and struggled with all his might, yet remained magically held in place. His heart pounded, helpless to do anything, he ground his teeth together. Two goblins appeared on either side of him. The four creatures ignored him as they watched the assassin and Eladonia, urging the man in black to kill the e lf.

Another man in black robes appeared in Aticus' vision on the right, causing the goblins to move away. He was a mage, and it was his magic that had him held fast. Aticus listened to the mage's lifeblood course through his heart as it pumped the blood into his body.

The man in black looked into Aticus' eyes with delight. Thud! Crimson spattered across Aticus' face and in his mouth.

Aticus glared into the mage's soul as it fled his body, eyes glazed over. He'd never forget the look. It was death. Aticus watched the mage's expression sag; a bloody arrowhead in his temple. Aticus knew the mage was gone, but listened to the thumping of his heart. It continued to beat as his body collapsed. The muscle fought for life, even though the mind had forgotten. Aticus licked the blood from his lips as the spell released.

Two of the four goblins ran into the woods when the mage fell, leaving the remaining two trembling with fear of what was to come.

The assassin pressed Eladonia, paused, and glanced back at his fallen comrade.

Eladonia used the distraction, striking the assassin across the jaw with a clenched fist, knocking him off balance. She followed with a kick to his groin, sending the killer to the ground.

Aticus reacted. He reached for the nearest goblin and twisted its head awkwardly, cracking the creature's neck.

"Aticus!"

Aticus heard Bryce calling his name, Toak screaming commands, and Aeotus chanting a spell, but all he could sense was the remaining goblin's blood coursing through its veins, and he wanted it to stop.

Aticus glared at the remaining goblin and screamed. "Stop!" He wanted the sound to stop. He needed the creature's heart to stop pounding in his head. He turned to face the goblin as a pair of fangs slid out, replacing two teeth and dislodging them from his gums. He felt the whoosh of an arrow pass behind him. He heard it strike, the assassin doubled over in front of Eladonia, and listened to the sweet silence when his heart burst from the impact of the arrow.

The goblin screamed and ran, horrified when he witnessed Aticus release his comrade's body.

Aticus knew he could make the sound stop—he had to, for his sanity. He lunged at the goblin, making up the distance faster than he thought he might.

He struck the goblin's head so violently that he launched the creature into a nearby tree, silencing the thunderous heartbeats in his head.

Aticus stood in calmness. He tasted the blood.

"Aticus!"

He heard his name again. It was Eladonia. She stood over the collapsed assassin, Gilanthos' arrow in his chest. Aticus studied her features for what seemed like an eternity. Her chest heaved from the battle. Her countenance conveyed a depth of emotion he'd never witnessed. Aticus understood at that moment he was a monster, and she saw him for what he was.

CHAPTER SIXTY

THE BATTLE

The battle cries echoed in the forest behind them as Aeotus addressed Bryce and Lorna. "The two of you hold back and keep an eye on them." He motioned toward Don and Sedric. "Gil and I will support Sung and Palias." He handed the reins of the two men's horses to Lorna and nodded as he turned his mount toward the fray.

Lorna tilted her head and studied Don and Sedric.

"Aticus and Eladonia need our help," Bryce replied, as Gilanthos slid from his saddle and notched an arrow; releasing it, he dispatched a goblin advancing on Sung. "Ela can handle herself."

Palias struck down one of the creatures with his sword, tossing it to the side like a child's doll.

"Besides, as long as we have the big guy clearing the rats, we'll be fine," Gilanthos declared, nocking another arrow.

Sung bound toward the advancing assassin, sword raised beside his head.

The two collided on the path as the sound of their steel weapons clanged with each exchange.

"The assassins are magically hastened." Aeotus slid from the saddle. "Gil, we've got incoming, and so does Ela! They're magic-users—she's going to need help!"

"I got her covered! You help Sung!" Gilanthos let loose a volley of arrows, killing two more goblins emerging from the forest. "I like these odds!"

"Two mages do not seem fair to me," Aeotus said as he studied the dwarf approaching. "I'm pretty sure the little one is a wizard."

"Yeah, but we got you," Gilanthos quipped.

"If you cut us loose, we can help," Don suggested.

Lorna studied Don; her brows sank inward. "Did you ask to be cut loose?"

Sedric rolled his eyes and shook his head.

Bryce guided his mount alongside Lorna and glanced at Don rigidly. "I'll take the reins, dear."

Sung sidestepped to the left, dodging the assassin's attack. The assassin's thrusts and parries came quickly. Sung darted right and evaded what would have been a robust strike. He had an opening and took it as he dropped to the ground, swung around, and kicked the assassin's leg out beneath him, sending him onto his back.

Palias moved to help Sung, clearing a path of oncoming goblins. Something grabbed hold of his legs and held him tight. Instinctually, he swung his sword back, assuming he'd missed an attacker, but instead struck tree roots encasing his legs. An unlucky goblin approached, believing it had the advantage. Unfortunately for him, Palias' reach was longer, and he removed the creature's head before it could pose a threat. "Sung!"

Yung Sung heard his friend and glanced back.

That was the distraction he needed. The assassin leapt to his feet and pressed Sung relentlessly.

Zander paused thirty paces from Palias. His magical chanting and hand motions drew tree roots around Palias, up and over his knees, stopping below his waist.

Aeotus sprinted beside Palias, distracting Zander from the large man. "I got this, big guy." Aeotus tapped Palias on the arm and grinned.

Palias folded his brows inward and lifted his arms in defeat. "You're not the one held by tree roots!"

Aeotus let his mouth crease, "It's just wood, do what you do best." He let his gaze fix on the dwarven wizard. "Smash your way out!"

Zander flicked his arms and prepared a spell, gazing at Aeotus. "You have the Bloodstone." Zander swallowed stiffly.

Aeotus recalled a spell, rubbed his fingers together, and prepared to speak the words as he moved away from Palias, forcing him out of the range of any spell the dwarf might cast.

Zander smirked and tipped his head to the side. "So you're a mage," he stated matter-of-factly.

Aeotus paused, squinting his eyes. "And you're here, why?"

"I've come to fetch the Bloodstone." Zander straightened and adjusted his shoulders. "If you give it to me, I'll let you and your friends live. After all, that is how this ultimately ends."

Aeotus chuckled as he listened to Palias tear away at the tree roots. "I have what you want, little man, but I won't give it to you," he said, waving his hand between the two of them. "How about you and I settle this, and I humiliate you. That's how this ultimately ends."

"Kill them!" Toak screamed at Zander and the assassins.

Aeotus glanced over Zander's shoulder at the crazed goblin king.

The dwarven wizard used the distraction and cast his spell. *"Acindra!"* Zander swung his hands toward Aeotus and summoned a globe of fire, launching it at Aeotus. He sneered as the blazing orb careened toward the elf.

Aeotus reacted too late. He had enough time to cross his arms, but the words to his spell were trapped in his mind; he failed to utter the mantra aloud.

"Aeotus!" Palias screamed as the fireball engulfed the elf. The heat of the flames was so great that he had to close his eyes and shield his face with his arms.

The roar from the fireball didn't distract Yung Sung as he deflected the assassin's onslaught. The magically enchanted killer showed no sign of tiring as the two danced a skillful death duel. Neither man could afford to make a mistake.

Gilanthos stood and glanced away from Sung at his friend encased in flames. "Aeo!" The magical fire exhausted itself as quickly as it had been summoned, revealing the elf. He survived! His arms crossed, crouched in a defensive stance. An azure shield surrounded Aeotus as static energy discharged into the air around him, absorbing what remained of the flames.

Gilanthos smiled with renewed vigor. He knelt, notched an arrow, and let it loose, striking a goblin approaching Yung Sung. "Come on, give me a window," he whispered, pulling his bowstring taut and closing one eye. The arrow nock rested between his fingers as he took sight of the assassin and concentrated on his breathing.

"Aticus!"

Bryce's scream distracted Gilanthos. He looked past the killer, engaging Sung, and focused on Aticus and Eladonia.

"Aticus!" Bryce screamed. "I need to help him."

Lorna took the reins from Bryce. "Go help your friend. I'll keep them," She said, looking at Don and Sedric.

Bryce spurred his horse toward Gilanthos and slid from the saddle, nearly tumbling beside him. "They need our help; they don't see the threat coming."

"I know, I know, I see the mage." Gilanthos' eyes darted between Sung, Aticus, and Eladonia.

"God, help them," Bryce whispered.

Aeotus straightened and examined his body.

"Impossible," Zander said, widening his eyes in disbelief. "The Bloodstone. I should have foreseen this," he grumbled and clenched his fist.

Aeotus straightened and twisted his hands, *"Tera'lack."* Twelve small spheres of arcane energy formed and sprang toward the dwarf.

Zander waved his hand to the side as an invisible shield deflected the magical orbs into the lush vegetation of the forest.

"Intriguing," Aeotus commented, admiring his hands and the power surging through him.

"Aticus! Behind you!" Bryce screamed as he watched Eladonia get pushed back, nearly tripping. "Gilanthos." Bryce placed his hand on the elf's shoulder.

"I got him." Gilanthos let loose the nock, striking the mage tormenting Aticus in the temple.

Bryce took a step to the side. "Good shot."

Gilanthos notched another arrow, targeting the assassin hunched over in front of Eladonia, but Aticus stepped in front of the shot, causing him to pause. "I don't have a line of sight."

Aticus reached for a goblin near him and snapped its neck.

"Aticus!" Bryce called. "No, God, no," he muttered.

Gilanthos closed one eye and focused on the target. The string of his bow sang like a finely tuned instrument as the arrow was released. As the assassin hunched over in front of Eladonia, the arrow found its mark.

Aticus ran down the last goblin, flinging the creature into a nearby tree, cracking bone and wood.

CHAPTER SIXTY-ONE

THE CHOICE

Horrified, Aticus stared at his bloodstained hands and the goblin's life force trickling from his fingertips. He took a breath and glanced through the canopy of leaves above him as the waning sunlight embraced his features; he exhaled. The world became oddly still, and an eerie silence enveloped the air around him. He let his gaze drift toward Eladonia as she stood motionless, searching his features for something she might recognize. He listened to her heart pounding wildly.

"Ah! Kill them, kill them!" The goblin king yelled.

Toak's shrill voice yanked Aticus back to a reality he desperately wanted to escape. He looked at the goblin king before glancing at his hands again, finally, at Eladonia.

A discharge of magic energy in the background caused Aticus to spin around. He watched Aeotus and a dwarf exchange magical attacks as Yung Sung battled against an assassin. Gilanthos released multiple arrows at Aeotus' magic opponent, only to have them reflect off an invisible force. Bryce ran toward him, and Palias ripped away at the tree roots wrapped around his feet. Aticus recognized Sedric and the man who tried to kill him in the forest outside Dewbrook. He tightened his jaw and clenched his fists. He heard everyone's heartbeats—except Vandeer's and Terra's. Aticus glanced at their bodies in the caged cart.

However, above all else, he heard Toak's voice, which became his point of awareness. Aticus focused on the goblin king as an uncontrollable rage enveloped him. Aticus sprinted toward the lone creature. He was the reason his people were dead. He would take Toak's life as payment for his sins, and so end his reign of terror. Aticus would no longer be a victim of circumstance. He ran his tongue over his teeth and tasted the mage's life force.

Aeotus held his arms across his chest as another burst of magical fire encased the shield surrounding him. Using the flames as cover, he contorted his fingers, remembering a spell he had learned from Gildon's book, and prepared to deliver its magical incantation.

The glow of the wizard's spell faded. "*Bla'th-Kol-tol,*" Aeotus uttered and raised his hands. Enhanced by the presence of the Bloodstone, eight spherical blades roughly the size of his hand appeared above him. He thrust his arms outward, pushing the magical incarnations at the wizard.

Zander knelt and raised his hands to reinforce the magical shield surrounding him, but the onslaught of energy cut through the invisible barrier, shattering it like glass. All but one of the blades were deflected. The only one to make it through struck Zander in the chest, knocking him off balance.

Aeotus slapped his hands together, "*Al'ian.*" A burst of wind pummeled the dwarf, tossing him back against an oak tree, cracking bones and wood on impact. Aeotus admired his hands and the power coursing through him.

Gilanthos concentrated on the remaining assassin, recognizing Yung Sung's fatigue. The adversary intentionally kept Sung between them, robbing him of a clear shot. Gilanthos pulled back on the arrow and held his line tautly.

The assassin parried Sung's attack and twisted the sword from his grasp, sending the weapon tumbling onto the path. Gilanthos held his breath. The killer swung his sword at Sung's head; there was no avoiding the attack. Sung did the only thing he could. He pushed back from the assassin, hoping not to lose his head. The tip of the blade tasted flesh. Gilanthos released the nock of his arrow. The fletching brushed the bowstring as it rushed toward its target; Gilanthos released his breath. Yung Sung fell to the ground in a spray of blood. The arrow passed the target, disappearing into the forest. The assassin smiled at his victory.

Gilanthos stood prepared to rush the killer, but Palias beat him to it. The large man grabbed the assassin's neck from behind and snapped it in his hands, dropping his limp body to the ground.

Gilanthos rushed to Yung Sung's side, surveying the battlefield. Sung's bloody hands shielded his face as he reeled in pain. "Let me see," Gilanthos said, pulling Sung's hands away to see the extent of the damage. Yung Sung looked into the elf's eyes. "Is it bad? There's blood everywhere." Gilanthos relaxed. "He knicked the bridge of your nose. I think you're going to live," he said, patting Sung on the chest.

"All I could do was push away! I thought I lost my eyes," Sung exclaimed, trying to catch his breath. He pressed his hands over his nose.

Palias slid to his side, dropping his sword. "Sung!" he shouted, looking at the blood running down his face. "Keep the pressure on it until we can get Bryce. Where's Bryce?" he asked Gilanthos. The two looked across the clearing as the dwarf ran after Aticus.

Aeotus sauntered over and knelt beside the broken and bloody dwarf.

Zander coughed up blood and swallowed what he couldn't spit out. His breaths drew shallow. "That spell—too powerful for you," he commented, understanding it was the Bloodstone.

Aeotus let his features sag. "Does it hurt?" he asked sarcastically.

"You have no idea what you're doing." Zander coughed up more blood as it ran down his chin.

"I have no idea what you're talking about."

"You will—and one day. You'll regret ever finding it."

"You're talking about the Bloodstone?"

"The only way to stop what's coming—is to leave it with me." Zander forced himself to breathe.

"Well, you're getting ready to leave, so—no." Aeotus shrugged.

"They will come. For my body," Zander said, ingesting more blood.

"Who, the Hands of the Shadow? Are you one of those hands?" Aeotus poked the dwarf, forcing him to take a breath.

Zander turned his hand over on the ground and revealed his bloody palm. "Last chance, wizard. Leave the Bloodstone with me, or you will suffer..." Zander's head slumped to the side as his last breath escaped and his eyes lost focus on the palm of his hand.

Aeotus pulled the Bloodstone out of his pocket and examined the brilliance of the swirling mist within. He felt the power it emanated. "I would never have been able to cast those spells without this," he whispered.

Aeotus studied the dwarf's open palm until he heard Bryce scream.

"Aticus, don't do it!" Bryce yelled, running toward the goblin king.

Toak shook. His back pressed against a tree.

Aticus looked down at the goblin. "You're no king! You're a murderer! I am going to kill you! Like you killed them," he said, pointing behind him at the caged cart and the bloody bodies.

Toak shuddered as Aticus grabbed the goblin by the throat and hoisted him against a tree.

Bryce arrived behind his friend. "Aticus, don't do this."

Eladonia reached Bryce's side but didn't speak, swords in her hands.

"I'm going to drag him into the forest and guarantee he never hurts another soul again!" His eyes glossed over, tears running down his face.

"Aticus, this is not you," Eladonia pleaded.

"Who am I?" Aticus asked. "I don't know anymore." He let his tongue brush against the fangs.

"I'll never hurt anyone again," Toak whined.

Aticus slapped the dented helmet from his head and dropped the goblin to the ground.

"Thank..." Toak misunderstood Aticus' actions as a form of mercy.

Aticus pulled the goblin's sword from its sheath, summoned a handful of Toak's hair, and began to drag him between two trees.

"Aticus!" Bryce yelled, holding out his hands to stop him. "Listen to me, to my voice. You have a choice. Listen to your heart. You know who you are, the man I know you to be."

Aticus stopped walking; his hand tightened around the tangled weave of goblin hair. Toak quivered in fear as he whimpered.

"Aticus, our choices in life affirm who we are. Don't let this moment define who you'll become." Aticus continued walking as he dragged the goblin by his hair. "Don't follow me," he said, disappearing into the foliage.

Bryce started to follow his friend, but Eladonia placed her hand on the dwarf's chest. "Let him go. He has to do this."

Gilanthos yelled for Bryce after Aticus disappeared into the woods. "Bryce, we need your help. Sung's hurt!"

Reluctantly, Bryce hastened across the battlefield, followed by Eladonia. Bryce suddenly stopped, and Eladonia almost ran into him.

"What's wrong, Bryce!?" she asked, drawing everyone's attention.

He pointed at where they had left Don, Sedric, and Lorna. "Where are the others?"

"Flack!" Aeotus cursed as he ran for the trail and climbed onto Konnos.

Gilanthos retrieved his bow and joined Aeotus, ascending onto Capasius.

"Wait for us," Palias announced, still hovering over Sung.

"We'll be fine," Aeotus declared as he and Gilanthos spurred their horses down the path.

Bryce and Eladonia arrived beside Yung Sung. "We've got you." Bryce knelt, placing his hands on Yung Sung. He began to chant as the azure glow stretched from his fingertips.

"Aticus?" Palias asked Eladonia.

She shook her head.

Bryce finished his chanting as the light faded from his hand. "How do you feel, son?"

Sung sat up and looked at his blood-covered hands. "Better. That was close." He glanced past Bryce, "Aticus."

Everyone turned and watched Aticus emerge from where he had taken the goblin.

"He didn't do it," Eladonia commented.

"What do you mean?" Sung asked.

"He didn't kill him. I can see it in his eyes. He didn't do it," Bryce added. "Thank you, Lord."

Chapter Sixty-Two

REVELATION

Don guided Lorna's horse off the trail near a tree.

"Hurry, Don, we don't have much time," Sedric declared, monitoring the path over his shoulder.

"Lorna, I'm not here to hurt you," Don reassured.

"You kidnapped me!" she said sarcastically.

"I had to take you, or you would've warned the others." Don secured her horse to a tree near the path. "I'm going to give you a bit of advice."

"Advice from a killer and kidnapper?" Lorna snapped.

Don finished tying the reins and glanced at Sedric.

"She has a point." Sedric shrugged, followed by a snarky expression.

"You're not helping, Sedric," Don quipped.

Don returned to his horse and climbed into the saddle. "You need to get away from these people. You can't win against the Hands of the Shadow. What you saw today is nothing compared to what they can bring to bear. How long were you held by the Hand?"

Lorna looked at the violet hues painted in the sky. "I don't know, years maybe," she answered.

Don focused on the darkening path behind them. "Let's go, Sedric," he said, studying Lorna. "If you want to live, you need to run and hide. Stay away from Aticus and the Bloodstone." With that, the two spurred their horses down the trail.

Lorna pulled on the rope, binding her hands to the saddle's horn. When she realized she couldn't free herself, she relaxed, letting her shoulders sag.

Not long after, Aeotus and Gilanthos rounded the path and found Lorna.

"Are you alright? Did they hurt you?" Aeotus leaped from the back of Konnos and began to untie the binding. "Where's Don?" he asked, looking around before letting her answer the first set of questions.

"I'm fine." Lorna calmly observed Aeotus remove the bindings.

Gilanthos slid off Capasius, rubbing her muzzle. "Good girl." He knelt on the path and studied the ground. Capasius neighed and shuffled her feet. "Stop it, girl. I can't play right now," he stroked her leg.

"What happened?" Aeotus asked.

"They cut free of their binding, grabbed me, and recovered their weapons while you were preoccupied. Then they brought me here, tied my horse to the tree, and went that way." Lorna pointed out the direction the two men went.

Gilanthos stood from examining the trail. "They went that way."

Lorna smiled at Gilanthos' response.

"We need to find them." Aeotus gave the reins to Lorna.

Gilanthos grabbed his friend's shoulder, "We need to regroup and figure out what happened."

Aeotus huffed and focused on Lorna. "Fine, let's get back to the others."

Aticus sat on a rock, his eyes glossed over, isolated from Bryce and Eladonia. He stared at Vandeer's hand hanging out of the wagon and Terra's body beside him.

Eladonia knelt near the edge of the path and watched Aticus.

Bryce was standing in the center of the trail, conversing with the nighttime sky, when torchlight and horses ambled from the darkness. "Palias, you found them!" He advanced toward the group.

"They were on their way back. Don and Sedric escaped." Palias glanced at Aticus.

Aeotus and Gilanthos lept from their mounts and rushed toward Eladonia.

"Ela!" Aeotus was the first to reach her.

Gilanthos was right behind his friend.

"Aeo, Gil." She embraced her friends, pressing their heads together. "Thank you for saving me." She placed her hands on her companions' faces before glancing at Palias and Yung Sung. "Thank you—all of you."

Palias smiled, holding a torch high above his head. "It's good to see you again."

Sung bowed his head.

Lorna silently sat on her horse and watched everyone bond before letting her gaze relax on Aticus, isolated and distressed. He filled the caged wagon with twigs and dried brush before throwing a torch on the kindling, igniting the wagon and the last of the Alarians.

The group moved away from the battle site before finding a small clearing to camp for the night. Everyone sat around the campfire, sharing stories about their adventures since parting last, except for Aticus, who sat by himself, legs crossed near the horses and out of presumed earshot. Bryce disappeared into the forest to meditate.

Gilanthos passed a bowl of berries to Palias. "Are we going to discuss what happened to Aticus, or will we all ignore him?" he spoke in a hushed tone.

Yung Sung leaned forward, "I've tried to speak with him, but I feel like he needs time to process what happened."

Eladonia nodded, "I have as well."

"He's different; there's no doubt about that," Aeotus commented before drinking and observing Aticus.

Eladonia laid her hand on Aeotus' leg. "You have no idea what we've been through; go easy on him," she said.

Lorna remained silent and studied Aeotus and Eladonias' interaction.

"I thought you were dead more than once, fighting that wizard today," Palias told Aeotus.

"I pictured us all dead more than once today," Aeotus chuckled.

"I've never seen you cast some of those spells," Gilanthos responded.

Aeotus glanced at Palias. "Palias and Sung gave me Gildon Prather's spellbook."

"King Eston's, Gildon?" Eladonia exclaimed.

Aeotus nodded his head.

Yung Sung crossed his legs. "We have other items of Gildon's. We obtained the spellbook and a few of his possessions when we discovered King Eston's sword."

Aeotus opened his backpack and retrieved the Bloodstone, balancing it in his palm. "This gemstone has the capacity to amplify my power exponentially," he explained. "I first noticed its effect when I cast a minor incantation. Rather than speaking the spell into existence, I merely remembered the words, and it worked." The light from the campfire refracted a red luster off the Bloodstone.

Lorna silently stood and walked toward Aticus.

"Do you feel different?" Sung asked Aeotus.

"No. I can sense the magical energy amplifying mine."

"What's the story with her?" Eladonia watched Lorna as she walked away.

Grinning, Aeotus leaned in and smiled. "You jealous?"

"Of you or her?" Gilanthos interjected, motioning toward Lorna.

Aeotus scowled.

"Why would I be jealous of either?" Eladonia asked. "I want to know who she is. She doesn't talk much."

"We found her and this in Oppack." Aeotus wiggled his hand holding the Bloodstone. "The Hands of the Shadow were using her ability for something she doesn't completely understand."

Eladonia wasn't listening as she watched Lorna sit down beside Aticus.

"Ela." Aeotus reacquired her attention. "She is a Lamarian. An Ancient."

Eladonia looked back at Lorna. "I remember studying the Lamarians and Padonians."

"I've heard of the Ancients in story, but the Padonians?" Palias inquired.

Aeotus replied, "Padonians were demon-like beasts who fought the Lamarians thousands of years ago during the First War; they nearly destroyed the world."

Palias nodded before addressing Aeotus, "You said the Ancients had an ability, and each one was different?" Palias retrieved a small, black book from his pouch. "I found references where the Hand used Lorna's ability to open doorways through mirrors. It mentions Meloorne, Kandar, and my homeland." He clenched his jaw, thinking about the death of his parents.

Aeotus analyzed the Bloodstone. "Lorna can open portals using mirrors." He held the palm of his hand out. Perhaps they used the Bloodstone to amplify her power?" He looked around at everyone. "Like it did with my magic."

"It's possible they used the mirror we found in Oppack for that reason," Sung suggested.

"If we know the king and queen of Meloorne…" Gilanthos paused, looking at Palias, "And your mother and father were killed, then we can surmise that the Hands of the Shadow used the Bloodstone and Lorna to open doorways to assassinate royalty."

"Palias, you mentioned Kandar in the book," Eladonia added. "For all we know, they may have successfully targeted the dwarven royalty as well."

"The Hands of the Shadow have already successfully pitted Meloorne and Asvernia against one another. If they were to create a division between the elves and dwarves, then there would be chaos in every corner of the realm." Palias paused, processing what he'd said aloud. "The orcs would go unopposed and conquer the land." He shook his head. "I need to inform my brothers about what we've discovered. We must mend our relations with Meloorne no matter the cost."

"We can speculate that the Hand may not have successfully targeted the elven or dwarven royalty based on their aggressive attempts to retrieve the Bloodstone and Lorna," Aeotus proposed, glancing at Lorna and Aticus sitting quietly. "That dwarven wizard gave his life to get it back, so it must be critical to their goals," he implied, staring at the g em.

"The world needs to know what we've discovered. I'll leave first thing in the morning for Veridian and find a way back home.

Everyone sat in silence, examining the Bloodstone in Aeotus' hand.

"I'm Lorna," she said to Aticus.

Aticus didn't answer.

"I understand you, and I have something in common." Lorna sat down, crossed her legs, and rubbed her hands together.

"Do we?"

Lorna nodded. "Neither of us remembers anything about our past."

Aticus looked at Lorna. "So."

She glanced at everyone around the fire. "I didn't feel like I belonged over there."

Aticus watched the group converse around the fire. "Maybe we have a few things in common."

Lorna sat for several moments, letting Aticus adjust to her silent presence.

"What did Don say to you?" Aticus pulled his knees up to his chest and wrapped his arms around his legs.

Lorna looked up at the stars shining in the night sky. "He told me to run from the Hands of the Shadow, the Bloodstone—and you."

"Me," he asked, looking at her silhouette against the campfire light.

"I don't know why I should run from you. I understand hiding from the Hand." Lorna studied the ground.

"How long did they have you?"

Lorna shrugged. "As long as I can remember, and even that seems like a blur. Years, if I had to guess."

"You don't remember anything about your past?"

"Parts, but it comes and goes. It's like looking in a creek after a heavy rain. Everything gets murky," she said.

"So, what are you going to do?" Aticus asked.

"About what?" she responded.

"Are you going to run?"

Lorna looked into the night sky. "I don't know."

Aticus stared at the sparkling, black canvas above.

"You didn't kill that goblin, did you?" Lorna uttered.

"No."

Chapter Sixty-Three

FAREWELL

Yung Sung sat up and rubbed his arms, brushing away the morning chill. He glanced around for Aticus, who'd taken the night's last watch. "Aticus?"

Palias stirred and yawned. "What is it?"

"I don't see Aticus." Sung got to his feet and searched the area. "Aticus."

Palias arose and peered around.

By now, everyone had begun to wake, and a search ensued.

"His horse is gone," Gilanthos announced, scanning for tracks.

"His belongings are missing," Bryce confirmed. "He must have left after Sung fell asleep."

Eladonia put her hands on the dwarf's shoulders. "Why would he leave us like that?"

Aeotus knelt beside Lorna. "What did you say to him last night?"

Lorna shrugged. "We talked about pasts we don't remember."

"That's vague," Eladonia added.

"He asked what Don said to me," Lorna responded.

"You didn't mention a conversation with Don," Aeotus added.

Lorna stood, straightening her shirt. "You never asked."

"And what did he say?" Bryce asked as he hobbled near.

Lorna glanced around. "He told me I should run away. Get away from the Bloodstone, the Hands of the Shadow, and Aticus."

Bryce huffed. "Did he go after, Don?" he turned and asked the canopy of leaves above.

"We've got to find him," Eladonia added.

Aeotus shook his head and raised his hands as he watched Bryce speaking to the leaves instead of them. "Maybe he doesn't want to be found. We need to give him space."

Gilanthos approached from the path. "I found tracks several hours old. I don't think he's following Don and Sedric. Aticus is going south."

"Why would he go south?" Sung inquired.

"Veridian, Dewbrook, Oppack. Look at where we've been in the last month," Gilanthos added.

"I'm traveling south to Veridian," Palias stated. "If I leave now, I might catch him." No one acknowledged Palias.

"Are you still going to Evermoure, Eladonia?" Yung Sung asked. "We can go together."

Bryce rejoined the conversation, "We need to go after Aticus."

Eladonia looked at Aeotus and Gilanthos. "No, I'm not going. I changed my mind."

Aeotus' mouth sagged open, "You're not going?" he smiled.

Palias glanced at Lorna as they watched the chaos develop around them. "Settle down," Palias commanded in a deep voice. "I will go to Veridian. The rest of you should find Don and bring him to the authorities."

Sung nodded reluctantly.

Gilanthos looked at Aeotus. "We can backtrack, and I can try to find their tracks."

"It's decided then; I'll be in Veridian securing passage home and looking for Aticus." Palias began gathering his equipment.

Eladonia approached him. "Palias, you have to find Aticus and protect him. He can't be alone now with what he's going through. We should have been there for him last night."

Palias comforted her. "I know. Aticus is much stronger than even he knows. If—when I find Aticus, I'll ensure Collet takes care of him until you make it back."

Eladonia placed her hand on Palias' arm. "Good luck finding your way home." She turned and walked toward Aeotus, Gilanthos, and Lorna.

"Sung, can I see you for a moment?" Palias motioned to his friend.

Sung nodded and followed the towering man to his horse.

Palias pulled a pouch of coins from his bag and handed it to Sung. "Use this for whatever you need. It should keep you for a while."

"Palias, I can't take this."

"Yes, you can." He placed his hand on Sung's shoulder. "Besides," he tilted his head and looked at Bryce. "Who's going to buy his ale?" The two men chuckled.

Palias fastened his gear to the horse and climbed into the saddle before he addressed everyone. "I wish you all luck. If I don't see you again before I return home, there is a place for all of you in Asvernia." Palias spurred his mount down the trail toward Veridian.

The remaining companions followed Don and Sedric's trail north into the early evening. They came to a fork in the road that led east and north.

Gilanthos dismounted for a better look, roaming the trails before declaring, "I've lost their tracks."

"What do you mean, you lost the tracks?" Aeotus shifted in his saddle, patting Konnos.

"They used one path and then crossed back into the forest and returned using the other route. I have no way of knowing which direction they took. I'm sorry."

"It's okay, Gil," Eladonia consoled, her attention drawn by a shimmer of light above Bryce.

"What's your source saying, Bryce?" Aeotus tilted his head and smiled.

"It doesn't work that way," Bryce responded without making eye contact.

Aeotus scrunched his lips and studied Eladonia, "doesn't work like that," he whispered.

Eladonia struck Aeotus before leaning closer, "Have you noticed a glow or brightness that draws your attention toward Bryce lately?"

Aeotus glanced at Bryce before considering Eladonia. "Glow? I only notice how bizarre he looks when he chats with the clouds. There's nothing bright about that."

Eladonia pursed her lips. "I can't explain it." The two watched the dwarf converse with the leaves. "I notice it out of the corner of my eye. I never see it when I look straight at him." She sighed, "It's happening all the time." She looked away from Bryce, watching him out of the corner of her eye. "I see it now."

Aeotus followed suit and focused on a tree, looking to the side at Bryce without moving his head. "I see nothing out of the ordinary." He shifted his jaw. "Other than him talking to himself, but that's normal."

"Perhaps we should stop for the night and decide what to do tomorrow," Sung recommended.

"I think we should leave the forest tonight. Go to Veridian," Bryce added.

"Veridian is a two-day journey from here. We've traveled all day. A good night's rest will do the horses and us good." Aeotus turned Konnos back down the trail. "We can find somewhere off the path."

"Aeo, Bryce has a point. You know this forest will be crawling with assassins in the next day or so. Why press our luck any further?" Eladonia confirmed.

"I agree." Gilanthos returned to Capasius and took the reins.

"We can eat and take care of the horses, but I recommend proceeding east and traveling the plains from there instead of back the way we came through the forest," Sung suggested.

Bryce leaned on his saddle and nodded in agreement.

Chapter Sixty-Four

Unbound

The gentle twilight glow enveloped the evening sky as a cool breeze from the west brought a sense of tranquility.

After taking a short respite, the six companions decided it would be wise to leave the forest and travel by night. They hoped to put distance between themselves and the forest before the Hands of the Shadow could pick up their trail.

Aeotus gathered his belongings and slung his bag over his back. He was unaware that the Bloodstone had slipped from his pack and landed in a patch of grass.

Lorna noticed the gemstone fall and knelt to pick it up. "You dropped this."

"I don't want to lose that." Aeotus recovered the Bloodstone and admired it, balancing in his palm, inspecting the multi-faceted reflections touched by the waning sunlight.

"Wait!" Lorna said, reaching for his hand. "I see something. There's an etching reflecting the light near the tip." Lorna pointed and leaned closer for a better perspective.

Aeotus narrowed his eyes and held the gemstone up. "I've never seen any markings, and I've studied it numerous times. Where do you see an etching?"

"There," she pointed, holding his hand so Aeotus would keep from turning the gem. "Hold it crown down, tip up with the sunlight behind it. You'll see it." The softness of Lorna's hand compelled him to focus on her. "See right here." She pointed. "Here," she said again with a crooked smile as she tenderly squeezed his hand to draw his attention back to the Bloodstone.

Everyone gathered around the two at the sound of her excitement.

"Look what Lorna found!" Aeotus grasped the gem by the top and turned it over, holding it against the waning light of day. "I'll be. I see it."

Yung Sung hovered over Lorna. "I can't see anything."

Lorna took the Bloodstone from Aeotus and held it up to inspect the etching. "The writing looks familiar to me." She squinted her eyes together, focusing. "It's a word."

"How can you see that?" Yung Sung asked.

She held it so he could rub his finger over the etchings.

"It feels like organized scratches." He glanced at Bryce proudly as if he'd discovered a new language and named it scratches.

Aeotus watched Lorna study the gem. The fading sunlight struck the gemstone, casting a crimson hue in her golden eyes.

Bryce stepped closer and tugged the sleeve of Aeotus' shirt. "You said it's magical?"

"Very much so," Aeotus responded to Bryce. "I would have never beaten the dwarven wizard without it." He pointed at the gemstone.

"I don't think you need to study it any further today," Bryce suggested as he backed away, listening to another conversation the others couldn't hear.

Gilanthos approached Aeotus. "I see it, but it's nothing I recognize. What do you think, Ela?" He shifted to better see Eladonia.

"No, that resembles nothing I've ever seen," Eladonia added.

Bryce glanced into the sky, "Why not?" He let his eyes crumble inward. "Don't read it?" Bryce's face relaxed with understanding. "Put the Bloodstone away, Aeotus!"

Gilanthos glanced at the dwarf, only half listening to him. "What's wrong, Bryce?"

"It's an ancient language," Lorna said as she tilted her head, trying to remember. "There is a name inscribed here," she spoke more to herself than to the others, hoping that saying it aloud would help her remember.

"Don't read it! Don't read it!" Bryce scurried over, grabbing at arms.

Gilanthos recognized the distress on Bryce's face. "Lorna..."

"Terr, Terru-mau-eru, that's..." Lorna started to speak, but instantly, a blinding light pulsed from the Bloodstone, projecting an invisible energy that sent everyone to the ground. It was as if a lightning bolt struck where they stood, accompanied by a thunderous crack.

The group found themselves blinded, deafened, and reeling on the ground.

Aeotus flailed in the grass. The ringing in his ears was overwhelming, and though his eyes were squeezed shut, it felt like he was looking into the sun. He struggled to regain his balance, but his body rejected the notion, forcing him back to the ground. "Ahhh!" he screamed, grasping his head between his hands. He sensed the power of the Bloodstone surrounding him; the air pulsated with energy, and the smell of blood hung in the air. He forced his eyes open, blinking through the tears, and glimpsed the shadow of something significant towering over a smaller, delicate silhouette. "Lorna!"

A pulsating red glow enveloped Lorna and the towering figure. Aeotus pushed to his knees and brushed away the tears. "Lorna's in trouble!" The ground shook, and the air buzzed.

Gilanthos stood, bewildered about where the dark shadow had come from. He heard someone call Lorna's name and rushed towards the shadowy figure, expecting to push it away from her. Instead, he collided with something solid that shoved him to the side.

Aeotus listened to Lorna's screams amidst the ringing in his ears. He recalled the words of a spell and spoke, *"Tera'Lack,"* he commanded, as six small spheres of arcane light materialized in his palms. He weaved his hands in circles, propelling the projectiles, one by one, at the dark, towering figure holding Lorna. It was hard to tell, but some of the arcane missiles struck the target; several missed their mark, impacting trees and sparking small fires that died as quickly as they were summoned.

Yung Sung was the next to get up. Despite the ringing in his ears, he turned and focused on the dark shadow, wiping the stream of tears from his face. Sung acted fearlessly, rushing the dark figure, leaping into the air, and kicking. There was a connection, and the clearing went dark as the crimson hue faded and the vibration in the air silenced. Still, before he could recover, something grasped his foot and hurled him into a tree.

Bryce found Eladonia and helped her to her feet. Eladonia drew her swords and charged at the shadowy figure. She missed as the creature sidestepped, throwing her off balance and sending her crashing into the nearby vegetation. She slumped to the ground, her ears ringing.

Gilanthos steadied himself, raised his bow, and notched an arrow. Tears clouded his vision, making it difficult to find a clear target. He held his bowstring, pausing to strike.

Sung regained his footing and closed on the creature again. He pulled his katana from its sheath and launched into action. Slicing at the hulking being, his weapon sparked with each strike. Suddenly, a mighty hand grasped his neck and lifted him off the ground, suspending him in mid-air. He dropped the sword and pounded the firm hand that held him. The red glow began to illuminate the clearing once more as Sung convulsed, and pain pierced through his body.

Aeotus focused his eyes wide, wiping them dry as the clearing glowed again with Yung Sung lifted into the air. He recalled a new spell and spoke the words, *"Eltoo-alha-vadin."* He crossed his hands toward the creature and pulled them back swiftly as one thread of arcane energy sprang from the ground, wrapping itself around the shadowy entity. Another and a third, then a fourth, banded around the creature, tugging downward as the magical spell slowly retracted into the earth. Aeotus concentrated on the spell, keeping his arms pulled tight at his sides, as if he himself were holding the magical bindings in place.

Gilanthos wiped his eyes on his forearm. The dark figure dangled Yung Sung by his neck. He released the bowstring as his arrow sliced through the air, striking the creature in the head, glancing off, and disappearing into the darkness.

Struck by the arrow, the dark entity released Yung Sung to regain its balance as the tension of the magical binders tightened downward. The red glow faded again, leaving only the illumination from the arcanic spell that held the creature in place.

Gilanthos fired another arrow; again, the arrow ricocheted off and struck a tree.

Ignoring Gilanthos, the creature flared a set of shadowy wings out and straightened, pulling on Aeotus' magical bindings. Twisting to the side, the beast seized a handful of dirt and thick brush, throwing it at Aeotus, knocking him over and disrupting his concentration, breaking the spell. With that, the enigmatic creature vanished into the darkened forest, snapping undergrowth and small trees as it fled.

Aeotus rushed to his knees and watched the forest line where the creature had dashed. He surveyed the clearing, looking for his friends. Everyone was stirring except for Lorna; she lay motionless, her body smoldering in the trampled and charred grass. He shuffled on his knees to her side and wiped his eyes with the sleeve of his shirt. "Lorna!" he gasped at what he saw. The skin on her face was charred and clung tight to her skull; a brume of smoke ebbed from her ears, and what was left of her eyes ran down the side of her face. The smell of burned flesh gagged him. Aeotus closed his eyes and choked. "Lorna!"

Bryce rushed beside Aeotus and Lorna. He knew there was nothing he could do. "I'm sorry, Aeotus," he consoled before focusing on Yung Sung, who held his neck, gasping for air. Bryce hobbled to Yung Sung's side and paused for a long breath, holding Sung's shoulders. "Something's different," he stated. Confusion crept across Bryce's face as he looked around at everything, as if for the first time.

"What's wrong, Bryce?" Sung gasped.

Bryce gazed at his hands and scanned the small clearing for something. Bewildered, he looked up, "It's too quiet," he remarked.

Yung Sung coughed and reached for the dwarf. "What's wrong, Bryce?"

Eladonia positioned herself defensively against Bryce and Sung, raising her swords as she watched the dark forest, the tears subsiding. "Sung, are you alright?" she asked, seeing he was in distress, and Bryce was abruptly distracted.

Yung Sung coughed and held his neck. "It burns; my neck feels like it's on fire," he commented.

Gilanthos approached Eladonia and pressed against her as he notched another arrow, scanning the forest line. "Lorna?" he asked.

"She's gone," Eladonia responded, glancing at Aeotus, who was on his knees, staring at Lorna's smoldering remains.

"Bryce, what is it?" Sung shook the dwarf when he refused to answer. "What the hell was that, and where did it come from?" He examined Lorna's body.

No one answered. For several moments, they remained silent.

"Bryce—Bryce, are you hurt?" Eladonia asked, examining him.

Bryce glanced around at the forest, his hands, and the sky. The expression of bewilderment weighed heavily upon his features. "Everything is so dark."

"He seemed fine a minute ago," Sung said, getting to his feet. "He's confused."

Aeotus' hands rested in his lap while he rocked back and forth, lamenting.

Gilanthos advanced toward where the creature had disappeared and surveyed the terrain. "I've never seen footprints like this!"

"What do you think it is?" Sung asked, comforting Bryce.

"Nothing I've ever seen. It has two feet." Gilanthos moved closer to the ground and shuffled debris back and forth. "And a tail," he paused, looking at the damage on the trees above his head. "I saw wings unfold before it fled," he finished before looking at his friends.

Everyone focused on Bryce when he broke the silence. "He's gone." Bryce let his hands drop to his sides as he looked at Sung. "I'm sorry, son. I can't help you."

"It's gone, and I hope whatever it was doesn't come back," Gilanthos stated, returning beside Eladonia.

Sung scrunched his eyes, confused. "There was nothing we could do to save Lorna, Bryce."

"I don't think he's talking about the creature or Lorna," Eladonia added. She knelt beside Bryce, gazing at the dwarf and scanning the air around him. "Who's gone, Bryce?" she whispered, holding his face between her hands.

Bryce glanced at Aeotus and Lorna before looking into the night sky. "God. I don't feel His presence."

Aeotus' eyes drifted to the ground near Lorna's hollow body. The Bloodstone had changed. It was no longer red or balanced but transparent and lying on its side.

The red mist that filled the vessel was gone.

Chapter Sixty-Five

Hands of the Shadow

Michael advanced through the monastery's stone corridors; he clenched an object in his hand, causing his knuckles to turn white. The rage he exhumed intensified the longer it took him to reach JoJung's quarters.

Michael rounded a corner to find Choluk, accompanied by one of the Hand's mages. "Make sure our contact in Shandar checks in before we go any further," Choluk added.

Michael stopped abruptly in front of the two men and glared at them.

Choluk glanced at the mage and nodded, dismissing him.

The mage bowed and kept his eyes on Michael while he continued down the corridor.

"Have you seen JoJung?" Michael spat.

"He's in his chamber." Choluk tried to defuse the situation. "I know we are all upset about Zander…"

Michael let his brows lean in, and his mouth sagged open. "The dwarf? I couldn't care less about Zander. He was no more than one of JoJung's fools." Michael pressed his finger into Choluk's chest, pushing him backward. "Like you are Choluk, a fool. But today, JoJung will answer for the years of his self-righteous arrogance. I will no longer be one of his pawns."

Choluk started at Michael's finger on his chest; his white hair fell forward, covering his face. His blue eyes pierced Michael, and his demeanor shifted. "We are not his pawns. We are all equal in this endeavor," he retorted.

Michael let his hand drop. "If you try to get into my mind, I will rip the arms from your body and beat you to death."

"Your idle threats mean nothing to me, Michael." Choluk tightened his jaw. "For far too long, you have created tension and unrest among the council. You should never have been allowed a seat at the table."

Michael let a smile crease the corner of his lips. "I've been on this council for far longer than you can imagine. Do you want proof that JoJung neglected his duties and put his legacy above others? Look no further than the obsession with finding his son, for what, so he can take his place at the table when JoJung's participation ends." Michael relaxed and took a breath. "Or perhaps fill the new void left by Zander. You want to see evidence that everything we've worked for has been in vain, and JoJung has single-handedly undone the work of all the previous councils before us?" Michael raised his clenched fist. "I hold proof of what you and the others fail to comprehend because you remain deceived by ignorance."

"Reveal this evidence you possess and prove we are as naive as you say." Choluk thrust his chest out and stood straight.

Michael smiled. "It makes no difference to me in the end. Perhaps I will let things end as they should." Michael turned to go around the dark elf. "Come, we'll show JoJung together what fate awaits him, the council, and the world." Michael strode down the hall and around a corner where JoJung's chamber was.

Choluk followed behind, giving Michael a wide berth.

Michael paused outside JoJung's door, relaxed his clenched hand, and studied the door. He took a breath and entered the room.

Choluk trailed behind Michael.

JoJung sat behind his large desk. The fire from the hearth cast a warm glow throughout the room. He looked up from a stack of papers he was examining to acknowledge the two as they entered. "Michael, Choluk, do we have any further word from our scouts concerning the Bloodstone yet?"

Michael walked to the side of the room and studied a painting depicting the interior of the dwarven stronghold of Kandar.

"Yes, I received word moments ago that we captured two individuals from Shandar. We will interrogate them once they return," Choluk responded to JoJung.

"Good. Perhaps our new guests will inform us about the Bloodstone," JoJung said.

"What are we going to do about the orcs now?" Choluk supported himself on the desk.

JoJung leaned back in his chair. "We can handle Mongole."

"We can't control Mongole. Talmet, yes, but not Mongole. Neacrom and his undead were our only counter against the orcs after they decimated the humans." Choluk straightened. "The orcs will advance unchecked once the human cities fall."

JoJung sighed. "Mongole will take the orcs back to their lands once Meloorne and the other cities fall into ruin, and there is nothing else to take."

"Neacrom was to use the army of undead and neutralize the orcs. Absorbing them into our ranks of undead and moving us one step closer to completing our plans," Choluk retorted.

JoJung stared into Choluk's eyes, determined to make him understand. "We need to concentrate on retrieving the Bloodstone and the Ancient. Once we have both of them in our possession, we will deal with the orcs."

"Over three hundred years ago, the council first implemented this strategy. That assembly of five helped bring the orcs back from extinction, aiding them by helping to kill the human savior, Endenden, favored by their god." Choluk tapped his chest. "We were responsible for ensuring that the orcs served their purpose before eliminating them, and now we no longer retain what's needed to dispose of that threat."

Michael chuckled while he examined the painting.

Choluk peered over his shoulder at Michael before addressing JoJung. "What about Zander?"

JoJung stood from his chair. "It's unfortunate what happened."

"Unfortunate—unfortunate is what I would say if a mission failed, but not if a council member died at the hands of thieves." Choluck glanced again at Michael, who silently continued to study the painting.

JoJung straightened his robe. "We're all soldiers fighting in a war that has raged for longer than we can comprehend." JoJung raised his hands in confirmation. "We will lose battles, but the outcome is what matters."

"Zander took it upon himself to go find the Bloodstone because he understood the significance of what could happen if we fail to retrieve the stone for safekeeping." Choluk glared at JoJung.

"Zander will be missed. He added a calmness to the council I feel will never be supplanted," JoJung added.

"What about his replacement? He has no heirs," Choluk addressed JoJung.

"I've given it some thought. It would benefit us if we had someone to tip the balance in our favor." JoJung sat and looked at the papers spread across his desk.

Choluk looked at Michael, who continued studying the paint's details, and then at JoJung. "You realize we are the majority in the room? There's only Gorgen left."

JoJung nodded. "If we placed my son on the council." JoJung paused, knowing Choluk would object, "hear me out."

Choluk's mouth slouched.

"During this time of unrest, we need all positions on the assembly filled until another council member is chosen to replace me."

Choluk looked back toward Michael, waiting for the version he confronted in the hall to emerge. "Are you mad?" He gazed at JoJung. "Do you understand what you're suggesting? There have never been, and never will be, two members of the same lineage occupying the council together. He is an outsider and knows nothing about our mission."

Michael laughed and turned to address JoJung. "You have set us on the path of destruction, JoJung." Michael took a step toward the desk. "You are the one who cast out Neacrom, knowing he would be the only one who could build the army we needed."

He took another step forward. "You are the one who permitted Neacrom to use the Bloodstone unsupervised." Michael stopped beside Choluk and glanced at the dark elf. "You and Zander gave JoJung the power and numbers he needed to lead us down this course we are on. You never listened to me when I told you what would happen." Michael glared at JoJung. "Because you lusted for power, you have thrust us into an impasse we may not be capable of removing ourselves from." Michael reached into his pocket and tossed an object on the desk. It was a shuriken.

JoJung scrunched his eyes together. "What is this?"

Michael bent his head and looked down at JoJung, "Proof your son is undermining our work."

JoJung regarded Michael with disdain. "The shuriken proves nothing."

Michael pointed at the metal star. "This weapon was found in Azrel, beneath Rocton, in Dumon's head—you remember? The man you placed in charge of the goblins, to mine the ore we needed. The mine we no longer control." Michael glanced at Choluck and raised his eyebrows.

JoJung pushed toward the desk. "This does not prove it was Yung Sung."

Michael turned to face JoJung. "There were goblins that survived, who said it was a giant man from Asverina and another from Satsun who attacked and killed Dumon in Azrel. Does that sound familiar?"

JoJung began to speak, but Michael slammed his fist onto the table, sending papers sliding onto the floor. "Because of you, JoJung!" Michael opened his hand and revealed the article he carried as he bore his fangs and hissed in disdain at what he held.

Choluk's eyes narrowed at the sight of the object. "I don't understand."

"You have unleashed hell on Idonia and, unfortunately, quite possibly sealed our fate." Michael dropped a grey medallion onto the desk for JoJung to see. Its turquoise hieroglyphs glowed brightly.

"What is that?" JoJung asked, contorting his face.

Choluk's face sagged, and he studied Michael.

"This confirms the Padonian is no longer a prisoner within the Bloodstone." Michael relaxed and turned away from the desk. "What I feared sixteen years ago, when we first acquired the Bloodstone, has come to pass."

CHAPTER SIXTY-SIX

DUNCAN

Duncan knelt before the grand cross in the chapel of Parador. The sunlight shone through the stained glass window of the sanctuary, bathing the surroundings in vibrant colors. The elongated shadow of the crucifix cast a darkened shadow over his features.

Duncan held his hands together on his lap as he prayed. "Lord, I come before you and humbly ask you to grant mercy. Forgive us for our shortcomings. Help us recognize what we must understand and overlook what we cannot change. Lord, I ask that you give us the strength to confront what is to come and grant us passage when it is our time."

He sat for many moments with his eyes closed, concentrating on his breathing. Duncan eavesdropped on the men outside the chapel as they expressed their fears about the coming war. He even listened to their heartbeat. He smelled food prepared in the eastern tower and listened to the smith's hammer beating steel in the northern tower.

Duncan heard footsteps approaching the chapel door. He knew it was Edden when the door opened. He could smell him. "What is it, Edden?" Duncan looked at the stone cross that towered above him.

"How do you do that?" Edden asked.

"Do what?"

"Know it's me when I come up behind you," Edden commented with a smile.

"You are the only person who ever interrupts me when praying. So, it's not difficult, and I can smell you."

"That's not true, and you know it on both counts," Edden challenged.

Duncan chuckled and stood as he turned to face his friend. "What is it?" He retrieved his sword from a nearby bench and secured it around his waist.

Edden's smile faded, and his expression held a darker cast. "We're getting reports from the front line that the orcs are assembling and preparing to push north."

"All of them?" Duncan's worst fears were becoming a reality.

"Yes," Edden replied.

Duncan peered into the wooden beams that supported the chapel's roof and sighed.

"Do you think he listened to you this time?" Edden inquired, widening his eyes.

Duncan let his eyes drift down and focus on his friend without moving his head. "He does. I asked for our swift transition into the afterlife when it's time."

Edden's shoulders sank. "You're not helping me feel any better about the situation. I hope you understand." His expression matched his posture.

Duncan approached Edden, and they walked out the chapel's door into the central courtyard of Parador.

The fortress comprised of three towers and three walls that connected the fortification to form a triangle. The northern tower contained the armory, blacksmith, officers' quarters, and the drake landing. The east and west towers housed the majority of the troops.

Edden stopped on the step before speaking, causing Duncan to pause. "I thought I'd let you know before you find out from anyone else, but we lost another Kabatra and drake last night."

Duncan glanced at the clouds passing overhead. "Groden and his dragon?"

"Yes, he's still hunting and killing them." Edden studied his friend's features.

Duncan placed his hand on Edden's back. "Let's see what plan the general has to get us out of this one.

The two men entered the northern tower and made their way to the war room. "Are we late again?" Duncan asked Edden.

"No, you were late. I was on time, the general sent me after you," Edden whispered as they entered the chamber.

General Edward Thorn stood around a table with twenty-six paladin and cavalier officers. His dark hair and full mustache betrayed his age. Lean and muscular for a man in his late fifties, Edward had seen thirty-six years of service, twenty-three as the general of Parador. "Duncan, good, we're all here. We can proceed. Thank you, Edden."

Edden nodded, "I'd follow that man to hell and back," he mumbled to Duncan.

"What about me?" Duncan asked, his expression stooped.

Edden shrugged and regarded General Thorn.

"Gentlemen, many of you have heard the orcs are mobilizing their entire army. Conservatively, we can now say the numbers may exceed one hundred thousand."

An audible gasp moved across the room in response to the general's words.

General Thorn held his hands up in reassurance. "I understand many of you may feel the odds are overwhelming, but we are knights of Parador. We will defend the crown and all seeking refuge." He lowered his hands and placed them on the table, supporting his weight. "Our forces on the front line have begun pulling back to reinforce here, in Parador."

Hushed undertones and exhalations sounded across the room once more. Men nervously shifted, glancing at one another; expressions of lost hope and despair blanketed the room.

"I acknowledge we've all suffered an incomprehensible loss with the murder of King Balen." General Thorn glanced at his desk in remembrance. "King Balen understood the importance of Parador and supported us with diligence. Although Timan is a child, he will be advised by Rath Inen. I have faith he will serve in the same capacity to assist King Timan."

"How can we defend against one hundred thousand orcs?" A voice in the crowd questioned.

General Thorn peered over his men, unable to determine who asked the question. "We've known this day would come and made plans. Our forces will pull back and reinforce the fortress. We will not have room for everyone, so we will absorb as many men as possible to hold the walls from a siege. The rest of the army will stage between Parador and Meloorne and reinforce. The cities have issued a decree to draft all non-disabled men, women, and children to reinforce the walls of the cities." General Thorn shifted and glanced at the paper littering the table. "We currently have enough resources to maintain Parador, so we will not pull any additional aid from any of our cities.

Duncan felt a vibration against his chest. He placed his hand on his leather tunic. "I'll be back in a minute," Duncan whispered to Edden as he exited the chamber and stepped into the hall.

Duncan found a corner where he wouldn't be disturbed and reached beneath his tunic. He pulled on a tarnished chain to reveal a small grey medallion. The center hieroglyphs pulsated a turquoise color. Duncan lost color in his face. "Flack." His hands began to sweat. "No, no, no. It's not happening." He dropped the medallion beneath his tunic.

"You look sick," Edden said as he stepped around the corner.

"I've got to go," Duncan said.

"What? What do you mean?" Edden questioned.

"I need to get to Meloorne as soon as possible." Duncan ran his hand through his hair.

"What's so crucial in Meloorne? The war is coming here, and you want to run!" Edden announced in a hushed tone.

Duncan stared at Edden. "I'm sorry, I can't tell you, but what I need to do could have repercussions that could affect the realm."

"And the war with the orcs won't?"

"I wish I could share with you what's happening, but I can't. Not yet," Duncan responded, as he started to take a step away.

"The general is not going to be pleased that you left for Meloorne without speaking to him about it," Edden said.

"Tell him I was called to Melooren by Rath for an emergency."

Edden took a deep breath and placed his hand on Duncan. "Go. I trust you. I'll tell the general something."

Duncan embraced Edden and shook his hand. "I will see you again, Edden." With that, he darted down the hall.

"Hey!" Edden shouted.

Duncan stopped and turned.

"I'd follow you to hell and back, too!"

"I know," Duncan replied.

Chapter Sixty-Seven

ATICUS

Aticus wandered the streets of Veridian for hours with his hands in his pockets. The night air was calm as the streets cleared of inhabitants, leaving the city oddly quiet.

He found his way outside the Wet Stag and studied the sign as he fought the urge to enter. *A familiar face right now might help. I could talk to Collet,* he thought. "Not yet," he whispered.

Aticus turned and studied the Skullduggery Inn across the street. He remembered the day he spent with Yung Sung and the others, before finding Normain's body.

The sound of laughter in the Wet Stag called to Aticus again, but the thought of a good night's sleep lured him onto the cobbled street and through the inn's door.

Aticus paid for a room with the last coins he had from Palias. He turned, ascended the stairs, and entered his room.

After closing the door, he removed his pack and sword, placing them on the table near the window. He fell onto the bed and stared at the ceiling. A flash of lightning illuminated the room, followed by the distant drum of thunder.

Aticus remembered Nicholas. He regretted that it had been so long since he'd thought of him. It wasn't that long ago when he sat on a wooden bench, longing for something better.

Bryce came along and rescued him. He showed him there was more to life than filling buckets with water or fastening chicken cages to a wagon.

He missed the Alarian people, despite their mistreatment of him.

Aticus yearned for another conversation with Rictor and wanted to gather more water for Terra. They were all dead now, so it didn't matter. He felt so alone, but this time it was different. This time, he'd run away from people who cared about him.

He closed his eyes and drifted to sleep.

Aticus felt someone touch his chest. "Bryce?" To his dismay, he opened his eyes to find the room empty and felt a vibration under his tunic. Aticus pulled the silver chain and medallion from beneath his shirt, casting an azure glow on the ceiling, illuminating the room. He pulled the necklace over his head and held it in his hands.

CHAPTER SIXTY-EIGHT

THE GOBLIN KING

Toak sat on a fallen tree; his teeth chattered from the chilly night air and the absence of fire. He didn't know how to make a flame; someone else had always done it for him. Now he was alone, his soldiers dead or routed.

Toak pulled his arms around himself for warmth. "You wait. One day, Toak will kill everyone who has wronged him. I will return with a larger army. Shandar will be my kingdom again." Toak shifted and rubbed his hands together.

"They will all regret the day they knocked Toak down and..." Toak paused when he heard something moving in the forest. "Who is that?" Toak stood; his voice quivered.

"Who's there?" He looked into the darkness, expecting one of his men to answer, but there was no response.

Fallen tree branches snapped underfoot as something shrouded in the night moved. "Who's there?" Toak swallowed hard and took a step behind the log.

He backed into a tree and hid behind the wooden shield; his teeth chattered.

The forest darkened as if a great veil had fallen upon the world, and the sounds of the forest suddenly muted.

Toak sensed a presence behind him. He turned to see a towering figure emerge from the shadows of the night, as a pair of wings unfolded, and a red luminosity blinded the Goblin King. The air hummed, and the ground trembled. Toak hugged the tree tightly. "What are you?" he screamed.

The humming grew louder as Toak's screams concluded, leaving the dark figure to bask in the brilliant swirling mist of what remained of the Goblin King.

Chapter Sixty-Nine

OPPACK

In the early evening, heavy rain streamed down, and thunder shook the palace in Oppack. Lightning flashed through the cracked windows, illuminating the throne chamber.

"I don't like it here. We shouldn't have come," spoke the man with a black patch over his left eye. He held a torch over his head to spread light into the shadowy corners, hoping to dispel his fears.

"I'm telling you, we're gonna make a profit from whatever we find here. Why else would the orcs come this far south?" This man uttered with a lisp. He held his torch behind him to avoid obstructing his vision.

Lightning brightened the chamber, shedding light into the room's dark corners.

"There, I saw something in the center of the room, on the steps," the man said with a lisp as he cautiously observed the circular stairwells hugging the walls.

"I don't like this. Can we go now?" The man with the eye patch questioned.

"There's nothing here that's going to hurt you. Nothing but your fear." The man with a lisp jerked his body to antagonize his friend.

"Stop it! I'll leave you here alone." Nervously, he repositioned his eye patch.

"Go then; that'll be more spoils for me."

The man with the eye patch nervously fumbled with his torch. He wanted to run but didn't want to find his way out of the palace alone. "Hurry. I don't have a good feeling about this."

"Here, I told you I saw something." The man with the lisp held out his torch and lit a raised area in the center of the chamber. A man's body in robes lay on the steps—an arrow protruding from his forehead. "Check his pockets." He urged his nervous friend forward.

"You check his pockets. I'm not searching the pockets of a dead man." He tugged at his eye patch.

The man with the lisp pulled his torch away from the corpse, shrouding it in darkness. "Why are you here? What could happen to you in an abandoned city palace where nobody has lived for eighty years?"

"He's here!"

"Yeah, and he's dead. By the looks of it, for a long time." His lisp was more pronounced the faster he spoke. He lowered his torch over the corpse and searched his robe for anything he thought might be of value.

The other man continued to pull nervously at his eye patch. "Nothing?"

"No, he's got nothing in his pockets."

"Hey, what about that arrow? Isn't it elven? It'll bring us something." He let go of his eye patch as it popped against his face.

Lightning flashed, filling the chamber with a blinding white light, followed by an earth-shattering clap of thunder.

The two shuddered at the sound. "That was close." The man with the lisp reached down, pulled the arrow free from the corpse, and placed it in his sack. "Come on; there's bound to be more here."

The two men cautiously approached the corridor and advanced into the darkness, holding their torches high.

The storm raged outside, and lightning danced with the shadows of the throne room, bringing life to the darkness.

Another burst of light flooded the chamber as Neacrom opened his eyes and inhaled sharply.

CHAPTER SEVENTY

POSTLUDE

Don sat on a wooden bench outside his parents' bedchamber. He swayed back and forth, incapable of understanding why Samuel wouldn't let him see his mother. Don wanted to be strong, but it was hard. He was only six.

Hours earlier, before dawn, his mother had died. Taken from them by a disease Samuel called consumption. Don called it unfair.

Her name was Elizabeth. Isolated from her family, she suffered from the disease for months before succumbing to it. Don hadn't seen her for fear of contracting the disease, so he never had the chance to say goodbye. However, hours later, word spread through the house and across town that a miracle had occurred—she was alive, and there was no sign of the disease.

Don watched as a continuous rotation of advisors, priests, and monks came and went from the room. He wanted to sprint through the door every time it opened.

Samuel stepped out of the bedroom alongside a friar from the local church. "Gather what you need and come back as quickly as you can. We'll be waiting for you in our chamber," he said, pausing, and reached for the friar before he departed. "Are you sure about this?"

"She bears the marks on her neck. We are certain there is no other way." The friar bowed and hurried down the hall, lifting his robe to avoid tripping.

Don watched the plump man disappear around the corner and out the front door.

"What's happening, father?" Don searched Samuel's eyes for answers.

Samuel sat on the bench beside his son and placed his hand on his leg. He remained silent for many seconds; his face contorted as he tried to find the words a six-year-old would understand.

"I want to see Momma." Don's eyes filled with tears. "I don't understand what's happening, Father."

Samuel peered into his son's eyes, "Don, I need you to be strong. Can you do that for me?"

Don straightened and rubbed his face dry. "Yes, Father, I can."

Samuel nodded, winked, and smiled proudly. "Good, I knew you could." He brushed his hand through Don's hair. "I'm going to take you to see Elizabeth. I know you couldn't say goodbye, but I need you to understand something before we go. The person you will see is not your mother. She will look like your mother, even sound like her, but it's not her." Samuel clamped his jaw, understanding nothing he could say would make sense to his son yet.

Don's eyes sagged, and sadness clouded his features. "I don't understand, Father."

Samuel took a deep breath, unsure if he'd made the right choice to include Don on this new quest of vengeance he was choosing. "The creature that occupies her body is not of this world but comes from the underworld." Samuel considered the wood floor. "What I'm going to show you is important because I promise, by everything holy, we will avenge what has happened to your mother."

Samuel stood and took Don's hand in his. "Be strong, yes?" Samuel nodded.

Don sniffed and gripped his father's hand tightly. "Yes, father." He didn't understand what his father was telling him, and he didn't care. He wanted to see his mother.

The two approached the door to Samuel and Elizabeth's chamber. Samuel grasped the handle and paused. Inhaling deeply, he turned the handle and pressed the door open.

Two priests and a monk stood alongside his parents' bed. Their somber expressions seized Don's gaze as he fought the urge to run to his mother.

"Don!" His mother's voice captured his breath, forcing the air from his lungs. The royal blue of the bedspread invited Don to climb aboard, but he kept his eyes fixed on the elegant fabric, avoiding her gaze.

"Don, it's me!" Elizabeth tried to move, but the rope restraints around her wrists held her in place against the headboard. "Samuel, why are you doing this?"

Don swallowed hard, his eyes twitching as he stared into his mother's deep chocolate eyes. Her long, chestnut hair framed her chiseled features, with an anguish reflected in her eyes that weighed on her like an unseen burden. He exhaled slowly, feeling a tremor deep in his chest. "Mama," Don murmured. He felt the firm squeeze of Samuel's hand when he noticed Elizabeth's teeth.

"It's me, baby. I've missed you." Elizabeth firmly tugged at the restraint that held her to the bed. "Samuel, please let me hold my baby." Her forced smile revealed sharp fangs.

Samuel avoided eye contact and glared at the priest, as if this were his fault.

The holy man shook his head and remained silent.

Don glanced up at Samuel. "Father?"

Samuel scanned the room, avoiding his wife's eyes, "This was a mistake," he said.

"Samuel, I beg you," Elizabeth pleaded, her voice trembling. Tears filled her eyes as she sank back, releasing the tension in the rope. "Please, I don't understand why you're doing this."

"Your son needs to understand," the priest intervened.

Samuel's eyes filled with tears. "I can't do this." He pulled Don close and brushed his hair, fighting the flood of emotion. "Elizabeth, I..."

"Samuel, you must be strong for the boy. He will need you," the second priest said.

Elizabeth began to sob. "Samuel, what's happening? Why won't you help me? What have I done to make you hate me so much?"

Samuel looked into his wife's eyes; tears streamed down his face. "I don't hate you—you died. You shouldn't be alive." Samuel clenched his jaw tightly.

Don shook uncontrollably as the flood of emotion overtook him, sobbing. "Mamma," he blubbered.

A look of confusion flooded Elizabeth's expression.

A knock on the door caused Don to swallow hard and wipe his tears. A man entered the room. Don recognized the chubby man as the friar he had seen earlier. He stared at the man's bag and the wooden stakes fastened on the side.

"The purification must be performed soon," a priest near the bed affirmed.

Samuel knelt and picked Don up. "We have to go."

"Samuel, please. Help me," Elizabeth whined. She tried to reach out, but the ropes kept her confined. "Please."

The man placed the bag on the bed before joining the monk on the other side of the room.

Elizabeth studied the bag and the weapons fastened to it. "Samuel, what are you doing?" Elizabeth tugged aggressively on the ropes, jolting the headboard. Her resistance visibly shook the priests and friars.

Samuel regarded Elizabeth. "I'm sorry. I've always loved you." Tears streamed down his face as he pulled Don tight and turned toward the door.

Don couldn't draw his gaze from Elizabeth's teeth. "Momma," Don whispered, and coughed back tears.

"It's time," the priest announced.

"Samuel! Don't leave me!" Elizabeth cried.

Samuel opened the door as Don watched over his father's shoulder, tears blurring his vision.

Elizabeth pulled on the ropes, causing the bedposts to creak under the strain as she hissed at the holy men surrounding her bed. "Samuel!"

The door clicked shut, but the wooden gateway could not obscure the screaming.

Samuel walked down the hallway leading to the foyer, holding Don in his arms. Elizabeth's cries clawed at him, tugging pieces of his humanity away. With each step and clenched jaw, his expression assumed a steely resolve.

Don settled his sights on the door as his father carried him down the hall. His mother's feral screams burned into his memory.

Samuel reached for the doorknob as her screams stopped. He paused before turning the handle as an eerie silence spread through the home.

"Father."

"Shh, we're going to make it right," Samuel reassured his son as he turned the knob and stepped outside. One door opened in their lives as another was about to close.

A man approached from the courtyard and stopped in front of the house.

Samuel glared at the man standing at the bottom of the steps. "Michael. What are you doing here?"

"Samuel," he bowed before continuing, "I'm here to offer you our condolences and assistance."

ACKNOWLEDGEMENTS

I want to express my profound appreciation to everyone who has supported me on this journey of a lifetime. Your encouragement and presence made this experience truly meaningful. To my wife, Nicole, for the years of listening to me talk about a world and people that never existed. You helped give me the courage to share my story with the world, and for that, I am genuinely thankful.

A heartfelt thank you to family and friends who served as beta readers: Adrianna, Carlie, Jacob, Jessica, Parker, Ralph, and Sean. Your thoughtful insight and constructive criticism helped me to bring these characters to life, and Robert, your guidance was invaluable. Thank you to everyone for the time you spent with me.

Additionally, I would like to thank 100 covers for the beautiful cover design. Your creativity and talent brought life to my world, and I genuinely appreciate your work.

And finally, to you, the readers. Without you, the words would just be words. Thank you for going on this maiden adventure with me and bringing these characters to life. They are like my children!

Everyone has a story to tell, and you have indulged me. Now tell yours.

Review this book on Amazon.

About the Author

J.R. Shepherd is an aspiring New York Times and USA Today bestselling author with Book One of the Bloodmoure Chronicles, in a series of YA fantasy novels, and multiple others in development.

During his influential years, Jason discovered a series of fantasy novels that sparked his imagination. Jump forward a few years, and he began scratching down concepts for an epic fantasy series and what will one day become that aforementioned bestseller. After a bit of self-prodding, Jason began writing on Wattpad in 2017. Along the way, he won multiple awards and gained a newfound confidence. All his hard work paid off on a chilly January morning in 2019 when he finished writing the first draft of book one. It was described as a magical moment.

Jason currently resides in a small village in southern Kentucky with his wife, son, and two cats, while working full-time in retail.

JRShepherd.com